On the Road to Nowhere

Robert Boyd

Granville Island
Publishing

Copyright ©2005 Robert Boyd

All rights reserved.
No part of this publication may be reproduced without express written permission of the publisher and author, except in the case of brief quotations embodied in critical articles or reviews.

Library and Archives Canada Cataloguing in Publication

Boyd, Robert, 1960-
On the road to nowhere / Robert Boyd.

ISBN 1-894694-34-1

1. Title.

PS8603.O985O6 2005   C813'.6   C2005-901002-9

Editing by Kathleen Holden
Proofreading by Arlene Prunkl
Book design by Fiona Raven
Cover design by Laura Kinder

First Printing March 2005
Printed in Canada

Granville Island
Publishing

Suite 212–1656 Duranleau
Vancouver, BC, Canada V6H 3S4
Tel 604-688-0320 Toll-free 1-877-688-0320
www.granvilleislandpublishing.com

*To the memory of my aunt Mildred Hanegan
whose love of reading was an inspiration
for me to take up writing.*

*To my former roommate Ray Picard
whose stories of life on the road
were a rich source of material for this book.*

*And, to my loving wife Gayle
who persevered despite
my long hours at the keyboard.*

1

June 1978

With obvious disappointment, Randy looked at the four remaining balls on the table—the three striped balls that were his and the eight ball.

Dave Sewell said in a cocky tone of voice, "Eight ball in the corner pocket."

All Randy could think about was, "Miss, you son of a bitch, miss!" But with the crack of the pool cue, the cue ball struck the eight ball with deadly accuracy and it sank into oblivion.

In a smug tone, Dave said to Randy, "That'll be twenty bucks, Watson." He asked Randy if he would like to make it double or nothing.

"No thanks, maybe some other time." He turned to his friend Gary and said, "Let's get out of here."

As they turned to leave, Dave said, "Hey, Watson, let's do this again sometime. My Camaro needs a new head gasket and I'm a little hard up for cash."

Randy muttered, "Up yours!"

As they left the Sportsman's Billiard Hall, Gary gave Randy a bad time. "What were you thinking of, taking on Dave Sewell? That guy is a pool shark—he practically lives there!"

All Randy could come up with was, "Hey, I was feeling lucky."

Gary told him that if he kept on feeling lucky like that, he'd soon end up broke. With that, they decided to head uptown to the 7-Eleven store and drown their sorrows in a Big Gulp.

That was a typical day in the life of sixteen-year-old Randy Watson. Randy lived in the town of Granby, British Columbia, located in the north-central Interior. With a population of a little over thirteen thousand, it was basically a two-industry town. Granby was built around the Bull Elk lead and zinc mine, and the Western Canadian Forest Products lumber mill, neither of which had been doing very well. The mine was due to shut down within five years, and the mill had laid off almost half its staff.

Randy was a high school dropout and worked periodically at the local recycling centre. His best friend, Gary McCallum, was on summer vacation from school. There was not much for kids to do around there. Granby didn't have a swimming pool, a recreation centre of any kind or even a shopping mall. So the young people of Granby were on their own when it came to finding ways to amuse themselves. The only real hangouts for teenagers were the 7-Eleven store downtown and the Sportsman's Billiard Hall on the town's southern outskirts. Needless to say, the crime rate in Granby was very high, especially when it came to youth crime. Randy himself had had a few run-ins with the law—two charges for shoplifting and one for vandalism—most likely borne out of frustration and sheer boredom.

When Randy and Gary arrived at the 7-Eleven, they met their twin friends, Bill and Brad Suarez. The twins' father had been part of the large influx of Portuguese immigrants who had settled in Granby when the mine was first established in the 1950s. He had worked at the mine for twenty-five years and was one of the foremen on the day shift.

After the boys loaded up with their regular staples of Big Gulps, potato chips and cigarettes, Bill invited Randy and Gary over to his place. He was bragging that he had recently purchased the new KISS album—their Double Platinum greatest hits package—and figured they would be interested in giving it a listen.

As they made their way along Commissioner Street, Granby's main drag, evidence of the town's floundering economy was everywhere. There were a lot of vacant stores and numerous places were having closing-out sales. A large number of the town's many unemployed spent their time in one of the four sidewalk cafés. It seemed that the only busy place in town was the Canada Manpower office in the post office building—that is, except for the Ministry of Social Services office on the last Wednesday of the month.

As the boys passed the King Edward Hotel, they fantasized about the day they would finally be old enough to go into the beer parlour or the day they could pass off a fake I.D., whichever came sooner. The recent addition of exotic dancers to hotel's entertainment lineup gave them added incentive. It was at this point that Randy spotted Kees Vandelaar coming in the opposite direction.

Randy said to the others, "Hey guys, look who's coming. It's the little Dutch boy."

Kees Vandelaar was an awkward kid. He was quiet and shy, and dressed differently than the other kids. His parents were immigrants from Holland who owned the local bakery. Randy couldn't stand him—he thought of him as a total dweeb. In fact, most of the other kids in school thought of him as a complete and total nerd.

"Hey, Dutch boy, nice outfit you got there! Did you get that at the Salvation Army for two bucks?" Referring to the violin case that Kees was carrying, Randy went on to say, "Look out guys, he's got a machine gun in that case."

Kees replied, "That's very funny, Watson. It just so happens that I am coming from violin practice."

Randy asked what he hoped to accomplish from this. Kees replied that he was expecting to get an audition from the Royal Conservatory of Music in the next couple of years.

Randy started laughing uncontrollably. He then began poking his finger repeatedly into Kees' chest and saying, "Look Vandelaar, you are nothing but a fucking loser and you will never amount to dick-all!"

With that, Randy proceeded to grab the violin case out of Kees' hand. The boys began playing catch with the violin case overhead. As tears formed in his eyes, Kees begged and pleaded for the boys to give him his violin back. Jack Morrison, the bar manager at the King Edward, heard the commotion and went outside to investigate.

"What's going on here?" he yelled.

"Oh, it's nothing, Mr. Morrison. We're just having a little fun!" said Randy.

He gave Kees his violin case back and said, "Here you go, wimp."

Jack Morrison went on to say, "Haven't you boys got anything better to do with your time, especially you, Watson? Your mom is a frequent customer of mine, so I'm sure she would be interested in this. So right now, I would just advise you to run along."

As they left, Gary said to Randy, "What kind of a name is Kees, anyway?"

"I think it's short for Cornelius," Randy replied.

Bill and Brad lived in a sprawling house in the Westview subdivision on a hill overlooking the valley. The view had been nice at one time, but now all you could see were the scars of open-pit mining on the mountains and the massive concentrator building. Their mom worked at the mine too, as a clerk in the administration building. They had more privacy now, for their older brother Manuel had moved out last year when he began attending the University of British Columbia. The house had a fairly sizable recreation room, which contained a very high-output stereo system. On many occasions the neighbours got quite an earful.

The Suarez twins always had a stash of marijuana. After passing around a couple of joints, the boys were all feeling fine.

"You know, I would really like to see KISS live someday," said Randy.

Bill said, "Brad and I saw them in Vancouver last summer."

Looking rather perplexed, Randy said, "I didn't know you guys went to Vancouver last summer!"

Brad replied, "Yeah, we went down when Manuel moved there, before he started at UBC. KISS was playing at the Pacific Coliseum and we managed to get tickets. Man, they are awesome on stage—they have one hell of a light show. It was cool when Gene Simmons made it look like his whole mouth was bleeding!"

Bill added, "Vancouver is an awesome city—there is so much to see and do there. Would you believe they actually have a nude beach there?"

"Are you shittin' me?" asked Gary.

"It's true. Brad and I went there one day. It's called Wreck Beach. It's right near the university. You should have seen it. There were lots of nice-looking chicks and none of them were wearing anything. I remember this one girl in particular. She was a really gorgeous blonde. She had a really nice set of tits and"—he pointed to Brad—"you should have seen this guy! For about the next half hour, he was walking around with this big erection!"

By now all of the boys were practically falling off their chairs laughing. After they had somehow managed to regain their composure, Gary asked if there was any possibility of KISS ever coming here, and the laughter erupted again.

Randy replied, "Oh yeah, I can see it now: Live at the Granby Civic Centre—KISS!"

Bill mentioned that if you were to ask any of the members of KISS, they would probably say, "Where the hell is Granby?" He then went on to say, "Who in their right mind would ever want to play here, out in the middle of nowhere?"

"Valdy and the Hometown Band played here at the fair last August," said Gary.

Once again Randy, Bill and Brad burst into uncontrolled laughter, while Bill added, "I bet you they needed to call out the riot squad for that concert!"

After a few minutes the laughter died down again, and Gary inquired as to how they could manage to get rid of the marijuana smell before his parents came home. Brad pointed to a ventilation fan in the ceiling and pulled out a can of Pine Scent air freshener from the coffee table drawer. Brad asked Gary why he wanted to know that.

"Because your mom is just pulling into the driveway!"

Brad yelled, "Holy shit," and began spraying the room vigorously.

They had all lost track of time and hadn't realized it was 5:30.

When their mom came downstairs, she said to the boys, "Are you boys hard of hearing or something? I thought one of you was going to mow the lawn today."

Bill and Brad both said that they had forgotten, and Mrs. Suarez replied, "How in the world could you possibly forget? The grass is starting to look like hay! Just make sure it's done tomorrow. Anyway, dinner will be ready in a half hour."

Randy and Gary decided to head home. Brad asked them if they would like to go up to the swimming hole sometime the next week, provided the weather improved. Randy and Gary both agreed and said they would give him a call when they knew which day.

Randy headed home—a home with bad memories. In this house, he lived with his mother, her fourth husband, William, and his younger brother, Mark. Randy's father had been his mother's first husband, but he had died when Randy was only five years old. He remembered his dad as a caring person who devoted a lot of his time and attention to him and his brother, despite working a lot of extra hours at the mine. Randy never stopped missing him.

His mom, however, was a controlling, self-centred person whose only concern was that everything in life should happen in her own best interests. Randy remembered that his dad had always gone out of his way to please her. He was the type of person who would give the shirt off his back for her. In return, she had just treated him like shit and was always blaming him for getting her pregnant so they would have to get married. After Mark was born things only got worse. She constantly complained that Randy's father had ruined her life, that she could have done something special otherwise. But instead she had got stuck in that dumpy town looking after two brats.

Randy's uncle (his father's brother) had a completely different story. He had told him about a particular weekend in the spring of 1961 when his mother and her best friend, Dana Adonis, travelled from Prince George to

Granby to attend a recreational hockey tournament. Dana's boyfriend was playing defence on the team representing the Canadian Forest Products mill in Prince George. Randy's uncle and dad were playing the team representing the Bull Elk Mine. His father was playing left wing.

After the tournament one of the members of the Bull Elk team threw a party at his house. It was there that Randy's parents first met. They hit it off immediately. After their first meeting, his mother travelled to Granby practically every weekend.

Barely two months into their relationship, his mother had booked a room at the King Edward Hotel. After a night at the hotel bar, his mother invited his father up to her room. She had smuggled a bottle of ouzo from her father's liquor cabinet. After at least seven shots of ouzo each, she conned Randy's father into a night of passionate lovemaking. The following morning she assured him she had taken a birth control bill the previous day (they were a fairly new invention back then). But six weeks later, she informed him that she was pregnant. Randy's father agreed to marry her.

Randy's uncle had concluded by saying that if his mom claimed to be so unhappy about the situation she had ended up in, she had nobody else to blame but herself.

Randy could still remember the awful sight that ended this part of his life. His father's employer (the mine) had been embroiled in a bitter labour dispute over the previous six months. On several occasions the strike at the mine had threatened to escalate into violence. At one point the mine's parent company threatened to close the mine down completely. The strike had taken a heavy toll on Randy's father, both emotionally and financially. With two little boys to support, it was difficult to manage on strike pay. Randy's mother was less than supportive, to say the least. Eventually the union caved in, so the settlement was not as good as they had hoped for. Randy's father was relieved to be back at work, but he had been transferred to the afternoon shift. Randy had just started grade one so he was only able to see his dad for one hour after getting home from school.

One week after the strike ended, Randy, as usual, hurried home from school so that he could spend some time with his dad before he headed off to work. On this particular day he was especially anxious to get home, as he wanted to show his dad a picture he had drawn in art class.

But when he got home, he found his father hanging from a rope tied to a branch on the oak tree in their backyard. Even at that age he had known something was wrong. He called out, but there was no response. So he ran to the garage and got out the ladder, but both he and the ladder were too short. He ran screaming next door to the Johnsons' house. Mrs. Johnson called for an ambulance. Mr. Johnson got his ladder, untied the noose and carried Randy's father to the ground. Randy remembered the paramedics and Mr. Johnson trying to revive his dad. All the while Mark, who was then one year old, was crying uncontrollably in his crib.

Randy's mom was nowhere to be found. It turned out that she and Randy's father had been fighting earlier in the day, and she had told him she was going over to a friend's place. In reality she had gone to the King Edward Hotel, where she spent the entire afternoon. When she learned that her husband had killed himself she didn't seem the least bit concerned. Even at the funeral she didn't seem very sad. By the way she acted, Randy figured she was glad it had happened. For Randy, the memory would last a lifetime.

Six months later, his mom had married a man named Dirk (Randy couldn't remember his last name). He worked for the local branch of the B.C. Ministry of Forests. The marriage lasted only a year before he ran off with a female co-worker half his age.

Two years after Dirk disappeared, his mom married Larry Braithwaite, who worked as a logger. He was a big, husky man with a very violent temper. Over the course of the four-year marriage, Randy and Mark both endured numerous beatings by Larry. Several times he beat Randy until he was black and blue all over.

One incident occurred on Christmas day. Larry had given Randy a G.I. Joe action figure and Randy had commented that the uniform colours had been changed slightly. Larry took it the wrong way and accused Randy of being ungrateful. He grabbed the action figure and beat Randy over the head and body with it, cutting him in several places. Another time when Mark was only four, Larry had beaten him so badly that he spent three days in the hospital.

Larry owned a large gun collection and had told Randy and Mark he would kill both of them if they reported him to anybody. Randy thought that his mom felt they deserved the beatings because on almost every occasion, she just stood back and watched. She never made the slightest bit of effort to stop Larry and always believed his side of the story. Not one of the incidents was ever reported, and it wasn't until Larry started beating her that she finally kicked him out of the house.

Barely four months after Larry had left, Randy's mom started dating William McGuigan. They went together for only two months before they got married. At the time of their marriage, William had been working steadily at the lumber mill, but for the last two years he had been off work and on disability because of a back injury. After that, all he did was sit around the house drinking beer and watching TV all day, which was strange because you could get only two channels in Granby. He made absolutely no effort to try to find another job, which seemed weird since he was only forty-one. His monthly disability cheque wasn't enough to pay the bills, so Randy's mom worked as a waitress at Kelly's Café.

Randy could not figure out why the two of them stayed married. They seemed to fight constantly, sometimes until late at night. He wished that someday she would throw the lazy bum out. But he suspected that even if William left, things at home wouldn't be much better. His mom had never been supportive of anything he did, and often she acted as if he wasn't even there. He quite often got the feeling that she didn't give a damn if he was alive or dead, and the only reason he was on earth was that abortion had been illegal in 1961.

Randy had contemplated running away from home many times and had actually made two attempts. But running away from Granby was not easy without a car. The only road that led out of Granby was Provincial Highway 55. It ran for forty-two miles south to join Highway 16 at Smithers. The only settlement in between was the Twin Lakes store and campground, twenty miles south of Granby. There was nothing else but wilderness.

Randy made his first attempt at running away when he was twelve by hiking along Highway 55. Along the way he had a near encounter with a grizzly bear. By the time he reached the Twin Lakes store, he was so cold, tired and hungry that he called his mom to ask her to pick him up, even though he knew what the consequences would be when he got home.

A year later he made another attempt. That time, however, he had saved his allowance until he could afford a bus ticket. But taking the bus out of Granby wasn't easy either. There was only one Skeena Coach Lines bus that left Granby each day; that was at 12:30 p.m. going to Smithers. When you reached Smithers, there was basically one direction you could go—east. If you headed west to Terrace, from there you had a choice to go south to Kitimat or farther west to Prince Rupert. But both of those destinations were the end of the line, unless you were really adventurous and tried to stow away on board a cargo ship!

When the bus from Granby arrived in Smithers, there was a six hour wait for the Greyhound bus that headed east. Randy found that out the hard way. He hadn't really been sure where he was going, so he thought he would go as far as he could with the money he had. At different times he made inquiries at the ticket counter about ticket prices. First, he asked how much a one-way ticket to Victoria cost, then he asked about Vancouver, Kamloops, Edmonton and finally, Prince George.

The man at the ticket counter became suspicious. He concluded that the kid didn't have a clue where he was going and that, judging by his young appearance, he had to be a runaway. So he called the police. When the police arrived, Randy wasn't suspicious at first. But when they began questioning him he realized they had come for him, and by then it was too late to run.

They took him to the police station and began asking him questions about problems at home. Throughout the interview Randy was very evasive. Even though Larry had left by then, things at home were still not good. The cops then had no alternative but to call his mom. Once again she had to drive down and pick him up. As with the previous time, they never said a word to each other on the way home.

After a few years, Randy started thinking of running away again because he felt older, wiser and better prepared. With some figuring he chose a destination—Alberta. He would make as much money as he could over the summer working at the recycling centre and leave by September at the latest. But he also prepared to leave on a moment's notice should the need arise. He loaded a backpack with spare clothing and a hundred dollars and stashed it under his bed.

As Randy walked into the house, his mom asked, "Where the hell have you been?"

"Over at Bill and Brad's place."

She told him that dinner was ready and that his boss at the recycling centre had called and asked him to come into work the next day. After dinner Randy and Mark went outside and tossed a football back and forth until it became dark.

The following week went fairly well for Randy. He got in four days' work at the recycling centre, mainly due to the separation of materials after the demolition of a building in town. But at the end of the workday on Thursday, Ned Pratt told him it was going to be very slow for the next while and he probably wouldn't be needed for the next several weeks. Randy wasn't worried one way or another—he was always paid in cash.

The following day was the first hot and sunny day in over a week, so Randy, Gary, Bill and Brad went to their favourite swimming hole. About one mile south of the city limits there was a spot on the Turgeon River (the river that runs through Granby) where the water was very calm, which made it a perfect spot for swimming. It was also the spot where the Canadian National Railway crossed the river. The railway was popular for diving, much to the chagrin of locomotive engineers. Randy, Bill and Brad took turns diving off the bridge, while Gary was content with swimming back and forth across the river. He didn't want to admit that he was afraid of heights. Randy was standing on the bridge when a northbound train suddenly appeared rounding a curve in the distance. Randy didn't jump immediately but instead waved at the oncoming train. When the engineer realized there was someone on the bridge, he began blasting the horn repeatedly. Randy finally jumped at the last minute. When he surfaced, he could see the engineer looking out the window and shaking his fist. Gary kept his head under the water the whole time. His dad was the foreman at the Granby C.N.R. switching yard and he was afraid the engineer would recognize him.

After awhile the boys decided to come out of the water and soak up the sun on the beach.

It was then that Randy made this proclamation: "Well boys, I have an announcement to make—I am finally getting my ass out of this one-horse town."

"Where have I heard this before? Where are you planning to go to?" Bill asked.

"Edmonton."

"Edmonton! Why in the world would you want to live there?" asked Brad.

Randy told them that the economy in Alberta was really booming because of the oil industry and that Edmonton was the main hotspot. He had seen on TV and read in the newspaper that they were really desperate for workers in Edmonton. Gary pointed out that he only had a grade nine education and didn't have any real skills. Randy told him it didn't matter—a lot of companies were willing to train workers. Bill asked Randy what kind of a job he hoped to find.

Randy replied, "Something in the construction field. But actually, I would be willing to take anything."

Randy pointed out that there was no future in Granby. He felt the town was going straight down the shitter. The others agreed. Bill said that his dad was going to get him and his brother a job at the mine when they finished high school, but Randy wondered what the point was in doing that. The mine only had about five years left. Brad then told them they had an aunt and uncle who owned an orchard in Osoyoos in southern B.C. They were going to have both of them work there over the summer, starting next year when they would be sixteen.

Bill seemed quite excited about it and said, "Osoyoos is a fantastic place. The lake there is really warm and there are beaches all over town. Over the summer hundreds of kids from Quebec go there to get jobs in the orchards and over half of them are women!"

Brad explained that the girls from Quebec were all quite attractive and the majority of them were in their age bracket.

Gary spoke up. "Well, I have you guys all beat. After graduation, I plan to go to California."

"What the hell do you plan to do down there?" Randy asked.

"Well, for one thing I'm going to do a lot of surfing and then I hope to make my mark in Hollywood. Who knows, I could become the next John Travolta," he replied, while doing disco dance moves.

The boys burst into uncontrolled laughter.

While laughing hysterically, Bill said, "Dream on."

"You just wait!"

The boys went for another swim. After they came out of the water, Bill said to the others, "Did you hear about the big party tomorrow night?"

Randy and Gary asked where it was going to be and Brad told them it would be at the gravel pit. He said there were supposed to be quite a few people going and that Manuel's friend, Rick, would be able to get them a couple of cases of beer. He also informed Randy that Tracy Sanchez would be there. She was the girl that Randy had admitted to having the hots for on several occasions.

Randy said, "Practically every guy in town likes her—you have to be pretty lucky to be able to get down her pants. That's another problem with this town—there are hardly any women our age, or any age for that matter."

Bill suggested to Randy that if he could get his driver's license they could go to Prince Rupert for a weekend.

Randy asked, "What for?"

"So we can get laid."

Bewildered, Randy asked, "What makes you think we can get laid in Prince Rupert? Why there and not anywhere else?"

The best explanation Bill could come up with was that since Prince Rupert was right near the ocean, there would be a lot of commercial fishermen living there. If they were out on their fishing boats for two to three weeks at a time, when they got back to Prince Rupert they would be pretty horny. Therefore, there would be a demand for hookers. Bill and Brad's father came from a seaport town in Portugal, where the main industry was commercial fishing. The town wasn't that much bigger than Prince Rupert, yet it had a fairly sizable red-light district.

Randy said, "That's all very interesting, but it's all speculation."

"There must be something there—we should go check it out," Bill replied.

"Bill, it's 250 miles from here to Prince Rupert, and how will we know about where to find hookers when we get there?"

"We'll ask someone!"

"Oh right, I can just picture it. We're walking along the Prince Rupert waterfront and I approach someone and say, 'Excuse me sir, where can a guy get a fuck in this town? Me and my buddies just drove over 250 miles and we are super horny!'" Randy went on to say, "I'll tell you what, Bill, you can do some research for us. Write to the Prince Rupert Chamber of Commerce and ask if Prince Rupert has any whorehouses. If so, ask them to please send a list that includes their addresses and the names of their madams."

After awhile Brad announced, "Well boys, I hate to be a party pooper, but we are having friends over for dinner, so my mom wants Bill and me to be home by 5:00." Pointing to Gary, he continued, "Besides, blonde here is starting to turn into a lobster!"

Bill commented that Gary looked about as white as Kees Vandelaar.

"Yeah, but at least I don't wear ugly clothes," Gary sneered.

The boys got on their bicycles and headed back into town. Once they passed the city limits, they took a shortcut through the Westview subdivision and rode along 14th Street. As they passed Kees Vandelaar's house, which was very recognizable because of the large windmill in the front yard, Kees was mowing the lawn, baggy shorts and all.

Randy yelled out, "Hey, Vandelaar," and flashed his middle finger as he rode by. Kees just ignored him.

When it came time for the boys to go their separate ways, Bill said to Randy and Gary, "Come by our place at 7:30 tomorrow night. Rick will give us a ride to the gravel pit and pick up some beer for us on the way."

"We'll be there!" they replied.

2

The gravel pit was actually the old Granby Public Works yard, located on a hill at the southern edge of town. The works yard had been moved across town five years ago and the old site had been vacant ever since. The site had become a popular party spot due to its wide, open space and its remote location. Its only drawback was that there were very few places to go to the bathroom!

Rick dropped the boys off at the gravel pit but he didn't stay himself. He was nineteen and old enough to go into the bars. He liked to go to the Lido nightclub downtown. The boys decided that when it came time to leave, they would either walk home or get a ride with someone else.

As usual, there was a big crowd—about eighty percent of the teenagers in Granby. Mike Thompson had a high-powered amplifier hooked up to the 8-track player in his truck, so the music was blasting throughout the site. The crowd made a huge bonfire. Everybody had brought their own booze and drugs. After an hour the boys had practically polished off both of their cases of beer. By then Randy got up enough nerve to go over and talk to Tracy Sanchez.

He nervously walked over and said, "Hi Tracy."

She looked up, smiled and said, "Hi Randy, I haven't seen you in awhile. Where have you been lately?"

Randy said, "Oh, I've been around. I'm not in school anymore—I'm working now."

"Oh, really? Doing what?"

"Oh, this and that. Lately, I've been working in the waste management business," he answered.

Randy gradually loosened up and then began blabbering away about his plans for the future, not paying any attention to whether she was interested. He even dropped the odd subtle hint that she might be interested in running away with him. But then the conversation was rudely interrupted by Randy's arch enemy, Arnold Becker. Over the years, Arnold had often been the butt of Randy's practical jokes. Despite all of the problems at home, Randy always maintained his sense of humour throughout his childhood. He was often the "class clown" and liked to play practical jokes on the other kids. Arnold was his favourite target. In the sixth grade he had put a rubber spider in his desk. In the eighth grade he had thrown a stink bomb in his locker. Last spring, he had put itching powder in his gym shorts.

"Well, fancy meeting you here, Watson," said Arnold.

"Yes, I am here, Arnold. Do you have a problem with that?" He added, "Oh, by the way, did you ever go see a dermatologist about your itchy nuts?"

Arnold, seething by then, said, "You really think you're funny, don't you? By the way, Tracy, don't waste your time with this guy—he's a fag."

"Oh, come on, Arnold. I was just having a little harmless fun, so quit being such a tight-ass. You can consider it a public service. I was just trying to help put a smile on that ugly face of yours."

Arnold was not amused and it was obvious to Randy that he was very drunk. He relentlessly taunted Randy, calling him every name possible. Randy realized that the only reason Arnold was standing up to him was due to the fact that he had been drinking heavily.

Then Arnold said, "How would you like me to punch your fucking lights out you, fucking retard?"

Randy had had enough. He let Arnold take the first swing and then the fight was on. Randy landed several vicious upper cuts and Arnold countered with a few fierce right hooks. The two combatants went toe to toe for what seemed an eternity. Randy eventually gained the upper hand by throwing Arnold to the ground and repeatedly punching him in the face with full fury. It took at least four guys to pry them apart, but when it was over Randy came out the clear winner. Arnold had managed to give Randy a busted lip, but Arnold himself was a bloody mess. He was bleeding from both his mouth and his nose, as well as above both eyes. He was moaning in pain and was barely moving. His friend Stan Sherman loaded him into his car and drove him to the hospital.

While everyone was praising Randy for his performance, Gary told him they had better leave. He knew Arnold had three older brothers, plus a brother-in-law who was one big, mean bastard. He was afraid that once Arnold was patched up, he would rally them together and come looking for revenge. Bill and Brad agreed and they all pleaded with Randy to get out of there. Randy reluctantly gave in.

As the boys made their way back into town, they had a difficult time calming Randy down. He was ranting that he wished he had killed Arnold and that he could have done the same thing to Larry, his ex-stepfather. Gary tried reassuring him by saying that Arnold got what he deserved and he wouldn't be giving him any more trouble.

"Just forget about it and let's enjoy the rest of the evening."

By the time they reached the city limits, Randy had settled down somewhat, so the boys started discussing what they wanted to do with the remainder of the evening. After all, it was only 10:00. One advantage to living up north was that it was still partially light out at 10:00 during the summer. As they walked along the street, they noticed a lone figure walking toward them in the distance. As they got closer, they realized it was Kees Vandelaar. Randy stopped him dead in his tracks.

"Hey Vandelaar, who the fuck said you could walk here? Don't you know this is our turf?"

"I can go wherever I want—this is my street!"

Kees tried to walk away, but Randy blocked his path and then blew cigarette smoke in his face. He asked Kees where he had been all night.

Kees replied, "That's none of your business, but if you must know, I went to the theatre, okay!"

"Boy, you and I have some unfinished business!" Randy threatened.

"What the hell is your problem, Watson? What did I ever do to you?" He asked.

"You don't have to do anything, it's just the fact that you're just plain ugly, stupid and you look like a fucking dork! You have no place in society!" He snarled.

Kees yelled, "Leave me alone, Watson!"

He tried to run, but Randy grabbed him and threw him to the ground. He jumped on him and began punching him in the face. He repeatedly pummeled him; then he got up and began kicking him.

Gary stepped in and said, "C'mon, Randy, he's had enough!"

Randy yelled back, "I'll say when he's had enough."

He continued his vicious assault on Kees, kicking him hard in the head and upper body. It was as if all his pent-up anger was being unleashed at once.

Gary stepped in again and yelled, "For fuck's sake, stop it!"

Randy pushed him away and was about to get in a few more shots, when a man from one of the neighbouring houses came running out toward them, yelling, "Hey!"

Bill yelled, "Let's get out of here," and the boys took off.

Gary took one look at Kees before he started running. He was lying motionless and had blood coming out of his mouth.

The boys ran for two blocks and then stopped to catch their breath. Gary spoke up. "What is your fucking problem, Randy? You could have killed him!"

"Yeah, so what?"

"So what? If he dies, that's murder! Don't you care? What did he ever do to you? He's just a little different, that's all!" Gary said angrily.

Randy responded, "Look, I just never liked him, okay!"

"That doesn't mean you had to beat the living bejesus out of him. You could have just ignored him. Frankly, Randy, I don't know what's gotten into you. Are you going crazy or something?" Gary asked.

"Look, just forget about it! What do you say we head downtown?"

"No, forget it! Leave me alone—I'm going home!" Gary said.

Bill added, "Yeah, me too."

"Fine, forget about it!" Randy replied.

With that they all went off in their own directions.

When Randy arrived home, his mom and William were arguing loudly, as usual. In fact, he could hear them from down the street. It seemed William's big mouth had gotten them into trouble again—they had been kicked out of the King Edward Hotel. Normally they would stay until closing time, but tonight they'd had to leave early.

When Randy went in, his mom said, "Where were you tonight? What the hell happened to you?" She continued, "Have you been drinking?"

"Look, I went to a party at the gravel pit and got into a fight, okay! Are you satisfied now?"

William piped in, "Don't you know that's private property? It seems you kids have nothing better to do with your time these days. All you ever do is drink, beat each other up and vandalize property."

He proceeded to talk about the constructive things he did as a kid until Randy butted in and said, "Look, I'm sick and tired of you always giving your opinion all the time. As far as I'm concerned, you're nothing but a goddamn loser and you don't know dick-all about anything!"

His mom said, "Don't you ever talk to William like that again! You should try something new and take his advice for a change!"

"Why are you always sticking up for him? Look at him, mom—all he ever does is sit around and spend your money! He's just a useless, lazy bum!"

His mom yelled, "Randy! You apologize to William right this instant!"

"Fuck you!" he yelled back.

She slapped him hard across his face and said, "You go straight up to your room and don't come out until I say you can!"

Randy ran up the stairs and when he entered his room he slammed the door hard behind him.

He sat in his room and stared out the window, listening to his mom and William argue downstairs. After an hour, he decided he'd had enough. He crept into the bathroom and removed his soap and toothbrush. After returning to his room, he reached under his bed for the backpack he had stashed there in preparation for this moment. He grabbed more clothes from his closet and drawers and added them to those already packed. He found the metal tin, also hidden under his bed, where he kept some of his money. He counted the money from the tin and his pack. He had a total of $212. He put a small amount in his pack, stuffed a few bills down his socks and put the rest in his wallet. Now he was all set. There was just one more thing he had to do.

He went across the hall and knocked on the door to Mark's room. Opening the door, he said, "Mark, can I see you for a minute?"

"Sure, Randy."

Randy sat down and said, "Look, I don't know how to tell you this, but I have to go away for awhile."

"You're not running away again, are you?" Mark questioned.

"I have to. I can't stay here anymore—there's too much shit going down. Besides, there's no reason for me to stay, there's no future here."

"Where are you going?"

"Well, I'm going to try my luck in Edmonton, and if things don't work out there I might head farther east."

With tears in his eyes, Mark pleaded, "Randy, please don't go."

"Look, everything's going to be all right. I'll tell you what, when I get settled and find a decent job you can come and live with me. After all, mom doesn't really give a shit about either one of us. To her we're just an inconvenience. But you have to understand, this place holds nothing but bad memories for me—I'm sure you feel the same way. I have to move on," Randy explained.

"I'm going to miss you, Randy."

"I'll miss you too, but I promise I'll write as often as I can. Hopefully you'll be able to visit me sometime soon," Randy assured him.

With that, they gave each other a big hug and they went into Randy's room. As Randy climbed out the window, he said to Mark, "Now you take care of yourself and be sure to close the window behind me."

He shinnied down the drainpipe and ran down the street in the direction of Gary's house.

When Randy arrived at Gary's, he went around to the back and tapped on his basement bedroom window. Gary was sitting in his room reading, and when he heard the tapping on his window he went over to investigate.

Opening the window, he said, "Randy! What the hell are you doing here?"

"Come on out, I need to see you," he replied.

Gary climbed out the window and immediately noticed the backpack. He said, "What's with the backpack?"

"I'm leaving town," Randy said, "and I need your help."

"What do you need me for?"

Randy blurted out, "Look, I have to leave *tonight*! I can't wait until tomorrow. The next bus for Smithers doesn't leave until noon tomorrow and by that time the cops will likely be after me. Besides, your mom would never let me stay here at your place. I was hoping you might have some suggestions. Do you know of anybody who would be willing to give me a ride to Smithers for a fee? How about your dad?"

"Are you kidding?" he said, "No way! He would get too suspicious."

"Look, I know first-hand that nobody drives on that highway at this time of night, so hitchhiking tonight is out of the question. Damn this isolated town! So, do you have any ideas?"

"Let me think for a minute!"

After a few minutes he came up with an idea. He asked Randy the time: it was twenty to twelve.

"Okay, here's the plan," he suggested. "It's a good thing my dad is the foreman at the rail yard. The train for the lumber mill will be leaving for Smithers in twenty minutes."

Randy asked, "You mean I'm going to have to hitch a ride on a train?"

"Well, it's either that or you're looking at one hell of an expensive cab ride," he answered. "Look, I know the whole routine. The train comes up here in the evening and drops off the empty lumber and woodchip cars. Then it picks up all the loaded cars. The switching is usually completed around 11:45. The engineer then goes into the station and picks up his orders. He almost always leaves right at midnight."

"Well, what are we waiting for? The rail yard is not that far from here. Let's go!"

"Wait a minute. You can't get on the train there; somebody will see us!" Gary added, "You have to get on at a spot where no one else is around, preferably somewhere outside the city."

"Now, hold on here. Are you telling me that I have to jump on the train while it's moving?"

Gary pointed out that it was his only choice. Reluctantly Randy went along with it, knowing he couldn't wait until morning.

"I know the perfect spot," Gary offered. "Do you know where Smethurst Road is? It's about a hundred yards past the railway crossing. The railway line makes a really sharp curve and because it's on a downhill grade, the maximum speed the train can handle is ten miles per hour. There are no houses there, so nobody will see us. C'mon, we better get going."

As they made their way to the rendezvous point with the train, Gary gave Randy instructions. He told him that it would be better to get on the front half of the train. This would give him time to get away after jumping off before the caboose came along.

"The first half of the train is lumber cars and the last half is woodchip cars," he informed Randy. "Usually the maximum length is thirty cars. Now, on the lumber cars there is a ladder on the back. It is only horizontal metal bars welded onto the back of the car. That's what you will be hanging on to."

Gary noticed that Randy looked somewhat nervous, so he tried reassuring him by telling him that he would be all right as long as he held on.

"What if I slip?" he asked.

"Then you're fucked."

"Gee, thanks for that reassuring tip."

As the boys walked along Highway 55, they passed by the sign that read "Welcome to Granby." Randy took one long look at it and realized he might never see it again. When they reached Smethurst Road they turned right and went up three hundred yards to the railway crossing. They then turned left, walked up the railway to the curve and hid in some bushes below the tracks.

"Wait until the last locomotive has rounded the curve. I will give the signal," Gary further instructed Randy. "When you grab onto the ladder, pull yourself up as quickly as possible. When you get to Smithers, be sure to jump off before the Bulkley River bridge. If you wait until after you cross the bridge, you will be right in the middle of the rail yard where you might get caught."

It was starting to rain. Randy confessed to Gary that he felt bad about what he had done to Kees. He admitted that he hadn't meant to beat him so badly. He hoped Kees would pull through okay.

"Well, there's not a lot you can do about it now," Gary said.

After a little while Randy remarked that it was five minutes past midnight. Just then they heard the sound of a train whistle in the distance.

Gary said, "Okay, the train's just leaving the yard."

A few minutes later, the whistle blew again, indicating that it was crossing Commissioner Street. It started raining very heavily. After a few more minutes they heard the whistle again; it was much louder. This meant it was approaching the Smethurst Road crossing. Then three large headlights came into view. The ground below began to rumble as four massive diesel locomotives passed above them. A couple of seconds after the last locomotive disappeared around the curve, Gary gave the signal, "*Now!*"

Randy bolted full tilt toward the train and ran alongside it, struggling to maintain his footing on the loose shale of the rail bed. He reached over and grabbed a ladder bar on the back of a lumber car. He swung his left arm around and grabbed the next bar up. His feet were dragging on the ground. Using every ounce of his strength, he pulled himself up to the next bar, his feet dangling in the air.

Gary was running alongside the train, yelling, "C'mon Randy, pull yourself up!"

Randy managed to pull himself up to the next bar and then swing his left leg up enough to set his foot on the bottom bar. He reached for the next one up, but his foot slipped on the wet bottom bar and his feet were dangling in the air again.

Gary yelled, "Randy! Pull yourself up! You can do it!"

Randy somehow managed to summon all of his strength and pulled himself up four bars until both feet could touch the bottom bar. When they were firmly planted on the bottom bar, Randy gave the thumbs up signal to Gary.

Gary gave a loud, "Yahoo!" and then yelled, "Goodbye, Randy!"

Randy knew the next hour would be the ultimate endurance test. The rain had turned into a torrential downpour and there was a strong wind. The train was accelerating rapidly and he was wondering how in the name of god would he be able to hang on all the way to Smithers. After awhile, he noticed the valley floor get farther and farther away as the train clung to the side of the mountain in order to maintain a one-degree gradient all the way to Smithers. Bolts of lightning lit up the sky. Some of them seemed too close for comfort. A bit later he noticed the ground disappear beneath him as the train crossed the bridge over Sonora Creek canyon. This was one of the longest and highest bridges on the entire C.N.R. system.

A half an hour later Randy was in sheer agony. The rain and the wind had numbed him all over and he was starting to feel delirious. Every so often he would get a brief respite when the train would pass through one of the ten tunnels along the line. He could see the lights of Smithers in the distance, so he kept telling himself over and over, "Hang in there, don't give up, it won't be much longer." He knew that if he let go it would mean certain death, so he did everything he could to stay focused. His main thought was that the trip would get better after this—no more riding on trains!

After what seemed an eternity, the train suddenly slowed down. He looked around the corner and saw the bridge over the Bulkley River dead ahead. He decided to take Gary's advice and jump off before the train crossed the bridge. The train had slowed down considerably, so he decided that now was his chance. He knew he had to jump clear of the train and get down the embankment as soon as possible. He said to himself, "Okay now, on the count of three—one, two, *three!*"

He gave a mighty leap and landed well clear of the train. He caught the edge of the embankment and rolled down until he landed in some prickly bushes. He scrambled down even further and hid until the caboose passed over. He stood up and checked to see if he had twisted his ankle when he landed. Everything appeared to be okay. He then climbed back up the embankment and proceeded to cross the river on the rail bridge. Even though it had stopped raining by then, the bridge deck was still very wet and slippery. The ties were treated with creosote and when they got wet it was just like a skating rink. He was having an awful time getting any footing. He looked up and saw the Highway 55 bridge in the distance. He thought, "What the hell am I doing?"

He crossed the highway bridge and when he reached the other side, he wondered where he was going to spend the night. It was a quarter past one, so he ruled out trying to get a room at the hotel. He looked over at the rail yard and noticed that there was nobody there. He thought, "What the hell was Gary talking about?" He noticed there were a number of sheds along the tracks, so he went over to see if any of them were unlocked. Sure enough, one of them was open. He opened the door, went inside and flicked his lighter. He thought, "Gee, what if this is the fuel storage shed!" Luckily it wasn't. The only things in there were a railway motor car and a bunch of tools. He sat down on the motor car, took off his wet clothes and put on some dry ones. Fortunately his backpack was waterproof. He hung his wet clothes on the motor car, then sat back and lit a cigarette. He thought, "So, how does it feel to be free?"

3

When Randy woke up it was 5:30. He could hear people talking nearby, so even though he hadn't slept much, he figured he had better get up and get going before anyone found him there. He put on his somewhat dry clothes from the previous night and stuffed his backpack with the dry clothes. He checked to see if anybody was around. The coast was clear. He left the shed and headed for town.

Downtown Smithers looked like a ghost town, but then again it was early on a Sunday morning. He thought he would wait until he got to Prince George before getting something to eat. Even though he had never successfully hitchhiked before, he knew it was common sense never to try for a ride in an urban area; always wait until you are outside the city. So he walked along Highway 16 until he saw the sign "Prince George 371 km." He turned, faced the highway, put his thumb out and said, "Well, here goes nothing!"

Randy was concerned his appearance might influence a potential driver against picking him up. In the bathroom mirror last night, he had seen his upper lip was cut, and the area under his right eye had blackened slightly. The black eye didn't look too severe—it looked more like a dark circle than a shiner. Because it was his right eye, he figured a driver would be less likely to notice it when looking at him from the left. Randy decided that if anyone asked about it, he would say he'd banged into a doorknob.

There wasn't much traffic at that time of the morning; several cars went by but didn't stop. However, a half an hour later a station wagon pulled over. Randy thought, "All right," and ran over to the car and got inside. It was a middle-aged man driving.

The driver asked Randy where he was heading, and he answered, "Prince George."

"Good, that's where I'm heading." He went on to say, "Hi, my name is Ralph Middleton."

Randy had to think quickly. He figured he shouldn't use his real name for fear that the police knew about his involvement in the incident with Kees and that it had been reported in the newspapers and on the radio.

"Hi, I'm Arnold Becker." He then thought, "What the hell am I using that goof's name for?"

Ralph asked him what had brought him to be out on the highway. Again he had to think quickly and make up a story. Saying he had run away from home just wouldn't cut it. He told Ralph that he was from Prince George and that he had gone to Prince Rupert to visit his girlfriend. He said he didn't have his driver's license and he couldn't afford a bus ticket. Ralph told Randy he was a sales rep for a line of vitamin supplements that he sold to drugstores, health food stores and some grocery stores. He was based in Vancouver and his territory was all of northwestern B.C. He was planning to call on several clients in Prince George and then head back to Vancouver. The part about heading to Vancouver sounded tempting to Randy, but his course was set—Edmonton was his goal.

After four hours they arrived in Prince George. Randy looked at his watch and noticed it was 10:30.

Ralph said to him, "Oh, Arnold. I'll tell you what, if you tell me where you live I can drop you off at your place."

It took a moment for Randy to clue in that he was Arnold. Again he had to think quickly. He told Ralph that he lived in an apartment near downtown, but his parents would be in church right now and he didn't have a key. Plus, he had planned to go out for breakfast. He told Ralph anywhere downtown would be fine.

When Ralph dropped him off, Randy thanked him and went into a nearby restaurant. He ordered the breakfast special since he hadn't eaten in awhile. Afterwards as he was leaving the restaurant, he noticed a map of the city hanging on the wall. He looked for the quickest access to Highway 16 heading east and determined how far he should walk before hitchhiking again. He figured that the best spot would be just past the bridge over the Fraser River.

Once outside, he got his bearings and made his way toward Highway 16. When he finally reached the bridge, he couldn't believe his eyes. He thought, "What the hell kind of setup is this?" It was strange that in the half mile before the bridge, all the cars heading east were stopped, yet all the cars heading west were moving. Then he realized that the bridge was only one lane! He took a closer look and noticed there was no sidewalk. Not only that, the roadway consisted of only two parallel metal decks just wide enough for a vehicle's wheelbase. The other half of the bridge was for the C.N.R. main line. He noticed the "No Trespassing" sign on the railway section, but his only thought was, "Screw you, I'm crossing."

After crossing the bridge, he walked up Highway 16 for a ways before putting his thumb out. He was standing there for quite awhile and the afternoon sun was really starting to beat down on him. He thought, "Man, what a contrast from last night!" After several hours a car finally pulled over. It was a late-model Volvo. When he approached the car the driver asked where he was heading.

"Edmonton."

The driver said, "Yeah, so am I."

This driver was younger than the other one; about in his mid-twenties. He was very neatly dressed and had short curly hair.

Almost immediately he asked Randy, "So, what's a young man like you doing hitchhiking? Don't you know it's very dangerous?"

"Well, I don't have much choice. I can't really afford a bus ticket."

"Look, there are a lot of kooks out there, and you being young and vulnerable, would be easy pickings," he said.

"Look, I can take care of myself, okay?"

"What do your mother and father think about you hitchhiking?" the driver asked.

"For one thing, my father is dead and for another, I couldn't care less what my mom thinks. She doesn't care about me."

A few minutes later the driver asked Randy why he was going to Edmonton. He explained that he was planning to look for work. The driver asked him how he expected to find a job dressed the way he was and with hair that long. Randy said that when he got to Edmonton he would change his clothes and get a haircut; he didn't plan to wear his good clothes while travelling. The driver also told Randy that he needed to change his attitude.

Randy then proceeded to take out a cigarette, and almost immediately the man said, "Hey, no smoking in my car!" A few minutes later he asked, "Have you accepted Jesus Christ as your lord and saviour?"

Randy thought, "Oh no, not one of those guys! That picture of the Virgin Mary hanging from the rearview mirror should have been a giveaway."

The driver continued, "If you haven't, you should. After all, Jesus died on the cross so you and I can be freed from sin."

"Whatever."

For the next while the driver gave Randy a constant, non-stop lecture on everything from proper etiquette to committing his life to Christ. All the while he spoke in a smug, arrogant tone of voice and acted like he was a leading expert on practically everything. For a time Randy just put up with it, but when the driver started telling him what he should do with his life, Randy had had enough.

He finally spoke up and said, "Look, if I had wanted your opinion, I would have asked for it!"

"Now, see here, young man. I was kind enough to give you a ride, so the least you can do is listen to some words of wisdom."

"Just because you gave me a ride doesn't give you the right to tell me how to live my life!" Randy said angrily.

"Well, somebody should because you sure aren't doing a very good job of it!"

"Fuck you!"

"Don't use that kind of language in my car!"

Randy, livid by now, said, "You know, I would rather walk to Edmonton than sit here and listen to your bullshit! Why don't you pull over and let me out?"

"Don't tempt me, young man. Maybe if you were more respectful toward your mother you would not be in this mess," he replied.

"That's it! Pull this Swedish piece of shit over right now! I said *now*, you fucking freak!" Randy shouted.

The driver pulled over onto the shoulder and as Randy was getting out he warned him, "You are going to be sorry! You are never going to make it anywhere in life!"

Randy shot back, "Go to hell, you fucking faggot!" He then slammed the door and as the car sped away, he yelled out, "Fuck you," and flashed both his middle fingers. As the car got further away, he muttered to himself, "Asshole. What a dipshit!"

After Randy had regained his composure, he decided that he would go to a nearby store and get something to drink before hitching another ride. But then he looked ahead and saw only road. He turned around to look the other way and saw the same thing—nothing but road. There was nothing but forest as far as he could see. He said to himself, "Where the hell am I?" His first thought was, "All right, don't panic here. There must be a town nearby." He looked down the road and noticed it went straight for about two miles and then curved left. He set off down the road, turning around and putting out his thumb whenever a car came by.

It seemed to take forever to reach the curve in the road. He wasn't having any luck getting a ride either. The traffic was awfully light, which was strange since it was summer and therefore tourist season. On the average there was about one car every two minutes. After the curve he realized that it was the same—nothing but road. The intense sun was really starting to get to him. He kept thinking about what had happened with the driver, and all that was going through his mind was, "I shouldn't have done that, or I could have at least waited until we were in Jasper before losing my temper." But he realized there was no sense in crying about it now, so he continued on down the road.

After walking another mile, he noticed a sign in the distance. When he got close enough he realized it was a mileage sign. It read "McBride 97 km; Tete Jaune Cache 162 km; Jasper, Alberta 263 km." He looked at it in utter disbelief, thinking, "You mean to say that there is no town *before* McBride?" Then he realized there was an intersection with a road entering from the left just ahead. Once at the intersection, he saw there was a sign that pointed to a place called Longworth. Just then a C.N.R. company pickup truck coming from the east slowed down to turn onto that road. He motioned to the driver to stop.

Rolling the window down, he asked, "Can I help you?"

Randy asked him if he was heading to Longworth and, if so, could he get a ride with him? The driver told him that was where he was going, then asked him why he wanted to go there. Randy asked what was in Longworth.

"Longworth is only a railway siding with some maintenance buildings. There are no stores or anything there. The only reason I am going there is that the rail replacement gang is stationed there right now and I am the foreman."

Randy asked where the nearest store or restaurant was and the driver answered, "Well, if you're heading east that would be in McBride, and to the west there is a store at Purden Lake, but that's still over thirty miles from here."

"So there's nothing closer?"

"Nope." He then asked, "How did you get out here in the first place?"

Randy replied, "It's a long story." He asked if there were any openings on the track gang.

"That's not up to me. You would have to apply at the C.N.R. regional office in Prince George. Besides, we are only going to be here two more days and then we're moving out. We will be working on the rail line into Granby next."

"Well, it was just a thought, thanks anyway," Randy said.

"I gotta go, good luck!" the driver finished.

Randy said, "Yeah, I'll need it!"

Randy felt sick knowing that he was stranded out in the middle of nowhere. He tried in vain to get a ride, but nobody was stopping. Afternoon turned into evening and he still hadn't had any luck. He realized that he would have to spend the night there and try again in the morning. He went into a wooded area back from the highway and found a spot under a large spruce tree. He knew he would be in for a rough night, being close to the highway. He also knew that it was going to be very cold that night. A few hours later he heard some twigs snapping nearby. He looked up and saw a mother bear and her cubs crossing the highway. He thought, "Oh no, not again!" All he could think about was that if it weren't for the severe chip on his shoulder, he might be in Edmonton by now!

Randy woke up at 5:30, the same time as the previous day. Needless to say, he hadn't gotten very much sleep. He made his way to the highway feeling quite groggy and very, very hungry. It had been almost twenty hours since he last ate anything. He immediately began hitchhiking, hoping that his luck would change. It appeared that he was having the same kind of luck, but after three hours his persistence finally paid off.

A car pulled over, and Randy said, "Oh thank you, thank you, thank you!"

The driver of the customized 1968 Oldsmobile Cutlass asked him, "Where ya headin'?"

"Edmonton."

"I can give you a ride as far as Jasper," the driver informed him.

"That's fine with me!" Randy said.

The driver was quite stocky and was wearing a baseball cap, big sunglasses and a leather jacket. He asked Randy, "What were you doing way out here in the sticks?"

"Well, I got a ride with some real asshole—a real opinionated bastard. He kept preaching the lord to me and told me I had a bad attitude. I can't take that shit!"

"Yeah, I know what you mean," he agreed. "You will run into people like that now and then, people who think they know everything yet they most likely know fuck-all! So, what's your name, kid?"

Randy decided to use his real name this time.

The driver said, "Pleased to meet you. My name's Torque."

Randy thought, "What the hell kind of a name is Torque?"

"Wanna do a toke?" Torque offered.

"Sure, why not?"

Torque asked what the big attraction was in Edmonton and Randy told him that he was planning to look for work there. He asked Torque what he did for a living.

"Well, a little of this and a little of that, whatever I can do to stay on top," was Torque's response.

Randy didn't feel satisfied with that answer. It was obvious that Torque had spent a lot of money customizing the interior and exterior of his car and it had one mean-sounding engine. The money had to have come from somewhere.

As they approached McBride, Randy asked if they could stop at a store and get something to eat. He was absolutely starving by then and smoking that joint hadn't helped.

Torque said, "I'll tell you what—when we get to Jasper we'll go out to eat and I'll buy."

Randy reluctantly agreed.

A little while later Torque asked, "You know something, do you ever have times when you just want to say fuck the world? I mean, we spend most of our lives paying our debt to society, and for what? We just get shit on in return. Sometimes I think life is just not worth it, know what I mean?"

Randy didn't have a clue what Torque was talking about. He rambled on and on about living in a totalitarian society and how the justice system and society as a whole had failed him. He was really starting to give Randy the creeps. He was drinking whiskey straight from a mickey bottle as well as popping amphetamines. He was driving well over the speed limit. Randy periodically looked over at the speedometer and noticed he was driving over ninety miles per hour. A couple of times he passed over a double solid line.

Just past Tete Jaune Cache they passed a mileage sign indicating that Jasper was only sixty-two miles away. Randy was quite relieved.

Torque took another swig of whiskey and offered the bottle to Randy saying, "Here, have a snort!"

"No thanks." Randy declined.

"C'mon what are you, a wuss?" Torque jeered.

Randy reluctantly took a drink. Straight whiskey on his empty stomach did not go down very well.

Down the road Randy caught his first glimpse of Mt. Robson. He was awestruck at the majestic sight. A little while later he saw the sign he had been longing to see for quite some time: "Welcome to Alberta." He thought to himself, "Well, at least I made it to Alberta!"

When they finally arrived in Jasper, Torque pulled up alongside a convenience store.

Randy said, "Excellent, I'm starving!"

"Whoa, not so fast there. Just wait here and when I get back we'll go to a restaurant," Torque stated.

"Look I'm really, really hungry!"

"Hey, I promised that I would treat you. I will only be a minute, so just wait here."

After about thirty seconds the rumbling in Randy's stomach was too much. Randy thought, "Fuck you, asshole! I want to eat *now*!" When he entered the store he was horrified to see Torque pointing a handgun in the clerk's face.

Torque shouted at him, "Hey!"

"Oh shit!" Randy yelled.

He bolted out of the store, ran to Torque's car, got out his backpack and took off at full speed down the street. He heard a shot and a few seconds later the squealing of tires. He ran around a corner, down half a block and then turned into an alley. The sound of squealing tires was getting closer, and all Randy could think was, "He's after me, he's after me!" He turned onto a street and into another alley, still running full tilt. He spotted some garbage cans, took the lid off one of them and jumped in. There wasn't much room for him and his backpack. He was only in there a minute when he got the feeling something was in there with him. He felt something crawling on his leg and yelled, "Oh fuck." He knocked the garbage can over, scrambled out and noticed two mice running away. He took off down the alley and a few houses down he noticed a tool shed in a backyard. He climbed over the fence and decided to hide in the shed for a few minutes until it was safe. All that was going through his mind was, "Why is this happening to me?"

If Randy had planned to spend only a few minutes in the tool shed, he shouldn't have sat down. It was very hot and stuffy in there and that, combined with his lack of sleep, caused him to nod off. An hour later an elderly lady came out to the shed. They were both completely startled when she opened the door. She let out a piercing scream and ran back to the house, yelling, "Help! Police!" Randy bolted out the door, jumped over the fence and ran down the alley.

He cautiously made his way downtown. Whenever he came to an intersection he looked very carefully both ways. When he finally reached the main drag, he poked his head around the corner of a building to see if Torque's car was parked anywhere. Since Torque had a car that stood out, he would have an easy time spotting it. He looked up and down the main street and saw no sign of it. He concluded that he had either split town or had been captured by the police. He didn't want to keep looking around suspiciously; anybody watching him would think he was weird.

Randy's next priority was to find a restaurant. He went into the first one he saw and the hostess asked if he wanted a table for one, smoking or non-smoking?

Randy said, "Smoking, definitely!"

He looked at the clock on the wall and noticed it was 1:00—he had forgotten about the time change, so he figured he had better order lunch instead of breakfast. He was so hungry by then that he was determined to order the biggest item on the menu. Those plans were quickly changed once he received a menu.

He looked with total shock and bewilderment at the prices of everything on the menu and said out loud, "Jumping Jehoshaphat, look at these prices!"

A hamburger or a grilled cheese sandwich at Kelly's Café would have cost about half that amount. But then again Granby wasn't exactly a tourist mecca. So all Randy ordered was a bowl of soup, albeit a large one. He figured that would hold him over until dinner, by which time he would find a cheaper place to eat, if there were such a thing in Jasper!

All the while Randy was in the restaurant, he kept looking over to the park across the street. He noticed a large number of young people hanging out all throughout it. All of them seemed to look around his age. When he left the restaurant he headed over there. After all, he had decided he would not attempt to hitchhike to Edmonton until tomorrow morning.

Randy went over to the park and sat under a large tree, hoping to be able to take a nap. Since there were so many other teenagers in the park, he was no more than ten feet from anyone else.

He was only there a few minutes when a boy sitting near him said, "Hey, how's it going?"

"All right, I guess."

The boy asked him if he had just arrived in town. Randy told him that was right. The boy informed him that he had arrived in Jasper a couple of days ago.

"My name is Craig."

Randy gave him his name. Craig asked if he had hitchhiked there and he told him that he had. When Randy mentioned that he was from Granby, B.C., Craig looked kind of puzzled, as though he had never heard of Granby. Randy informed him that it was a small mining town in the north-central Interior of B.C., between Prince George and Prince Rupert. You had to turn north at Smithers and then it was another forty miles. Craig said that he was from Chatham, Ontario, about fifty miles east of Windsor.

Craig asked Randy how his trip was going.

"Well, I spent the first part of the trip hanging on to the back of a rail car in a driving rainstorm, spent the first night in a C.N.R. shed, got a ride with a crazed holy-roller, spent the next night in the woods in the middle of nowhere and to top it off, I got a ride here with some psychopathic robber! Other than that, the trip is going just fine."

Craig told him it had taken him five days to get there, and he had run into a few assholes along the way, but most of the people he had gotten rides with were cool. He even got a ride with the same person all the way from Saskatoon to Edmonton. Then Randy said he would be heading to Edmonton the next morning.

Craig suggested, "Why don't you stay here? There's lots of work available."

He inquired as to what jobs were available and Craig told him that restaurants needed waiters, cooks and dishwashers; gas stations needed gas jockeys; hotels needed bellhops and banquet staff.

When Randy pointed out that most of those jobs would not pay any more than minimum wage, Craig said, "So what? I'm only here for the summer. I just want to make some extra money."

"You see, it's different for you. You will be going back to school in the fall. As for me, I'm not in school anymore. I need a job that is permanent and that pays a lot better. I'm interested in something in either construction or the oil industry. Something that pays big bucks."

Craig asked him if he would be interested in taking a tour of Jasper and Randy said that he would be delighted. He wasn't exactly sure if Craig was doing this with the intention of persuading him to change his mind. So Randy got the grand tour, seeing all the attractions of Jasper. Craig seemed quite knowledgeable about all of the sites around town, considering he had only been there for two days. As they passed by the Jasper Park Lodge, he told Randy that he had a fairly good job prospect working in the kitchen there. He was supposed to call them back in the next couple of days. If that job didn't pan out, he knew of a couple of restaurants that were hiring dishwashers. He also pointed out that most places provided accommodation for their workers, which included room and board. They just took a little bit off each paycheque. So you could actually save most of the money you made over the summer. Randy found this quite interesting, but he still wasn't changing his mind.

"I've also heard that Jasper is a great place to party, and from what I have seen so far, there are lots of nice looking babes here."

Randy said, "You know something, this friend of mine back home said the exact same thing about Osoyoos. I'll tell you what, when I get settled in Edmonton I'll come up here for a weekend sometime."

After Craig had showed Randy practically everything there was to see in Jasper, Randy asked if he knew about any places to eat that were cheap. He wondered if they had an A&W.

"They don't have an A&W but they do have a Dairy Queen."

"That's all right with me. What do you say we go have an early dinner?" Randy replied.

When they got to the Dairy Queen, Randy ordered three double cheeseburgers and a large order of both french fries and onion rings.

"Holy shit!" Craif said. "You really must be hungry!"

"You better believe it!"

He asked Craig where he crashed at night, and he replied, "In that park where you first saw me."

"Are you sure you're allowed to do that?"

"They're used to it here. It happens here every summer. Kids from all over Canada come here looking for summer employment. As long as we don't bother the local residents and merchants and don't cause any trouble, they don't mind us. Why do you ask?"

"Well, I need some place to crash tonight."

Craig said, "Hey, no problem!"

After they left the Dairy Queen, they went back to the park. Later that evening a large group of teenagers gathered there. Three of them were playing guitars and one was playing the harmonica. They had one gigantic sing-along which lasted well into the night. Randy was really enjoying himself. Deep down inside he would have liked to stay in Jasper, but he knew that if he had any chance of making it in the workforce, Edmonton was the place. Jasper was a nice town, but the work was mainly just seasonal. Edmonton was his goal.

Randy woke up at 6:30 the following morning. Once again, he hadn't gotten much sleep. The group had partied until after 1 a.m. and the location of the park hadn't helped either. It was right next to the C.N.R. tracks and a train had gone by practically every hour. He woke up Craig, who was sleeping next to him.

"Hey, what's going on here?"

Randy said, "Wake up, sleepyhead!"

"Randy, what do you think you're doing?"

Randy answered, "Look, I'm heading out. I just wanted to say goodbye."

"You mean I couldn't talk you into staying?"

"Look, I really like Jasper, but my destiny is only 130 miles away."

"Well, at least I tried," Craig said.

Randy went on to tell him not to make the same mistake that he had. "You be sure and go back to school in the fall and go until you graduate."

Craig assured him that he would.

"You take care of yourself and thanks for all your hospitality."

"Hey, it was my pleasure. Good luck in Edmonton."

They shook hands and Randy headed off.

Before he left Jasper, he stopped in at a convenience store and got a coffee and a doughnut to go. As he walked out of the store, he thought to himself, "Boy, I sure have been eating good lately." He walked about one mile past the edge of town before putting his thumb out. It was three hours before a car finally pulled over. This time it was a man and a woman in a late model sedan.

The man asked him where he was heading and he said, "Edmonton."

"You're in luck—that's where we're heading."

The ride was more enjoyable for Randy this time around, mainly because neither of them tried to get into a conversation with him. He didn't really like it when anybody asked him a lot of questions and pried into his personal life. In his mind it was none of anyone else's business. Throughout most of the trip they just let him sit back and enjoy the scenery, which gradually changed from mountains to prairie. He also enjoyed having the whole back seat to himself.

About the only time they spoke to him was when the woman asked him if he planned to take in any of the events at the upcoming Commonwealth Games in August. Randy said that he hadn't given the matter any thought.

After three hours he got his first glimpse of Edmonton in the distance. This was the first time he had seen any real skyscrapers. The tallest building he had seen up until then was the Inn of the North Hotel in Prince George. About a half an hour later he saw the sight he had been looking forward to since leaving Granby—the sign saying "Welcome to Edmonton, Host City of the 1978 Commonwealth Games."

All that was going through Randy's mind was, "I made it! I made it. For everyone who doubted me, I proved them wrong!"

The man then said, "So, what part of Edmonton are you going to?"

Randy asked him if he knew of a place to stay that was cheap and the man asked, "How cheap?"

"The cheapest place possible."

"That would be the Single Men's Hostel. I hear that a room there is only about four bucks a night."

"That sounds great! Whereabouts is it?"

"It's downtown somewhere near 99th Street. It's probably not the best place in the world, but for four bucks you can't lose."

Randy asked them if they were going downtown and the man said, "No, we're not. We live near Westmount Shopping Centre, which is at 111th Avenue and Groat Road. But there is a bus that stops right in front of Westmount that will take you right downtown. When we get there, I'll point it out for you."

They arrived at the shopping centre and pulled up in front of the bus stop. The man told him that the bus would be coming by shortly. He thanked them for the ride, got out of the car and the couple left. A few minutes later the bus arrived.

As the bus made its way toward the downtown core, Randy stared in awe at all of the tall buildings. He had never seen anything like it before; this was by far the biggest city he had ever set foot in. As the bus went along Jasper Avenue he kept a lookout for 99th Street. One thing he noticed about Edmonton was that the streets were easy to follow, such as 112th Street, 111th Street, 110th Street, etc. He got off the bus just before 99th Street and when he reached it, he realized he could only turn left.

If he turned right he would end up in the North Saskatchewan River! He went up for a couple blocks but couldn't find the hostel. He approached a man walking the other way and asked him if he knew where the hostel was. The man told him to go up another couple blocks and then turn right. He did as the man instructed and eventually saw a large brick building with a sign on the front that said: "Alberta Ministry of Social Services Single Men's Hostel." As Randy approached, he saw a sign on the door that said: "Hostel Opens at 5 p.m." That was still two hours away. He went to a nearby coffee shop and waited there.

Randy arrived back at the hostel a little before 5:00. There was already a lineup outside the door. When he finally got up to the counter, he asked for a bed for the night.

The man at the counter said, "That will be four dollars and that comes with a meal ticket." But before Randy got out his wallet the man said, "Look kid, are you sure you want to stay here?"

"Well, of course I do!"

The man, looking concerned at Randy's youthful appearance, said, "Look, I don't think you should stay here, it's not safe."

"Hey, I don't care if this place is safe or not. I need a place to stay tonight! I can take care of myself, okay!"

"Very well, then. Gordon will show you to your room. Dinner will be served at 5:30."

Gordon, the assistant, showed Randy and about ten other men to their rooms. When he saw the room he would be in, it didn't look too appealing. There were sixteen bunks crammed into a small room and it stank to high heaven. There were a bunch of unsavoury-looking characters sitting on the bunks.

He proceeded to put his backpack on one of the top bunks, and just then a huge man came up to him and said, "What the fuck do you think you're doing, boy? That's *my* bunk!"

This man was quite scary looking. He had scars on his face and neck and had a mass of tattoos.

Randy said, "Hey man, what's the big deal? It's just a bunk!"

"Are you getting lippy with me, you little fucker?" He then grabbed Randy by the collar, put his fist near his face and said, "How would you like it if I rammed your fucking head right through that wall, huh? Maybe that might teach you some respect, you piece of shit!"

"All right, take the bunk, it's yours!"

Randy placed his backpack on the lower bunk. He heard the big man mutter, "What a sissy."

As Randy was having his dinner in the cafeteria (which consisted of runny stew and a ham sandwich), he contemplated turning in early as he hadn't had much sleep lately. He knew that wouldn't be easy with the big asshole sleeping right above him. He wasn't enjoying his dinner very much; he was still kind of shaken up over the earlier incident.

He went back up to his room after dinner. He thought about reading for awhile before turning in. He had brought along the latest edition of *Road and Track* magazine so he would have something to read during the trip. He noticed that every bunk in the room was taken. In fact, it was so crowded that four men were sleeping on the floor.

Throughout the evening, most of the men in the room were being very noisy. At one point two of them got into a heated argument that resulted in a pushing and shoving match. Randy couldn't believe his eyes when he saw one man actually taking a piss right in the corner! He felt tempted to go over to him and tell him that the goddamn bathroom was down the hall!

Even after the lights in the room went off, most of the men were still yapping away. Since you had to bring your own bedding, Randy just slept in his clothes and used his backpack for a pillow, just like when he was on the road. Even though the light in the room had been turned off, the hallway ones were still on and the door was open, so it was far from dark. He tried to go to sleep but it wasn't easy. As he was trying to close his eyes, he noticed that the man who had the lower bunk next to his was standing and staring down at him.

"May I help you?" asked Randy sarcastically.

"You want to have some fun?"

"Not with you, I don't," snapped Randy.

The man had a real scraggly appearance and a terrible body odour. When he smiled you could see that half of his teeth were missing.

He said to Randy, "C'mon, boy. I just got out of jail. Been locked up for fifteen long years. I'm in the mood to party!"

"Well, you'll have to party with someone else. You can forget about me. Now shut up and go back to bed, asshole," said Randy.

The man would not take no for an answer. He knelt down and got right into Randy's face.

He said, "Don't make this any harder, boy! I want you!"

The man's bad breath was making Randy gag. He realized that this called for desperate measures. He reached into his backpack and got out a little something he had brought along, to be used only in the event of an emergency. It was the hunting knife that Larry had given him.

He pointed the knife right in the man's face and said, "You get your ass away from me or I'll slit your fucking throat! Now get away from me, you fucking asshole!"

Randy swung the knife wildly in front of the man's face. When he realized Randy meant business, he backed away.

After that incident Randy had an even more difficult time trying to fall asleep. He kept the knife tightly held in his hand. After a couple of hours he did finally fall asleep, but it was short-lived.

Three men burst into the room, yelling repeatedly, "Everybody up!"

They were all very drunk. They began kicking at the men sleeping on the floor and shaking each bunk. One of the men cuffed Randy in the side of the head.

Randy got up and yelled at one of them, "Hey, what is your fucking problem?"

The man slapped Randy across the face real hard and yelled, "Wanna do something about it, you little punk?"

"I've had it with this fucking place! I can't take this shithole anymore," yelled Randy.

He grabbed all of his belongings, brushed one of the drunken men aside and stormed out of the room and the building. He checked to make sure he had put his knife back into his backpack. As was the case when he had left home, even though he had departed in a rush, he still made sure he hadn't forgotten anything.

Randy looked at his watch and realized that it was only 3:30 in the morning. He thought to himself, "Now what?"

It was too late to get a room anywhere else; nothing would be open. So he went for a long walk through the deserted streets of downtown Edmonton. He walked from one end of the downtown to the other and back several times. One time he walked all the way to 120th Street. By then he was an absolute wreck. He had not had a decent night's sleep since he had left Granby. He was at the point where he could hardly function.

He kept walking until after 8:00. He went into a magazine shop and bought a city and a transit map. He went into a coffee shop next door and ordered breakfast. He studied both maps, focusing on the main roads and the corresponding bus routes. He also made the decision to splurge a bit and get a reasonably priced motel room in an outlying area for the next night. He had originally planned to start looking for work that day, but last night had changed his plans. He was definitely in no condition to try and find work.

After what he had been through the last few days, getting a room would be a real treat.

He left the restaurant, went to a phone booth, looked up the motel listings in the yellow pages and phoned several of them. There was one in the south part of town that had a vacancy and was reasonable, so he chose that one. He checked his city map for its location and found out from the transit map which bus went out that way.

When he arrived there the desk clerk gave him a strange look, asking, "Can I help you?"

Randy thought he would humour him by doing his imitation of Inspector Clouseau and said, "Yes, I would like a rhhuummm!"

The clerk gave him a real puzzled look and asked, "A what?"

The man obviously didn't get it. They probably had never shown any of the Pink Panther movies in India. He said he had called earlier to see if there were any vacancies and how much their rates were.

He asked Randy for his driver's license and Randy replied, "I don't have one, I don't drive."

The clerk asked for some other form of identification. All Randy had was his student I.D. card from Granby Junior Secondary School. It indicated that he was only sixteen and that he was in grade nine.

He took a look at Randy's I.D. card and said to him, "So, where are your parents?"

"Well, my father is dead and my mother is back in Granby," said Randy.

He then asked Randy if he had a girl with him.

"Look, would I come all the way from Granby, B.C. if I had a girl? I mean, they have motels back there!"

"Good point," said the desk clerk as he wrote out the room request form.

"So, you're from Granby," said the desk clerk, acting as if he had never heard of the place.

Randy figured he had better get used to it. Granby was not exactly a household name. After all, no great event had ever happened there and nobody famous had ever come from there—yet.

Before going to his room, he purchased the latest edition of the *Edmonton Journal* from the front desk. After he settled into his room, he spent most of the afternoon looking through the Help Wanted ads. He was amazed that there were over four pages of ads; he had the pick of them all. In the *Granby Sentinel,* if there were two ads that would constitute a good week. This made Randy feel very upbeat about his future there. With that in mind he tried to take a nap, but to no avail. He was like that. No matter how tired he was he could not sleep in the daytime.

That evening he went to a nearby McDonald's for dinner. Afterward he thought about making a phone call. But first he inquired at the office as to how it worked with long-distance calls. The desk clerk said the cost would be added to the bill for his room. He then phoned Gary's place and his mom answered. She recognized Randy's voice and asked him where he was.

"I can't tell you," said Randy.

He asked if he could speak to Gary and his mom called him to the phone.

With great enthusiasm Randy said, "Gary! It's me, Randy!" Gary asked him where he was and he said, "I'm in Edmonton! I bet you didn't think I would make it here, did you?"

His friend asked where he was calling from and Randy told him that he was staying at a motel. Gary told him that his mom had come by the other day and asked if he knew where Randy had gone.

Randy asked what he had told her and Gary answered, "All I told her was that you were running away and you didn't say where you were going. She didn't ask any more questions after that."

"Well, that's good. I don't want her to know where I am."

He finally worked up the nerve to ask Gary about the condition of Kees Vandelaar. He told him that he was still in a coma but was showing vital signs. He warned him that when Kees woke up, he would be able to identify them.

"Yes, I realize that, but I don't like to be reminded of it," said Randy.

With that, he thought he had better end the conversation. But before he hung up he asked Gary to do him a favour. He asked him to tell Mark that he was doing all right and that he had made it to Edmonton. He'd write to him as soon as he could. Gary said that he would be glad to pass the message along. After he hung up the phone, Randy had a long, hot shower and hit the sack early.

Randy slept like a log that night. When he finally woke up it was 9:30. Since checkout time wasn't until 12:00 he went to a truck stop down the street and had a leisurely breakfast. Afterward, he went back to his motel room, gathered his belongings and went to the office to pay for the room and the telephone call.

The desk clerk asked, "So, how was your stay?"

"I feel like a new man!"

4

Feeling fully rejuvenated, he caught the bus that headed toward downtown.

During the bus ride, he kept thinking about this place he had passed by during his long walk the day before. It was called Labour Force Temporary Employment Services and he recalled that the name had appeared several times in the want ads in the *Journal*. He had made a mental note of where it was and decided to check it out when he arrived downtown. He didn't really know what to expect at first. When he walked into the place, all he saw was a large room with chairs lined against the walls and a counter that looked like the one in the Granby post office. There was a man sitting at a desk behind the counter and another man standing in front of the counter.

The man behind the counter said, "Can I help you?"

"Yes. I am interested in applying here."

"Very well, then, just fill this out," he said, handing Randy an application form.

It didn't take him very long to fill it out. After all, he didn't have an address and there wasn't much he could put down regarding past work experience. He filled in as much as he could and handed it to the man behind the counter.

"Okay, here's how we operate. We open at 6:30 every morning, you come in here at that time and if we have work available we'll send you out. We provide the transportation to the job site. We are very busy right now—there's lots of work available. So if you get here right when we open, you're pretty well assured of getting work. But there's just one other thing—do you have a pair of steel-toed work boots?"

"No, not yet," Randy answered.

The man told him, "Well, you had better get a pair! They're a necessity on most jobs."

"Okay, I'll buy some."

Randy asked him if it was okay that he didn't have a fixed address. He told him he had stayed at the Single Men's Hostel the other night but hadn't liked it.

The man in front of the counter, who must have been a regular client there, finally spoke up and said, "Oh, don't stay there, that place is a dump!"

"Tell me about it!" Randy agreed.

He told Randy that if he was looking for a place to stay temporarily, the Salvation Army was a good place. The price was the same as the hostel but they wouldn't let anybody in if they were drunk, there was no noise allowed after 11 p.m. and anyone who was being a troublemaker was kicked out right away. They also had a thrift shop next door where he could get a pair of boots fairly cheaply.

"That sounds great! Where is it?"

The man told him to turn right when he got outside and to go straight for three blocks.

Randy was fortunate enough to find a pair of boots his size at the Salvation Army Thrift Store. They were actually in fairly good condition. He then went next door to the Harbour Light Centre to register for a bed for the night. The attendant showed him which room he would in. He noticed that the setup was similar to the hostel's, but this place was much cleaner. The other men in the room pretty much kept to themselves, which was a good thing. He was able to turn in early and get a decent night's sleep.

He was up bright and early the next morning. He got dressed, put on his new work boots and headed to Labour Force. He stopped at a convenience store along the way and got a coffee and a muffin to go. He got to the Labour Force office right at 6:30, and sure enough, they found work for him almost immediately. The job involved doing cleanup work on a construction site. The work was kind of repetitive but otherwise it wasn't too bad. It was Friday, so he would have to wait until the following Monday before getting any more work. Fortunately, Labour Force paid their workers weekly, so Randy would receive a paycheque the next Friday for the wages he had earned that week.

Randy had come to the conclusion that the long-term prognosis for Edmonton looked very good, so he decided to look for a more permanent place to live. On the day he had gone for a long walk, he had seen a large older-style house at the other end of town with a sign on the front door offering "Rooms for rent—weekly or monthly."

On Saturday, he went to check the place out. The landlord told him that there were still a couple of suites available and Randy was shown one of them. He asked him if he wanted to rent by the week or by the month. Randy said that he would rather pay the rent monthly. The rent per month was $120 but the landlord was willing to give him a deal. Since it was already the eighth, he would only charge $80 for the remainder of July.

"Great, I'll take it!"

The landlord said, "Good, welcome aboard. Now, here are the rules. The rent is to be paid on the first of each month, there is to be no excessive noise, no drugs, no wild parties—and I would like this place kept reasonably clean. If you need anything, my suite is on the ground floor. By the way, my name is Ben."

"Pleased to meet you, Ben—my name is Randy."

Ben asked Randy when he wanted to move his stuff in. Randy pointed to his backpack and said, "This is it!"

Ben looked rather surprised, and said, "Well, that should make moving in easy!"

The setup there was that of your basic rooming house. There were four suites on each floor and there was a shared kitchen and bathroom. The rooms were fairly small and only had a single bed. Randy figured this would be adequate for awhile, but when he got established in the work force he would consider getting something bigger. Randy was inspecting the kitchen area when a man came out of the room next door.

"Oh, you must be the one who just moved in next door," he said.

"Yes, I am."

"Hello, I'm Conrad."

"Hello, I'm Randy."

Conrad asked him how long he had been in Edmonton, and Randy told him that he had been there exactly four days. He then asked him where he was from.

Randy replied, "I hail from a small mining town in northern B.C. called Granby."

"Well, I'm originally from Dartmouth, Nova Scotia, which is the reason I talk funny. I've only lived in Edmonton a few months but I lived in Calgary for many years."

Randy asked him if he liked living in Edmonton and he answered, "I don't mind it here, Edmonton is an all right city. As for this place, it's not too bad—at least the rent is cheap. I think you'll like it here, it's pretty quiet. The location is quite handy to everything. There's a Safeway a block away from here and there's both a pizza and a Chinese take-out place right nearby."

Randy thought to himself, "Safeway?" One thing he had overlooked before he left home was that he didn't know the first thing about cooking. He realized that now was the best time to learn.

Monday morning rolled around, and Randy was ready to tackle Labour Force once again. On Saturday he had made it to the Salvation Army Thrift Store before closing time and had picked up a couple of pots, a frying pan, a can opener, some utensils and an alarm clock. So far the only item he had actually used was the alarm clock. He had planned to get groceries the following day, but found out the hard way that the Safeway store was closed on Sunday!

The work week went very well for him. From Monday to Wednesday he worked on a construction project doing foundation backfill. On Thursday and Friday he helped with setting up tent-like buildings for the upcoming Commonwealth Games. Also on Friday he got his paycheque for his previous week's work. He wondered whether he should venture into a bar and celebrate. After all, he was only two years underage instead of three. After much debate, he decided to wait awhile longer.

When he got back to his apartment on Friday afternoon he asked Conrad how one could get a telephone. Conrad suggested that they both share his phone line. They could split the monthly cost fifty-fifty and pay for their own long distance calls. He figured that it would be much easier than having many different phone lines running into the same building. Randy thought that was a great idea—he was anxious to call Gary again.

"If you want to call your friend, be my guest," Conrad offered.

Randy enthusiastically called Gary and this time his dad answered.

He said, "Randy—is that you? Where the hell are you?"

Randy said, "I'm somewhere out of town. I would rather not say."

"Look, your mother is worried sick about you!"

Randy thought to himself, "Yeah, right!" He then said, "My mom will be just fine; she can take care of herself. Now can I please speak to Gary?"

He heard Gary in the background saying, "I'll take it upstairs, dad!" He lifted the receiver on the upstairs phone and said, "Hi Randy!"

"Is your dad off the line?"

He heard a click in the background and then Gary said, "Now he is."

Randy went on to tell him that he had his own place and had been getting temporary work. After asking Gary what was new and exciting in his life, he listened to him talk for awhile.

Gary said, "Well, I hate to put a damper on everything, but the day after you phoned the last time, I learned that Kees Vandelaar came out of his coma. I have since heard that he is expected to make a full recovery without any permanent brain damage. So far he claims to not remember anything. I'm not sure if he's telling the truth or if he's just afraid. That man that yelled at us didn't get a good look at any of us—he claims it was too dark."

"Well, that sure is a big relief!"

"Relief? What the hell are you talking about, Randy? It's only a matter of time before Kees will be able to identify us! Then we're in really big trouble!"

"Look, I'm really sorry I got you guys into this. Let's just wait and see how things go. But if he says anything, I promise I will take full responsibility," Randy offered.

"You're right, let's just see what happens. But let's stay in touch, okay?"

"You got it!" Randy agreed.

With that their conversation ended.

Randy looked visibly upset, and Conrad asked, "Is there anything wrong?"

"Oh, it's nothing. Look, I'm going back to my room. Thanks a lot for letting me use your phone."

After Randy went back to his room, a deep feeling of uneasiness began to overwhelm him. Reality was setting in and he was facing the fact that his newly found freedom might be short-lived. At any time he could be sent back to Granby to face assault charges.

The following Monday he decided to try something different. Instead of going to Labour Force, he thought about trying to find a job on his own. The previous week, while riding in the Labour Force van on the way to a job site, he remembered overhearing a conversation between two other workers concerning the Canadian Fiberglass plant. One man had said they were hiring and the other man had commented that the work was quite hard. Randy made up his mind to give the place a try and he figured out how to get there on the map.

When Randy arrived at the plant, he was amazed at how big it was. At the front desk he inquired about applying for employment. The receptionist handed him an application form and directed him to an adjacent room where he could fill it out. She then called the plant manager.

After he finished filling out the application, the plant manager met with him, asked him a bunch of questions and then asked, "Can you start tomorrow?"

"Yes, yes I can!"

"Good, welcome aboard. My name is Ted Williams. You will be reporting to Simon, the foreman. See you tomorrow."

Randy left the place feeling very excited. He kept thinking, "Wow, I finally found a real job. Now I can make some decent money for a change."

Randy made it there right on time the following morning, which was a challenge since the starting time was 7 a.m. He reported to Simon's office and Simon showed him what he would be doing. He would be working the bagging machine. When three bales of insulation came off the assembly line, he would stack them and put them into a bag.

It was very boring, repetitious work. At the end of the day his arms were itching like crazy from the insulation. After a couple of weeks he realized that nobody stayed there for very long, but he vowed that he would tough it out. But after three weeks he couldn't take it any more. The repetitious movement and noise, compounded by the insulation dust and the itching, were making Randy go crazy. Plus Simon was a real prick. So on the Friday of his third week there, he told Simon that he was quitting.

Simon just said, "Okay, no problem."

Randy figured that he was quite used to hearing that. On the bus ride home he kept thinking about what to do next, and eventually he decided to go back to good ol' Labour Force.

Over the next three weeks Randy continued to plug away at jobs provided by Labour Force, but he had become quite discontented. None of the jobs were steady; the longest one lasted three days. Most of the jobs were for just one day. The majority of them involved digging or throwing stuff away. As an example, on one job he spent the whole day throwing old pieces of drywall into a dumpster. As for finding another job on his own, he wasn't having any luck with that either. He had applied at several different industrial plants but they were either not hiring or were not interested in him. His young age and the fact that he only had a grade nine education didn't help.

One evening when he was visiting Conrad, he told him about his situation. He explained to him that things weren't working out and Edmonton was not proving as promising as he had thought. He said that he wasn't really sure what he should do; should he stay in Edmonton or move on? Conrad suggested that he might want to give Calgary a try. Randy asked why Calgary would be any different.

Conrad said, "Well, I lived in Calgary for six years and I know that there are always lots of opportunities there. The economic base is more diversified. There are more different types of industries there. The only reason that I am living here is that my job transferred me here."

"Well, that might be worth looking into. But tell me something. You told me that you work as a heavy equipment operator, right? You must make pretty good money, so why do you stay in this place?" Randy asked.

"For one thing, I have to pay child support for my kids in Ontario; for another I am not sure if I want to stay in Edmonton. That's what I like about this place. I am not stuck with a long-term commitment. With the rent being this cheap I am able to save some money, because someday I might move to Ontario so I can be closer to my kids."

"It must be nice to be able to save your money. I should learn to start doing that. Look, I think I'll turn in for the night. What you said about Calgary—I'll definitely think about it."

The next day Randy went into a magazine store downtown and bought a copy of the *Calgary Herald*. When he got home he took a look through the want ads. Sure enough, it was an absolute gold mine. There were at least six pages of want ads and many of the jobs posted were right up his alley. It didn't take much to convince him that Calgary would be worth a try. There was just one thing, though. His rent was paid up to the end of August and there was still almost a week to go before the end of the month. He decided that he would just take it easy for a week. He then went downstairs, and told Ben, the landlord, that he was moving out in a week.

Later that day he told Conrad what his plans were.

"That sounds great. You will like Calgary. I enjoyed living there. But don't get me wrong, you will be missed around here."

"Yeah, I think I will just lie low for a week."

"So, will you be taking the bus to Calgary?" Conrad asked.

"I have a cheaper mode of transportation—thumbnail express," Randy replied, indicating his thumb.

"I don't think that is a good idea—there are a lot of kooks out there," Conrad warned.

"I think I can take care of myself."

When the last day of August came around, Randy was ready and raring to go. His backpack was all packed, which included most of his recently acquired cookware. Since he didn't have room for it, he left one pot behind. He gave his room key back to Ben and went up to say goodbye to Conrad.

Conrad told him to get in touch with him if he was ever in Edmonton again and to have a safe journey. Randy wished him all the best.

Randy took the city bus as far south as he could and then he walked south along Highway 2 until he saw the Edmonton city limits sign. He went a little farther before putting his thumb out. It was over three hours before a car pulled over, and Randy's first thought was, "Hey, I'll be riding in style—it's a BMW!"

A man and a woman who looked about in their mid-thirties were in the car. The man asked him where he was heading, and Randy replied, "Calgary."

The man said, "Good, so are we."

Randy noticed that they were both fairly well dressed. The woman was wearing about ten pounds of makeup as well as a generous amount of perfume. He couldn't tell if they were married or just dating, but it was obvious they didn't get along very well with each other. Over the course of the trip, they argued constantly about everything from money, friends and relatives to the theory that he was not attracted to her anymore. She even ran off a long list of potential younger women he could be more attracted to. All the while Randy was doing his best to try to ignore them, but it was getting on his nerves. He also realized that the woman was repeatedly looking at him in the rearview mirror.

After awhile the woman asked Randy, "So, how old are you?"

As usual, Randy overstated his age by two years and said, "Eighteen."

She then asked, "Tell me something, have you ever made it with an older woman?"

Randy was totally stunned and a few seconds later said, "No, I can't say that I have."

The man shot back by saying, "Listen here, punk! Don't you get any ideas, okay?"

"Now see here, I never said anything, she did! Lady, I am no jailbait for you!"

The man said to the woman, "What's the matter—am I not good enough for you? This was your idea to pick this kid up! What is it, are you more attracted to him than to me?"

Randy could see Red Deer in the distance and made a sudden change of plans.

He said to the man, "Oh, don't forget, I'm getting off in Red Deer."

"I thought you told me you were going to Calgary."

"I changed my mind," Randy said.

"I can take you to Calgary—it's not going to be any problem."

Randy could see a series of gas stations straight ahead and noticed that they appeared to be on the outskirts of town, so he figured he had better speak up now.

"I said I want to get off in Red Deer. Pull this fucking car over *now*!" he yelled.

The man pulled the car over and before Randy slammed the door he said in a sarcastic tone, "Thanks for the ride!"

After the car sped away, Randy thought, "I can't believe this! The only reason they picked me up was so that crazy bitch could use me to make her old man jealous! What a couple of head cases! Maybe Conrad was right—there are a lot of kooks on the road. Well, that settles it. I'm going to take the bus the rest of the way."

He went into a nearby Shell station and asked the clerk where the bus depot was. The clerk indicated it was downtown.

Randy asked, "Now where would that be?"

The clerk replied, "You go straight ahead on this road, Highway 2A. It eventually becomes Gaetz Avenue. You just keep going straight ahead for almost two miles and it's on your left. You can't miss it."

The two-mile walk into downtown Red Deer seemed like an eternity, but Randy felt that it was better than the alternative. His only thought was, "I would rather be doing this than spending another two hours riding with those two mental cases!" Eventually he made it to the bus depot. The next bus for Calgary didn't leave for another two hours. When the bus came and he got on, he was amazed at how comfortable the seats were, not to mention that they could also recline. He had never been on a Greyhound bus before; they were sure a big improvement over Skeena Coach Lines. He got to thinking, "Gee, I should have used this method of travel all along. Just imagine, I am assured of getting a ride and I don't have to worry about encountering a crazy driver. Unfortunately, it also costs more."

An hour into the bus ride, Randy caught his first glimpse of the Calgary

Tower in the distance. When the bus pulled into the Calgary depot, he decided to put his backpack into a locker until he got settled for the night.

As he was putting his stuff into the locker, a man approached him and said, "Hello there."

"Hello," Randy said warily.

The man said, "I was wondering if you would be interested in working for my company?"

"Well, I could be. What exactly is your company?"

"I would prefer to talk about that in private."

Randy said, "Why don't you give me your business card? When I get settled I'll call you and then we could set up an interview."

"Actually, I was wondering if you would like to join my family and me for dinner tonight. We could talk about it then."

"Sure, I would like to, but does your wife mind?"

"No, she doesn't mind. I have guests over quite often. I figure this is the best way to meet potential new employees. My wife knows it's all part of doing business."

"Well, I'll go along with that."

"What are we waiting for—let's go!" As they were leaving the depot, the man continued, "Oh by the way, my name is Tom Smith."

"I'm Randy Watson."

Randy started thinking, "Man, this is really something. I know the economy in Calgary is good but I didn't think it was *that* good! Imagine, somebody is so desperate for workers that he is recruiting people as soon as they get off the bus!"

During the drive to Tom's house, Randy became inquisitive about the company that Tom owned.

He commented that the company must be doing really well, and then said, "I don't get it. You don't even know me and you don't know anything about my background. I mean, I'm only eighteen, I never finished high school and I don't really have any job skills. What could I possibly have to offer you?"

Tom said, "Young people have to start somewhere and I like to give them a chance to get started. Not very many companies do this, you know. The way I see it, they have their whole lives ahead of them and I can make a difference by helping them get their first big break. You know, you ask too many questions. Why don't you just sit back and enjoy the ride?"

Randy still had one more question, though. He said, "Your family, what do you have?"

Tom replied, "I have two daughters."

Randy asked him how old they were, and Tom replied that they were twelve and ten. Randy thought, "Oh, shoot. I was hoping they would be my age." Tom didn't look that old either. Randy estimated that he was in his mid-thirties at the most.

When they pulled into the driveway at Tom's house, he said, "Donna is taking the girls to soccer practice today, so I'll be making dinner."

Randy noticed that he had a really nice place and it looked to be in a fairly upscale neighbourhood.

As they went inside, Tom said, "Donna and the girls should be home by 6:30, so just make yourself at home."

Randy commented, "My, this is a really nice place you have here!"

"This is a fully restored Edwardian home. In fact, we did most of the restoration. Here, let me take your coat and just pull up a chair. Would you like a beer?"

"Yes, I would."

A couple minutes later Tom brought out a huge mug of beer, and Randy said, "Holy mackerel!"

"It's homemade. I brewed it myself."

Randy took a sip and said, "It has a peculiar taste!"

"You're probably used to the beer you get at the liquor store. This is different. It is completely unpasteurized and has no preservatives."

Randy thought, "Oh, what the hell. I'm really thirsty anyway."

By the time he had drunk half the mug he began to feel weird. The peculiar taste he had noticed earlier seemed kind of familiar. He started seeing things in double images and eventually multiple images. The room started to look like it was spinning around. He wondered what was happening to him and then it dawned on him. He remembered what the peculiar taste was. Last Christmas when Bill and Brad's older brother Manuel was visiting from Vancouver, he had brought some acid with him. One night when Randy had gone over to their place, they had all tried a couple of hits.

He finally put two and two together and realized, "That son of a bitch put acid in my beer!"

By then the room looked like it was spinning out of control. He then felt a pair of hands unbutton his pants and unzip the fly. He felt his pants being pulled down to his ankles, followed by his underwear. He looked up in a haze and saw Tom leaning over him.

Tom started to rub Randy's penis and Randy muttered, "You put acid in my beer, you lousy fucker! What is your wife going to say when she gets home?"

"What wife? What kids? We're all alone, it's just and me, Randy. You're mine—all mine!" Tom leered.

"You fucking bastard!"

He knew he had to think of something fast, but that wouldn't be easy considering how stoned he was. He was totally in never-never land. Tom continued to rub Randy's penis and was enjoying himself. Randy knew Tom's intention was to rape him, so he swung his fist toward him, but missed. He saw at least seven images of him; he wasn't sure which image was the real Tom. Tom just laughed. Randy managed to work up enough strength to force himself off the chair and push himself right into Tom. The force knocked Tom to the ground. He tried to run but he didn't get very far. His pants were down at his ankles, which caused him to trip and fall. Before he could pull his pants up, Tom jumped on him and pinned his arms to the ground. He had since taken his shirt off and began trying to kiss Randy. During one of Tom's attempts Randy managed to head-butt him. He knew where Tom's head was, so he swung his fist and this time he connected. He swung his other first and hit him again. He pushed Tom off of him, pulled up his pants and got to his feet. He made a run for what he thought was the door, but he ended up running right into the wall. Before he could get his bearings Tom tackled him again.

They wrestled on the floor for what seemed an eternity, and all the while Tom said repeatedly, "You're mine, you're mine!"

Despite being stoned, Randy was putting up a good fight. Luckily Tom wasn't a very big guy. He eventually rolled on top of Tom, and using his left hand, felt his way to find Tom's face. He took his right hand and landed several hard shots. He seized a picture that had fallen off the wall and busted it over Tom's head. He got to his feet again and made another attempt to find the door. But before he could find it, Tom grabbed him again. He elbowed him in the stomach, turned around and gave him a good swift kick, nailing him right in the genitals. He gave him another kick that landed on his jaw. He then felt along the wall until he found the door. As he ran out, he tripped and went head over heels down the stairs.

He ignored the pain, got up quickly and ran in a zigzag pattern toward the street, still stoned from the acid.

As he made it to the road, he still had no concept of where he was. In fact, he only knew he had reached the road because he had run into a parked car. He was aware that one of the side effects of acid was a surge in adrenaline. So he picked himself up, turned left and began running at full tilt, unaware that he was heading right down the middle of the road! He didn't realize it until he saw a car coming right toward him. He got out of the way in the nick of time. All he could hear was the loud screeching of tires and the sound of a horn honking.

The driver yelled out, "What the hell is your fucking problem, kid?"

Randy realized he had better slow down because he had reached a main thoroughfare. He saw a bus stop just up the street and thought he had better sit down for awhile and let the effects of the acid wear off. He had only been there a few minutes when a bus pulled up.

He asked the driver if the bus was going downtown.

"No, I'm going to Chinook Centre. If you want to go downtown you will have to catch the bus across the street," the driver told him.

Randy decided to go for a long walk. He walked up the street for four blocks before crossing. By then most of the effects of the acid had worn off. He thought about going to the police, but then he realized that he didn't have much to go on. Besides, there were no witnesses. Also, he had learned from an early age not to trust cops. But what really irked him was that he had left his jean jacket behind. It wasn't so much the jacket; it was worn out and was getting too small for him. It was that he had almost a full pack of smokes in the pocket!

He caught the downtown bus, and when he arrived there he figured out where the Salvation Army hostel was. He asked the man at the front desk if there were still any beds available.

The man answered, "Yes, we have lots, but I'm afraid you missed dinner."

Randy asked if he could come back in an hour and the man said, "That's okay."

He went to a nearby submarine shop and ordered a foot-long sub with the works. He knew that another other side effect of acid was that it made you very hungry. After eating, he went to the bus depot to retrieve his backpack out of the locker and then returned to the hostel. Since he was still quite sore, he decided to check the extent of his injuries after he got his bed. Luckily, all he had was a few scratches and bruises; there were no broken bones. He considered himself very lucky. After all, it could have been much worse.

5

Randy had arrived in Calgary just in time for the Labour Day weekend. He wouldn't be able to start looking for work until the following Tuesday. Therefore, the next morning he made no effort to get up early. Right after he left the Salvation Army hostel he went into the thrift shop next door and bought himself a "new" jean jacket.

He was determined to try something different this time around. He had learned while living in Edmonton that the YMCA in larger cities rented rooms. He hadn't realized that until after he had moved into the rooming house (Granby obviously didn't have a YMCA). He decided that he would stay at the YMCA until he found a decent job and would then get an apartment.

He spent the Labour Day weekend taking in the sights around Calgary and getting to know the city. He went up the Calgary Tower and visited Heritage Park and the Zoo. He also noted where all the temporary employment agencies were. There was one agency in particular that he made an extra effort to find. It was called "Tempo Industrial Labour," and Randy noticed that its ads appeared in several different places in the *Calgary Herald*. Judging by how the ads were worded, it seemed as though the agency was pretty desperate for workers since they all emphasized "no experience necessary." He made a note of how to get there from the YMCA and decided that he would go there first thing Tuesday morning.

Tuesday morning came around and Randy, unfortunately, had slept in. When he woke up and realized that it was after 9:00, he said, "Oh shit!"

Since he had not worked in the past week, he had not been accustomed to setting the alarm clock. He decided to check the place out anyway so he went downstairs, had breakfast and then walked over to the Tempo office. He figured there might be a faint hope that there would still be some jobs available.

When he arrived at the Tempo office it was after 10:30. He asked the man behind the counter if there were still any jobs available for that day.

The man replied, "No, there's nothing left. However, I can get you to fill out an application form and then maybe we can set you up with something tomorrow."

Randy filled out the application and as he turned it in, the man said, "We open at 7:00."

Randy said, "See you tomorrow."

The next day Randy made sure that he got up early. The night before, he had checked several times to see that the button on his alarm clock was pulled and set for 6:00. He was at the Tempo office right at 7:00. There was a different man at the counter this time—someone much younger. When it was Randy's turn, he gave his name to the man behind the counter. He pulled out Randy's application form. He then told him that he had a job for him on a construction site. It was at a new townhouse development being built on Southland Drive and the job involved moving sheets of drywall.

"That sounds great," Randy said. "What time does the van leave?"

"What are you talking about? We don't have a van. You have to provide your own transportation."

"Oh, that's great! How am I supposed to get there?"

"You can take the bus there. When you go out the door, turn left and go up the street for two blocks. From there you catch the number 3 bus, which goes straight down Elbow Drive. When you get to Southland Drive, go west for three blocks and it's on your left."

"How will I know which way is west?" Randy asked.

The man, looking kind of annoyed, said, "Put it this way, go up Southland Drive and if you see mountains, you're heading west. If you see prairies, you're going east!"

"I should be able to find it." Before Randy left, the man said, "When you get there, report to Klaus Gutmann."

During the bus ride, he kept a lookout for Southland Drive. When he got there he figured out which way was west. Three blocks later, he saw on his left a huge townhouse development under construction, with five huge stacks of drywall sitting near the curb. He reckoned that must be the place. He went up to an ATCO trailer and knocked on the door.

A man answered the door and said in a German accent, "So, you must be the person from Tempo."

"That's right, I'm Randy Watson. You must be Klaus Gutmann."

"That's right. Okay, here's what I want you to do. You see those sheets of drywall? I want ten sheets placed in each entranceway," he said, pointing to the entrances of each townhouse.

Randy figured that would be easy enough, but then he noticed that there was a fair distance between the stacks of drywall and the building, and the ground in between was quite muddy. It was unseasonably cold that day and it was quite windy. His only thought was, "Okay, let's get this over with." It wasn't until he picked up the first sheet that he realized how heavy they were. Even with both arms completely outstretched, he could barely get a grip on both ends of the sheet. The wind wasn't helping either. At times it felt as though the wind would pick up both him and the sheet and carry them away.

By the time he had carried his fifth sheet he was exhausted, but he knew he had a long way to go. At that point it started to rain. After an hour, he had moved only sixteen sheets. After he had given Randy his instructions, Klaus had gone to another part of the complex.

He came back to check on Randy and said, "Is that all you have done? I've got the drywall workers coming this afternoon, and I am not paying them to sit around. C'mon, man, move faster!"

Randy was obviously annoyed, but he vowed to plod onward. By then the rain was coming down harder and the ground was turning into mud. After he struggled with three more sheets, the rain turned into wet snow. He looked in utter disbelief, thinking, "What the hell is going on here? It's only the first week of September!" By then the ground had turned into an absolute quagmire. Every time he took a step he would sink almost up to his knees. Carrying those big, cumbersome sheets of drywall made things even worse. All the while Klaus was watching him from inside the trailer.

When he saw Randy trudging back to the drywall pile, he stormed out of the trailer, came up to him and began yelling, "What the hell is the matter with you? Can't you move any faster?"

Randy yelled back, "I'm going as fast as I can, but the ground is too muddy and these sheets are too big for one person to carry!"

"Oh, bullshit! I can carry those no problem! That's no bloody excuse! You're just plain lazy, that's all!"

With that, he stormed back into the trailer. Randy was very pissed off and his only thought was, "That's easy for you to say, you fucking asshole! Sitting there warm and dry in your little office!"

He struggled with three more sheets after his "lecture" from Klaus. However, by the time he placed the third sheet inside the building, he was completely exhausted. He was gasping for air and he felt like he was ready to keel over any minute. His hands were completely numb from the cold, and his arms were so sore that he could hardly move them. Even the walk back to the drywall pile was agonizing, due to the excruciating pain in his legs. When he made it back to the drywall pile, Klaus was there waiting for him, and he had a very angry look on his face.

He said, "Jesus Christ! I don't know what your fucking problem is! That saying is right—never send a boy to do a man's job! You are completely hopeless!"

Randy couldn't take it anymore. He took the sheet of drywall that he had just picked up and threw it onto the muddy ground.

He then yelled out, "I've fucking had it with you! You think you're so goddamn tough, then you finish it!"

Klaus yelled back, "Don't you talk to me like that!"

"Fuck you, you fucking kraut! I don't need this bullshit!" Randy shouted.

With that he started to walk away.

"You walk away from me, you don't ever come back, you hear?"

"You go to hell, you fucking Nazi, I quit!"

He then stormed off the job site.

As he made his way along Southland Drive, he had difficulty walking. Aside from his legs being very sore, his boots were still caked with mud. He felt like he was wearing lead boots, and his main thought was, "They'll never let me on the bus like that. I have to find a way to clean them off." As he looked around, he wondered what month it was. It had snowed enough to cover the grass and the roadway, so it actually looked like December. He kept thinking, "Am I really going to like it here?"

He found a gas station nearby with a hose outside. He was able to clean off most of the mud from his boots. When he reached Elbow Drive he caught the bus going downtown. He then realized that he hadn't had his time card signed. He figured, "Ah, to hell with it. I probably won't get paid anyway. Besides, I'm never going back to that outfit anyway."

During the bus ride, all that was going through Randy's mind was, "That does it! I have had it with temporary employment agencies! From now on either I find a job on my own or I don't work at all!" He remembered when he had gone into the Canada Manpower office on the previous day. All of the bulletin boards were loaded with job prospects, which was a far cry from the Canada Manpower office in Granby. From the time he'd dropped out of school until the time he'd left Granby, there had been only one job listed on the bulletin board and that was for selling vacuum cleaners on commission! He concluded there were plenty of job opportunities out there, and it was up to him to look for them.

He decided he would focus on one particular industrial area each day until he found something. On that day he planned to check out the industrial areas in the northeastern part of the city. Some of the places he applied at sounded promising, but most of the responses were either "We'll call you in the next few days" or "We'll keep your application on file." At the end of the day he didn't have a concrete job offer. The next day he focused on the Ogden area in the southeastern part of town. At first it seemed as though it would be the same as the day before, but when he applied at Ace Industries, an asphalt shingle manufacturer, the receptionist told him to take a seat and wait. A few minutes later a man approached him and introduced himself as Glen Tompkins, the manager. He led Randy into his office and reviewed his application. He asked him a few questions and then inquired if he would like to start on Monday.

"Yes, definitely!"

"Very well, then, welcome aboard! Be here at 8:00 Monday morning."

Randy was ecstatic. He had always known that persistence eventually paid off in the end. He intended to give this job a one-hundred-percent effort. He would make sure the alarm clock was set for Monday morning.

He was right there at 8:00 on Monday morning. Glen Tompkins introduced him to Doug Halvorson, the foreman. He was a big, burly man with really long, scraggly hair and big glasses. He put Randy to work on the packaging line, making bundles of ten asphalt shingles and placing them on a pallet. The job was fairly fast-paced and, as at the insulation plant, very repetitive. But he was determined that he would make a go of it and hoped that he would be in this job for the long haul.

The first couple of days went all right as far as the job was concerned. What he noticed most about working there, however, was Doug. The guy had a mouth on him like you wouldn't believe. He was constantly yapping both during work and on breaks. It seemed that he had a one-track mind too. All he ever talked about was sex. Actually, that wasn't correct; there was something else he talked about as well. He was a devout racist, which explained why there were no visible minorities working there.

During coffee breaks and lunch, Doug would either talk about getting laid or wiping out a certain minority group (a different one each day). At first Randy just took it in stride. After all, when he was in school, whenever he got together with the other guys, they talked about sex a lot. But not to the extent that Doug did, and sometimes he would be so full of himself that it would get annoying. He liked to brag that he was a real stud in bed and that women really liked him for his huge penis. He would either brag about the sexual experience he had had the night before or about one he was going to have. When Randy was listening to this, all that would be going through his mind was, "What woman in her right mind would ever want to have sex with that fat pig?" On a few occasions he felt tempted to say to Doug, "Do we have to keep hearing about your goddamn sex life all the time?" If he said that, however, Doug would no doubt have the perfect retort—"at least I *have* a sex life!"

On the fourth day of the job, Doug started directing his lewd comments toward Randy.

In the morning they happened to be working together, and Doug said to him, "Wow-wee! Did anybody tell you that you have a nice ass?"

Randy said, "No, I can't say that they have."

"Oh, that's too bad, 'cause you have a nice, tight little ass. So when are you going to let me fuck you up the ass?"

Randy gave him a very disgusted look and said sternly, "Never!"

"Aw, c'mon. You know something, you're cute, and you're young. I like them young."

Randy started wondering, "Is this guy a fag too? I better try to keep my distance from him as much as possible!" As it turned out, he wasn't the only recipient of Doug's perverted comments. The guy who operated the asphalt-mixing tank, who didn't look very much older than Randy, was also a target. Doug repeatedly asked him when he was going to let him fuck his girlfriend. Randy thought that was very bizarre. If he had a girlfriend he sure wouldn't let her anywhere near that fat slob!

By the start of the second week the verbal abuse from Doug had become even worse. He was repeatedly asking Randy when he was going to let him perform anal intercourse on him.

Randy would always answer, "When hell freezes over!"

On several occasions in the lunchroom, Doug announced to the other workers that he planned to stick his twelve-inch dick up Randy's little ass.

One time when two truck drivers came into the plant, Doug said to them, "You see this guy here?" He pointed to Randy, "Someday soon, I plan to fuck him right up the ass!"

Randy said angrily, "Like hell you will!"

Doug and the truck drivers just laughed. One time Doug snuck up behind him, grabbed him from behind, practically put him in a bear hug and started making a humping-like motion with his pelvis. He was starting to get pretty fed up with this treatment, but he wasn't sure if this would constitute sexual harassment. He thought that applied only to incidents between males and females. He was kind of afraid to say anything to Doug due to his sheer size. To make matters worse, Doug was also making derogatory comments about his workmanship. Whenever Doug was working alongside Randy, he was constantly telling him to, "Give 'er shit!"

On several occasions after he had completed a pallet of shingles, Doug came up to him and said, "That stack looks like shit! How am I going to be able to pile them five high? Now stack them properly, or else!"

In every case, Randy hadn't thought there was anything wrong with the stack.

On the Thursday of the second week Randy finally snapped. Just before the morning coffee break, Doug came up to him and began ridiculing his work again.

He concluded his lecture by saying, "You know what you need, boy? You need a good fuck up the rear end and I would love to give it to you!"

Randy looked at him and said, "Are you some kind of homosexual or something?"

Doug glared at him for a few seconds, then ran toward him, knocked him down and sat right on top of him. He grabbed Randy's throat with his right hand and put his massive left fist right in his face.

He began yelling, "You take that back, you fucking little puke! Take it back!" Randy could barely breathe, but he managed to squeak out, "I take it back!"

Doug then yelled out, "Now you say you're sorry, punk!"

Doug's three-hundred-plus pound frame was squeezing the life out of him, but he managed to say, "Okay, I'm sorry! I can't breathe!"

"Now you better watch your mouth around me, boy!" Doug said as he got up off Randy and let him get up. "Otherwise, I'll ram your fucking head right through the wall! You understand me?"

"Yes, I'm sorry."

At first Randy was just going to let it go. But when they were walking past the shipping area on the way to the lunchroom, Doug turned around, unzipped his fly and whipped out his dick (with the overhead doors wide open).

He said to Randy, "Wanna suck it?"

Randy said nothing and instead turned and walked the other way. He headed up to the front and stormed into Glen Tompkin's office.

He said to Glen, "I would like to file a complaint against Doug!"

Glen peered out from his glasses and said, "What seems to be the problem, Randy?"

"Doug keeps making lewd comments toward me and just now he attacked and threatened me!"

Glen said calmly, "Well, according to what Doug has been telling me he finds you kind of slow."

"Slow! What are you talking about? I work my ass off out there! I'm telling you, Doug is harassing me sexually! I don't care if he's queer or not, but I don't like it!"

"Well, I don't know. Doug has been with this company for eight years now and I have never heard any complaints about him. I know he may be brash at times, but he is a good worker. He runs the production department very well and that's what I like about him. Just don't take him so seriously, that's all. He just has an offbeat sense of humour."

Randy could not believe what he was hearing. He relayed to Glen what Doug had been saying to him and added, "Doesn't that count as sexual harassment? I shouldn't have to put up with this bullshit! You should do something about it!"

"Now see here! We are in the business of making quality asphalt shingles and getting them to the customer on time. Doug has an excellent track record of meeting production deadlines and maintaining quality standards. He is a good man. It's just that sometimes you have to take what he says with a grain of salt. Now my suggestion to you is that you do what he tells you!"

With disgust, Randy said, "I can't believe you're sticking up for him! In other words, you don't plan on doing anything about it."

"No, absolutely not. Now get back to work!"

Randy yelled out, "Well, as far as I am concerned, you can take this job and shove it up your fucking ass!"

He stormed out of Glen's office, grabbed his jacket from his locker and burst out of the building.

Later that afternoon, while Randy was having coffee at the YMCA cafeteria, he began to contemplate his future. At one point he began to wonder if moving to Calgary had been such a good idea. He had been there only two weeks and had already walked out of two jobs. He figured he had definitely not started out on the right foot. But after taking a long walk, he regained his composure and decided to give it another try with a different company. There were hundreds of different industries in Calgary and all of them were run differently. He decided to start looking again the next day.

The following day he tried his luck at the Meridian Industrial Park in the eastern part of town. Lo and behold, at the third place he applied, he got lucky. He was hired at Prairie Agro Services Ltd., a cattle feed manufacturing plant. The hiring process was the same as with his previous job. After he had completed the application, the manager called him into his office and introduced himself as Angus McVittie. This time, however, the foreman was also present for the interview. His name was Danny Tamaka and he asked most of the questions. Both Angus and Danny explained to him that the job was very labour intensive and was also very dusty. They wanted to make sure he would be able to handle the work. Randy told them he would be able to handle it and he would do everything possible to prove himself. They told him that he could start on Monday.

The first couple of days there went all right. But there were a few occasions when Randy wondered if he had put his foot in his mouth. They had him working on the packaging line, stacking feed bags on a pallet when they came off the line. Each bag weighed fifty-five pounds, and they often came off the line at a fast and furious pace. For the first couple of days he was pretty stiff and sore by the end of his shift, but by the end of the week he was getting used to it. The dust didn't bother him since he always wore a breathing mask. By the end of the second week he thought, "So far, so good." He was getting accustomed to the workload and Danny seemed to be satisfied with his work performance.

Now that Randy had found a job where the long-term prognosis looked good his next objective was to move out of the YMCA and into his own apartment. He figured the timing was right—it was just about the end of September. He spent the weekend looking at apartments and basement suites. He wanted to look at a whole bunch of places before deciding. There was one question, however, that was asked by most of the landlords that had him rather perplexed—"Do you kick holes in the wall?" He couldn't figure that one out. He thought that if somebody wanted to vandalize something, why would it be the wall in their own apartment? Plus, they could break their foot doing that!

Randy eventually settled on a small bachelor suite in an apartment building near the Holy Cross Hospital. The rent was reasonable and he had the whole place to himself (no sharing the kitchen or bathroom). There was a bus stop right near the front of the building, and when that bus reached 9th Avenue he could transfer to another one that went to the Meridian Industrial Park. A week after he moved in, he got a phone installed. As far as he was concerned he was officially settled. He was hoping that everything at his apartment and at work would all work out in the long run.

Two years later

It was 1980 and things hadn't changed that much for Randy, now eighteen. He was still living in the same place and still working at Prairie Agro Services. It appeared that he had achieved all of his objectives.

But although he had managed to stay in Calgary, he was not happy there. He felt as though he didn't fit in, and being from a small town, he was still finding it hard to adjust to life in a big city. In the two years he had lived there, he had not made any new friends. He hadn't even got to know anybody else in his building. It seemed as though the other tenants couldn't be bothered to give him the time of day.

During the previous March, Randy was in seventh heaven when he turned eighteen. This meant that he was of legal drinking age, which was one year earlier than in B.C. But the euphoria was short-lived. It seemed that every time he went to a bar or nightclub, somebody would pick a fight with him and he would almost always oblige them. As a result, on three different occasions he had to spend the night in the city lockup. Because he had a slightly dark complexion, many people thought that he was a native and that appeared to be the main cause for provoking him to fight. Someone would come up to him and start making racist comments, and before he could convince the person that he was not a native, the fight would be on. The fact was, Randy's paternal grandmother was Armenian and his mom's maiden name was Goustopholous. Besides, he figured that even if he was native, what was the big deal? Some of the comments he heard really annoyed him. Back in Granby a lot of the workers in both the mine and the lumber mill were from the Twin Lakes Indian Reserve. The vast majority of native people that Randy knew were hardworking, industrious people. Some of the attitudes he had encountered toward them in Calgary made him very annoyed. He felt that was another reason that he didn't belong there. So he didn't go out on the town that much anymore. On the weekends he usually bought a case of beer or a bottle of rum and drank them in his apartment.

The previous year he had seen his first Calgary Stampede. He'd found it quite exciting but also fairly overpriced, so he didn't go again this year. By far the most exciting event that had occurred over the last year, as far as he was concerned, was when Gary came up to visit for a couple weeks. Gary had driven to Calgary all the way from Granby and stayed at Randy's place. They had a year's worth of catching up to do and they also had a great time reminiscing about the good ol' days in Granby.

One thing that Gary talked about that had Randy rather perplexed concerned Kees Vandelaar. Apparently Kees claimed to have no memory of the beating incident. Gary wasn't sure if he was telling the truth or was just saying that out of fear of retaliation. His best theory was that somehow he had learned Randy had left town and figured as long as he never saw Randy again, that was good enough for him. Gary thought Kees actually knew more than he said he did. He told Randy about what had happened a couple weeks after school had started the following September. He had approached Kees in the hallway and started to tell him how very sorry he was about what happened and that Randy hadn't really meant to do it. Kees just turned and walked away without saying anything.

Since Gary's visit, he, Bill, Brad and Kees had all graduated from high school. Randy wished he could have been part of it, but even if he had stayed in school, he wouldn't have been in that graduating class because of failing a grade. He still phoned Gary on a regular basis and wrote to Bill, Brad and Mark quite often. He never phoned Mark anymore; whenever he had phoned in the past, either his mom or William would answer and he would never get a chance to talk to Mark. Randy found that keeping in touch with his friends helped him get over the loneliness. The one thing he missed about Granby was his friends; he didn't miss the town itself one bit.

Since he had been in Calgary he had made virtually no attempt to find a girlfriend. In fact, he had hardly even tried to lose his virginity. He found this particularly frustrating—it seemed as though he had everything going against him in that department. He found he was quite shy and awkward around women, and he could never think of himself as being that great looking. Before he had turned eighteen, he hadn't thought there were many places in the city where he could meet girls. Since turning eighteen, none of the bars or nightclubs he had been to had been that great either. In every place he had been to so far, there appeared to be ten times as many women as men. Yet whenever he had asked a girl to dance, she wouldn't politely say, "No thank you." Her response would be anything from "Get lost" to "Fuck off." In one particular place, he had gone within two feet of a girl, and she had said to him, "Get away from me, you ugly puke!" Luckily, he had managed to restrain himself from hitting her.

At his workplace, all of the workers in the plant were male; the only female there was the receptionist, who happened to be the wife of the sales manager. In Randy's apartment building there were a few girls who were single mothers, but they were a lot older than him. As a result of all these circumstances, one night his hormones got the better of him. He took some money he had saved over a couple of months, and went to the part of town where the high-priced hookers hung out. He figured that if he was going to get his first lay, he was going to do it in style. As it turned out, the girl he approached just happened to be an undercover cop. He was charged with soliciting and was given a hefty fine. He had not made another attempt since then, and the only solace he found was in his collection of *Playboy* and *Penthouse* magazines.

In terms of acquisitions, he hadn't bought very many things for himself over the past two years. He had bought a few things for the apartment, such as a coffee table, a cushioned chair, a single bed, a portable black-and-white TV set, a clock radio, a table and chair set for the kitchen and some more kitchen utensils. But perhaps his greatest purchase was a car. A year and a half ago, he had bought a 1972 Dodge Colt station wagon from one of the many used car lots along 17th Avenue S.E. But before he could buy it, he first had to get a driver's license. In his case, it wasn't easy, since he hadn't had a family member to teach him how to drive. He had to learn through a driving school, and the instructor had to drive him to the Motor Vehicle Office when he took his driver's test. He passed the test with flying colours, and bought the car shortly afterward. It ran not too badly, but it burned a lot of oil. In addition, it had difficulty starting when it was very cold outside, even with the block heater plugged in. Randy considered it his prized possession, and he found it a big improvement over taking the bus.

As for the job, Randy was still plugging away at Prairie Agro Services.

His work was divided between the bagging machine and one of the mixing machines. For the longest while, it appeared as though he would be there for the long haul. That all changed when the Calgary mill, which had been in operation since the early sixties, was sold to Simmons and Sattler, a large American grain conglomerate based in Sioux City, Iowa. Prairie Agro Services had built a state-of-the-art mill in Olds, forty-five miles north of Calgary, and then had amalgamated it with the Calgary mill. As a result, their Red Deer mill, one hundred miles north of Calgary, was closed. Angus McVittie, the manager, and Danny Tamaka, the foreman, had been transferred to the Olds mill. Randy wanted to take a job there as well but he didn't have enough seniority.

A new manager was appointed for the Calgary mill. His name was Dick Suderman; he had previously held a position at corporate headquarters. There was also a new foreman. His name was Dory Hoskins and he was the former plant manager at the Simmons and Sattler mill in Appleton, Wisconsin. Ever since the management change, things had been going steadily downhill, especially for Randy. It seemed as though Dory had it in for him right from day one. He had been reprimanded on numerous occasions and his work was constantly being ridiculed. Dory appeared to think that he was a completely useless tit. On several occasions he had called Randy into his office, slammed his hand hard onto his desk, and told him to start towin' the line or he'd fire him. Randy didn't know how much more he could take; he knew that Dory had something personal against him. After all, while Danny was foreman he had never once complained about Randy's work performance.

Randy was seriously considering quitting, but he was not sure what course of action to take. There were still a lot of job opportunities in Calgary, so he would have no problem finding work. The thing was, he didn't really want to stay in Calgary. He figured there had to be some other cities besides Edmonton and Calgary where there were a lot of work prospects, but he was not sure where. There was one city, however, that he had given some consideration. He had learned about it from a co-worker named Cyril. Cyril was the only colleague that Randy ever had regular conversations with. He had been born and raised in Saskatoon. He had frequently told Randy stories about his early days there and always bragged about what a really nice city it was. Yet he preferred to live in Calgary, mainly because his ex-wife lived in Saskatoon and he was estranged from his family—something Randy could relate to. According to Cyril, Saskatoon was not too big, not too small and the people were friendly. But he never said very much about the local economy. Either way, Randy was giving the possibility of moving to Saskatoon some serious thought.

One typical Monday morning Randy went into work and, as usual, Dory was on his case. By then, he was at his breaking point, so at lunch he asked Cyril what the economy was like in Saskatoon. Cyril wasn't quite sure since he hadn't been there in five years. He pointed out that when he had lived there the economy was always fairly stable and he never had any trouble finding a job. However, he suggested that it might be a good idea to drive up there for a weekend first. That would help Randy get somewhat familiar with Saskatoon. He brought that up because the Heritage Day long weekend was coming up, so that would be a good time to visit. It took six to seven hours to drive there, so the extra day would be helpful. Randy said he would give it some thought, but for the moment he just wanted to wait and see how things went. He said that deep down inside he would like to stick around for just two more months so he could say he had worked there for two years. But being realistic, he knew that was highly unlikely. He told Cyril he would wait until the next time Dory gave him a bad time and would take it from there.

As it turned out, Randy didn't have to wait very long. Two days later Dory called him into his office—again.

He told Randy to sit down, and said to him in his southern drawl (he was originally from Louisiana), "You know something, Randy, I have tried to be patient with you, but you don't seem to be working out here."

Randy thought he would seize the opportunity and get in a few shots.

"Look, I've busted my ass here for almost two years! I don't know what's the matter with you, but Danny never had a problem with me—he was always happy with my work!"

Dory responded with, "I don't know if you realize this, but Danny is not in charge here anymore. I am! I don't know what Danny's expectations were. You may have lived up to his expectations, but you aren't living up to mine."

"It seems that with you, nothing I do is ever good enough!"

"Randy, I have my own standards and you are just not meeting them. Therefore, I have no choice but to let you go."

"Fine, see if I care!" Randy said.

With that, he stormed out of Dory's office, said goodbye to Cyril and left the plant for the last time.

That evening he mulled over whether to stay in Calgary or move to Saskatoon. He realized that this was a major decision and there was an element of uncertainty as to what to expect in Saskatoon. But by the following morning his decision was final—he was moving to Saskatoon.

Then there was the question of what to do with his apartment. There was still one week left in July and his rent was paid for the rest of the month. In addition, he hadn't given the manager any notice that he was moving. So he went down to the manager's suite and told him that he was leaving at the end of the month. He told Randy that he was supposed to give one month's notice and his apartment must be cleaned up. Otherwise he wouldn't get his damage deposit back. Upon hearing that, Randy thought about changing his plans. For awhile he considered doing temporary work until the end of August and moving out then.

But by the next day his decision was, "Fuck this, I want to move out NOW!" He figured that the amount of the damage deposit was not worth sticking around there, especially if he was not happy. He went to the manager's suite again and informed him that he would be leaving the next day. The manager decided to go easy on Randy. He said he would only withhold half of the damage deposit since he had otherwise been a good tenant. He asked Randy to give him his new address when he got settled in Saskatoon so he could forward a cheque.

Later that day Randy went to his bank, withdrew all his money and closed his account. He went home and began packing his belongings. The next morning he loaded everything into his car except the coffee table. It was too big and bulky to fit in the car, so he decided to leave it behind. Besides, he had paid only five dollars for it at a garage sale. It was a good thing his car was a station wagon, but even with the back seat folded down, there was little room to spare. The bed and the kitchen table took up most of the space.

After he finished loading the car, he turned in his apartment key to the manager and then took off. As he was heading out of town, all that was on his mind was, "This is great! No more standing by the side of the road with my thumb out, no more not knowing whether I will get a ride and no more risk of getting a ride with a weirdo. I can now travel on my time, at my pace. Yes, I am now in control!"

6

Instead of taking the more direct route to Saskatoon via Highway 9, Randy decided to take the Trans-Canada Highway to Regina and then head north. That way he could spend a few days in Regina (and maybe even Moose Jaw) and see what things were like there. This was the first time he had driven his car outside of Calgary. In fact, it was the first time he had set foot outside of Calgary since he'd arrived there nearly two years ago. As he made his way eastward, he thought to himself, "This is strange. I have been in Alberta for two years now and this is the first time I have seen genuine, honest-to-goodness prairie." The farther east he went, the flatter the terrain became. Past Brooks there was nothing but flat land as far as the eye could see. All he kept thinking was, "Man, dig this crazy scenery!" He decided he would make his first pit stop in Medicine Hat, which was still sixty miles away.

Just after he passed Suffield, he noticed the red light on the dashboard indicating "Oil." He decided that when he stopped in Medicine Hat he would put in a quart of oil. Whenever that light had come on previously that was how he had dealt with it. But usually the light would only stay on for only a few seconds. This time it stayed on persistently. A little while later, he started having difficulty maintaining normal highway speed. A few miles further down the road the engine started making a funny clunking noise. By then he was getting pretty worried. He could see the town of Redcliff in the distance and thought about finding an auto repair place when he got there. But as he got closer he decided to try to make it to Medicine Hat since it was only about four miles further on. By then the car was only able to achieve a top speed of forty miles per hour.

Shortly after he passed the turnoff to Redcliff, smoke started coming up from under the hood. Randy immediately pulled over, got out of the car and opened up the hood. Smoke billowed from the engine block and the stench was unbearable.

He yelled out, "Holy shit! Oh man, this looks serious!"

He walked back a half mile to the turnoff to Redcliff and went into a gas station at the intersection. Randy explained his situation to the attendant.

"We do only minor things like oil changes and tire rotations here. You will definitely need to be towed. Your best bet would be to have it towed into Medicine Hat," said the attendant.

He let Randy use his phone. He called up a towing company, and a half an hour later a tow truck arrived.

The truck driver assessed the situation, then said, "Yes, you definitely need a tow! Are you an A.M.A.?"

Randy asked, "What's that?"

"Are you a member of the Alberta Motor Association?"

"No, I'm not."

"Well I can take you into Redcliff, or I can take you to Medicine Hat, but no matter what it'll cost you fifty bucks," the driver told him.

"Fifty bucks! That's outrageous!"

"Well, that's why it pays to belong to the A.M.A."

Randy reluctantly gave in and requested that his car be taken into Medicine Hat. He asked where there was a good place to service his car and the driver recommended a garage on Railway Avenue near the downtown.

As they drove into town, Randy explained to the driver what had happened. The driver told him that the indicator light meant there was no oil pressure, which implied that the oil pump had given out. When that happened there was no oil getting over the cylinder heads and that resulted in increased friction. This eventually caused the motor to seize. When that light comes on, you are supposed to pull over and shut the engine off immediately. When Randy told him the light had come on just after he'd passed Suffield, the driver couldn't believe that he had actually driven twenty miles with no oil pressure. He was amazed it had lasted as long as it did. He told Randy that there was a good chance that the engine had seized up completely.

Once they were at the garage, Randy hung out in the waiting room for what seemed like an eternity. After awhile a mechanic came into the room looking grim-faced. He asked, "Are you Randy?"

And Randy replied nervously, "Yes."

"Well, I'm afraid I have some bad news. All of the piston rings are shot and there is considerable damage to the cylinder heads. You have two alternatives. I can either do a complete piston ring job or I can put a new engine in. Either way it will cost at least a thousand dollars."

Randy's jaw dropped and he yelled out, "A thousand dollars! Hell, I only paid six hundred dollars for the damn thing in the first place!"

Randy was absolutely flabbergasted; he didn't know what to think.

"I'll give you some time to think it over."

Randy thought about it for a little while, but it was not a difficult decision to make. He went into the garage area and told the mechanics not to bother, that the car was not worth spending a thousand dollars on. Besides, he didn't have a thousand dollars. He asked them if they knew of an auto wrecker who could take it off his hands. One of the mechanics had a friend who owned an auto wrecking yard and he could arrange to have one of their workers come and pick the car up. He then asked Randy what he planned to do with all the stuff in his car, since he had noticed it looked pretty loaded. Randy was fully aware of this, and had tried his best to think of something earlier—he had expected this outcome. He realized that his only choice was to get rid of everything. He had noticed on the drive into town that there was a second-hand shop about two blocks back. He told the mechanics he would be right back and left to check the place out. When he got there, he told the proprietor he had some furniture and kitchen utensils he wanted to sell. He told Randy to bring them in.

Randy could carry only one item at a time and had to make at least eight trips. The bed alone took two trips—one for the mattress and one for the box spring. He must have looked pretty silly lugging a piece of furniture or a box for two blocks down the street. At the second-hand store, he put all his stuff in a pile in the middle of the floor. The only things he planned to keep were his backpack and all of his clothes. By the time he had brought the last box in, he was completely exhausted. He asked the proprietor how much he would give him for the whole lot.

The man inspected everything thoroughly and then offered, "Forty bucks."

"You have a deal," Randy agreed.

As he was handing him the cash, he asked Randy, "So, why are you selling your belongings?"

"I'm moving to Saskatoon."

The man gave him a funny look and asked, "What in the world would you want to live there for?"

Randy asked, "What's wrong with Saskatoon?"

"Well, it's too hot in the summer and too cold in the winter and during summer the place is overrun with mosquitoes. At least here you get chinooks in the winter."

"I'll be the judge. I'll see for myself whether or not I like Saskatoon."

"Suit yourself. So, how are you planning on getting there?"

"I'm going back to my old method of transportation—thumbnail express!" he said, indicating his thumb.

By the time Randy arrived back at the garage, someone from the auto wrecking yard was there. He asked the guy if he could get a least a little something for what was left of his car.

The man said, "Well, I notice that you do have some new parts in it, and there are some other parts that are salvageable. So, I'll tell you what—I will give you forty dollars for it., but to be honest, I am being generous. Normally, and this applies to any vehicle, once the motor is toasted, the vehicle is completely worthless. So that's my offer—take it or leave it."

Randy reluctantly agreed, and the man gave him forty dollars. He then took all of his remaining items out of the car, which included his backpack loaded with all of his clothes, his heavy winter coat and his heavy winter boots. He tried to stuff them all into his backpack—no easy task. Every compartment was jammed full and he could hardly do up any of the buckles. It was absolutely bulging at the seams, which made it difficult for him to mount it on his back. He took a look at his car for the last time and then went on his way.

For some reason Randy didn't feel like taking the city bus; he wanted to walk instead. It could have been because he was pissed off or that he didn't know the city's transit system or a combination of both. When he was in the waiting room in the garage, he had studied a map of Medicine Hat on the wall. He made his way over to Kingsway and then headed south. He knew it would eventually turn into Dunmore Road and that in turn would lead to the Trans-Canada Highway. All he kept thinking about was how he had been royally ripped off. He felt that he should have gotten more for his car; that guy from the auto wreckers was nothing but a bloody con artist. But obviously Randy knew nothing about auto mechanics, so how would he have been able to argue his point? In terms of his belongings, however, that wasn't quite so bad. He had bought all of his things at garage sales, so when he sold them he almost broke even!

Randy began to wonder if walking was such a good idea after all; Dunmore Road seemed endless. His backpack was three times heavier than it was two years ago. The late afternoon heat didn't help either. When he reached the Trans-Canada Highway, he went into a nearby gas station and bought a pop. When he came out, he noticed a man standing next to a semi-trailer truck watching his every move.

He remounted his backpack and started heading toward the highway when the man called out, "Hey kid!"

The man approached him, and Randy turned around and said, "Yes?"

"Whereabouts are you heading?"

Randy said, "Well, first I'm going to Regina, and then I'm going on to Saskatoon."

"How would you like to go to Winnipeg?" he asked.

Randy thought about it for a minute and then said, "Why not—what have I got to lose?"

"Great, get on!"

Randy had never been inside the tractor unit on a big rig before. He was amazed at the large number of gauges and buttons on the dashboard and couldn't get over how high up he was.

The driver climbed in and said, "And we're off!"

He introduced himself as "Del, which is short for Delbert."

He said, "I sure hope you like to talk."

Randy asked, "Why is that?"

"I left Edmonton first thing this morning and picked up my load in Calgary. I will be off-loading in Winnipeg, then driving to another part of town to pick up a load there, and then I head back to Edmonton. So I need you to help keep me awake."

"Wait a minute, aren't you going to stop and go to sleep for awhile?"

"Look, son, us independent truckers are not paid by the hour; we're paid by the trip. We have to pay for all of the gas and maintenance on our rigs and when you have a mortgage and a family to support, you've got to try and make as many trips as you can."

Randy could see his point and so for the next couple hours he talked constantly on everything from growing up in Granby to his time in Calgary.

Eventually Del said, "Look, Randy, that may be of interest to you, but it is of no interest to me. I know, tell me about the best fuck you ever had!"

Randy was too embarrassed to tell him he was still a virgin, so he had to think of something fast. He relayed a story he had read from the "Forum" section of one of his *Penthouse* magazines and made it sound like it had happened to him. Judging from the look that Del gave him, it appeared that he didn't believe his story. Randy figured, "What difference does it make? Most of those stories are made up anyway!"

Then Del started to tell Randy stories of some of his "conquests." He made it sound as if he had mistresses in every major Canadian city and even some in the U.S. It seemed as if all of them had fantastic bodies and enjoyed sex often. He found this kind of strange, since he thought Del had told him that he was married and had a family. Anyway, he didn't want to say anything about it.

But after awhile, he finally spoke up and said, "You know something, there's somebody in Calgary that I used to know that you really oughta meet!"

They stopped and had dinner in Moose Jaw, and after they passed Regina it became dark. Randy commented that now he would not be able to admire the breathtaking scenery again until morning. It was obvious to Del that he was being sarcastic. After awhile he ran out of things to talk about, so he told Del that he wanted to give his tongue a rest for a few minutes. He then put his head back and closed his eyes and that's the last thing he remembered.

When Randy opened his eyes, he felt groggy and disoriented. He tried to focus and see where they were, but it was still dark out.

He asked Del, "Where are we?"

Del, looking pretty peeved, replied, "Well, for your information, we crossed the border into Manitoba a half an hour ago!"

"I don't remember that."

"That's probably because you fell asleep five hours ago! I thought you were supposed to be keeping me awake!"

"Oh, I'm sorry!" Randy apologized. "Okay, now where did I leave off?"

"Hey, don't worry about it. Actually, I pulled over and went to sleep for a couple hours myself just outside of Moosomin. The warehouse that I will be dropping my load at doesn't open until 7:30, so I thought I would take advantage of being early and get some sleep while it was still dark out. I would have slept a little longer if it weren't for that damn train. I'm amazed that you slept through it!"

"Yeah, I must have been really tired."

By the time they passed Brandon, the first hint of daylight had emerged. When they reached Portage La Prairie, the sun had come up over the horizon. As they passed by the town, Randy noticed a very large building near the highway that had "Campbell's" written on the side. He asked Del what that building was, and he told him that it was the Campbell's Soup factory. Randy thought to himself, "Wouldn't that be nice if I could get a job there. I would love to live in a small town again. Only this time I would be living in a town with a future." He decided to give that place serious consideration if things didn't work out in Winnipeg.

An hour later they arrived in Winnipeg. Del told him that the warehouse he was taking his load to was not far from the downtown area, so he offered to drop him off right downtown.

He said, "I'll tell you what. I can let you off at that famous intersection of Portage and Main."

Randy said, "That sounds all right, but I can never figure out why that intersection is so famous. I mean, it's just an intersection."

"I don't really know why, either. You would have to ask someone who is a native of Winnipeg. At least my timing is good. The rush hour is just beginning. I should be able to make it to the warehouse right at opening time."

He let Randy off at the corner of Portage and Main, and as he left Randy said, "Thanks for the ride and you have a safe trip back to Edmonton."

Randy looked at his watch and saw that it was only 7:00, so for the next two hours he walked all through downtown Winnipeg. He started asking himself, "What am I doing here? The main reason I left Calgary was to escape the hustle and bustle of the big city. Sure, Saskatoon is a big city, but not the magnitude of Calgary and Edmonton. Here it's a case of the same shit, different city!" With that, he decided to stick to his original plans and make his way to Saskatoon. But he wanted to go to Portage La Prairie first. He remembered from looking at a map of Western Canada in Del's truck that the Yellowhead Highway started out just west of Portage La Prairie and from there went directly to Saskatoon. He figured that would work out just fine. The question was how to get to Portage La Prairie from there. He didn't know his way around Winnipeg and didn't know any of the bus routes. Plus, it had seemed to take Del forever to get to the downtown area from the western city limits. Therefore, Randy decided to take the Greyhound bus to Portage La Prairie. He remembered where the bus depot was, and when he arrived there he found out there was a bus heading west in a half an hour.

After the bus arrived in Portage La Prairie, he got a room at the Albion Hotel. He planned to use that place as his "address" when filling out job applications, so he asked at the front desk what their street address and phone number was. He also asked if they could take any phone messages for him. He then made his way over to the Campbell's Soup plant and asked at the front desk for an application form. After filling it out, he met with the human resources manager, who happened to be a woman. She introduced herself as Angela Simpson and began asking him questions about his background. The main thing she noticed was that he had lived in B.C. and Alberta, but not Manitoba. She asked Randy how long he had lived in Portage La Prairie and Randy said hesitantly, "One day."

She then asked him if he planned to take up permanent residence there, and Randy replied, "I am hoping to."

She said, "The thing is, we do not have any openings right now, but that could change. People come and go here all the time, so openings do come up. We just don't know when. So if a position does become open, how are we going to contact you?"

"I'll see what I can do. Maybe I can find a part-time job here for the time being."

Angela said, "All I can do is keep your application on file for three months and you can check back here if you get a permanent address."

Randy decided to try to find a job that would hold him over until he could get on at the Campbell's Soup plant. He applied at a number of restaurants, gas stations and convenience stores, as well as a grocery store, all of the grain elevators and even an elevator that handled dehydrated peas, but no luck. He then went to the Canada Manpower office and spoke to a counsellor there. She told him that about the only place in town that was hiring at the time was the Manitoba Mental Hospital.

The job involved working with mental patients, and Randy's reaction was, "I think I'll pass on that one!"

As he left the office, all he kept thinking was, "Well, at least I tried."

That evening he decided to check out the hotel bar. He figured that he might as well, since he didn't have to go very far afterwards. He also thought that since it was going to be his only night there, he might as well live it up. He struck up a conversation with a local man named Joe Snider. He was a truck driver for a local feed mill and had lived in Portage La Prairie all his life. Joe appeared to be quite intrigued by Randy's stories about his adventures on the road, mainly because he had not travelled very much. They even shot a few games of pool. At 9:30 Joe told him that he had to pack it in, since he had to start work early the next morning.

When Randy said he would be leaving in the morning and heading for Saskatoon, Joe replied that he had to take a load to a farm near the town of Gladstone, which was on the way. He offered to give Randy a ride as far as Gladstone and Randy accepted. As it was to be his first run of the day, Joe told Randy to meet him in front of the hotel at 7:30.

Randy went up to the front desk and asked for a wake-up call for 7:15 the next morning. But instead of going up to his room he decided to go back to the bar and have a couple more beers. As it turned out, he had a lot more than just a couple. The band was playing lively country-rock music. He played a few games of pool and he even got to dance a few times. He was really enjoying himself, and all night he kept thinking, "Man, I wish I could stay here!" He ended up staying there until closing time at 1:00, and by then he was pretty drunk. He somehow managed to stagger up to his room.

The telephone rang at precisely 7:15, and to Randy it sounded ten times louder than it really was.

He struggled to reach the phone by the fourth ring and said in a weak voice, "Yes?"

The voice at the other end said, "You requested a wake-up call for 7:15?"

Randy mumbled, "Oh right, thank you."

His head felt like a two-ton weight had been dropped on it. He'd had hangovers before, but this had to be the granddaddy of them all. He struggled to drag himself out of bed, managed to get his clothes on and load his backpack. He then stumbled down the stairs and turned the key in at the front desk. When he got out the front door, he was greeted by a large hopper truck with "JL Feeds" written on the side.

He climbed into the cab, and Joe said, "Good morning! For awhile there I thought you weren't coming." He took a look at Randy and then noticed the distinct smell of booze on him. "Holy shit, you must have really been living it up last night! How late did you stay there?"

Randy said, "I was there until closing time. Oh man, I feel like shit!"

"That serves you right."

On the previous night Randy had forgotten to ask Joe if the feed mill he worked for had any job openings. He told him he had two years experience working in a feed mill and some job experience with a mixing machine. Joe said that his company had a pretty stable workforce, so the staff turnover rates were very low. In fact, several of the employees had been there over twenty years. Randy said that the company he used to work for was like that until this Yankee outfit took over. After that it was practically a revolving door.

"You don't mean Simmons and Sattler, do you?" Joe asked.

Randy said, "That's right—you know them?"

"Of course, I know them all too well. They are systematically trying to take over the cattle feed industry in Canada and the U.S. one piece at a time, mostly by buying up smaller companies. When old James Langham retired—that's what the JL stands for—they made him an offer they thought he couldn't refuse, but he wouldn't have any part of it. Luckily, he found a local interest to buy the company. Simmons and Sattler are notorious for cutting corners too. For instance, in their mills in Texas and Oklahoma, practically all of their workers are illegal Mexican immigrants. They pay them next to nothing and if they complain, the company reports them to immigration. Also, they quite often dehydrate dead animal guts, grind them up and mix it in with the feed in order to make it stretch further."

"Yeow, that's gross!"

"Yeah, they are one scummy outfit. You should consider getting fired from there a blessing in disguise!"

As they approached the village of Gladstone, Joe told Randy that he would be heading north from there. He offered to drop him of right in the village, where there was a coffee shop nearby. Randy thanked him for the ride and then went into the coffee shop to have breakfast. He planned on having at least a couple of extra cups of coffee in hopes that it might relieve his hangover.

After he left the coffee shop he headed out to Highway 16. It was a beautiful, sunny day, not a cloud in the sky. But surprisingly there was very little traffic. Randy couldn't believe how few cars were going by. For the first three hours he walked down the highway whenever there weren't any cars coming. One thing he noticed about the prairies was that you could always tell where the next town was from a distance, grain elevators being the indicator. He could see a series of them straight ahead and another three off to the right. He decided not to walk anymore; he figured that the town ahead could still be several miles away. So he turned, faced the highway and kept his thumb out.

Morning turned into afternoon and Randy still had no luck getting a ride. The afternoon sun beat down on him mercilessly; it felt like it was a hundred degrees Fahrenheit. He began to wonder if he was coming down with sunstroke; he was feeling woozy at times. But then he figured that it might just be the lingering effects of his hangover. In addition, he was absolutely dying of thirst.

Later in the afternoon, Randy noticed that the air had become very humid. In fact, it was downright sticky. Also, he kept hearing a rumbling noise that sounded like thunder. He thought that was strange since there wasn't a cloud in the sky (in the east anyway). Heading west, he decided to start making his way toward the next town. He still wasn't having any luck getting a ride, so he figured that he would reach town by dinnertime. Then he turned around and looked up and his jaw dropped.

He yelled out, "Holy shit! Where the hell did that come from?"

There, in the western sky, was this huge, jet-black cloud heading straight for him. In a panic, he started walking fast toward the town up ahead. In fact, he was practically running. He could also see in the distance a sign pointing to the town off to the right. But he soon realized he wasn't going to make it to either town in time. Just then out of the corner of his eye he noticed a car coming. He turned and began waving his arm with his thumb out frantically.

"Gimme a ride, gimme a ride goddamn it, give me a ride!" he yelled out. As the car sped by he continued, "Asshole!"

By then it was starting to rain, and he knew he had to take cover somewhere fast. He saw a lone tree in a nearby field, but immediately thought, "A solitary tree in a thunderstorm, I don't think so!" He then noticed a small stream coming out from under the highway. He decided to take refuge in the culvert that ran under the highway. He scrambled down the embankment, but when he reached the culvert he realized that he wouldn't be able to stand up straight inside it. He made his way inside and the water went up to his ankles. Just as he made it inside, the floodgates opened. The rain was coming down so hard that Randy imagined he was standing under Niagara Falls. Lightning bolts were coming down all around him. A few minutes later he noticed that the water in the culvert was beginning to rise. The heavy downpour was putting too much of a strain on the creek, so the water had nowhere else to go but up. The water eventually went up past his knees and up to his waist. He took his wallet out of his pocket and held it above his head. The water kept on rising and he was getting worried. He realized that if the rain didn't stop pretty soon he could be completely submerged.

After a couple minutes the rain did stop, but not the way he wanted it to. The only reason it had stopped raining was because it had turned to hail! Randy couldn't believe his eyes as he looked outside and saw hailstones the size of golf balls coming down. He looked up and to his horror saw what looked like a funnel cloud. He started thinking, "Oh great, that's just what I need, to be carried up to the land of Oz!" Fortunately, the funnel cloud never touched the ground. The hailstorm lasted several minutes. Hailstones floated on the surface of the creek as it went through the culvert. This made the already freezing water even colder. By the time the rain finally stopped, the water was chest deep. Randy emerged from the culvert thoroughly soaked. He noticed that the landscape had completely changed; the ground was a blanket of white from the hailstones. It looked like it had just snowed. Randy couldn't believe it. He kept thinking, "I don't fucking believe this place! One minute it's hotter than hell out and ten minutes later, it's raining—ice!"

He trudged up the embankment toward the highway. The slope was very slippery and he was so cold that he had difficulty moving. He couldn't stop shivering; he wondered if he was starting to get hypothermia. By the time he reached the highway the sun had started to poke through the clouds. This helped warm him up a little bit. He then saw a pair of headlights coming his way, so he weakly put his arm out. Lo and behold, the vehicle pulled over! Randy thought, "Wouldn't you know it, NOW I get a ride!" It was a Volkswagen van and there was a young man driving.

He said, "Hey man, where are you heading?"

"Saskatoon."

"I'm only going as far as Yorkton," the driver said.

"That'll do just fine."

Soon after they headed off the man said, "Whoo-wee! Did you see that storm back there, man? It was raining so hard I couldn't see the road! And the hail, it was just a coming down like bullets!"

He looked at Randy and noticed that he was soaking wet and looking rather annoyed.

"No shit?" Randy said sarcastically.

"Oh, I see, I guess you got caught in it. It's too bad I didn't come along this way sooner."

"Oh, don't worry about it. Can you please turn the heat up?"

They arrived in Yorkton a little over an hour later. Randy's clothes were still damp. The man dropped him off downtown, and from there Randy went to look for a hotel for the night. The hotel he checked into was aptly named the Yorkton Hotel. Once he got up to his room, he emptied his backpack and sure enough, everything inside was soaking wet. He hung it all on the towel rack and on the shower in the bathroom. Before he had left the restaurant in Gladstone, he had bought a package of cigarettes and had only smoked two. The other twenty-three were soaked. This made him very mad. He was determined not to waste them, so he carefully laid out each one on the counter, hoping they would eventually dry out. Besides, his book of matches was wet too, so they were useless. He took off all his clothes, placed them over the heat register and sat on the bed and watched TV, stark naked. An hour later he was so hungry that he couldn't stand it any longer. So he put his still-damp clothes back on and walked a couple blocks to a Kentucky Fried Chicken outlet.

When he arrived back at his hotel room he took off his clothes again, hung them up and turned on the TV. He realized that the hotel was not hooked up to cable, so he was limited as to what he could watch. Over the course of the evening he kept thinking, "Dear diary—here I am, sitting in a hotel room in Yorkton, Saskatchewan, buck naked, dining on Kentucky Fried Chicken and watching the Tommy Hunter Show. Man, is this living or not?"

Randy woke up the next morning feeling a lot better than he had the day before. For obvious reasons he had decided to abstain from going drinking last night. He figured that he would save his energy for when he got his first paycheque from his new job in Saskatoon. He enthusiastically put his clothes on and loaded his backpack, knowing he was only two hundred miles away from his goal. On his way out of town he grabbed his traditional on-the-road breakfast staple of a coffee and doughnut from a convenience store. From there he headed up Smith Street (which was part of Highway 16) to the city limits and put his thumb out. It was over two hours before a car pulled over. It was a young couple in a late model Buick. The woman asked Randy where he was heading.

"Saskatoon," he told her.

"Good, that's where we're heading," she said.

During the trip, Randy contemplated what strategy he was going to use in his job search. He thought about using a different approach this time around. Instead of trying to get temporary work and risk getting a job he didn't like, he would get welfare for a month and then he could take his time and find a job he did like. But whatever approach he was going to take, he wasn't going to be able to do anything about it because today was Saturday. So all he could do for the present was to hold that thought until Monday.

Three and a half hours after Randy was picked up, they arrived in Saskatoon. Randy was quite relieved, as he hadn't been able to have a conversation with either of them. Throughout the whole trip they had blabbed away to each other in French. For all he knew, they could have been talking about him the whole time without him knowing. He eventually spoke up and asked if he could be dropped off as close to the downtown core as possible. The man told Randy he wasn't planning to go downtown and the best place he could drop him off was at the corner of College Drive and Cumberland Avenue, right by the University of Saskatchewan. He told him he could get downtown from there, but it was a bit of a walk. Randy figured, "What the hell, I've got the rest of the day, anyway."

After they dropped him off, Randy made his way downtown. Later that day he checked in to the Salvation Army hostel. On Sunday he went for a long walk through the downtown area and along the South Saskatchewan River. That seemed to be his traditional method of familiarizing himself with his new surroundings.

7

On Monday morning Randy went to the nearest Social Services office. After a lengthy wait, he finally got to see a social worker. She reviewed his application and commented on the fact that the last place he lived in was Calgary.

She asked, "What did you leave Calgary for? There are a lot more job opportunities there than there are here. Personally, I feel that you would have been better off if you had stayed there."

"I found Calgary too big and impersonal. I didn't feel like I fit in there," he answered.

The social worker then asked where he lived, and he told her that he didn't have a place yet.

"Before we can give you any money, you have to be committed to a place for at least a month. Otherwise, how do I know if you are going to take off back to Calgary tomorrow?"

She handed Randy a form for the landlord to fill out once he found a place. She told him that once the form was filled out and returned he could then receive a cheque for one month's worth of rent and living expenses.

Randy set off to find a place. He decided to look around in that neighbourhood first, and if nothing turned up then he would look at ads in the newspaper. He headed down the street for a couple blocks and came upon a huge Victorian-style house. On the front door was a sign that read "Furnished Rooms for Rent" along with a phone number. The house had a real gothic look, like something out of a horror movie, except it had stucco siding that gave it a more modern appearance. He knocked on the door, but there was no answer. So he wrote the number down and went to the nearest pay phone. When he called a man answered. He inquired about the rooms for rent.

"Sure, we still have two suites available. Would you be interested in looking at one?" he asked.

Randy said, "Yes, I would."

"Well, look, I live in another part of town, but I was planning to come up there anyway. So I will be there in an hour. Oh, by the way, my name is

Marvin Drinkwater." As Randy hung up the phone, he thought to himself, "What the hell kind of a name is that?"

He parked himself in a nearby coffee shop for an hour, and then went back to the house. Shortly afterward, a short man in a plaid jacket, fedora and bow tie appeared.

He asked, "Are you the one who called about the suite?"

"Yes, I am," Randy said, realizing that this must be Marvin Drinkwater.

Marvin stretched his arms out toward the house and said, "Well, what do you think?"

Randy said, "I don't know. I've only seen it from the outside."

"Well, let's take a look inside."

As they went inside, Marvin pointed to a door on the left. You could hear a TV blaring on the other side.

He said, "That's where Henry lives—he's the caretaker. If you ever need anything he's right there."

They went up a stairway and started walking down a long corridor. Randy kept thinking, "Gee, how many apartments did they cram in here?"

Marvin said, "They're a pretty decent bunch living here. I think you'll like this place. Oh, by the way, you're not native, are you?"

Randy gave him a very annoyed look and said, "No, I'm Scottish, Greek and Armenian. Why should that matter?"

"Normally, I don't particularly like renting rooms to Indians."

Randy didn't want to get into an argument about discrimination, so he said nothing.

Marvin unlocked the door marked "2F" and showed Randy the suite. The first thing he noticed was how small it was. At first he wondered where the bed was, but then he realized that the room was L-shaped and the bed was around the corner. He asked where the stove was, and Marvin pointed to an old, two-burner hot plate on the counter. Randy thought, "That's just great. How am I going to make TV dinners and frozen pizzas? I guess I will have to cook for a change!"

He then asked where the bathroom was and Marvin said, "It's down the hall—there's only one bathroom per floor."

Randy was thinking, "Oh wow, man, that's just wonderful!"

Reluctantly he decided to take the place. He figured it would do for the time being. He told Marvin he was interested, and then asked him if he could fill out the rent form provided by Social Services.

"What? You're not on welfare, are you?" Marvin asked.

"It's only temporary—I fully intend on looking for work!"

Marvin filled it out and then asked when he could get his rent money.

Randy asked him if he was planning to stick around here for awhile and Marvin said, "Well, I could."

Randy told him that he would take the form back to the Social Services office, and then he could get a welfare cheque. He said that he would be "back in a flash with the cash!"

He returned to the Social Services office, and after a lengthy wait he got to see the same social worker as before. After processing his form, she presented him with a cheque for one month's worth of welfare. From there he went to a cheque-cashing place two doors down. He kept thinking, "How convenient it is, and what a coincidence that they would locate this place here!"

When he got back to the house Marvin asked, "What took you so long?"

"They were very busy," Randy replied.

He handed him the rent money, and as Marvin left he said, "The place is all yours—have fun!"

Randy wondered, "What did he mean by that?"

He spent some time looking around to see if anything had been left behind. He looked through all of the cupboards and there was not one utensil to be found. He noticed that the refrigerator was a real antique. It reminded him of the one in his house when he was a little kid. He hadn't realized Firestone made refrigerators—obviously before his time! He looked inside and then opened the door to the freezer compartment. It had not been defrosted in ages—there was practically no room to put anything. Also, it had not been cleaned since god knows when. He then went over to the window and admired the view—the brick wall of the building next door!

After spending the next couple of hours in his room reading, Randy decided to go and order dinner. He figured that the last time it was the Colonel so this time it would be a take-out pizza place. As he was leaving his room, four men were entering the room next door. They all looked like bikers and one of them was carrying a rifle. The man bringing up the rear was especially scary looking.

Randy must have been looking at him a little too long because the man said to him, "What the fuck are you looking at, punk?"

Randy didn't say anything; he just walked cautiously down the hall. Just before he reached the stairs he met up with another creepy-looking man standing in the doorway of his room. He gave Randy a real dirty look. Randy wanted to say something, but instead he just kept on walking.

When Randy arrived back at his room from the take-out pizza place, he could hear the men next door talking. In fact, he could hear every word they were saying. It sounded like they were up to no good, perhaps planning a robbery. He could also hear a familiar metal-clinking sound. It soon dawned on him why that sound was so familiar. When his mom was married to Larry, he used his rifles frequently during hunting season. Whenever he came home from a day of hunting, he would spend the evening cleaning the rifle he had used. Randy realized they were cleaning their rifles next door. This made him feel very uneasy. He did his best to try and tune them out, but it wasn't easy.

He decided he would turn in early so he could get a head start on his job hunt bright and early the next morning. He planned to buy a new sleeping bag the next day, since he had sold his old one to the man in Medicine Hat. For tonight, he would sleep in his clothes. Shortly after he turned out the lights, he was lying awake and looking up at the wall when he noticed something moving. He immediately thought, "Holy shit, what the hell is that?" He turned on the light, and saw a gigantic cockroach crawling down the wall. He used his shoe to kill it and then ran down to tell Henry about it. When he reached Henry's room, he knocked on the door, but there was no answer. The door was slightly ajar so he went inside. He knew Henry was home because he could hear the TV. As he went inside he noticed a very messy room and the floor was littered with beer and whiskey bottles. There, slumped in an easy chair, was an old, grizzled-looking man in a severely drunken state holding a bottle of Jack Daniels.

Randy said, "So, you must be Henry. Look, I just moved into room 2F and there was this big, fucking cockroach crawling down the wall."

Henry looked up at him, and when he opened his mouth Randy noticed that the guy didn't have any teeth.

Henry said in a barely audible voice, "So, kill it."

"I did!"

"So, what the hell do you want me to do about it?"

"Well, can I borrow some bug spray? Can you come up and check to make sure there aren't any more?"

Henry answered in a very slow drawl, "Look, if you see any more, just kill them. Now quit bothering me!"

As he left Henry's room, Randy grumbled, "If you need anything, he's right there—my ass!"

Randy tried again to go to sleep, but he was having another problem this time. Even though it was nighttime the heat was still unbearable. In addition, the humidity seemed close to one hundred percent. He felt like he was in a sauna. He eventually opened the window, hoping that would cool things down a bit. It did help, but then he could hear all the sounds coming from the street. The house was on a busy thoroughfare and there was lots of traffic—even late at night. In addition, he could hear sirens practically every two minutes. He also heard a man and a woman arguing at the top of their lungs up the street. A little while later he felt stinging sensations all along his arms and hands. When he turned the light back on, he realized he was being eaten alive by mosquitoes! With that he decided he'd better shut the window.

He did eventually go to sleep, but it was short-lived. He heard the voices of a man and a woman coming from the room on the other side. When he heard the woman say, "I need the money now," he came to the conclusion that she must be a hooker. His first impression was, "Hey, this could come in handy!" A few minutes later he could hear the sound of bed springs squeaking. He could also hear both of them making moaning sounds. He figured the man must really be enjoying himself. A half an hour later the man give out a loud groan followed by, "Oh, yes!" He assumed that the guy must have shot his load. He kept wishing it was him, so he made a note to pay that girl a visit when he got his first paycheque. After they got dressed and left, he made another attempt to go to sleep.

Needless to say, Randy didn't get a lot of sleep that night and he woke up a little later than planned. However, he was still determined to get out and look for work.

He went to the Canada Manpower office; on the job board there was one particular ad that got his attention. The job was for labourers to work on a landscaping project at the local brewery. When he inquired about the job the counsellor told him that it was only temporary; it would only last until September.

"The brewery is undertaking a major project to create a large botanical garden on the grounds. However, the workers have been on strike since last May, so all of the grounds have been behind a picket line. The strike was settled last week so now they want to get the project underway. Even though they won't be able to start planting until next spring, they want to complete the garden layout before fall. So, are you interested?"

Randy said, "Sure, I'll give it a try."

The counsellor gave him a form with the brewery's address and told him to report to Jeff Parkins in the trailer in the parking lot.

When Randy arrived at the brewery, he saw a large ATCO trailer in the parking lot. He went inside and asked to see Jeff Parkins.

The receptionist said, "He'll be here in a minute. Just have a seat."

A few minutes later Jeff came in. Randy introduced himself and told him that he was interested in the landscaper job. Jeff took him into his office and started asking him a few basic questions, such as, "Are you good with a shovel and a pick?" Randy informed him that he was, then Jeff took him outside and showed him the project. As it turned out, it was going to be quite a project—it would be spread over three acres. After showing him all that would be involved, Jeff asked Randy if he would like to start the next day.

"Yes, I would!"

Jeff said, "Okay then, be here at 7:30 sharp."

As Randy left the site of his new-found employment, he kept thinking, "Now, that wasn't so hard, was it? It may be temporary, but at least it will get my foot in the door here." Later he went into the Army & Navy department store and bought a sleeping bag, cooking pot and can opener. After all, he was now relegated to eating only canned and packaged goods.

That evening, as Randy was dining on canned stew, he could hear the guys next door at it again cleaning their rifles. He could also hear two guys down the hall yelling at each other at the top of their lungs. In addition, there was thumping and music playing up above. He was hoping that he would be able to sleep that night since he had to get an early start in the morning. Just like the night before, it was unbearably hot with nearly one hundred percent humidity. He still made a point, however, not to open the window.

Just after he turned off the light and lay down, he heard one of the men in the neighbouring suite scream out, "Hey don't fuck with me, man!" A few seconds later another man yelled out, "You want a piece of me, asshole?" Then what sounded like a scuffle ensued. He was quite worried because he knew they had guns. He was afraid that if one of them took a shot at the other and missed, the bullet could come right through the wall.

Fortunately, one of the guys stepped in and said, "Hey you guys, cool it!" He then started giving them a pep talk about how they could only get the job done if they worked as a team. Somehow Randy thought that maybe it would have been better if they had killed each other.

Eventually the men left, but Randy was still on edge. After awhile the heat really got to him so he took all of his clothes off. A little while later he heard the girl in the suite on the other side come in. He also heard a male voice so that meant that she had a customer with her. This time the customer repeatedly haggled over the price. The guy must have been some kind of cheapskate; he was trying to get as much as he could for as little as possible. Randy could tell that the girl was getting kind of annoyed. In a voice he could hear clearly, she said, "Look, if you want a blowjob that will cost you extra!" Randy had to restrain himself from laughing. Eventually the man gave in and settled for a straight lay. As he heard the bed squeaking, Randy again wished he was the one fucking her, so he began to masturbate. Both the customer and he managed to climax at the same time. After his neighbours had both dressed and left it was quiet, at least for the moment.

The alarm went off at 6:30 and Randy struggled to his feet, a little worse for wear. He'd had two rough nights in a row. This would be his first day at the new job, so he had to make a good first impression. He figured he had better drink a couple of extra cups of coffee.

When he started work, he learned that he would be digging a channel for an artificial stream. He would load the dirt into a wheelbarrow, carry it two hundred yards and dump it where they would be building an artificial hill. Come to think of it, everything on this project was artificial—before there had been nothing there but grass. One unique feature though, was that the north end of the property backed onto a hill. At the top of the hill a pond was being built. From there the water would go over a large waterfall, a stream would travel from one end of the project to the other, and another pond would be built at the end. The water would then be piped back to the other end. Therefore, the water would be continuously recycled.

It seemed as though he had to use the pick more than the shovel; the ground had more rocks than dirt. The two hundred yards that he carried the dirt and rocks in the wheelbarrow seemed more like two hundre miles. He wondered why there were only five other people working on the project; he didn't think it would be possible to finish by early September.

By the afternoon the heat was unbearable. The region was in the midst of a severe heat wave with no signs of it letting up. He was finding the work very hard and backbreaking; the lack of sleep didn't help either. By the end of the day he was stiff and sore all over. He was completely exhausted and just wanted to go home and go to sleep. On his way home he stopped at a drugstore and bought a bottle of insect repellant. That way he could open the window that night.

When he arrived back at his place, the man who lived down the hall approached him just before he got to his room.

He asked, "Hey man, can you spare a few bucks?"

"Why don't you do like I did and get a fucking job? Now get out of my way!" Randy sneered.

After he went into his room, Randy slathered on some insect repellant, opened the window and lay down. He immediately fell asleep and didn't wake up until 9:00. When he awoke he decided to make dinner (canned stew again) and then go back to bed before the next edition of "sex for the theatre of the mind." He figured that listening to the girl next door was the equivalent of a blind man going to a porno flick!

As Randy turned the water on to rinse out the pot, he noticed a sudden drop in water pressure. He then heard what sounded like water spraying coming from underneath the sink. He opened the cupboard door and got a shot of water in the face. The pipe had sprung a leak; the pipes were so badly corroded that the rust had worn right through. The shut-off valve was designed in such a way that it couldn't be closed off by hand. He needed a wrench. He ran down to Henry's room and pounded on the door, but again got no answer. He then opened the door and noticed Henry passed out in his recliner. He tried to wake him up, but to no avail.

He yelled out, "Oh, for fuck's sake," and began looking frantically around the room for any tools.

He noticed a pair of vice grips hanging on the wall and took them. He also saw a sponge lying by the sink, so he helped himself to that too. He ran back to his room and, using the vice grips, closed off the valve. By then there was an inch of water on the floor all through his room.

He heard a voice from the hallway saying, "Holy shit! Somebody really pissed himself!"

Randy muttered, "Shaddup!" He then said to himself, "Oh that's just great! Now I don't have any running water!"

It took him over two hours to mop up all of the water. By then he was really pooped. He ate his dinner right out of the can with a plastic fork.

He noticed that the bikers next door were not home; he hoped they would be out all night.

Barely an hour after Randy had gone to bed, the girl on the other side came in. When he heard her, he started thinking, "Oh no, here we go again!" But this wasn't the case. The man she was with must have said something to her she didn't like (Randy didn't catch what he said), because she started getting very angry. After a short argument she yelled out, "Get your fucking ass out of here, you sick piece of shit! Go on, get out—you're disgusting!" He stormed out, but she stayed behind. As Randy was listening to this he kept thinking, "Gee, that's weird. How can some woman who makes a large part of her income by sticking guys' dicks in her mouth find anything disgusting?"

The alarm clock went off at 6:30 as usual, and Randy felt worse than he had the day before. He deliberately left the alarm clock ringing for a few extra minutes, hoping it would piss off the guys next door. They had come in at two in the morning and for several hours argued vehemently about what went wrong on their latest "job."

On his way to work, Randy started to seriously consider leaving that place. Even though his rent was paid for the month, he knew that he would not be able to stay there that long. He was the only one in that building who worked, and it was obvious that nobody there gave a goddamn about anybody but themselves. He decided he would try to tough it out until payday, but it wouldn't be easy.

He continued to work on digging the channel for the stream. The fatigue was really starting to take its toll on him, so he had to use every ounce of stamina. He figured he was able to hold up as well as he did because he was so young. Just like yesterday, it was a scorcher outside. This made the work even more challenging. In the afternoon Jeff approached him and asked if he would like to work for four hours on Saturday. He said there would be two trucks coming that would be loaded with bags of concrete and they had to be unloaded by hand. One would be coming tomorrow, but the next one wouldn't arrive until Saturday morning. The job required about four hours. Randy told him that he would be interested in doing the work.

When he arrived back at the rooming house, there was a big, fat man sitting on the bottom of the stairwell. He was so big that he took up nearly the entire width of the stairs. Randy tried to get around him and when he said "excuse me," the man just gave him a dirty look. This guy was exceptionally creepy looking, so Randy tried not to do anything to make him mad. As he went up to his room he kept wondering who he was and what was he doing there.

He didn't have to worry about dinner, since he had already eaten at a restaurant. He thought he would try to turn in early, with emphasis on the try part. He noticed that in all the excitement of last night, he had forgotten to give Henry his vice grips back. He was going to give them back to him, but then he thought, "I wonder if that old fucker will even notice that they're missing!" He decided to wait and see.

The bikers next door were at it again, cleaning their rifles and talking in their booming voices. He could tell that he was in for another rough night. Around 10:00 his prediction came true. The hooker next door came home with a man. He heard him say, "Look, bitch, I've been waiting forever for you to get here." She said, "I'm sorry, but I had some other business to take care of." Randy realized that the man was that fat guy he had seen sitting on the steps. He then heard the man say, "Yeah, Tito referred me to you. I just got out of jail so I want to make up for lost time!"

Randy was taking all of this in and thinking, "This is just great. I wonder how long he was in jail for? Tito—I guess that must be her pimp." He also kept wondering what kind of "business" she had to take care of. With her, the lord only knew. It wasn't long before the sound of squeaking bedsprings started and the man repeatedly said, "Oh yes, oh baby!" A half an hour later Randy (and probably everybody else in the building) heard a loud, "Huh-huh-huh-huh-huh-huh-huh-ahhhh!" Randy was thinking, "Finally the fat pig shot his load. Now I can go to sleep!"

But that was not the case. After a smoke break, the man said, "That was great, let's do it again!" Randy said to himself, "Oh shit, not again!" It was the same routine, and a little over a half hour later, he made the same "Huh-huh-huh" sound when he climaxed. But he wasn't done yet. Randy counted a total of eight times that the guy climaxed. He kept thinking, "How the hell can one guy come that many times in one night? He must have been in jail for quite a long time!" After the eighth climax the girl said, "I'm getting sore, I think I've had enough." Randy was expecting the guy to say "listen bitch, you're done when I say so," but actually the guy seemed tuckered out himself. Besides, he probably didn't have any come left in him. He said, "Oh man, I've waited so long for this. Let's do this again sometime." The girl said, "Sure, you know where to find Tito—just let him know."

Randy looked at his clock and realized it was 3:45 and he still had not slept one wink. When he heard the man leave, he thought, "Oh good, now I can get some peace and quiet for the next three hours." The girl left several minutes later, but she had the audacity to leave her clock radio on, at a fairly high volume. He couldn't believe it. He did everything he could to drown out the sound of the radio, but to no avail.

When it came time for him to get up he was a complete wreck. He had not slept one wink and kept thinking, "How the hell am I going to be able to work today?" He knew that he couldn't call in sick, since it was only his third day there. He would just have to make the best of it.

On the way into work he bought a copy of the *Saskatoon Star-Phoenix*. When he got the chance he was going to read through the "suites for rent" ads. It was obvious that he couldn't take that place anymore. Fortunately he hadn't told the lady at the welfare office about the money he had from when he closed his bank account. If he absolutely had to, he could use it for one month's rent, if the place was cheap enough. But he wouldn't have much to live on until he got his first paycheque.

That day at work was a nightmare. The truck loaded with bags of concrete came on schedule. Half of the bags had to go to a nearby storage building, but the other half had to be placed by a cement mixer that was situated by the upper pond. This meant carrying the bags uphill. Once that was done, Jeff asked Randy to help with cementing the basin for the upper pond. His job involved emptying the bags of concrete mix into the cement mixer, adding four shovelfuls of sand and then adding water. Once the cement was mixed, he loaded it into a wheelbarrow and took it to where the other guys were spreading it out. This was all very labour intensive, and for Randy it was a struggle just to stay awake. There were times when he momentarily forgot where he was and many times he felt like collapsing. He had to utilize every bit of stamina that he had, and he tried not to let on how tired he was, especially to Jeff. This was about the worst feeling that he could possibly have; it was like he was on really cheap drugs.

Randy was very relieved when 4:30 came and it was quitting time. All he wanted to do was go home and go to sleep, if that was possible. On his way home, however, he periodically got disoriented and ended up going the wrong way. At one intersection, it was only when a truck came barreling toward him blasting its horn that he realized he had started crossing the street on a red light. He made it to the curb just in the nick of time. He had to grab onto a lamppost for support.

It was then that a man came up to him and asked, "Hey kid, are you all right?"

"Yeah, I'm okay," he answered.

At that point Randy concluded that if he lost any more sleep he would be out of that suite as soon as possible.

When he finally found his way back to his place, he opened the window, put on some insect repellant and flopped down onto the bed. As far as he was concerned he was too tired to eat. When his back hit the bed, it was painful both internally and externally. The constant lifting made his back sore on the inside and taking his shirt off early in the afternoon had resulted in one hell of a sunburn.

He woke up four hours later, only because the bikers had come home. He decided to eat his last can of stew and then go back to bed. He noticed that the guys next door were in a festive mood this time. He guessed that their latest "job" had been successful, so they were in the mood to party. He climbed back into bed, but he wondered why he even bothered. The guys next door turned their stereo on and had it cranked right up. Every few seconds, one or more of them would yell out, "YEE HAW!" There were sounds of crashing and banging. Normally, this being a Friday night, Randy wouldn't really care how late they carried on, since he could sleep late the next day. But since he had to work the next morning, it did matter. For the next couple of hours he lay awake and listened to the goings on next door. Then he heard the girl on the other side come in. When she and her customer started doing their thing, Randy finally snapped. He got up, put his clothes on and started rifling his things into his backpack. Once he had everything loaded inside and had fastened on his sleeping bag, he savagely kicked at the wall separating his room from the hooker's, nearly putting his foot through the paper-thin veneer. He must have kicked the wall pretty close to her bed because he heard a male voice call out, "Hey!"

Randy screamed back, "Go to hell, you fucking goof!" As he left his room, he yelled out to the bikers next door, "Fucking assholes!"

He stormed down the hall and was met by the creepy-looking guy that lived down the hall.

The guy blocked his path and said, "Where the fuck do you think you're going?"

Randy grabbed him by his shirt and flung him full force into his door. He went down hard and Randy went for his knife, pointed it in the guy's face and screamed out, "C'mon, motherfucker! You want a piece of me?"

The man scrambled to his feet, ran into his room and shut the door. He had a real frightened look on his face—it was like he was dealing with a crazed psychopath.

After Randy left the building he looked at his watch and realized that it was only 1 a.m. He thought to himself, "Gee, this seems kind of similar to that incident at the hostel in Edmonton. It's like what Yogi Berra said: 'It's déjà vu all over again!'"

He went to a park that bordered on the South Saskatchewan River and managed to find a small clearing behind some bushes (which wasn't easy in the dark). He laid out his sleeping bag and crawled into it. He decided not to wind up his alarm clock; he was afraid the ticking sound would give away his position. He figured that he would take a chance and hopefully not sleep too late, even though he had not slept much in the past while.

When he woke up it was 6:50. He felt quite relieved when he looked at his watch. He had plenty of time to make it to work by 7:30; the site was not far away. When he arrived at the job site, the truck hadn't shown up yet. Jeff was there and he told him that the truck would not be there until 8:30. Randy decided to go to a nearby café and have breakfast. The truck arrived at 8:30 and was completely unloaded by 12:30. Afterward he made several phone inquiries about a place to rent. One call sounded quite promising—it was for a one-bedroom basement suite in the south part of town. He decided to check it out.

When Randy arrived at the advertised place, he rang the doorbell and a man answered. He told him that he was interested in the suite for rent. The man introduced himself as Gavin Alsbury and took him around to the back. The place had its own entrance, which was a bonus in itself. It looked very bright and spacious, and he would have both the kitchen and bathroom all to himself. The rent was also very reasonable. Randy started questioning how quiet the place was. He pointed out that he was a responsible working person and he needed to get up very early each morning. He wanted to be assured that he would have peace and quiet. Gavin thought that was very strange—a teenager giving *him* the third degree on how quiet the place was. Gavin told him that he had nothing to worry about. He was a widower and all of his kids had grown up and moved out. It was just him living there now.

He asked him if he would ever have any parties, and Randy said, "How can I? I don't know anybody here!"

Gavin told him he could have the suite if he wanted it. Randy said he would take it. He gave Gavin the money for one month's rent and told him that he would pay the damage deposit when he got paid on Friday.

Randy slept practically half the day on Sunday. He found it a really great relief to be once and for all out of that dump. At least from now on he would be bright-eyed and bushy-tailed when going to work.

The following Friday Randy got his first paycheque. Since it was only for the first three days, it wasn't very much. After he gave Gavin the damage deposit, there wasn't a lot left over. Even so, he decided to go for a beer that night. He went to a lounge that was a couple of blocks from his place. Before he could order though, the bartender asked him for some ID. He nonchalantly got out his driver's licence and showed it to the bartender.

He looked at it for a few seconds and said to Randy, "I'm sorry, but you're not old enough."

Randy looked bewildered and asked, "What are you talking about? I'm eighteen!" Noticing that it was an Alberta driver's licence, the bartender said, "The legal drinking age in Saskatchewan is nineteen." Randy couldn't believe it and the bartender added, "You're in Saskatchewan now, so you'll have to wait until next year."

As he left Randy kept wondering, "Why is it that some provinces have the legal drinking age at eighteen and others nineteen? Why can't they all be the same?"

The landscaping project continued until September 15th, at which time everything was completed. All that was left to do was the planting, and that wouldn't be done until next spring. Randy found himself looking for work again; this time it took him over a week before something finally paid off. He found a job at the Glengarry Meats packing plant working on the loading dock. On his first day he didn't really know what to expect. He assumed that he would be loading packages onto a truck in the form of beef roasts or hamburger. He was surprised to learn that Glengarry Meats was merely a slaughterhouse, and all of the beef was shipped out as carcasses. Actually they were shipped out in quarters, but they still weighed over two hundred pounds. So when a load of carcasses was delivered to the loading dock, Randy had to pick one up, carry it into the trailer and place it into the back. Needless to say, it was extremely hard work and as he continually worked up a sweat in the cold environment, the work became even more unpleasant.

After he finished work on his first day, all he could think was, "Who do they think I am, Hercules?" His arms and his back were really stiff and sore. At times he wondered why he kept ending up with these scummy, hard-labouring jobs where he was pushed to the max physically. But then he concluded that he had no one to blame but himself. With only a grade nine education and no real job skills or trades training, he realized that this was about the best he was going to be able to get.

By his third day there, the hard, physical work was taking its toll on Randy. At lunch he was talking about this to a co-worker named Harold. Harold pointed out to him that he should consider himself lucky; there were some jobs in the plant that were even worse.

Randy said, "Oh yeah, what could be worse than lugging around those big carcasses?"

Harold told him that they could have had him doing Joe's job.

"Who's Joe?"

Harold said, "Joe is someone who used to work here, but doesn't anymore, for obvious reasons. His job involved shovelling all of the guts from the cows and pigs, which included the brains, lungs, spleens, intestines and shit like that; anything that's not used for meat. He had to shovel it into this large holding tank and once a week the tank would be emptied. Don't ask me where they take it or what they do with it 'cause I don't know, and frankly, I don't give a shit. To give you some idea how awful it is working there in the days before the tank is emptied, the stench is so bad it's like working around a thousand dead bodies!

"Anyway, one day he was standing a little too close to the edge and he somehow slipped and fell head first into the tank. It was on the day before it was to be emptied so it was pretty full. Still, he fell a good twenty feet before landing in all the guts. When he finally surfaced he started screaming his head off. Hans and I heard him screaming and when we realized what had happened, Hans ran to get a rope. We lowered the rope and yelled at Joe to grab on to it, but the guy was just fucking hysterical. We finally coaxed him to grab the rope and then pulled him out. When we got him out, he was covered in blood and had maggots crawling all over his clothes, his face and in his hair."

Randy was practically turning green by then and he felt like he was going to lose his lunch.

"Oh, jeez! Gross me out, why don't you? Okay, you made your point! Maybe I should count my blessings. Maybe my job isn't so bad after all!" he said, and decided that if they ever assigned him to that job, he would be out of there pronto!

He decided that he would tough it out there for the time being. One bright spot was that he got the occasional respite from lugging the heavy beef quarters. The plant also slaughtered hogs so he periodically loaded sides of pork, which were not quite as heavy. He figured that he would work there at least until something better came along. Unfortunately the management had other ideas. After one and a half weeks there, the plant manager decided that Randy was not living up to company standards. So on that Friday afternoon, he called Randy into his office and told him that he would have to be let go.

It took Randy a week to find another job and it was only part-time and paid minimum wage. The position was a counter person at the concession stand at a local ball park. Fortunately it involved only evenings and weekends, which enabled Randy to look for a full-time job during the day. At first he was quite busy. It was early October and the high school football season was in full swing. He was working practically every evening and all day Saturday and Sunday. But over the next several weeks his hours dwindled. The weather was getting colder and fewer games were being played.

By the end of October he was only working for four hours on Saturday afternoon. He was having absolutely no luck finding a full-time job and he didn't want to apply for welfare again. He didn't like the thought of spending the winter in Saskatoon with no job. On November 1st he didn't have enough money to pay the rent. Gavin warned him that if he didn't come up with the rent money in the next few days, he would have to leave. By November 5th Randy still hadn't succeeded in finding a job. Finally Gavin told him that he would have to move out. Feeling he had no alternative, Randy made the agonizing decision that he would have to return to Calgary.

8

Gavin let Randy stay there one more night. He got up early the next morning and loaded his backpack. He gave Gavin his room key and then said goodbye. From there he caught a bus going downtown and transferred to one heading toward the western outskirts. He would have liked to take the Greyhound bus to Calgary, but unfortunately he didn't have enough money. So it was back to his traditional mode of transportation.

Unlike other times when he had left a particular city, he actually felt sad. He really liked Saskatoon and had had high hopes that he would be able to make a go of it there. He figured that he might try his luck in Saskatoon again in a few years after he got some more work experience. But for now Calgary was the place where the opportunities were, and he would just have to learn to accept it.

He took the city bus to its most westerly point and from there walked six blocks until he reached Highway 7. He walked up the highway a little ways until he reached the Petro-Canada truck stop. He decided to stop in there and have breakfast and then head out to the city limits.

While he was in the truck stop, he got into a conversation with the man sitting next to him. The man noticed that he had a fullyloaded backpack with him and asked him if he was planning to take a trip somewhere. He found it rather unusual that anyone would want to be hitchhiking this time of year; he figured it would be pretty cold standing by the highway. Randy told him he didn't want to spend the winter in Saskatoon if he wasn't working, so he was heading to Calgary. At least there he could find some kind of work. The man told him he lived on a farm near the town of Kindersley, which was 120 miles west. He said he had come up to Saskatoon first thing that morning and had gone to a cattle auction. He got a really good deal on four Simmental bull calves and was heading back to Kindersley. He told Randy he would be willing to give him a ride as far as Kindersley.

Randy said, "That's okay. At least that will get me part way to my destination."

The man seemed to be in a rather jovial mood. He was telling him that the Simmental bull calves were an absolute bargain and he couldn't pass the deal up. He then went on and on about all of the advantages that Simmentals have, mainly in the area of breeding ability and beef quality. Randy didn't have the heart to tell him that he was from the city and didn't know one breed of cattle from the other; to him a cow was a cow.

They both finished eating around the same time.

Pointing to a covered five-ton flat deck truck in the parking lot, the farmer said, "You see that truck over there? You meet me there in ten minutes. I have to make a few phone calls."

Randy was thinking, "That's good—now I have time for another cup of coffee and a cigarette."

Then when he went over to the truck, he didn't see any sign of the man anywhere. After awhile he started muttering to himself, "Where the hell is that guy? I want to get going!" A few minutes later the man showed up, and Randy said, "Ahh, there you are! Okay, I'm ready to go."

He started to open the passenger side door when the man said, "What do you think you're doing?"

"I'm getting in your truck. You said you were going to give me a ride to Kindersley!"

"You're not riding in the cab!"

"What's the matter? There's lots of room and I don't bite!"

"Nope, the only one who gets to ride in the cab with me is my favourite travelling companion."

"Yeah, and who the hell would that be?"

The farmer whistled and called out, "Satan, here boy!"

"Who the hell is Satan?"

Just then, a huge Doberman came running from the other side of the truck. The man grabbed him by the collar just before he was about to take a run at Randy. He couldn't believe how big the dog was; it was giving Randy a look like it wanted to tear him limb from limb.

The man said, "You see, there wouldn't be enough room in the cab for all of us, and besides, he'd rip you to shreds."

"Just for the record, where exactly am I going to be sitting?"

The man seemed quite dumbfounded that Randy hadn't figured it out. "In the back."

"Are you out of your fucking mind? You want me to ride in the back with the cows?" he asked incredulously.

"Do you want a ride or don't you?"

Randy reluctantly gave in, and as he climbed into the back of the truck he muttered to himself, "I don't believe this! The dog gets to sit in the front and I'm stuck back here!"

He sat himself down on a hay bale, and as the man came around and put the tailgate up he said, "Don't worry, they won't bother you. And one other thing, no smoking."

During the ride the calves constantly gave Randy a funny look. He was tempted to say "What the hell are you looking at?" but that wouldn't do any good. Since the back was open, vehicles travelling in the same direction would be able to see him. Anyone following the truck would wonder why he was sitting in the back instead of the cab. He found this embarrassing. The cover provided no protection from the elements whatsoever. It wasn't really cold out, but it was cold enough to make the ride unpleasant. He did whatever he could to try and stay warm.

Two hours later the truck slowed down, turned right and then pulled over. The farmer came around to the back and asked him if he wanted to go right into Kindersley or be let off there. Randy said he wanted to get off there. Even though he would have liked to stop somewhere and have lunch, he realized it was now afternoon and he wanted to reach Calgary before the day was over. He didn't really have the money to spend the night anywhere, and there was no way he was going to spend the night outside this time of year.

Right after the man took off, Randy went over to Highway 7 and put his thumb out. He hoped he wouldn't have to wait long; he was still feeling half-frozen from the ride from Saskatoon. He didn't really care who picked him up as long as their vehicle had heat. As it turned out, he had to wait an hour and a half before a truck pulled over. It was a middle-aged man driving, and he asked Randy where he was heading

"Calgary."

"I can give you a ride as far as Drumheller."

Randy figured that it was better than nothing, so he got in.

During the ride he didn't get into much of a conversation with the driver, whose name was Tony. Randy did, however, comment on his vehicle. His pickup truck was a 1953 Chevy, fully restored. He was amazed that it looked to be in mint condition. Tony pointed out that he had spent a lot of time and money on it over the years and it had paid off. The truck had won first prize at three classic car competitions thus far. He said that he had a whole collection of classic cars and invited Randy to come out to his farm north of Drumheller to have a look sometime. Randy said that he would be delighted and would definitely make a note of it.

When they arrived in Drumheller, it was 5:15. It was already dark by then and Randy commented that he might not be able to get a ride into Calgary until the next day. Tony said, "Actually, you're in luck. There is a Greyhound bus that goes to Calgary and it stops here at ten to six. It shouldn't cost that much to go to Calgary from here—it's only sixty-five miles."

Randy said, "I'll be all right money-wise. What's more important is that I get to Calgary today."

Tony dropped him off at the downtown bus stop and Randy thanked him for the ride.

The bus arrived right on schedule at 5:50. After he got on the bus, all Randy could think about was what he would do if he encountered that "Tom Smith" character again at the Calgary bus depot. All that was going through his mind was, "If I ever see that fucking pervert again, I'll kill the bloody bastard!" Even though the incident was over two years ago, it was still fresh in his mind.

The bus arrived in Calgary at 7:30. Fortunately, that guy who called himself Tom Smith wasn't there, so Randy had nothing to worry about. His only concern then was if there were still any beds available at the Salvation Army hostel. Sure enough, there were a few. He would begin his job search the next morning.

He was up early the next morning, and after breakfast headed straight for the Canada Manpower office. As usual, there were hundreds of different jobs available. In comparison with Saskatoon, Randy thought, "Now this is more like it!" After scanning the job boards for awhile, one particular ad got his attention. It was for Amoco Canada, and they were looking for people to work on oil rigs in northern Alberta. He remembered hearing from a number of different sources that oil rig workers made really good money and they have all their living expenses paid for. He decided to check it out.

The counsellor gave Randy a rundown on what the job involved and then reviewed his background. She was pleased to note that he was young, single and not tied down to any place. Judging from his past work record, she realized that he was no stranger to hard, physical work. She asked him if he would have any problem working in an isolated area.

"No, I wouldn't," he replied.

The counsellor said, "You seem to fit the criteria they are looking for."

She filled out a referral slip and told him to take it to the seventh floor of the Amoco building and report to Graham Fisher.

When Randy arrived at the Amoco Canada office, he asked at the reception desk to see Graham Fisher. The receptionist told him to have a seat and that Mr. Fisher would be with him shortly. After a lengthy wait, Graham Fisher came out, introduced himself and asked Randy to come into his office.

He asked Randy quite a few questions, most notably, "Have you ever worked on an oil rig before?"

Randy replied, "No, I haven't."

As with the girl at the Manpower office, Graham also asked him if he would have any problem working in a remote area away from civilization.

Once again Randy said, "No, that wouldn't be a problem. I'm okay with it." Graham also asked him if he minded working outside in minus-forty to minus-sixty-degree weather.

"Well, that shouldn't be a problem as long as I am insulated."

"Very well then, what I will have you do now is get a medical examination. I want you to take this referral slip and go see Dr. Solheim. His office is right across the street from here; it's on the second floor. When you get to the reception desk, just tell them you're with Amoco. When your examination is completed, report back here."

Randy did as Graham instructed. The nurse told him to take a seat and that Dr. Solheim would see him shortly. Once again he had a lengthy wait. He didn't exactly know what to expect, since it had been at least four years since his last medical checkup and he hadn't exactly been leading a healthy lifestyle in the meantime. When the doctor called him in, he had him undress and get up on the examination table. He did all the usual examination procedures and even gave him a blood test. In the end he concluded that Randy was in fairly good health, although he was underweight. He said not to worry about that since they fed you pretty well in the camp. As was expected, he also told Randy that he should lay off the cigarettes.

He returned to Graham Fisher's office. When he finally got to see Graham he showed him the results of his examination.

Graham took his time looking over it, and finally said, "Welcome aboard! This is going to be a record year for oil drilling, so we really need workers."

He asked Randy if he had any questions, and the only one Randy could think of was, "Why do they do drilling in the wintertime when it's really cold out?"

Graham said that in the region where he would be working, in the far northern part of Alberta, the land was mostly muskeg. In the winter the ground was frozen and was therefore suitable for drilling. In the summer the ground was too soft and the rigs would sink.

Next he gave an overview of the job. The camp was located sixty-five miles east and then twenty miles north of the town of High Level. The nearest settlement was Jean D'or Prairie, about thirty miles away. Everything was provided for in the camp, including living accommodation and all meals. He would be working ten days on and then would have four days off. On his days off he would be driven into High Level; he could either stay there or take a plane into Edmonton They didn't recommend that the workers stay in the camp on their days off. There wasn't much to do there.

As he handed Randy a plane ticket, he said, "Okay, here's your plane ticket. You are to be on Time Air flight 37K leaving from the Edmonton Municipal Airport tomorrow morning at 10:00, bound for High Level. When you arrive there you will meet up with Gunnar Ericksson. You can't miss him—he's a big Norwegian. There will be six other men starting along with you. Gunnar will be driving you and the others out to the job site."

He handed him a prepaid bus ticket to Edmonton, saying, "Well, I wish you the best of luck. But there is something I must be totally honest about. There is an element of danger in the job. At any time the drill bit can hit a high-pressure pocket of oil or natural gas, so you have to have your wits about you at all times. Anyway, I will be up at your camp sometime in the next month, so I'll see how you're doing."

On his way out of the Amoco building Randy didn't know whether he should feel ecstatic or apprehensive. In fact, he didn't know what to think. On the one hand, he would have a well-paying job with his living expenses paid for. But on the other hand, he would be working outside, up north, in the middle of winter and he didn't know yet what the actual job would be like. He kept thinking, "Why did Graham have to say that last part, the part about the element of danger. I didn't need to hear that." Randy had also never been on a plane before. This was definitely going to be a new adventure for him.

He went back to the Salvation Army hostel to retrieve his backpack, and then went to the bus depot and caught the 4 p.m. bus to Edmonton.

He arrived in Edmonton at 7:30 and then checked into the Salvation Army hostel there. He was up early the next morning so he would have time to figure out which bus went to the Edmonton Municipal Airport. Fortunately, there was an airport bus that stopped nearby the hostel and it left every fifteen minutes. He arrived at the airport with plenty of time to spare. At the information desk, he asked where the Time Air check-in counter was, and the girl pointed him in the right direction.

He arrived at the Time Air counter and checked his backpack as baggage. When the man at the counter processed his ticket, Randy noticed that it didn't specify where his seat was.

He said to the man, "Gee, I sure hope my seat is in the smoking section!"

"Do you want a seat in the smoking section?"

"You betcha!"

"Well, you're in luck. Your plane will be boarding from Gate 10 in a half an hour."

When Randy arrived at the gate, he looked out onto the tarmac and noticed a small, twenty-seat propeller-driven plane with the words "Time Air" written across the side. He wondered, "I'm going in that thing?" When he had boarded and found his seat, he waited nervously for the plane to take off. He kept thinking, "Oh, man! Get me there in one piece!" When the propellers started up and the plane started moving, it made one hell of a racket and there was lots of vibration. When the plane finally took off, Randy dug his fingernails hard into the armrests and hyperventilated severely.

The man sitting next to him said, "Let me guess. This is your first time in an airplane."

"Yeah, what was your first clue?"

As the plane gained altitude Randy nervously reached into his jacket pocket to get out his pack of cigarettes. However, before he could take one out, the stewardess came up to him and said, "Oh sir, you can't smoke until we have reached cruising altitude."

A few minutes later the plane leveled off. It was obvious that Randy was still nervous as he nearly put the wrong end of the cigarette in his mouth. When he went to light it, his hands were trembling so badly that he couldn't make his lighter work.

The man sitting next to him said, "Here, let me help you with that." Later, he added, "Don't worry about it, flying takes a little getting used to.

It's best to start out on a jumbo jet as they fly a lot smoother. These small planes are more suited to someone who is used to flying a lot."

When they finally landed in High Level, Randy was greatly relieved. Because it was snowing, he couldn't see the runway lights until thirty seconds before the plane landed, so he wasn't exactly sure where they were. When he got off the plane he almost wanted to kiss the ground. Once inside the terminal, he retrieved his backpack and then noticed a large, blonde man holding a sign that read "Amoco." He figured that he must be Gunnar Ericksson.

He went up to him and asked, "Are you Gunnar Ericksson?"

The man replied, "Yes, I am." He then got out his clipboard and said, "Okay, which one are you?"

"I'm Randy Watson."

Gunnar looked on his list and said, "Okay, here you are."

Another man who had been on the same flight as Randy came up and said he was there for Amoco. Gunnar told them they would have to wait until the flight from Grande Prairie arrived because there were three more new people on that plane. It would be arriving in twenty minutes.

After the last three people had arrived, they all piled into a van and headed out. They quickly left civilization behind; the surrounding countryside became more and more desolate. Highway 58 was one lonely road. Randy noticed there were barely any buildings along the way. He learned from Gunnar that Highway 58, heading east from High Level, went for 90 miles until it reached Wentzel River and then came to a dead end. That was why Highway 58 was nicknamed "the highway that goes nowhere."

An hour after they left High Level, the van turned left onto a gravel road. You could tell it was a gravel road even though it was covered in snow. For the next half hour they passed nothing but trees; then they came into a huge clearing. There was a whole bunch of ATCO trailers and three oil derricks.

As they pulled up to one of the trailers, Gunnar said, "Okay, gentlemen, come with me."

This was the bunkhouse they would be staying in. He assigned each person a bed and told them dinner would be served at 5:30. Wake-up time was 5 a.m. and work began at 6:00. He told everyone that by December there would be so few hours of daylight that it wouldn't matter what time they started.

Randy made a vow that he was going to do his very best to make a good impression on this job. After all, this was by far his best-paying job, and the long-term potential looked promising. But on his first day he was really put to the test. For most of the day they had him packing one-hundred-pound bags of barium sulfate (drilling mud) up onto the platform. At other times they had him assist with holding the brace in place when they changed the drill bit. Whenever the drill bit came up out of the ground, everyone would get sprayed with dirt and drilling mud. At the end of the day he was covered head to toe with mud. His foreman, as it turned out, was Gunnar's twin brother Andreas. So he really had to be at his best. This ranked right up there as one of the toughest jobs he had ever had; there had been a few occasions on his first day when he'd felt like packing it in. But he was determined to tough it out; it was a good thing that he had had some hard, physical jobs in the past, as they had helped prepare him for this one. Even so, he was downright exhausted by the end of the day.

Life in the camp was all right. As long as his trailer had heat and he got lots to eat, he was happy. They had satellite TV and a pool table in the recreation room so he spent most of his off hours there. Most of his co-workers were from Newfoundland. The way they spoke made it seem as if they were talking in a different language. Randy had trouble understanding them a lot of the time. Plus, all they ever talked about was their way of life back home—something he couldn't relate to.

After his tenth day on the job, Randy got his first time off. He opted to stay in High Level rather than fly to Edmonton. He would have liked to, but he was virtually broke. He decided to wait until he got his first paycheque. So on his days off he pretty much just stayed in his motel room and watched TV. The motel had a pinball machine in the laundry room, but that room wasn't very well heated. He did manage to scrape up enough money to buy a six-pack of beer. He made a note that he was going to make up for it on his next time off.

He got his first paycheque the day before his next four-day break. It was only for his first ten days of work, but it was still pretty good. He told Gunnar he wanted to go to Edmonton this time. Gunnar told him that when they got to High Level he would have to open a bank account before he took him to the airport.

When Randy cashed his paycheque, he only put about half of it into the bank; the rest he kept for himself. He had one goal in mind once he got to Edmonton—he was going to once and for all lose his virginity. The fact that he still hadn't had his first sexual experience was really starting to get to him. He kept thinking, "Here I am, three months away from my nineteenth birthday and I still haven't done it yet!" As long as he had been on his own he had remained tight-lipped about it, and he had been lucky so far that nobody had found out.

When he arrived in Edmonton, he checked into a cheap hotel only two blocks from where the hookers were known to hang out. He hoped he wouldn't have to resort to that, but, just in case, he wanted the women to be at hand. That first night he was going to try to do it the hard way. He planned to go to a nightclub and hoped he could pick up a girl there, and either go to her place or to his hotel room. He learned about this new nightclub that had recently opened up in the Strathcona area and he hoped there would be lots of girls there. When he thought back to his success (or lack of it) in meeting women when visiting the nightspots in Calgary, he didn't feel overly optimistic, but he still planned to give it a shot.

The nightclub was jam-packed. It just so happened that it was a Friday night. There were lots of women there, but then again, there were lots of men there too. He did get to dance a few times, but as far as having a conversation with any women was concerned, he wasn't having much luck. He tried to get something going with this one woman by telling her that he worked on an oil rig and by offering to buy her a drink. She in return told him to get lost. Throughout the evening he was really belting down the booze, so he got pretty blitzed.

A man sitting next to him at the bar asked, "Hey man, why the long face?"

"Let's face it man, I have the charm and sex appeal of a fucking fencepost!"

"Hey, I know. Why don't you go after that girl over there?" he said pointing to this big, fat, ugly woman dancing with another woman.

Randy said in a very annoyed tone, "Very funny!"

Realizing that he was not going to get lucky there that night, he decided to pack it in. Having lost track of how many drinks he'd had, he hoped that he would be able to walk out of there. Once outside, he hailed a taxi and told the driver which hotel he was staying at.

As they drove away, Randy began his spiel about what he hadn't accomplished that night by saying, "Wow, man, what does a guy have to do in order to get a good fuck in this city?"

Judging by his slurred speech, it was obvious that he had drunk too much. It wasn't until after he had blurted out this question that he realized the cab driver was a woman.

She said in a disgusted tone, "I beg your pardon, young man?"

He said, "Oh, nothing. I was just muttering to myself."

She said, "I think you have had too much to drink tonight. It's a good thing you're not driving!"

The cab driver dropped him off at his hotel and he staggered up to his room. He decided not to try and pick up a hooker that night, mainly because it was already 1:30 and also because he was so drunk, he probably wouldn't have known what he was doing anyway. At least when he went to bed, he didn't have to worry about getting up early the next morning. He had all day to sleep it off.

He woke up the next morning with one lulu of a hangover. This one felt worse than the one in Portage La Prairie. He looked at his watch and saw that it was 10:00. He went back to sleep for two more hours. When he finally dragged himself out of bed, he went down to a restaurant two blocks away that served breakfast all day.

That evening he was ready again but he was still a little nervous. He decided to loosen up with a few drinks so he went into the hotel bar. He had planned to have only two or three beers, but he ended up drinking eight. He figured he had better stop there; he wanted to be able to know what he was doing. From there he went down to the street where the hookers' stroll was. There were quite a few ladies to choose from.

An attractive brunette came up to him and said in a polite tone, "Hello there. Would you like to go out?"

"Hey, I sure would!"

He asked her what she charged. She told him it would be sixty dollars for a straight lay and eighty dollars for a half-and-half. Randy was too embarrassed to ask what a half-and-half meant, so he played it cool and told her he would like a straight lay. Even though he was trying to act cool, he was sure that he had "first time" written all over his face. He told her that he was staying at a hotel just two blocks away and they could go to his place. She told him that her place was just up the street and it would be easier to go there.

The place where she "worked" was an old, run-down residential hotel. Inside there was an old man at the counter who signed them in. They then went into an ancient, wrought-iron elevator (the ones that were opened and closed by hand) and went up to the fifth floor.

Once inside their room, she said to him, "I will need the money now." After he handed her the money she asked him what his name was. Randy told her his name and then she said, "My name is Laurisa."

From the outset Randy thought he had picked up a real winner. She was quite nice looking and had long, flowing black hair. But she did have kind of a husky voice. She had a long, fancy dress on, so it was kind of hard to tell what kind of a body she had. When she took off the top part of her dress he noticed that she had almost nonexistent tits, but he didn't give it a second thought. He turned his back to her and started to remove his clothes. When he turned around, he was completely shocked to discover that "she" had a dick.

"Y…You're a guy!" he shrieked.

The hooker said, "I thought you knew!"

Randy said in a disgusted tone, "No, I didn't know!"

He angrily put his clothes back on, and the hooker asked, "What are you doing?"

"What the hell does it look like? I ain't doing anything with you!" When he finished getting dressed, Randy added, "Gimme my money back!"

"No way, you already paid me!"

"Now look! I wanted a goddamn woman and you don't fit the bill! The deal is off, so give me my fucking money back now!"

"Hey man, you gave me the money, so it's mine now. I guess them's the breaks. We could have still done something, but you've wasted too much time."

Randy was getting pretty angry by now and said, "I told you, I don't want to do anything with you! Now for the last time, give me my fucking money back or I'll…"

The hooker interrupted him at that point and said in a snarly tone, "You'll what?"

"I'll kick the living shit right out of you! What do you think of that, you fucking faggot?"

"What did you say?"

Randy screamed out, "Are you deaf or something? I said I'm going to kick the living shit out of you! Let's go right now, you fucking freakazoid!"

The hooker sneered at him and said calmly, "Just try it!"

"Okay, I will!"

With that, he wound up to take a swing at the hooker, but he blocked it with one arm, and using his other arm, gave Randy a karate chop across the face. He then gave him a kung-fu kick right in the stomach. Next it was a flying kick in the side of the head. With Randy stunned by then, the hooker backed up, then came right at him and nailed him with a flying kung-fu kick right between the eyes. That knocked Randy out cold.

He came to fifteen minutes later, staggered to his feet and reached into his pants pocket. Then he cried, "Jesus Christ! What happened to my wallet?"

Realizing that his wallet was missing, he frantically searched all through the room. Since he was still feeling groggy, he made sure he searched every square inch several times. He then went out into the hallway, where he found his wallet on the floor. He picked it up, looked inside and was shocked to realize that all his money was gone. Even after paying the hooker, he'd still had over a hundred dollars left. He started feeling sick to his stomach knowing that scumbag had stolen all of his money. All he had left was eighty-five cents in change and he still had two days to go. At least he had his return plane ticket and his hotel room was paid for. Otherwise, he would have been really screwed. He figured that guy must have had at least a third degree black belt in karate, so going after him had been a big mistake.

Randy slept in quite late the following morning. In fact, he didn't feel like getting out of bed at all. It was a good thing the hotel had complimentary coffee. He went to a convenience store down the street where they had doughnuts for twenty-five cents each, so at least he was able to have a complete breakfast. With only three cigarettes left, he decided to ration them and have two that day and one the next morning. As it turned out, he was able to bum one from the desk clerk.

That evening he felt that it was a lucky coincidence that it was Sunday. He reluctantly went to the weekly free dinner and church service at the Union Gospel Mission. He felt two feet tall—here he was employed in a well-paying job, taking part in a dinner normally reserved for people down and out. He decided that he would make it up to them. On his next visit to Edmonton, he would come back and make a contribution.

He was up early the next morning even though his plane didn't leave until noon. He had no other choice but to walk all the way to the airport. When he arrived in High Level, Gunnar was there to pick him up.

"So, how were things in Edmonton?" he asked. Then, noticing the big bruise in the middle of Randy's forehead, he added, "Jeez, what the hell happened to you?"

Randy said, "Well, if you must know, I got into an argument with a transvestite!"

Gunnar gave him a funny look, thinking he had made that up. Randy asked if he could stop at the bank on the way out.

When Randy went into the bank he requested a withdrawal, but the teller told him that he would not be able to make a withdrawal until the account had been with the bank for two weeks. When he asked why, all she said was that it was company policy. He left the bank in a huff and asked Gunnar if he could borrow twenty bucks until next payday. Gunnar started giving him a lecture on the fact that blowing one's paycheque was a sign of irresponsibility. He had seen many such cases with young guys who had worked for him before. He said that they kept blowing their paycheques, and by the time they left, they had nothing to show for it. He reluctantly loaned Randy twenty dollars, but he warned him that he had better start putting some money away for a rainy day.

9

As expected, Randy spent his next four days off laying low in High Level. He had planned to go to Edmonton again on his next time off. But it turned out that right around that time, the company was shutting down for the Christmas break. They would not be starting up again until January 3rd. Gunnar asked him if he would be spending Christmas with his family, and Randy told him he didn't have any family and he just wanted to remain in High Level for the holiday. Gunnar thought that was very strange; he thought that Randy would have at least some family he could have shared Christmas with. He didn't think being alone at Christmas was a good idea. Randy figured being alone at Christmas was a hell of a lot better than watching his mom and William fight. After all, that's how he had spent the previous two Christmases. To him it was just another day. Besides, he still had vivid memories of that incident with Larry. Even though it had happened a long time ago, every Christmas it felt like it had been only yesterday. Whenever he thought about that incident, he vowed that he would kill Larry if he ever met him on the street. But to show that he had not completely lost all of his Christmas spirit, he still sent Mark a present every year. Over the years, he found it harder to decide what to get him since he wasn't a little kid anymore (he was fourteen by now). That year he had got him a t-shirt with a "Molson Canadian" logo emblazoned across the front. He wasn't sure how big Mark had grown, so he had taken a chance and bought a medium.

On Christmas day Randy sat in his motel room watching TV and drinking beer. He had found out the day before that everything in town would be closed on Christmas day, including all restaurants. That made things kind of hard for him because the motel room didn't have a stove or a fridge. On Christmas Eve, he had eaten dinner early—all the restaurants closed by 6 p.m. He had managed to get to the bar before closing time and had bought a couple of cases of beer at the off-sales. Luckily, the Red Rooster store was open on Christmas day, so he had bought some food there. His Christmas dinner consisted of three pieces of Chester Fried Chicken, jo-jos and coleslaw. To him it was no big deal. The last time he remembered having a turkey on Christmas was when his dad was alive.

For the next week he rarely ventured outside his motel room. The daytime high temperature was only minus forty-nine degrees Fahrenheit, and there were only a few hours of daylight. For dinner he would order in either pizza or Chinese food. However, on New Year's Eve he did decide to venture out. He wanted to live it up and ring in 1981 in style. The motor hotel up the road from where he was staying had a nightclub, and it was hosting a big New Year's Eve bash.

The nightclub was filled to capacity that night, but there was one small problem. The crowd was about ninety-nine percent men. Randy couldn't believe how few women were there and wondered why they had even bothered bringing in a live band. The crowd was mostly oil rig workers and local farmers. He recognized some of the men from the camp where he worked. Throughout the course of the evening tension slowly built between the local guys and the oil rig workers. The lack of females added to the pressure. After midnight, a number of fights started breaking out; it eventually turned into an all-out free-for-all. The combatants far outnumbered the bouncers, so there was nothing they could do. Another man, who worked in the same camp as him, had been mouthing off to Randy all evening.

When the fighting started, he came up to Randy and said, "A fucking retard like you has no business working on an oil rig!"

Randy snapped back, "Who the hell are you calling a retard, you ugly piece of shit?"

"Yeah, do you wanna fight about it?"

Randy gladly obliged. He was wishing that if he were going to fight anyone from work, it would be that annoying guy on his crew who constantly sang that song "Oh it's forty below and I don't give a fuck," but this guy would do. For the next several minutes they exchanged some vicious upper cuts and they fought with the intensity of a bout between Muhammed Ali and George Foreman. At one point Randy managed to get on top of the guy and deliver some hard shots to the head. Then the other guy somehow reversed the manoeuvre and started doing the same thing to him! They knocked over at least three tables and even broke a couple chairs. For what seemed an eternity, they kicked and punched each other in the head and stomach and there was nobody available to break them up. It was not until the police arrived that order was restored.

Eight RCMP officers entered the bar and one of them shouted out, "All right, that's enough! The next one that throws a punch will be spending the night in jail!"

Since the High Level RCMP had only one paddy wagon, the officers decided to let the guys off easy.

The officer said, "Okay, I'm going to go easy on you guys! If you all leave and go your separate ways, you won't get charged. But if any of you decide to carry on your altercation in another place, we'll be right there. You will then be spending the next few days in jail. You get my point?"

All of the men quietly left the bar, including Randy. The last thing he needed was to end up in jail. He could tell that he had been cut above his left eye and his lip was also busted open. So he walked the two blocks in the minus forty degree weather to the local hospital. When he arrived there, he got the nurse to check if he needed any stitches and to see if his jaw was broken. As it turned out, all he needed was a couple of bandages and some antiseptic. When he was ready to go back to his motel room, he decided against freezing his ass off, so he called a cab.

When he woke up the next morning he was in a lot of pain. His face was really sore and he could barely move his jaw. In addition, his left eye was swollen right shut. Only after looking in the mirror did he realize the full extent of the beating he had taken. His face was a mass of welts and scabs and his lower lip was so swollen that it looked ready to explode. Needless to say, he didn't feel like eating anything—he was hungover as well. That was good because, once again, all of the restaurants were closed.

Later in the day he ventured over to the Red Rooster store and bought a jug of orange juice. He tried his best to ignore the fact that everyone in the store was staring at him. Fortunately, nobody said anything.

The following day, Gunnar picked him up at noon.

One of the first things he said was, "Good lord, what the hell happened to you?"

"What does it look like? I got into a fight on New Year's Eve, okay!"

"Oh, you were involved in that big punch-up at the nightclub on New Year's. Yeah, I heard about that. Some other guys from the camp were involved too. Frankly, I don't know what I'm going to do with you guys! Personally, I don't find beating the hell out of each other entertainment!"

When he was in the mess hall at dinnertime, who should he come across but the guy he had gotten into the fight with. He looked pretty worse for wear himself and judging from his appearance, Randy had given him a pretty good beating. That showed that he could dish it out as well as take it. As the guy approached Randy braced himself.

"Hey, hey, it's all right. I didn't mean to say what I said the other night.

I was just drinking too much." He extended his hand to Randy and said, "My name is Tony."

He nervously shook his hand and said, "I'm Randy."

Tony went on to say, "Jeez man, where did you learn to fight like that? I've been in quite a few scraps in my day, but you put up one of the greatest fights I've ever had."

Randy told him that he came from a rough town and he'd had a troubled childhood. Tony informed him that they occasionally had amateur fight nights at one of the arenas on the Edmonton Exhibition grounds. It was a great opportunity to make some really big money. Randy said that he would give it some thought.

It was late January before Randy decided to venture to Edmonton again. It was not for lack of money, but because it had been snowing so much. The road going to High Level was very treacherous, and planes had been having difficulty taking off and landing at the airport.

He planned to accomplish what he had failed to do on his last trip to Edmonton, but this time he did some research ahead of time. For the past several weeks he had been asking different people in the camp if they knew of a place in Edmonton that was great for picking up girls. He also tried to find out if anyone knew of a way he could pick up a prostitute without getting caught. In other words, he was trying to find out if there was a brothel anywhere in town. He eventually hit a home run. A colleague named Bill, who had lived in Edmonton for the past ten years, told him about a woman named Chantelle who ran an escort service in the south part of town. Actually, it was a one-woman operation. She was a really gorgeous blonde with a fantastic body. Bill also pointed out that she only did outcalls. That way she could keep her home base a secret. Randy figured that this could be the break he had been looking for.

The day before he was to head off to Edmonton, Bill gave Randy Chantelle's phone number and a list of instructions. The most important one was to bring lots of money, since she was very expensive. Yet she was worth every penny. He said to phone early in the evening because she might be booked up later on. He needed to book a motel in the south part of town with a room that opened to the outside. If she had to walk past the front desk that wouldn't look good. Randy made a mental note of everything.

That following morning Randy wondered if he was going to get out of the camp, let alone get to Edmonton. It had snowed heavily during the night, and in the morning none of the roads had been plowed. Fortunately, by mid-morning the snow had stopped and by late afternoon the road to the highway was plowed. This was a major relief to him; he had been cooped up in the camp since the day after New Year's and he was getting a severe case of cabin fever. He was also relieved when it stopped snowing, not only because he was anxious to get to Edmonton, but he wanted to get there alive. His flight to Edmonton was delayed by one day, but that didn't really matter. He would still have three days to spend there.

When he arrived in Edmonton, the temperature was a balmy minus four degrees. To Randy, that practically felt tropical because at camp and in High Level the temperature had not risen above minus forty degrees since before Christmas. He made his way to the south end of town and checked into a motel just one mile from the place he had stayed at two years before. He then went to a nearby liquor store and bought a bottle of wine.

At 7:00 that evening he figured the time was right. As he picked up the phone, he said, "Well, here goes nothing!" He dialed the number and a few seconds later a woman answered. He asked to speak to Chantelle, and the lady said in a sexy voice, "This is Chantelle."

"Great, super, excellent! You are just the person I am looking for! I...I was, um, just wondering if—you know, if you—um, would—"

She interrupted him at that point and said, "You wanna go out?"

"Yes, you betcha, I would love to!"

"Where do you live?"

"Well, right now, I am staying at the Bel-Air Motel in room twelve. It is at 4900 Calgary Trail. You can't miss it—it's right on Calgary Trail at 49th, I guess. Anyway, you probably know Edmonton better that I do. You most likely know where it is."

Chantelle said with a giggle, "Yes, I know where it is."

Once they settled on a price she asked him if 10:00 would be all right.

"Ten o'clock will be just groovy. I will be looking forward to your arrival." After they hung up, he thought to himself, "Man, she must have thought I was a complete and total yutz!"

Randy waited what seemed an eternity for Chantelle's arrival. He made a point to go easy on the wine. He did not want to get totally shit-faced and not know what he was doing. At about five minutes after ten, he heard a knock at the door. When he opened it he became instantly bug-eyed; she was drop-dead gorgeous.

He stood in the doorway mesmerized for several seconds until she said, "May I come in? It's freezing out here."

"Oh yes, by all means, come on in! Pleased to meet you, I'm Randy."

"Yes, I know."

Randy offered to take her coat. She removed it and he started getting an erection when he saw her low-cut dress.

He offered her a glass of wine, and she then said, "I will need the money up front."

He handed her the money, and she asked him to tell her a little about himself. Randy rambled on and on—often in an incoherent tone—about life in the camp and his family history. Eventually, she interrupted him by asking him if he was nervous.

"Nervous? Me nervous? Hell no, I'm just as cuke as a coolcumber!"

"Here, let me help you unwind and put your mind at ease."

She helped him slip off his shirt and told him to lie down on the bed on his stomach.

Just before he lay down he said, "Can I ask you just one question? Are you sure you're a woman?"

Chantelle gave him a rather surprised look and said, while motioning her large breasts, "What do you think?"

"Yes, I believe you!"

She gave him a sensuous massage, which greatly helped him to loosen up.

A little while later she said to him, "Tell me something, have you ever been with a woman before?"

"Yes, I have."

"I mean, have you ever made love before?"

Randy tried to be cool and said, "Have I ever made love? Huh, huh! Have I ever made love?"

Chantelle whispered into his ear, "The truth."

"Okay, yes, I have, but only with my right hand!" he reluctantly admitted.

"Don't worry about it—it's nothing to be ashamed of. It happens to the best of people. Besides, you're still young. It seems such a shame, though. You're kinda cute and you have a great body. Are you a shy person?"

"In a way, I am. But living in a camp where there are only men doesn't help either."

"Well then, let's get down to business!" she said.

She helped him remove his jeans and socks, and then she slipped out of her dress. When she took off her bra, Randy's underwear looked like the launching pad at Cape Canaveral! She dropped her panties to the floor and he took off his underwear. Chantelle went into her purse, took out a condom and slipped it on his penis.

"Do I have to wear one of those?" he asked.

"Of course! I don't want to risk spreading any diseases, and besides, I don't want to get pregnant!" She then climbed into bed and said to Randy, "Aren't you going to join me?"

Randy cautiously climbed on top of her; it was obvious he was not very confident. He told himself once and for all to relax, which he did. He began to caress her breasts and she guided his penis into her vagina.

"You can begin the motion now," she told him.

"How do I do that?" he asked.

"Use your ass—move it up and down!"

"Oh right. I guess that makes sense. Why didn't I think of that?"

He began to move his butt up and down slowly and asked her, "How's that?"

She said, "You're doing fine!"

Randy felt like he was getting the hang of it, so he started to move up and down faster. A few minutes later he came to a climax.

He let out a loud, "Oh, yes!" and flopped onto his back.

Chantelle leaned over him and said playfully, "Now, that wasn't so hard, was it?"

Almost immediately she got up and began putting her clothes back on.

"What are you doing? We were just getting started!" he asked.

"Honey, I'm a working girl. I have other clients to deal with. Besides, it takes awhile for your hormones to get back to normal," Chantelle informed him.

"I didn't realize that it would only be for a short while. How much extra would it be for the whole evening?"

"Honey, if you wanted me for the entire evening that would cost you over a week's wages. I'm not cheap, you know."

"In this place I was staying at in Saskatoon, there was this hooker who had the room next to mine. One night this guy stayed with her all night. I oughta know because I heard him orgasm eight times!"

Chantelle asked him what this girl looked like, and he replied, "I don't know, I never saw her."

She pointed out that the girl was probably not that great looking and therefore could be bought at a low price. She also mentioned that the guy must have been faking it at least twice. Any man who was able to come eight times in one evening would be practically setting a world record!

Chantelle put on her boots and then her coat.

She said to Randy, "Well, you have my business card. Give me a call the next time you are in Edmonton. I really had an enjoyable time tonight. It was nice to see you. But I have to go now. Goodbye!"

With that, she hurried out the door. Randy, still lying on the bed, had mixed feelings; on the one hand he felt euphoric in that he had finally done it, but on the other hand he felt discouraged that the woman who had provided him with his first sexual experience was so quickly gone with the wind. He looked down at his penis and realized he still had the condom on.

"I guess I can take this damn thing off!"

Later he noticed that they had barely touched the wine; there was still three-quarters of a bottle left. He thought, "Good. Now that it's over, I can get pissed."

He spent most of the next day lying around in his motel room nursing his hangover. The following day he headed back to High Level. Back at the camp he ran into Bill while having dinner in the mess hall.

"Well, how did it go?" he asked.

"Man, you were right, she was fantastic!" Randy replied.

"Hey, would I lie to you?"

"No, but there was one thing that I wasn't too crazy about. I hardly got to spend any time with her. I only got to see her for about a half an hour at the most."

"C'mon, man, don't expect to have a long-term relationship with her! She is extremely popular. There are quite a few men who are her regular customers. If you ask me, I think you were lucky to get that much time with her. If you want more time with her, you have to shell out more money."

Randy took that into consideration and got together with Chantelle again exactly one month later.

Work on the oil rig continued until the middle of April. By then, the temperature had warmed up to the point that the muskeg was too soft for drilling. Only the workers with the most seniority got to work on the rigs in southern and central Alberta where drilling happens all year around. Everyone else would be laid off, including Randy. He had been warned about this ahead of time, so for the past month he had been saving his money. But as it turned out, he might not remain unemployed for too long. He heard about a potential job prospect from Cameron, the man who slept in the cot next to his. A friend of his ran a construction company that had recently been awarded a contract to build a massive townhouse complex in northwest Edmonton. There would probably be enough work to last throughout the summer, and they were severely short of workers. If Randy applied he would probably be assured of getting a job there.

Cameron gave him a card that contained the construction company's name and where to contact them. His friend's name was Ron Savoie and he recommended Randy contact him as soon as he got to Edmonton. Randy was very appreciative of the information, and said that he would definitely give Ron a call.

On the last day of work in the camp, Graham Fisher came up from Calgary and met with all of the workers. He assured everyone they would all be hired back once the ground froze again. He promised that next winter would be just as busy as this one had been. This felt like a tonic to Randy—for the first time he felt as though his future was secure.

When he arrived in Edmonton, he got a small apartment not far from the downtown core. The next day he contacted Ron Savoie. He told him that he had worked with Cameron and he was interested in working on the construction project. Ron asked him to come in for an interview that afternoon. Sure enough, Randy got the job and, unlike the last construction job he was on, he wouldn't be just a gopher. He was going to be doing some actual construction work. He started the following day.

Cameron's prediction that the job would last throughout the summer held true. He was busy all summer long. In fact, he even got lots of overtime. But the real highlight of the summer was when Mark came to visit. He took the bus from Granby to Smithers and then caught the train to Edmonton. Randy almost didn't recognize him when the train arrived; he had grown so much. After all, it had been three years since he had last seen Mark; he found it hard to believe that Mark was now fifteen. Needless to say, it was a very emotional reunion.

They had a lot of catching up to do. Mark talked mainly about what had been going on back home since Randy had left. Nothing much had changed. Their mom was still married to William, and he still wasn't working. In fact, he was as lazy as ever. All he did all day was sit on the couch, watch TV and drink beer. They were considering cutting him off his disability, claiming that he was physically able to work. The problem was that he had no interest in working whatsoever. Besides, he blew most of his money at the bar and on bingo. Their mom barely made enough to cover the rent and living expenses as it was, and losing the disability would make things even worse. Mark admitted that he wanted to get away from home in the worst way and, like Randy, he wanted to leave Granby permanently. But at the same time, he also wanted to finish high school. He still had three years to go and that would be an endurance test. Randy suggested that, starting next year, he should spend the entire summer with him. At least in Edmonton he would have a much better chance of finding a summer job.

Mark stayed for a total of three weeks. During that time, they took in all of the sights around Edmonton. It took longer than usual since Randy didn't have a car. They even spent a day at Klondike Days. When the day came for Mark to head home, Randy felt sad. As they parted, he promised Mark that they would get together every summer.

The construction project lasted until the end of October. Judging by the building inspector's report, it was a complete success. As luck would have it, Randy wasn't unemployed very long. Two weeks after the project ended he was called back to work on the oil rig. The cold weather had come early in northern Alberta, so the ground was hard enough for drilling.

The camp had been moved four miles west of where it had been the previous season. Their objective this season was to drill six new wells. This was good news to Randy, since it meant he would have steady work until next spring.

On New Year's Eve he attended a dinner and dance at the High Level Community Hall. Unlike the year before, he decided that he would behave himself and not get into any fights. Therefore, he went easy on the drinking. The police presence influenced his decision. When the clock struck midnight, Randy joined everyone in toasting the New Year, and he hoped that 1982 would bring as much promise and prosperity as 1981 had.

For the first month of 1982 his wish came true. They were busier than ever on the oil rig. But that all changed at the end of January. One day Graham Fisher came up from Calgary and called a meeting for everyone in the camp. Judging from the grim look on his face, Randy knew this wasn't going to be good news. Graham announced that the full extent of the National Energy Program imposed by the Trudeau administration had kicked in. As a counter-measure to this program, the Alberta government had announced that oil production would be cut back drastically. As a result, Amoco was shutting down all of its oil drilling projects effective immediately.

A hush fell over the packed mess hall; everyone was in a state of shock.

Graham concluded by saying, "Look, let's not get in a panic. I am hopeful that this issue can be resolved shortly. I am sure this is only going to be a temporary setback. There is still lots of oil in the ground and the price of crude oil is still high. But right now, we will just have to wait and see."

Randy found little comfort in him saying that, and everyone else probably felt the same way. He was thinking, "Here he is, telling me I've just lost my fucking job and he tells us not to get in a panic?" His thoughts then shifted to, "Now what am I going to do?" At least this time he wasn't being singled out; everyone else was in the same boat.

The next day he packed his belongings and arranged for a plane ticket to Edmonton. He decided he would settle there for the time being. He learned he would be receiving one week's worth of severance pay, which would help in the short run. Since being rehired last November, he hadn't made any trips into Edmonton, so he had saved most of his money. He would have enough to live on for the next while. He figured there was also a chance that he might find another job.

When he arrived in Edmonton he took an apartment in the same building he had lived in the previous summer, but in a different suite. The landlord had stored some of his belongings over the winter, anticipating his return. He decided to lay low for awhile, with the hope that he would eventually be called back to work. However, since he had a substantial amount of money saved up, he wanted to live it up as much as possible. He frequently went out to nightclubs and had two more intimate encounters with Chantelle. He maintained the attitude of "spend for today, for tomorrow will look after itself" all throughout February. When February turned into March and there was still no word from Amoco, Randy started to become worried. He called Graham Fisher and was told that the situation was very grim. All oil exploration in Alberta was virtually shut down and there was no relief in sight. He made it clear to Randy that there was absolutely no hope of him being rehired for a long time to come.

After his conversation with Graham, Randy finally got a grip on reality and realized that he would have to find another job. He began to look through the classifieds of the *Edmonton Journal* and noticed with dismay that there were hardly any job ads. He kept thinking, "Man, what a contrast from when I came here the first time." Out of the few ads he found, the only one that he was remotely qualified for was at a restaurant in the east part of town. They were looking for dishwashers and bus people. This wasn't something Randy would normally be interested in, but he decided to give it a shot anyway.

When he arrived at the restaurant he noticed a large crowd standing in front of the building. He wondered what was going on. He was just about to walk inside when a man stopped him.

"Are you here to apply for the job?" he asked.

"Yes, I am."

"Get to the back of the line, dude!" he was ordered.

Randy then realized that the lineup went around the block and down the street. He thought to himself, "This is ridiculous!" He thought about turning around and heading home, but then he figured, "Well, it's like a contest. You can't win if you don't enter. Plus, I have all day."

The following day, he decided to check out the Canada Manpower office. As it turned out, the job boards were virtually empty. He was starting to come to terms with how serious the situation was there, and it was making him uneasy. About the only ad he found that was worth inquiring about was for a new resort in Jasper that was opening the next month. There were over a hundred openings, with jobs ranging from kitchen staff to maintenance people. He decided to check it out. The counsellor told him the interviews were being conducted the following Monday. She put Randy's name on the list and told him to be there at 1:00 on Monday afternoon.

When Randy returned the following Monday the place was jam-packed. There must have been over 500 people there, all applying for work at the same place. Once again he initially thought the situation was hopeless, but then he decided to stick it out and be interviewed. Even though he was there right on time, he still had to wait what seemed an eternity; the interviewers were running way behind schedule. He had to keep reminding himself that he had nothing else to do that day. He got into a conversation with the man sitting next to him which helped break up the monotony.

"Man, there sure aren't very many jobs here anymore!" the man said.

"Don't I know it!" Randy responded.

The man went on to tell him that he was an apprenticed electrician and he had not been in a job in his field in over a year and he hadn't had any work in the last three months. In turn, Randy talked about his last job on an oil rig.

"No kidding! How long did you work there?" the man asked. Randy replied that he had been there off and on for two years.

"You know what? You really should be up in the Peace River area."

Looking puzzled, Randy asked, "The Peace River area?"

"Yeah, you know, around Dawson Creek and Fort St. John."

Randy wondered what the big attraction was there. The man told him that they were doing a lot of drilling for natural gas and they were severely short of people to work on the rigs. He told him that with his experience he should be able to get a job there no problem.

"Is that a fact?"

"Yeah, I would head up there as soon as possible if I were you."

Randy said he would give it serious consideration. He noted that at the rate things were going, there was not much point in staying in Edmonton,

Over the next couple weeks, Randy gave a lot of thought to what that man in the Manpower office had said. It sounded encouraging all right, but his rent was paid until the end of March. Because of that he didn't want to leave right away. In addition, he didn't want to completely give up on Edmonton just yet. He still held a faint glimmer of hope that some kind of job offer would come up.

Ever since he'd moved back to Edmonton, he had been somewhat apprehensive about calling Ron Savoie, the contractor fromr the previous summer. This was understandable in light of all the discouragement he had incurred lately. One day he got up the nerve to call. He asked Ron if there were any new projects coming up and if so, would he be needed. Ron told him that he had nothing on the go at the time, and he had very few new projects lined that year. He had barely enough work to keep his top ten carpenters busy, and he made it very clear to Randy that there was no chance he would be hired back anytime that year. After he hung up, Randy almost regretted making that call.

When April 1st rolled around, Randy didn't have enough money to cover the rent. As a result, the landlord told him he would have to move out. But by that time his fate was already sealed. With no job and virtually no chance of finding a job, there was no point in staying in Edmonton anymore. His decision was now final—he planned to head to Dawson Creek.

The landlord let him stay one more night, which gave him an opportunity to dispose of his TV set, chair, coffee table and cookware. Luckily, he found a second-hand store in the yellow pages that had pick-up service. He didn't want to repeat what he had gone through in Medicine Hat. The man from the second-hand store gave him a reasonable price for the items, which would help with the travel expenses.

10

Randy was up early the following morning. He hadn't slept that well since he'd had to bed down in his sleeping bag on the floor. He loaded his backpack and left his apartment for the last time. He took the bus to the western outskirts of town, walked past the city limits and put out his thumb. He was hoping that whoever picked him up would be going in the same direction as he was heading. Otherwise he would have to be let off at the Highway 43 turnoff.

Two hours later, a man driving a Subaru pulled over. He asked Randy where he was heading, and he replied that he was going to Dawson Creek. The man was on his way to Jasper, but he could give him a ride as far as the Highway 43 turnoff. That was exactly what Randy had been afraid of, but he accepted anyway. As they sped away Randy turned around and took one last look, wondering if this was to be the last time he would ever see Edmonton. In a way he felt a sense of sadness in having to say goodbye to Edmonton. After all, it was where he had found his first real taste of freedom.

The driver dropped him off at the intersection of Highway 43. From there he began walking up the highway, only putting his thumb out when a car would come by. He figured that if nobody picked him up he could at least make it to Onoway. As it turned out, that wasn't necessary. After an hour a pickup truck pulled over. A native man was driving. The driver was heading in that general direction of Dawson Creek and could give him a ride part of the way, and Randy accepted the offer.

Once inside the car, Randy asked him what he had meant by giving him a ride part of the way.

"Exactly how far are you going?" Randy asked.

"Well, I live in a place called Little Smoky."

"Where is that?" Randy inquired.

"It's between Fox Creek and Valleyview."

Unlike on previous journeys, Randy had made sure he had a map this time. He reached into his backpack and took out the one of Alberta. He followed Highway 43 from where he had been picked up until he saw where

Little Smoky was. He noticed that it was nothing more than a little dot on the map and it was the only place between Fox Creek and Valleyview.

He asked the driver, "So, exactly how big is Little Smoky?"

"It's just a gas station and a store."

"You mean they don't have a hotel or anything?"

"Nope, nothing."

"How far is it from there to Valleyview?"

"Twenty-five miles."

"And from there to Fox Creek?"

"Twenty seven miles."

Just for the record, he asked the driver what was in between and he responded, "Not much of anything!"

Randy began to feel uneasy. He didn't want a repeat of what had happened on Highway 16 east of Prince George. He was debating whether he should play it safe and get off in Fox Creek; it didn't sound as though there would be any place to take refuge for the night in Little Smoky. It was still unseasonably cold outside and the forecast predicted snow that night. He managed to get up enough nerve to ask the driver if he could spend the night at his place if he couldn't get another ride. The man looked at Randy and began to laugh.

"You've got to be kidding! For one thing, I live on an acreage ten miles west of the place. I have five kids so there wouldn't be any room for you. Besides, my old lady would not approve of it."

Randy said, "Thanks anyway."

Despite that he decided to take a chance and ride with him all the way to Little Smoky.

After they passed Fox Creek, the surrounding countryside became nothing more than dense forest. There was very little traffic in either direction and quite often they had the whole road to themselves. Randy knew he was gambling and he wondered if he had made the right decision. It was already 3:00 in the afternoon so he only had about three hours of daylight left.

He was dropped off in front of the store in Little Smoky. He looked around and thought to himself, "Man, he wasn't whistling dixie! It's too bad there isn't a Big Smoky!" He decided to make a refueling stop, since he had hardly eaten anything all day. When he went into the store the clerk gave him a funny look. He was probably wondering why he would get off there if he was hitchhiking. Randy looked over the merchandise, hoping there was something that was "ready to eat." In the end all he ended up buying was a chocolate bar and a can of Coke.

As he put the items on the counter, he said to the clerk, "Yup, gotta load up on them there carbohydrates!"

Randy was tempted to ask the clerk what they did for fun around there, but decided against it. He took the items outside and consumed them then and there. After a smoke break he figured it was time to hit the road. It was 3:30 by then, so he kept his fingers crossed and hoped for the best. The only time he put his thumb out was when a car came by, which wasn't very often. The clerk in the store kept staring at him through the window and this made him feel very uneasy. He felt tempted to give the guy the finger, but figured he'd better not. For all he knew the guy might call the cops.

Luck must have been on Randy's side, for after only an hour a car pulled over. In fact, luck was really on his side. The car was a red Firebird and inside it were two attractive young ladies. The girl driving asked Randy where he was heading.

"I'm going to Dawson Creek."

"We're only going as far as Valleyview."

"That's all right, that will be no problem!"

As Randy got into their car, he thought that he had died and gone to heaven. All he kept thinking was, "Man, are they pretty! Oh please, let them be single!" He kept wondering why they would pick him up. Normally, it's kind of unusual for women drivers to pick up male hitchhikers—it's far more common the other way around. The theory he was hoping for was that they were into threesomes. He figured that would be a real bonus; he had a hard enough time getting lucky with one woman, imagine making it with two!

Five minutes later, one of the girls finally spoke up. "So, do you have friends or relatives in Dawson Creek?"

"No, I have a job offer there."

She asked him where he had started out from and he told her Edmonton.

"What a coincidence, that's where we came from! It's too bad we didn't meet you in Edmonton, we could have given you a ride from there."

Randy was thinking, "You sure got that right!" She went on to tell him that they had both had a couple days off, so they had decided to check out West Edmonton Mall. She added that it was such a shame that their husbands hadn't wanted to come along.

Randy said in a dejected tone, "Husbands."

The girl driving said, "Yeah, they would rather spend their spare time sitting around the house watching television than getting out of town."

Randy was thinking, "I knew my hopes were too good to be true."

"It's always good to have a man come along for the ride. There are a lot of weirdos out there, and you never know who you will run into on the road," the driver continued.

"Yeah, but you don't know me," he said.

The other girl said, "You don't seem the type, and besides, there's two of us and only one of you."

"I see your point," he said.

The driver said, "This road is so goddamn boring. Sometimes it's nice to have another person to talk to. It makes the trip less monotonous."

When they arrived in Valleyview, the girls dropped Randy off downtown. He checked into a hotel and then had dinner in the hotel restaurant. He decided against going to the bar that night—he wanted to conserve his money until he got settled. So he turned in early, hoping to start out early the next day.

He was up early the following morning. After having breakfast in the hotel restaurant, he made his way out of town, heading for Highway 34. Two hours later a car pulled over. It was the complete opposite of his last ride. This time there were two men in the car. The car they were in was a far cry from what the girls had; it was a Volkswagen.

After learning of Randy's destination, the man driving said, "We're only going as far as Grande Prairie."

Randy figured that it was better than nothing, so he said, "That will be all right."

It was a bit of a struggle when he got into the car since it was so small. Randy and his backpack took up the entire back seat and he barely had any legroom. When he saw the sign indicating how far it was to Grande Prairie, he was thinking, "Oh, thank god I will be cooped up in here for only an hour!"

When they arrived in Grande Prairie, the men dropped him off at the junction of 100th Avenue and Wapiti Road. The driver told him that 100th Avenue was part of Highway 2 and it eventually lead to Dawson Creek. It took Randy a little while to get feeling back into his legs, and when he realized it was still early in the day, he decided to take a coffee break. He went into a truck stop, and while he was having coffee he decided to check out the employment situation in Grande Prairie. He purchased that day's edition of the *Grande Prairie Herald-Tribune* and scanned the want ads. That didn't take very long since there were very few. In addition, the front page carried an article about massive layoffs at the town's largest lumber mill. He got to thinking, "So much for that idea! I think I will stick to my original plan."

He made his way to the western outskirts of Grande Prairie and then put his thumb out. After an hour, a farm truck with a covered flat deck pulled over. Randy's first thought was, "Oh no, not again!"

When he climbed on the deck and opened the passenger door, the middle-aged man driving asked, "Where are you heading?" Randy told him that he was going to Dawson Creek, and the man said, "I'm going as far as the town of Pouce Coupe, which is only eight miles from Dawson Creek."

"That's great!"

"Jump in!"

"Are you sure it's okay to ride up front?"

The driver said, "Sure, I don't see why not. You can ride in the back if you want, but I'm sure it will be too damn cold."

As they headed down the road, Randy explained that he had gotten a ride from Saskatoon to Kindersley in a truck similar to his, but the driver made him sit in the back with the cows.

"Some people have no consideration for others, have they?" the driver commented.

An hour into the ride, Randy saw a very welcome sight, a sight he had wondered if he would ever see again. It was the sign that read "Welcome to British Columbia." He realized that he was setting foot on British Columbia soil for the first time in almost four years. Scenically it wasn't any different, though, as the landscape was still prairie.

He said to the driver, "Ahh, home sweet home! It sure feels good to be back in my home province."

"So what's bringing you to Dawson Creek?"

"Well, I heard they are doing a lot of drilling for natural gas around there and since I have experience working on an oil drilling rig, I can easily find a job."

"I see," the driver said with a puzzled look, as if he didn't know what Randy was talking about.

His response, along with the fact that jobs were practically nonexistent in Grande Prairie, was starting to make Randy somewhat suspicious.

After being dropped off in Pouce Coupe, he decided to walk the remaining eight miles into Dawson Creek rather than trying to hitch another ride. It didn't look that far away—he could see the town's grain elevators in the distance. In the end he wished he had tried to hitch a ride; it took him almost two hours to reach Dawson Creek. By the time he got there he was half frozen. In addition, it was already 3:30. He figured that he had better get into the Canada Manpower office soon before they closed.

When he walked into the Canada Manpower office, he made a request at the front desk to speak to a counsellor. It must have been pretty obvious that he was a drifter—the backpack was a dead giveaway. When he finally saw a counsellor, she asked him how she could be of service. Randy asked if he could get the names of the companies that were drilling for natural gas in the area.

"What are you talking about?"

"You know, with all of the natural gas drilling that is going on, I want to know which companies are in charge of the wells. Is it the government or are private companies involved?" Randy asked.

"I still don't know what you're talking about. There is very little drilling for natural gas right now due to the National Energy Policy. I don't think there will be very much, if any, activity in the natural gas industry for quite some time."

"But, that's not what I heard!"

"Randy, where exactly did you hear about this?"

"Well, when I was in the Manpower office in Edmonton, this guy sitting next to me told me that there was a lot of drilling for natural gas up here and that they were desperate for workers."

"Who was he? Did he work there?"

"No, he was there applying for the same job I was. I never knew his name."

"Let me get this straight. You came all this way because of something you heard from someone you had never met before? I mean, where did he get the information from? For all you know, he could have just been making it up, or he could have not known what he was talking about. You should have done some research first."

"There wasn't much point in me staying in Edmonton anyway. There wasn't any work there. There must be some other job opportunities here besides natural gas drilling?"

"It's not any better here. The Louisiana-Pacific Lumber Mill recently laid off half its staff, farmers are suffering because of low commodity prices, and construction is at a standstill due to high interest rates. In all honesty, Randy, you wasted your time coming up here."

"Oh, I don't think it's a total waste. I mean, I can head up to the Yukon from here." She asked him what he would want to go up there for, and Randy replied, "To find a job."

She said, "In case you don't realize it, the big mine in Faro just closed, putting over four hundred people out of work. Needless to say, the economy is depressed there too. You would be wasting your time if you went up there."

Randy had heard just about enough by then. He got up to leave and said to her, "Thanks for your help."

"My pleasure."

Before he left the Manpower office Randy decided that it ain't over till it's over. He obtained three dollars' worth of change at the front desk. He went to the pay phone at the front of the office and called the Prairie Agro Services mill in Olds. He asked to speak to Angus McVittie.

When he came on the line, Randy said, "Hello, Mr. McVittie? This is Randy Watson. Do you remember me? I used to work for you at the mill in Calgary."

Angus said, "Yes Randy, I do remember you. How is everything going?"

"All right, I guess. Listen, I was wondering, are there any job openings at the mill right now? I'm not working at the moment."

"Randy, we have not had any openings here in quite some time and we have a stack of applications a mile high. I don't see anything coming up any time in the future."

Randy said, "Thanks, anyway," and hung up.

He went back to the front desk and asked for three more dollars' worth of quarters. Then in an act of sheer desperation, he called the Simmons and Sattler mill in Calgary and asked to speak to Dory Hoskins.

"Dory, it's Randy Watson. Remember me? I used to work for you. Look, I have been doing some serious soul-searching over the last year and I have come to the conclusion that you were right. I wasn't putting in a good enough effort, but if you give me another chance, I promise I will put in a much better effort."

Dory said, "Randy, we are not doing well financially. This mill has been losing money like crazy in the last couple of years, and the head office is seriously considering shutting us down. We're all worried about keeping our own jobs here, so there's no chance of us hiring any more people."

"Oh well, I thought I would give it a shot," he said and hung up.

As he hung up he started feeling sick to his stomach. He felt that he'd hit an all-time low by actually resorting to grovelling to that scumbag.

When he walked out of the Manpower office, he felt like a complete and total jackass. He figured the lady must have thought he was a total idiot for coming all that way for nothing. He parked himself in a nearby coffee shop and spent the next several hours pondering his future. He was facing the reality that he had reached the end of the road; the economic well that had provided him employment over the past four years had finally dried up. It was a really nauseating feeling. He could go north, east or west and the results would be the same. He realized that going to the Yukon was out of the question, so he eliminated that option. He thought about going to Calgary and riding out the economic slump there. But then he figured that if he was going to be unemployed anyway, he might as well be in Vancouver. At least there the climate was better.

After four cups of coffee and a half a dozen cigarettes he decided that he had to make a move. Staying in Dawson Creek was definitely out of the question, so he narrowed it down to two cities—Calgary or Vancouver. He figured the best way to settle it was to flip a coin.

He said, "Okay now, heads Calgary, tails Vancouver."

He flipped the coin and it came up heads—not the outcome he was hoping for.

"All right, let's make it two out of three."

He tossed the coin again and it came up tails. As he prepared to flip it a third time he kept thinking, "This is it, this is the deciding factor!" Lo and behold, it came up tails!

He said joyfully, "Well, that's it! My decision is final—I'm heading to Vancouver!"

By then it was after 6:00 in the evening and it was starting to get dark. He debated whether or not he should get a hotel room for the night and start out early the next morning. But then he had to remind himself that he was running low on money, and he didn't know how long it would have to last him.

He made his way along Highway 97 to the eastern edge of town. Once he was past the city limits, he put his thumb out. There was very little traffic at that time of day and, as expected, nobody picked him up. By 9:00 he was ready to give up for the night. He realized that getting a ride would be hopeless until the next day. But he wasn't the least bit tired. After four cups of coffee, he was still pretty wired. He thought about walking back into town and wandering through the downtown for the next few hours, but he didn't want to risk having the cops pick him up and charge him with vagrancy. On the other hand, it being so cold out, the thought of spending the night in a warm jail cell seemed almost appealing. But then he began to wonder if, since he was back in B.C., there might still be a warrant out for his arrest for what he had done to Kees Vandelaar. So he decided to stay put and keep trying. He stayed there until 11:00 and by then he was numb from standing in one spot. He couldn't get over how cold it was, especially since it was April 3rd. All he kept thinking was, "Man, I can't wait until I get to Vancouver! It will sure be nice to get out of this iceberg!"

He started heading back toward town, hoping he would be able to find a place where he could take refuge for the night. He made his way toward the grain elevators, thinking one of them might have a door open. He took a shortcut through a used car lot, and as he walked past a 1967 Plymouth Valiant, he noticed that one of the back doors was unlocked. He decided to take advantage of the situation. He opened the door and crawled into the back seat.

He said, "Man, this is roomy. I wish I had the money to buy this car."

He took some of his extra clothes out of his backpack, laid them over top of him, put his head down and went to sleep.

That night the temperature went down to minus four degrees. When he woke up he was so cold he couldn't move. When he managed to look at his watch he saw that it was 6 a.m. He knew he had better get up before any of the employees of the car lot arrived. He struggled with every move and it took him a half an hour just to sit up. He was worried that one of the employees would come in early, and he would be nailed for trespassing. He wondered who would be buying a used car this early in the morning, but he still didn't want to take a chance. Using every ounce of his strength, he managed to get out of the car only to fall into the snow. He picked himself up and put on his backpack.

He said to himself, "Okay now, if anyone who works here comes by, I'll say that I'm just looking."

The truck stop across the highway seemed ten miles away. All he could think of was that the place had heat. The fact that he was hungry was secondary. His legs were so stiff from being frozen in one position all night that it made walking difficult. When he reached the edge of the highway, he waited until there was a major lull in the traffic because running was out of the question. Inside the restaurant it felt like paradise; heat had never felt so good. His mouth was still frozen, so when the waitress asked if he wanted a menu he could only nod his head in agreement. It was the same when she asked if he wanted coffee. After ten minutes he had completely thawed out and was able to order some food. After breakfast and two more coffees, he was thoroughly warmed and strengthened. By then the sun had come out and it began to warm up outside. Randy thought, "Vancouver, here I come," and headed out to the highway.

He waited along the highway with his thumb out for over an hour before a car pulled over.

The middle-aged man driving asked him where he was heading and Randy said, "Prince George."

"Well, I can give you a ride as far as the Highway 39 turnoff, which is ninety miles west of here."

Once again, Randy thought, "It's better than nothing," so he said, "Okay."

During the ride he confessed that he was actually heading to Vancouver and Prince George would only be a stopover. The driver told him he was one of the operations managers at the big pulp mill in MacKenzie.

Randy looked upon this as a golden opportunity and took advantage of it by asking, "So, would you be the one I would talk to if I was looking for a job?"

"No, that would be our human resources manager. But I can tell you right now, there's not much of a chance you will find a job there. Business has been quite slow lately so we've had to lay off some of our production staff. As a matter of fact, the reason I was in Dawson Creek is that the local Credit Union is one of our biggest creditors and I spent all day yesterday in meetings, trying to persuade them to give us an extension of our credit. I'm not sure yet how the meetings turned out. Only time will tell. So, I don't mean to be the bearer of bad news, but I don't think you should get your hopes up."

"Oh well, it was just a thought."

Once they passed Chetwynd they were into the Rocky Mountain foothills. This was a real treat for Randy since he hadn't seen any big mountains in quite some time. This was the type of topography he had been accustomed to while he was growing up, so he felt that he was finally back in his home province.

The driver dropped him off at the junction of Highway 39 and Highway 97. He told him that if he failed to get a ride before the day was over, the town of McLeod Lake was only fifteen miles west. There was a store and a restaurant, as well as a place that rented cabins for the night. Randy thanked him for the tip and the ride. He decided he would just wait and see, and if he didn't get a ride by 3:00 he would start making his way to McLeod Lake.

For the next two hours he waited patiently beside the highway with his thumb out. He nervously looked behind every few minutes—he knew there were bears in the area. At least the cold was easing up. The traffic was moderate, but nobody was stopping. Finally a pickup truck pulled over. It was an old Ford, circa 1955. It was painted red, but had lots of rust. It looked like something out of *Sanford and Son*. There was a fair amount of junk in the back. The driver was a man in his forties with long greyish hair and a scraggly appearance.

He said to Randy, "Hello there young feller, where are you heading?"

"Prince George."

"Great! That's where I live—hop in!"

As they drove off, the truck sputtered and chugged as it struggled to reach highway speed. Whenever he changed gears the whole truck would shudder.

Randy said sarcastically, "Man, is this thing going to make it?"

"Of course it is! I rebuilt the motor myself!" He went on to say, "So, what's a good-looking young man like you doing travelling all by yourself?"

"I don't know, I guess I couldn't find anyone to travel with."

"So, are you going to Prince George to visit anybody?"

"No, I am going to see what the job situation is like there and if nothing pans out, I am going to go on to Vancouver."

"Well, if you're interested, you can work for me," the driver offered.

"Oh really? What exactly do you do for a living?"

"Well, I do a number of different things. One thing I do is I pick up scraps of wood from the lumber mills and sell it as firewood. I also pick up scrap pieces of gyproc from construction sites and sell them to the recycling centre in Prince George. I even sell used auto parts on the side. Yep, there's some damn good money to be made there."

Randy said again in a sarcastic tone, "Oh yes, I can see that you are making damn good money! This new vehicle of yours was a dead giveaway!"

The man gave Randy an annoyed look and said, "You think you're real smart, don't you? You probably don't know what it's like to put in an honest day's work!"

"Don't start in on me! I know what hard work is like, okay!"

The man went on to tell him that he had spent the day fishing in Williston Lake. Randy asked him where his boat was and he told him that he used an inflatable raft.

"So, where's all the fish?" Randy asked.

"In the lake," the driver informed him then went on to say, "I was thinking, how would you like to stay with me for awhile? I live twenty miles outside of Prince George out in the country. There's no big-city stress there, just total solitude. It'll be just you and me."

"That's what I'm afraid of!"

"C'mon, you'll like it at my place. You can come and work for me and we'll have lots of fun."

All that was going through Randy's mind was, "Yeah, right! The last thing in the world I want to be is that asshole's personal sex slave!" He said, "Thanks anyway, but I prefer the big city and all the conveniences that come with it. Vancouver is the place for me."

"Ah, that's too bad."

He then put his right hand on Randy's knee. Almost immediately Randy grabbed the guy's hand and removed it. A few seconds later he did it again, only to have Randy remove it again. This procedure was repeated four times, and each time the man put his hand closer to Randy's thigh.

After the fourth time, Randy finally said, "Look, do you mind?"

The man appeared to stop, but a few minutes later he made another move on Randy, this time putting his arm around him. He tried to pull away, but the man drew him even closer. Randy was by then right up against him.

He yelled out, "Will you get your goddamn hands off of me!"

"C'mon kid, relax, take it easy!"

The man continued to alternately rub his shoulders and stroke his hair.

"Jesus Christ, man! When the hell was the last time you had a goddamn bath?" Randy blurted.

He noticed that the guy had a huge bulge in his crotch, but that wasn't the worst thing. He looked at the speedometer and saw that the truck was going eighty miles per hour!

Randy shouted, "I'm telling you, let go of me, you fucking pervert!"

"Take it easy kid! I really want you to come and stay with me! I need some company and you're the one!"

Randy could tell from his mannerisms that this guy was horny as hell. Plus, his body odour was making Randy's eyes water. He knew he had to take some drastic action. He decided it was time to get out the heavy artillery. He managed to break free from the man's grip, reach into his sock and pull out Larry's hunting knife. He took it out of the scabbard and pointed it right in the man's face.

The guy freaked out and said, "What are you doing? Are you crazy?"

"Look who's asking who's crazy, you sick piece of shit! Now let's get this straight! You're taking me to Prince George, okay. You'll drop me off when I say so and if you put your hand on me one more time, I'll slit your fucking throat! And another thing—slow down or else this old clunker will blow up!" Randy threatened.

"Don't you know that what you're doing is illegal? I can have you charged with kidnapping and threatening me!"

"Go ahead! There aren't any witnesses so who's going to believe you anyway? Besides, I'll tell the cops what you tried to do to me. In addition, you don't even know my name and you know what, you aren't ever going to know my name. As far as you're concerned, my name is Mister X!"

The man said nervously, "Pleased to meet you, my name is Bill."

Randy said, "I don't give a fuck what your goddamn name is. All I know is, if you touch me one more time your name will be Mud!"

As they approached the northern outskirts of Prince George, Randy said, "Okay, you can drop me off here. I can walk the rest of the way. Now, once you drop me off, I want you to just keep on going and don't look back, got it?"

They pulled over and as Randy got out of the truck, Bill said, "I hope you burn in hell!"

"I know you will!" Randy retorted then added sarcastically, "Oh, by the way, thanks for the ride!"

As the truck sped away Bill flashed his middle finger out the window and Randy returned the favour.

He then held the knife in front of him and said, "Ahh, my new best friend. Popeye has his spinach, I have this!"

After the incident in Edmonton at the Single Men's Hostel when Randy had to produce his knife in self-defence, he had hoped he wouldn't have to do that again. He thought it weird that these kinds of situations kept happening to him.

11

It took Randy nearly an hour to reach the downtown core of Prince George. He had forgotten just how far the city spread out in all directions. He found it hard to believe it had been nearly four years since he last passed through there. Still, it felt great to be in a familiar place again. He noticed that the downtown hadn't changed much since his last visit—he could easily recall where everything was. He remembered where the Salvation Army was located, and with this being a major city, they had a hostel adjoining the citadel. He checked in there and got a bunk for the night. Having dinner in the dining hall was a real treat, since this was the first decent meal he'd had since he left Edmonton. He was quite impressed as they went all out. They served turkey with mashed potatoes, gravy and stuffing. This was better than what he had ever had at home on Thanksgiving. He decided that he would stay there at least two nights and the next day he would check out the employment situation in and around the city.

He was up early the next morning; he knew he had a lot of ground to cover. Most of the industries were in the outlying areas past the limits of any bus lines. He was going to make an effort to apply at all three of the pulp mills and, if possible, all of the lumber mills.

In the afternoon he applied at a lumber mill located on the western outskirts of town. As expected, it was a long walk from the last bus stop. As he walked along Highway 16, he saw a road sign indicating the distances to the various cities westward. What got his attention the most was where it read "Smithers 370 km." This really made him realize just how close to home he was. He began to wonder just what would happen if he were to hitchhike back to Granby. Would his mom accept him and let him back in the house? Would he be able to get a job at the mine or the lumber mill?

Those thoughts were almost immediately dashed, and he made a declaration by yelling out loud, "The day I set foot in that stinking shithole again and the day I go crawling back to that fucking useless bitch will be the day hell freezes over!"

All the while Randy was yelling this out, he pointed his finger wildly at the road sign. Someone in a house across the road was watching him and must have thought he was some kind of nutcase. When he noticed them watching him he felt kind of embarrassed.

At the end of the day he felt like he had done a pretty good job in his search for employment. He had covered quite a bit of ground, applying at all three pulp mills, most of the lumber mills and even at B.C. Rail. However, the same couldn't be said for the results. Perhaps the main reason he was able to apply at so many places was that he was never very long at any one place. Most of the time he was there just long enough for the receptionist to tell him they were not taking any applications. In the end, not one place gave Randy even the faintest glimmer of hope that there would be any job openings then or in the future. It seemed like every industry in the city was laying off workers.

He managed to find some time in the afternoon to look in the local Canada Manpower office. But the results were the same as in Edmonton and Dawson Creek—the job boards were virtually empty. After he left, he finally came to terms with the fact that he had no chance of ever finding a job there. As much as he liked Prince George, he had no reason to stay. But at least he gave himself credit for trying. So then it was back to his original plan—it was Vancouver or bust.

He made his way to Highway 97 at the crack of dawn the following morning. He wanted to get an early start so there would be the possibility that he might actually make it to Vancouver that day.

As expected, it took forever to reach the southern city limits. Once he passed the city limits sign, he parked himself beside Highway 97 and sat on top of his backpack. It was a warm, sunny spring morning; a big contrast to what it had been like in Dawson Creek three days before. He sat beside the highway with his thumb out for nearly two hours before a vehicle pulled over. It was a station wagon with two men inside. When Randy got up close to the car, he noticed that the two men had long beards and were wearing black robes. The passenger, speaking in a heavy accent, asked Randy where he was heading.

He told him Vancouver and the man said, "Good, that's where we are going."

Randy immediately recognized his Greek accent since, after all, he was half Greek.

A few minutes after they headed out, the driver asked Randy if he had friends or relatives in Vancouver. He replied that he didn't really know anybody there, he was only going there to try and find a job.

The driver went on to say, "In case you haven't noticed, we are Greek Orthodox priests. Our parish is based in Vancouver, and we have another parish in Prince George. We make a point of visiting them at least four times a year."

Randy recalled that when his Grandmother Goustopholous was alive, she had gone to the Greek Orthodox Church. Prince George had once had a sizeable Greek community, and that's where his mom hailed from. But he didn't want to let on to the priests that he was half Greek. It was a good thing too. When the priests were talking between themselves, they used Greek. What they didn't realize was that Randy understood every word they were saying! His grandmother had started teaching him the language as soon as he could talk and continued until just before she died eight years ago. The lessons were finally paying off. As it turned out, the priests were talking about him and practically all of it was negative. They were constantly making derogatory comments about his long hair and the way he dressed. They commented that he didn't appear to be very intelligent and that he likely didn't have a very good education. They didn't think he had much chance of ever finding a job and that he was going nowhere in life. At first Randy just tried to tune them out. But over time he started getting more and more pissed off. He desperately wanted to say something, but he wanted to wait until they were in a populated area before doing so. He decided there was no chance in hell he was going all the way to Vancouver with those two assholes!

As they approached Quesnel, Randy finally spoke up. He really let them have it—in Greek. When they realized that he spoke fluent Greek, they looked at him in total disbelief. It was then that it dawned on them what they had done.

Translated into English, Randy said, "Just who the hell do you flicking assholes think you are, talking about me behind my back? Ha! I bet you didn't think I could speak Greek, did you? For your information, I am Greek on my mother's side! Surprise, surprise, eh? You flickers call yourselves men of the cloth? If you ask me, you have no goddamn business being priests! As far as I'm concerned, you're nothing but a couple of flicking hypocrites! Now pull this piece of shit over—I'm not riding with you anymore!"

One of the priests, still obviously flabbergasted, tried to tell Randy that he was sorry, but Randy was having no part of it. He was absolutely livid and just wanted to get away from them. After repeated demands they finally pulled over.

As Randy got out of the car, he screamed out, "I hope you motherfuckers both burn in hell! Now get out of my flicking sight!"

As the car sped away, Randy yelled out, "fuck you" and flashed both his middle fingers. When he turned around, he realized he was standing right in front of a crowded restaurant. Most of the patrons inside were looking at him, including two police officers. He felt like yelling out, "what are you looking at," but decided against it. Instead, he decided to make the best of a bad situation and look around town.

He headed into downtown Quesnel. He decided he would check out the employment situation there even though he didn't hold out much hope. But in Quesnel he thought he just might have a possible ace in the hole. His uncle Jack had worked at one of the lumber mills there until he had retired five years ago. He had then moved to Vancouver Island, settling in Parksville. Randy was trying to remember the name of the mill, but couldn't think of it offhand. In a phone book, he looked up the listings for all of the lumber mills in town, hoping that would jog his memory. He came across one particular mill and remembered that it was the one. Looking at a local map, he determined how to get there from where he was.

When he arrived at the mill, he asked to speak to the foreman, who, a few minutes later, invited him into his office. Randy explained he was looking for work, and he wanted to apply for a job. The foreman informed him that there was virtually no chance that they would be hiring anybody for quite some time. In fact they had laid off a number of workers recently.

Randy said, "Well, I thought I might have at least a remote chance. Do you remember Jack Watson?"

"Yes, I remember Jack quite well. He worked here for over thirty years. He was a very dedicated worker. What does he have to do with all of this?"

"Jack is my uncle," Randy told him.

"That's very interesting, but just because a relative of yours worked here does not give you special privileges. There have been cases where sons of men who worked here many years have asked for a job and there's been nothing I can do for them. The fact is, the forest industry is in a very severe slump and that applies to everywhere. To be honest, I don't know if this mill can survive much longer unless the economy improves."

As expected Randy felt dejected, and as he got up to leave he said to the foreman, "Thanks anyway."

Before he left, the foreman said, "If you're ever in Parksville, say hello to Jack for me."

Randy was still determined not to give up. He went back to the downtown area and into the Canada Manpower office. As was the case in Prince George and Dawson Creek, the job board was practically empty. At this point he thought about giving up on Quesnel completely, but then he decided to make one last-ditch effort to find a job there. He had more gumption than brains. He decided to apply at the pulp mill and if that didn't work out, it was onto Vancouver.

The walk from downtown to the pulp mill seemed to take forever. He realized that it was actually a good idea to locate the pulp mill away from the city—that way the local residents wouldn't have to put up with the smell all the time. He reasoned that he might have a chance at the pulp mill because, even during a recession, people still read newspapers and used other paper products. After all, anybody who had lost their job would still prefer to use toilet paper rather than their fingers!

When he arrived at the pulp mill he felt that the large number of cars in the parking lot was a good sign. He went into the office and asked to speak to the human resources manager. When she came out of her office, she told Randy straight out that they were not taking any new applications at that time. He commented that it appeared as though they were doing quite well. Yes, she said, the mill was indeed doing well and they were quite busy. The problem was that the mill was the only bright spot in the local economy. Therefore, everybody wanted to get on board there. They had eventually ended up with so many applications that they stopped taking any new ones two months ago. The majority of applicants had lived in Quesnel all their lives, so it was doubtful they would hire anyone from out of town. In addition, with the economy being the way it was, the people who were already working there were staying put. When he heard this, he said nothing. He just turned and left.

After he left the premises he yelled out, "That's it, and this time I mean it! It's Vancouver or bust!"

He made his way back to Highway 97. He decided to wait until he was at least two miles out of town before putting his thumb out. As he was walking along the highway, a police car drove past him very slowly and pulled over a hundred feet ahead.

Randy tried not to pay any attention to it, but when he walked past the police car the cop driving called out, "Come here, boy!"

Randy turned around and looked at them, and the policeman said, "I'm talking to you! Get over here!"

Randy approached the car, and when he got up to the driver's window the driver said, "Where are you going to?"

"Vancouver."

"It sure doesn't look like it! We've noticed you wandering around town all morning!"

"I just wanted to have a look around here, but I'm leaving now."

The cop on the passenger's side said, "Why aren't you taking the bus?"

"I don't have the money for bus fare."

That same policeman said, "How do you expect to get a ride all the way to Vancouver if you treat people who give you a ride like that?"

The other cop said, "We saw you when we were in the restaurant. We heard you swearing at them and saw you giving them an obscene gesture!"

Randy interceded by saying, "Look, they were making fun of me, okay? I couldn't take it anymore. I do have some dignity, for god's sake!"

The driver said, "Look kid, there are laws against vagrancy, and as far as I am concerned, you have been hanging around here too long!"

Randy struggled to maintain his composure. He knew that if he said one wrong thing he would end up in the local lockup.

He managed to politely say, "Okay, I promise I'll leave. I assure you that I will keep on going and I will never come back"

The policeman on the passenger side said, "You do that! When we come back if you are still here, you are going to be in big trouble. Now don't show your face around here again, understand?"

"Yes sir, I'm on my way!"

He waited until the police car was out of sight and screamed out, "Fuck you pigs!" and then flashed both his middle fingers.

For the next hour he walked steadily at a very brisk pace. He was so mad he hardly even looked up. Eventually he reached the village of Kersley. At that point he thought to himself, "Whoa! At this rate, I'm going to end up in Williams Lake!" He stopped walking and put his thumb out. He looked at his watch and realized that it was 3:00. He said to himself, "Oh man, I'm never going to make it to Vancouver today!"

A half an hour after he had started hitchhiking, a pickup truck pulled over. The man driving rolled down his window, and when he heard Randy's destination, he offered, "Well, I'm going to Kamloops, but I can give you a ride as far as Cache Creek."

"That's okay with me!" Randy said.

During the ride, he asked Randy what was taking him to Vancouver. He told him that he was going there to look for work.

"Well, I can give you a tip. Cache Creek is a real going concern in the summer. Since it is located at the junction of Highways 1 and 97, it's a popular stopping place for tourists. There are a lot of motels, restaurants and gas stations there and they're always very busy in the summer. It seems like most places have trouble filling all their positions, so experience doesn't matter. They will hire anybody who is willing to work."

Randy found this very interesting, and said he would give it serious consideration.

"It might be a little early in the year now. It doesn't get busy there until at least late May," the driver added.

"If nothing pans out in Vancouver by then I might make a trip up there. One place I'm definitely not going to is Quesnel!"

"Oh, is there a problem?"

"There sure as hell is! Two cops started hassling me for no reason! They threatened to charge me with vagrancy—in fact, I was job-hunting! I wasn't doing anything. They were just being a couple assholes!"

"Well, I can't say I blame them. You see, they have been having problems lately with people from eastern Canada coming out here hoping to find work, and when they get here, they find there isn't any. There has been an increase in robberies and vandalism, and there have been a lot of complaints from local residents that they are being harassed by panhandlers. It isn't just in Quesnel; it's happening all throughout the Cariboo. The reason I know all of this is because my dad is the Crown prosecutor in Quesnel!"

"I see your point. I assure you that I will not pass this way again until I am employed."

Four hours later they arrived in Cache Creek. Randy thanked the driver for the ride and didn't realize until later that the man hadn't told him his name. It was evening by then, and he decided to wait until the next day before hitching a ride to Vancouver. His number one priority was to get something to eat. He had not eaten anything since morning, so he was really starving. Out of the many restaurants in town, he chose the Husky Truck Stop. At least with them, he didn't have to worry about an early closing.

After dinner he wondered where he was going to bed down for the night. He didn't feel like spending money on a motel. He looked up into the hills surrounding Cache Creek and even though it was dark, he could tell that there were a number of wooded areas in amongst the sagebrush. He decided to build a makeshift campsite far enough away that he wouldn't be noticed, yet close enough that he could run for help if he was attacked by a bear. He didn't worry about it getting cold that night, since he was still wearing his winter coat. Besides, he knew that it wouldn't get anywhere near as cold as it had in Dawson Creek.

As he made his way up the hill, the going was fairly easy in the open area—it was a clear night with a full moon. Once he got up a fair distance, the view of the lights of Cache Creek was quite spectacular. However, as he entered a wooded area, the going became rough. He was constantly tripping over twigs and fallen trees. When a raccoon jumped out of a tree right in front of him it scared the living daylights out of him. He eventually found a small clearing and proceeded to lie down, using his backpack as a pillow. He kept his winter coat on, hoping that it would keep him warm enough.

Surprisingly, Randy slept pretty well that night, even though it was quite uncomfortable with all those twigs underneath him. It was very peaceful there and the day before had been very long. When he woke up his back was killing him, so it took him awhile to be able to stand up straight.

Even though he had been told that the businesses in Cache Creek would not be busy until May, Randy decided to give it a shot anyway. He figured that he was in town then and wasn't sure if he would get up that way the next month. He noticed it was only 8:00. That would give him some time to look around. He hoped his appearance would not work against him—he hadn't had a shave or a shower since leaving Prince George.

He applied at six different gas stations and five restaurants, but the answer was always the same. It was not the tourist season yet and wouldn't be for at least another month. After he received a negative response at the Husky Truck Stop he decided to give up. It was time to have lunch and then start thumbing a ride to Vancouver.

12

He made his way to the southern outskirts of town, which wasn't very far away, and put his thumb out. Two hours later a van pulled over. There were no windows on the back and it had a customized paint job. He could hear music blaring from inside.

He approached the van cautiously and when he got up close a young man in the passenger seat said, "Hey, dude, where are you heading?"

"Vancouver."

"Right on, man, that's where we're going! C'mon in!"

The sliding door along the side opened, and when Randy looked inside he noticed that there were two more young men in the back.

One of them said, "C'mon in, man."

When Randy climbed inside he noticed that all four men looked around his age. The back part of the van was completely carpeted. There wasn't anything he could sit on, so he made a stool out of his backpack.

The young man driving said, "Welcome aboard! My name is Chad and the guy beside me is Kirk. The two rowdies in the back are Greg and Kelly."

Randy said, "Pleased to meet you," and shook hands with all of them.

After they headed off, he commented how nicely the interior of their van was decorated and also noted that it had quite the sound system. He asked them if they were all from Vancouver and they all said yes.

He then asked if they were on vacation, and Kirk said, "Well actually, we went to Calgary on a business trip."

Greg said, "What he means is, we went there to sell the magic mushrooms we had stored in our place since last fall!"

Chad yelled out, "Way to go, Greg! How do we know this guy ain't no fucking narc!"

"Hey, don't worry about me! I would never lower myself to that level!" Randy reassured them.

Greg then said, "Good! In that case, do you want to smoke a joint?"

"Sure thing!" Randy said.

He went on to tell them he had lived in Calgary for two years. Chad asked him if he liked living there, and Randy said that he could take it or leave it.

Chad asked where he was living at present, and Randy said, "Right now, I'm not living anywhere. That will all change once I get to Vancouver."

Kirk asked Randy if he had a place lined up.

"Well, I will probably stay at the Salvation Army hostel until I can line up some temporary work," Randy replied.

Kelly said, "We all share this two-storey house, which also has a self-contained suite in the basement. Right now, nobody's living in it. It has everything, like your own kitchen and bathroom, but it's kinda small. Do you think you might be interested?"

Randy thought about it for a minute. Kelly offered him a beer, and of course Randy accepted. He said that he liked the offer, but he didn't think he could manage the rent until he started working.

Chad said, "Wait a minute! When was the last time you had a job?"

Randy told him, "I was laid off from my last job three months ago."

Chad asked how long he had worked there, and Randy replied, "I worked there off and on for over a year and I had another job in between."

Chad said, "Did you know that you can collect Unemployment Insurance?"

"No, I wasn't aware of that."

Kirk asked if he still had his separation slips from his last two employers. Randy asked, "You mean those pieces of paper that each of them gave me on my last day? Yes, I still have them. In both jobs they told me to hang on to them since they were very important, so I did."

Chad said, "So all you have to do is go to the nearest Canada Manpower office once you're in Vancouver and apply. It should only take about two weeks before you get your first cheque."

Randy tried to look out the window and admire the scenery, but that wasn't easy since the van had hardly any windows. Plus, he was sitting pretty low, making looking out the windshield difficult. This was especially frustrating since they had just passed the sign that read "Entering Scenic Fraser Canyon." Just beyond that a mileage sign indicated that Vancouver was only 258 kilometresm away. Randy thought to himself, "I'm almost there!"

Kirk was curious about Randy's last job. When he responded that he had been working on an oil rig, Kirk said, "Holy shit, man, you must have made damn good money!"

Randy said, "Yes, and unfortunately I squandered most of it."

"The amount you make on Unemployment Insurance is based on a percentage of your income. I'm not sure, but I think it's at least sixty percent. Even at that rate you'll still be living pretty good," Chad informed him.

"That suite in the basement is pretty cheap. If you take it you'll have it made. You will have all this money left over and won't even have to work for it!" Kirk said.

Randy said, "It sounds great, but I won't have enough money for my first month's rent!"

Greg said, "Jim Leung, the landlord—he's a pretty cool guy. He's quite easygoing. He'll let it slide for a couple weeks as long as you have enough money for a deposit or even a portion of the rent. Besides, if he says no, he'll just be flicking himself up the ass. There is an overabundance of rental space now since more people are leaving Vancouver than moving there. The way he sees it, it's better to get a portion of the month's rent than none at all."

Randy decided to accept their offer. Greg then handed everyone a beer so they could make a toast to their new downstairs neighbour. He wondered how they would explain themselves if they were ever pulled over by the police with having open beer cans in the vehicle.

Chad said, "You'll like the place, but I've got to warn you, we have a lot of parties on our floor and we can get pretty fucking wild!"

The four guys let out a simultaneous "Yeehaw!"

Kirk said to Randy, "Of course, you're always invited. We always have lots of booze, lots of drugs and lots of chicks—everything a man could ask for!"

At first Randy wondered what he was getting himself into. But then he figured, "What have I got to lose?"

After three hours on the road, Randy got his first glimpse of the Greater Vancouver area as they crossed the Port Mann Bridge. A short while later, he saw the sign he had been looking forward to seeing since leaving Dawson Creek—the sign that read "Entering City of Vancouver."

Chad said, "I'm not sure how familiar you are with Vancouver. We live only one block off Commercial Drive."

"That doesn't mean a damn thing to me. I've never been in Vancouver before in my whole life," Randy said.

"Commercial Drive has lots of shops, cafés, pubs—it's a real trendy place. Everything you need is within walking distance. We're not that far away from Hastings Street, where you can catch the bus that goes downtown," Chad said.

"In due time you'll get to know Vancouver. If there's anything you need to find, just let me know," added Greg.

Ten minutes after they exited the freeway, the van pulled up to a ramshackle two-storey house. Judging by the design of the house, Randy figured it must have been at least eighty years old.

"Well, this is it!" Kirk said.

"Welcome to the end of the road!" Randy said.

Chad said, "The house is in pretty good shape. It just needs to be painted."

Randy thought to himself, "He sure got that right, and it could use a few other things too."

Kelly took Randy around to the side of the house and showed him where the entrance to the basement suite was. He told Randy that he didn't have a key—he would have to wait until Jim Leung arrived before he could see inside. He invited him upstairs in the meantime.

Reaching the main floor entrance involved climbing a long flight of very rickety stairs. Randy was very careful of where he stepped, especially with carrying his heavily loaded backpack. This was made even more difficult by the fact that during the ride he had drunk four beers and they had passed a joint around three times. He was feeling pretty pie-eyed. Still, he was trying not to go head over heels when climbing the stairs.

Once inside, the first thing Randy noticed was that the living room reeked of marijuana. There was a huge Confederate flag pinned on the wall. Both the floor and the coffee table were littered with hash pipes, roach clips, beer cans, candy wrappers, you name it. The place looked like an absolute pigsty.

"So, is there a place to eat nearby?" asked Randy. "I'm starving!"

"We're going to order a pizza," Greg said. "If you want to chip in I'll order an extra one."

Randy agreed to go along with it.

Greg asked him what he liked in the way of toppings, and Randy said, "Anything but anchovies!"

Right after Greg ordered the pizzas, he called Jim Leung. Greg told him there was someone interested in the suite downstairs, and Jim said he would be there in an hour.

Greg offered Randy another beer, and Randy said, "Whoa there! If I am going to meet the landlord, I don't want to give him the impression that I'm some kind of drunk!"

Kelly said, "Oh, don't worry about him. As long as you pay the rent and don't destroy the place, he doesn't really give a shit. I think he inherited this house from his old man, so he doesn't have to worry about a mortgage or anything like that."

That the boys were not making the slightest effort to clean the place up attested to the fact that Jim cared only about the rent.

Randy said, "Okay, I'll have a beer."

When Greg opened the refrigerator door, Randy noticed that they had plenty of beer, but not much else.

He asked the boys where the nearest Canada Manpower office was, and Kirk told him it was twelve blocks west—on Broadway. Randy said he didn't want to stay up too late that night, since he wanted to be there first thing the next morning.

Kirk said, "Jeez, dude, you must have been on the road too long! If you go there tomorrow, you'll have one hell of a long wait!"

Randy asked, "And why is that?"

Chad said, "Because tomorrow is Sunday! Today is Saturday!"

As they all laughed their heads off, Randy looked at the calendar on his cigarette pack and exclaimed, "By golly, it is!"

An hour later there was a knock at the back door. It was Jim Leung. When the door was opened, Randy noticed that there were only two steps leading to the alley. He made a note that whenever he came up there in the future, he would use the back door. Jim asked him if he was the one interested in the suite, and Randy told him yes.

Jim said, "Okay, come with me. I'll take you through it."

The grand tour of the suite only took a minute—everything was all in one room except for the bathroom. Jim pointed out that it contained all of the basic necessities. The bed looked fairly new and there was even a microwave oven.

Randy said he would take the place and Jim responded, "Good. Now, Greg told me you will soon be receiving U.I. Is there anything you can give me right now?"

Randy said that he could give him seventy-five dollars.

Jim said, "That will be all right, as long as you can give me the balance of the rent plus the damage deposit as soon as you receive your first U.I. cheque."

The following Monday, Randy walked down to the Canada Manpower office and filled out all of the necessary forms. He spent the next two weeks looking for work, but the search was completely fruitless. He couldn't even find any temporary work. Eventually his first U.I. cheque came. He gave Jim the remainder of what he owed and he still had a substantial amount left. That night he decided to celebrate by paying a visit to the neighbourhood pub down the street. Toasting his new-found wealth, he kept thinking to himself, "Man, life doesn't get any better than this!"

One year later

It was 1983. Randy was twenty-one and still on the federal government payroll. In other words, he hadn't found a job. Even so, he was far from destitute. The fact that his last job had been so lucrative sure had helped. He was still in the same place and since the rent was very reasonable, it meant he had more money for himself. In July of last year he had bought a car. It was a 1971 Ford LTD and it was in much better condition than his last car. He had also bought a portable colour TV.

In the past year he hadn't been completely unemployed. Shortly after he had bought his car, he got a job picking raspberries on a farm near Abbotsford. He was paid in cash so he hadn't reported it on his U.I. report card. While he was working there, he camped out on the farm and only went back to Vancouver on weekends. In early August of last year, he had gone to Osoyoos for three weeks. Brad, his old friend from Granby, had been there working at his aunt and uncle's orchard. He gave Randy a job picking peaches (also paid in cash). He went up there again in late September when the pears were ready for harvesting. Randy was hoping that Bill, Brad's brother, would be there as well, but he had been staying with relatives in Oporto, Portugal.

One of the main things that Randy and Brad liked about working in the orchard was that their fellow pickers, most of them from Quebec, really liked to party. They had many memorable evenings. Another bonus was that the orchard was right on Osoyoos Lake, and on most evenings the pickers liked to go skinny-dipping. That applied to both the men and the women. Randy and Brad were amazed at how uninhibited they were. Unfortunately, all of the women pickers had boyfriends so all they could do was look. Even so, they didn't mind. One thing that did bother them though, was that they never understood what the other pickers were saying. Despite the fact that both of them were bilingual, neither of them spoke French. Randy was hoping at least one of them would speak Greek. Brad and his uncle gave them a taste of their own medicine by always conversing in Portuguese.

Right after Randy had returned from his first trip to Osoyoos he got a pleasant surprise. Gary had stopped in when he was passing through Vancouver. He had been in Granby visiting his parents and was returning to California where he attended university. It was the first time Randy had seen him since he had visited Calgary four years ago. He was amazed how far Gary had gone since they had last met.

When Gary started at Granby Senior Secondary School he began to excel in basketball. Randy had always known that he was good at the game, but once he got to senior high school, his skill level had really taken off. In his senior year (the year after he had last seen Randy) his team had gone to the provincial senior boys' high school basketball championship tournament. Granby Senior Secondary finished in eighth place and Gary had led the team in scoring. He was chosen as the team's most valuable player. As a result, he received a basketball scholarship to California State University, Fullerton campus. He was majoring in electrical engineering, and when Randy saw him, he was about to begin his third year. Randy was quite blown away by all of this and he told Gary that he was really proud of him.

There was, however, one thing that had concerned Randy. He was worried that when they were kids he had led Gary astray with all of the trouble they had gotten into. Gary assured him that he had never inspired him to pursue a life of crime. In fact, he admitted that they'd had a lot of fun. He told Randy that he had brought some excitement into his life, which likely would never have happened if they had never become friends.

Randy jokingly commented that he had always thought that he would follow in his old man's footsteps and work for the C.N.R.

Gary responded by saying, "Are you kidding? Not a chance!"

"Well, that's good, because their lumber cars are a bitch to ride on!"

"Did you hear that Kees Vandelaar was accepted into law school at York University two years ago?" Gary asked.

"No kidding?" Randy said with surprise. "Man, he must be doing quite well for himself!"

When Gary left, Randy had wished him well. Afterward he started questioning his own destiny in relation to where his friends were heading. Brad would someday take over the family orchard and when Bill returned from Portugal in December, he was going to start York University in January. Randy kept thinking, "They're all doing well and here I am, an unemployed bum with a grade nine education!" Despite these thoughts, he wasn't inspired to make any changes in his life.

Since last summer Randy hadn't done much of anything. Whenever he had been in Vancouver last summer, he had spent most of his time at the beach—Wreck Beach. In the fall and winter, he had sometimes taken the bus downtown or driven to Stanley Park. The rest of the time he spent sitting in his suite watching TV and drinking beer. Trying to find a job had been pretty much a hopeless case—there were very few jobs available. The house he was living in was party central. Just about every week the boys upstairs threw a wild party. There was always a really large crowd and lots of booze and drugs. Quite often members of the Hell's Angels had been in attendance, and on several occasions there had been hookers in the crowd. Whenever they were, there Randy had taken advantage of the situation and had invited one of them down into his suite so they could have a party of their own. The house had become quite well known to the police. On at least two occasions they had warned Jim Leung that they would shut the place down. Luckily, they never followed through. Whenever Randy attended the parties, he usually stayed until around three or four in the morning and then slept in until noon.

As his first anniversary as a Vancouverite approached, he started receiving notices in his Unemployment Insurance statements informing him that his claim was soon to expire. At first he didn't pay that much attention to them, but when he received one that had the banner headline "Final Notice," he figured that he had better investigate.

When he brought this up with the counsellor at the Canada Manpower office, she seemed kind of amused.

"Did you actually think that you could stay on U.I. permanently? A claim lasts a maximum of one year!"

Randy seemed quite surprised and then said, "Then what?"

The counsellor said, "Well, you have basically three options. One, you can find a job. Two, you can go back to school or take a trades training course. Then there is the third option."

Randy, in suspense by then, asked, "What is that?"

"Welfare."

Randy said, "I see, I should have expected that. After all, I briefly received welfare when I lived in Saskatoon. So, how much is it now?"

The counsellor told him, "For a single male—three hundred and seventy-five dollars a month."

"Are you out of your mind? That's less than what I made in Saskatchewan three years ago!" Randy said incredulously.

She pointed out to him that over the past few years there had been an influx of people from other parts of Canada coming there looking for work and most of them ended up staying, job or no job. As a result, the provincial welfare budget had gone through the roof. Most people who were unemployed figured that if they were going to be out of work, they might as well be in British Columbia since the climate was better. The most likely reason they were more generous with welfare in Saskatchewan was that if someone was living there and not working, it was highly unlikely that he or she would remain there. In addition, the low amount served as a deterrent to staying on welfare for a long period of time. It was designed to encourage people to do something with their lives. She suggested that he put in more of an effort to find a job, or else consider moving to another province.

Randy said, "No thanks, I would rather stay here. I'll give it my best shot."

He decided he had better make a last-ditch effort to find a job. He figured the monthly amount for welfare was barely enough to live on. The odds were definitely not in his favour. There wasn't even a full page of "Help Wanted" ads in the *Vancouver Sun* and there weren't very many ads on the job board at the Canada Manpower office. Like a fool, he fell for a particular ad in the *Sun* that read "Busy executive looking for someone to learn his business and assist in its growth, no experience necessary." When he called, the man on the phone told him to meet him in meeting room "D" at the Sheraton Hotel downtown that Thursday. As it turned out, the man was trying to recruit new Amway distributors. When Randy realized that, he stormed out of the room, swearing his head off. On his way home all he kept thinking was, "What a waste of time! It'll be a cold day in hell before I hustle that garbage!"

It eventually dawned on Randy that he had two years of experience working in a feed mill. He remembered noticing there were several large feed manufacturing facilities near Abbotsford when he had the raspberry-picking job last summer. He went to the nearest branch of the Vancouver Public Library and looked them up in the Abbotsford telephone directory. Sure enough, there were at least four mills of major significance. He then checked out the Chilliwack telephone directory and found one major mill there as well. The next day he drove out to Abbotsford and applied at all four of the mills there, then drove on to apply at the one in Chilliwack. None of the places gave Randy any encouragement that they would be hiring anytime soon but, as they always said, they would keep his application on file for three months. He often wondered if they really meant that. While he was in both cities he also inquired at the Farm Labour Pool offices, hoping to find some kind of farm work. That didn't go over very well, since he was not from a farm, he had never worked with livestock (living, that is) and he had never driven a tractor.

For the next two weeks he desperately tried to find work, but nothing seemed to go right. With the high interest rates, the construction industry was virtually nonexistent. He tried every stevedoring company on the waterfront, hoping to find a longshoreman job. He even went out to Steveston and applied at all of the salmon canneries. He inquired at almost every industry he could think of, but his search was completely fruitless. After two weeks he received his final U.I. cheque. The U.I. well had finally dried up.

The following week he went down to the nearest Social Services office and applied for social assistance. He was assigned a social worker, who gave him all of the necessary forms to fill out. She also gave him a form that the landlord had to fill out. Randy was thinking, "Oh great! I have to get Jim Leung to fill this out. He'll be pleased about that!"

Later that day he went over to Jim Leung's house and asked him to fill out the landlord's form. He returned it to the Social Services office the following day. The social worker told him he would receive his first cheque on the last Wednesday of the month (three weeks from then). After he returning home, he kept thinking, "Oh well, the honeymoon's over!"

One year later

Another year had passed, and nothing much had changed. Randy still didn't have a job and there were very few prospects on the horizon. The hardest thing for Randy was adjusting to having less income each month, which involved having to give up certain luxuries. For Randy that meant buying less beer and cutting back on cigarettes from one pack to a half a pack a day. But perhaps the greatest sacrifice he had to make was selling his car. After being on welfare for three months, he had found he could no longer afford the insurance payments. To add insult to injury, he had to declare the amount he received from selling the car and it was deducted from his welfare cheque.

The last summer had been the same as the previous one. He had gone to work picking raspberries on the same farm near Abbotsford, and afterward he had gone to work on the orchard run by Bill and Brad's aunt and uncle. The only differences were that he had to take the bus to each of those destinations and he had to declare every dollar he made to Social Services. When they had made the necessary deductions, he hadn't been that much further ahead. It seemed as though Social Services wanted to know his every move, and that was something Randy was not too thrilled about.

In June, Mark came down to Vancouver to see Randy. He was eighteen by then and had been living in Prince George for over a year. This was the first time Randy had seen him since his visit to Edmonton three years ago. As with Randy, there had been a lot of changes in Mark's life during that time.

Mark had dropped out of high school after one semester of grade eleven. At first he'd tried to get a job at the lumber mill in Granby, but they weren't hiring. He had then moved to Prince George, and managed to land a job at a lumber mill there. Randy was quite surprised to learn which mill it was, because ten months previously he had tried to get a job there himself. He asked Mark how he he'd been able to get work there. Mark said that he had learned about the company from his best friend Pete McGowan. Pete's uncle had been the plant manager and Pete figured his uncle could pull some strings for him. He put in a good word to his uncle about Mark and as a result he had been hired. Randy commented that Mark had been really lucky and he should be counting his blessings that he had a job, period. Randy wished he could be so lucky. Mark pointed out that the trick to finding a job amounted not to what you know, but who you know. There were jobs out there, but you needed to have the right connections.

As for things on the home front, nothing had changed one damn bit. Their mom was still married to that lazy pig William. Randy shook his head in disbelief.

Mark commented, "That useless tit wouldn't know what work was if it jumped up and hit him in the face!"

Mark was glad that he'd found a job in a city other than Granby—he couldn't stand being anywhere near the guy anymore. That practically answered Randy's next question. At first he had thought it was strange that Mark would drop out of high school with only three semesters left to go, but then Randy could see his point. Mark explained that he wasn't worried about finishing high school for the present. He was going to see how the job at the lumber mill went, and then he would consider picking up his remaining credits at the local community college.

13

Mark stayed with Randy for a week. Just before leaving, he told Randy that he would keep his ears open to any job possibilities that might come up at the mill; if he heard of any openings he would put in a good word for him. Randy told him that he greatly appreciated that and he wished Mark all the best with the job and his future endeavours. He also said he would make a point to try and get up to Prince George sometime in the near future. With that, they both said goodbye.

As July approached, Randy decided that it was not worth pursuing the fruit harvesting jobs he had held the previous two summers. With the amount that welfare deducted from each job he was no further ahead in the end, and besides, he had to pay all of his travel expenses. When he stayed in Osoyoos he spent most of his money on beer anyway. Overall he was becoming increasingly lazy; he rarely got up before 10 a.m. His social worker had really been getting on his case. She was constantly getting after him to go back to school or take some kind of training course. She kept telling him that he was throwing his life away; he should do something with his life while he was still young. That had never appealed to Randy. He had never liked school or thought of himself as a good student. Besides, he didn't know what he would take, since he didn't really know what he wanted to do with his life.

Since moving into his place, he had been puzzled about the guys upstairs. In the two years he had lived there, he had never really gotten to know them on a personal basis, even though he had partied with them on many occasions. One thing he had never learned about them was what they did for a living or for that matter, it they even worked at all. It seemed as though they were always home except for when they went out at night. Yet their money had to come from somewhere because whenever they had parties, they always went all out. There was always plenty of alcohol and drugs for everybody. They also had a lot of nice things in their place. They had a brand new top-of-the-line stereo system with a huge record collection and a 27-inch floor-model television set with the full cable package. Randy would have given anything to be able to have any of those things.

Another thing Randy found strange was the recent acquisition of a fifth person. Three months ago some guy named Doug had moved in. He couldn't figure out where the guy slept, since the upstairs had only four bedrooms. Even more bizarre was the way in which Chad introduced him. Randy had gone upstairs for a visit and Doug was sitting at the kitchen table.

Chad said, "Randy, this is Doug. He's moving in with us. This guy is one bad-ass motherfucker! Whatever you do, don't fuck with him!"

Randy gave Chad a strange look and said to Doug, "Pleased to meet you."

It got even stranger. As it turned out, Doug was only seventeen and he had been in and out of Juvenile Hall regularly since he was fourteen. In fact, he had just been released from the Willingdon Road Youth Detention Centre after serving six months. Since all of the other guys were over nineteen they were able to supply him with booze, which Doug most likely appreciated. What Randy noticed the most about him was that he had a really cocky, know-it-all attitude that rubbed him the wrong way. He couldn't figure out for the life of him why the guys would want to have him around in the first place.

One day Randy decided to pay them a visit. Even though it was early afternoon they offered him beer. It was then that Randy decided to speak up.

He said to them, "I was wondering, where do you guys work?" They stared at him blankly, and he continued, "I mean, what exactly do you guys do for a living?"

Doug began to laugh, and Randy asked, "Did I say something funny?" He continued laughing and Randy added, "Look, I know you wouldn't be able to manage this whole house on welfare even with five of you. There must be some other way you earn income."

Greg spoke up then. "You're a nosy son-of-a-bitch, aren't you?"

"No, I'm just curious, that's all. You guys all seem to be living pretty good."

Doug continued to laugh his head off, and when he regained his composure he said, "Oh Randy, you are so funny! Did you realize that?"

"Is that so? Since when did I become a goddamn comedian?"

Doug said to the other guys, "What do you think, boys? Should he come along with us tonight?"

The four of them talked among themselves for the next couple minutes, and then Kelly said, "Sure, why not!"

Doug then said to Randy, "Okay, be up here at 9:00 tonight. You'll get to see us at work. Just don't ask any questions, got it?"

"Sure, I'll be here."

Randy had a bad feeling about this. He didn't really know what to expect, but still, he decided to see for himself. He went upstairs right at 9:00.

Doug said, "Good, you showed up. All right boys, let's go!"

As they were leaving, Randy was tempted to ask Doug, "Who the hell appointed you king shit of turd mountain?"

After piling into the van, they spent the next hour driving around the south part of Vancouver. They eventually ended up in the Kerrisdale district, and Chad began driving slowly down the residential streets. They covered at least six blocks, carefully examining each house they passed by. Eventually Chad turned down an alley and parked in front of a garage.

"Okay, Greg you cover the front, Kelly you cover the back, Chad and Kirk follow me. Randy, you stay here and watch to see if anyone's coming. Here, get in the driver's seat. If anyone comes by and asks what you're doing just tell them you're waiting for a friend. C'mon guys, let's move!" Doug ordered.

Randy couldn't believe his ears. He was thinking, "Who the hell does that little punk think he is, bossing us around like that?" He was seriously tempted to tell Doug off.

About ten minutes later the boys returned. When the back door opened, Randy was astonished. Chad was carrying a television set and Doug and Kirk were carrying a stereo system. In addition, Greg had a stack of records. Chad told Randy to get out of the driver's seat. When Chad climbed in they took off.

As Randy looked over the merchandise, he asked, "Where did you get this?"

Doug gave him a disgusted look and said, "Are you stupid or something? The fucking tooth fairy gave it to us! Where the fuck do you think it came from, dipshit? Now I suggest you keep your fucking mouth shut! You're starting to piss me off!"

They drove for about six blocks and then they parked in another alley.

Doug said, "All right guys, same procedure. Randy, you stay here. Let's move it!"

After the guys left, it really started to sink in with Randy that they made their "living" by breaking into people's houses! Randy didn't quite know what to make of it, but for the time being, he figured he had just better play it cool.

A few minutes later they returned with more "loot," which again consisted of a television set and stereo equipment. This time, however, they had also stolen some jewellery and even an IBM computer! They repeated this procedure one more time at a house six blocks away and then decided to call it a night. They told Randy that they would be going out again the day after tomorrow and they wanted him to come along.

Back home, Randy tried to come to terms with the fact that the guys upstairs were criminals. He didn't really know how to respond to the fact that they wanted him to participate. The funny thing was that he wasn't reacting in a way he expected a normal person would if he or she had encountered this type of situation. Sure, what they were doing was illegal, but Randy's attitude seemed to fall more into the category of "so what" rather than "they must be stopped." The more he thought about it, the more he realized that, while he was growing up, he had never really been taught the difference between right and wrong. He hardly, if ever, had any sense of morality. He remembered the times he had shoplifted at various stores in Granby. He had never felt any remorse about it, and the thought had never crossed his mind that what he was doing was wrong. When he considered his troubled childhood and adolescence, he could understand why he didn't have much of a conscience. Another way he looked at it was that once out on his own, he had been determined to make it in society the legitimate way, but society had let him down.

One other thing he realized was that even if he did have any morals, reporting those guys to the police would be completely out of the question. He would most likely have to go into hiding for the rest of his life because Doug would probably hunt him down to the ends of the earth.

Two nights later he went upstairs precisely at 9:00. The guys were waiting for him. They had spent the previous day selling some of stolen merchandise at various pawnshops around town. They all piled into the van and headed for the Point Grey district. There were many upscale homes in that area, and that meant greater chances of obtaining big-ticket items. Doug had a keen sense of detecting the houses that had alarm systems and those that didn't. Again Randy was appointed the lookout. They knocked off four houses, yielding another stash of televisions, stereos, jewellery and even some cash.

After they finished "work" for the night, they decided to head to

Spanish Banks beach. They had a cooler of beer in the back and decided to throw an impromptu party. It was after midnight and the beach was completely deserted. Randy wandered down to the water by himself, but he was close enough to overhear Doug talking to Kirk.

Doug said, "That Randy guy—he doesn't seem all that bright."

Randy marched right over to where Doug was standing and shouted out, "I heard that! So you think I'm not very bright, eh?"

"Jeez, you got pretty good hearing!" Doug said.

"Look, you don't even know me! I'm a hell of a lot smarter than you think I am!"

"Hey, ain't I entitled to my opinion? I have a right to my opinion and my opinion is—you have stupid written all over your face!"

"I didn't appreciate that!"

"What are you going to do about it?" Doug asked.

"I'm going to kick your ass!"

Randy flung off his jacket and put up his dukes to challenge him. Doug swung his right leg and nailed Randy in the side with a martial arts sidekick. Then, using his other leg, he nailed Randy in the forehead with a kung-fu kick. He went flying to the ground. As he lay there face down in the sand moaning, Doug went up to him and jeered, "Now, if I say you ain't too bright, then that means you ain't too bright! What I say goes, got it? Now you better shape up."

After that incident, he lost interest in being part of the boys' crime wave. He told them straight out that he didn't give a shit what they did, but they could count him out. Over the next several days he was quite on edge. He even had trouble sleeping at night. He was worried that Doug was trying to convince the other guys that he knew too much and therefore must be done in. At times he was even afraid to leave his place.

Two weeks after the incident, Greg paid Randy a visit. He tried to talk Randy into coming back with them. Greg told him that he and the other guys had put in a good word for him with Doug, and they had convinced him that Randy should join them again. Randy finally spoke up and asked him why they kept letting Doug call the shots all the time. Greg pointed out that Doug was a pro and that he knew what he was doing. Greg made it very clear that all of them had gone out on a limb for him, so the least he could do was to take them up on the offer. Greg was really happy when Randy agreed to go along with it.

As they shook hands, Greg said, "Welcome back to the team!"

Over the next two months, Randy became a willing participant. They were all operating like a well-oiled machine. Their hand signals and timing were becoming very efficient, and not once did they even come close to being caught. The guys eventually decided to move on to bigger and better things. They started breaking into businesses that were closed. One night Doug suggested that they knock off a wholesale distributor of records and cassettes. He claimed that he knew the layout of the security system and where the safe was. He also pointed out that records and cassettes fetched a big price on the black market.

They arrived at the warehouse around 2 a.m. and parked in the alley. They had brought a ladder so they could climb in through one of the upper back windows. Doug went first, and when he reached the window he pried it open with a screwdriver and then tied a rope around the windowsill. He motioned for everyone else to follow him just before he scaled down the rope inside. Randy brought up the rear, and as he was scaling down the rope he let go prematurely. He landed on a table, slipped and fell onto the floor, setting off the alarm.

Doug yelled out, "Let's get out of here!"

They all quickly climbed up the rope and down the ladder. Doug brought up the rear, untying the rope before he climbed down the ladder. All they had managed to take was eight cassettes.

Back at the house, Randy tried to tell Doug he was sorry, but Doug went ballistic. He yelled out, "You fucking retard! You can't do anything right! I don't know why I let these guys talk me into letting you back in the group! You're nothing but a fucked-up, retarded, useless piece of shit!"

Randy yelled back, "Now see here! That's the only time I made a mistake! It was an accident, okay? That doesn't give you the goddamn right to talk to me like that!"

"I can talk to you any way I want, and there ain't a fucking thing you can do about it!" Doug jeered.

Randy was ready for Doug this time. He knew some karate himself and was determined to beat him at his own game.

He gave Doug a hard shove and said, "C'mon, let's go!"

He put up his arms in a martial arts stand-off stance and went to make a move on Doug, but he was just too quick for him. Besides, Doug had a lot more experience in martial arts. He nailed Randy with several kung-fu kicks to the head and chest and once he had Randy on the ground, he grabbed his hair and yanked his head back. Then, using his other hand, he pulled out his switchblade and put it right up to Randy's throat.

"You remember what Chad said when you first saw me? What did he say, huh? You got a short memory! In case you forgot, he said I'm a bad-ass motherfucker and then he said don't fuck with me. Why did you think he said that, huh? Did you think he was just pulling your leg? There's a reason why he said that and from now on you had better listen to him! I can cut your throat open if I want to. I don't give a fuck! If you even try to run away from us I'll find you and when I do, I'll cut you into a million pieces, got it?"

He loosened his grip and drove Randy's head onto the floor. As he walked away, he said, "Get this useless fucking idiot out of my sight!"

After that, Randy realized just how crazy Doug was. He didn't know what to think and moving out was out of the question. He knew what Doug was capable of doing, so he found himself looking over his shoulder practically all the time. He was losing a lot of sleep over it. For example, one day Randy stepped out of his suite and Doug was there, sitting on the back steps.

He got up, approached Randy and yelled out, "Where the fuck do you think you're going?"

Randy said, "I'm going to the grocery store. I gotta eat!"

Doug glared at Randy and said, "You better not be too long or I'll come looking for you!"

Randy realized there was no way out for him, so he figured that the best thing to do was just play it cool and do his best to cooperate. He thought that if he could save more of the money he received as his "cut" when they sold the stolen merchandise, he could buy a one-way plane ticket to the Bahamas.

One evening when the guys were having one of their many parties, a group of Hell's Angels were in attendance, as was often the case. One particular biker named Duke had been talking to Chad most of the evening. At one point, Chad asked Randy to accompany him and Duke to one of the rooms upstairs. When they entered the room it was just the three of them.

Randy asked, "What are we doing?"

Chad asked Duke to close the door. Randy was getting kind of nervous by then.

Chad said, "Randy, I think it's time you got yourself a heater."

Duke placed a metal suitcase on the dresser and opened it. Inside was a collection of handguns.

Chad told Randy, "Take your pick."

Randy said to Duke, "Wow, where did you get these?"

Duke gave him a dirty look and said, "That's none of your business!"

There was a fairly diverse selection of guns to choose from. There was everything from a Colt .45 to a .44 Magnum. He asked how much the .38 Special cost. Duke told him that he would sell it to him for three hundred dollars. Bullets were ten dollars each. Randy said that he was interested in buying the .38 Special and three bullets. He went down to his suite and took three hundred and thirty dollars from his secret stash. Returning to the room upstairs, he paid Duke. As Duke handed the gun over to him, he told him to be very careful with it. The trigger was very sensitive; he wanted to make sure he didn't accidentally shoot one of his friends.

He said to Randy, "Remember, it is only to be used to scare people. You don't want to end up with a murder rap!"

Randy said, "It's been a pleasure doing business with you!"

With Randy's newest acquisition, the boys wanted to move on to bigger (but not necessarily better) things. They devised a plan whereby, using Randy as the hold-up man, they would rob various businesses. The plan would be as follows: earlier on in the day, Doug, Greg or Kelly would check out a certain business — for example, a corner store. They would examine the layout and check to see if the place had any surveillance cameras. Then, later in the evening, Randy would enter the store and perform the robbery. Doug figured he would have an easy time persuading Randy to go along with this since he believed that he had him brainwashed by then.

Doug's prediction turned out to be bang-on. The boys decided to throw a party in Randy's honour three days after he purchased the handgun. They got him good and drunk (as well as stoned) and managed to sweet-talk him into joining them the next night. Their planned target was a corner store on Fraser Street in the south part of Vancouver.

When they arrived at that store the following evening, Chad drove the van around to the back and parked in the alley. Doug showed Randy a diagram of the store's layout and told him the only way in and out was through the front door. Randy was quite nervous, but the boys assured him that they would keep watch and be there waiting for him.

Randy made his way to the front door and just before entering he put on his balaclava. He then burst into the store, pointed the gun at the clerk and demanded that he put all the money into a paper bag. The clerk quickly complied. Randy yelled at him to hurry up and when he said he didn't have any more money, Randy grabbed the bag, turned and ran out the door. He ran as fast as he could around to the back and into the van. Chad quickly sped away and for the next half hour drove like a maniac through the side streets of South Vancouver, hoping to throw the police off their trail. After that, they drove straight home. All the time they were in the van, Randy never once looked inside the bag to see how much money he had obtained.

Back at the house, Randy looked inside the bag and realized that he had stolen over five hundred dollars! For the first time, Doug actually complimented Randy on his efforts.

Doug said to him, "You know what? I take back all those things I said to you. You're cool, man. You did an excellent job tonight!"

Three nights later, they made a repeat performance at a corner store in North Burnaby. Four nights after that they knocked off a convenience store in Surrey. In both instances, everything went off without a hitch. With each robbery Randy was gaining more confidence. What was really scary, though, was that each time he committed a robbery, it gave him an adrenaline rush. Judging by the way he acted after each hold-up, it seemed to be going to his head. None of the other guys were complaining, though. In fact, they were delighted.

Four days later, Doug called everyone to a meeting in the living room. He announced that the next target would be the Mr. Submarine Shop on West Broadway. When he had gone there the night before, there was only one clerk on duty. The store stayed open until eleven and there was a door that led to the back alley.

That evening they arrived at the Mr. Submarine shop around 10:30. As usual, Chad parked in the alley. Randy got out of the van, put on his balaclava and snuck in through the back door.

He went up to the clerk, pointed the gun in her face and yelled out, "All right, give me all your money and put it in this bag," as he threw a paper bag on the counter. She quickly opened the till and started putting the money in the bag. Her hands were trembling like crazy and she was fumbling.

Randy yelled out, "C'mon, don't fuck with me! Move it!"

The clerk, almost crying, said, "Okay, okay!"

Randy nervously looked at the front door every few seconds, hoping no one would come in. Fortunately, there were no customers in the place.

When the clerk put the last bill in the bag, she cried out, "That's all there is, I swear to god!"

Randy turned to leave, but kept the gun pointed at her.

He yelled out, "Don't try any funny stuff! Just turn around and don't look!" and he bolted out the back door.

When he got outside, he was shocked to discover that the van was gone! He yelled out, "Where the hell are those guys?"

He turned left and ran down the alley to the nearest side street. He looked down the street both ways and still didn't see any sign of the van. Then he heard sirens. He realized at that point that the shop must have had a silent alarm. He turned and ran down the alley the other way, but before he could reach the next street, a police car with its lights and siren going pulled up in front of the alleyway.

"Oh, shit," yelled Randy, as he turned and ran in the opposite direction.

Another police car turned into the alley from the other end and he realized he was boxed in. He didn't know where to run then.

Police officers from both cars got out and came toward him with their guns drawn.

One of the officers yelled out, "Don't move, and keep your hands in the air where I can see them."

Randy was petrified and did not move a muscle. When the police officers got right up to him, they searched him and found his handgun in the inside pocket of his jacket. They found his balaclava in one of his other pockets. The bag containing the stolen money was lying on the ground. One of the policemen picked it up and looked inside.

When he noticed the large amount of money, he said, "You're under arrest!"

One of the other officers handcuffed him, read him his rights and stuffed him in the back seat of his squad car. Throughout all this, Randy kept thinking, "They deserted me! Those dirty bastards deserted me!"

He was taken to police headquarters, where he spent the night in a holding cell. The following morning, when it was determined that he didn't have the money to post bail, he was transferred to the Vancouver Remand Centre. His trial would be held in one month. In the meantime he was appointed a lawyer through Legal Aid.

Over the course of the next month, he met on several occasions with his lawyer. He made it very clear to Randy that the evidence against him was overwhelming and his best option was to plead guilty. He had been caught red-handed and that would definitely not stand up in court in his favour. As for the clerk, even though she hadn't seen his face she would still be able to identify him by his eye colour, his height and what he had been wearing. In addition, someone living across the alley from the shop had seen him running out the back door. The attorney was very blunt with him, telling him that he didn't stand much of a chance. Randy tried to explain to him that he hadn't acted alone, that the five guys who lived upstairs from him were in on it too. They were supposed to have been waiting for him in a van out behind the Mr. Submarine shop. The lawyer told him that he was the only one seen at the crime scene, and the witness claimed that she had never seen a van.

Randy was determined that if he was going down, the other guys were going down as well. He gave the lawyer his address and asked him to give it to the police. He told him to let them know that there were drugs and stolen merchandise all over the place. He wanted the cops to try and make them confess to being in on the robbery. The lawyer told Randy that that would be highly unlikely. The guys would deny any involvement in the robbery, and, with no evidence linking them to the crime, there was nothing the cops could do. Randy had to accept the fact that he had been played for a fool and now he must face the consequences.

When he had his day in court, he did what the lawyer recommended and pleaded guilty. He knew that he had no chance of beating the charge so a lengthy trial would just be a waste of time. The judge sentenced him to two years in prison to be served at a provincial correctional facility. In B.C. that meant only one place—Oakalla Prison.

14

The day after his conviction, Randy was transferred from the Remand Centre to Oakalla. The ride there seemed like the longest ride of his life. As they approached the prison, the building looked like a castle on the outside, but he knew it was anything but that on the inside. The main building spread out in four directions and had one guard tower in the centre.

Once they were on the prison grounds, Randy (along with five other men being transferred at the same time) was taken inside, had all his information processed, was fingerprinted, strip-searched and ordered to take a shower. Next, he was issued his prison uniform and had his mug shot taken. Two guards ordered him and the others to follow them. They were being escorted to their cells.

The first thing he noticed when he entered the cell block was the smell. It stunk to high heaven in there, as though the place hadn't been cleaned in ages. The block was four tiers high and the cells were accessed via narrow catwalks. As he walked passed the cells he couldn't believe how small they were, and yet there were four men to each one.

Once he and the others were in full view of the other prisoners they all started letting out howls and catcalls.

Several different men yelled out, "Here comes fresh meat!"

Randy actually had a good idea of what to expect in this place. When he was in the Pre-Trial Centre his cellmate had filled him in on what Oakalla was like. He had been there for six months two years ago, and he described the place as the closest thing to hell on earth. He told a number of horror stories about his time there. He'd had to endure it for six months, for Randy it would be four times that much hell. He had also given Randy some tips on how best to survive there.

The most important tip was never, never to back down from a fight, no matter how big the other guy was. Standing up to him shows that you have guts, and that gets you respect even if it means getting the living shit kicked out of you. If you back down you will be labelled a coward, and everyone will be after you. Since prisoners do not have any rights, they will jump at the opportunity to have power over someone if they know they can get away with it. Any feeling of domination is like a tonic for them. As for the guards, forget about them protecting you—they don't give a shit. They are only worried about covering their own asses. Perhaps the best advice he had given Randy was to not take any shit from anybody. Along with that, he also warned him to watch his back at all times and above all, don't trust anyone.

After they walked down the corridor a little ways, they stopped in front of a cell and the guard yelled out a six-digit number.

Randy didn't pay that much attention to him, but then the guard yelled out, "Watson! That's your number, goddamn it! Get your ass over here now!"

Randy walked up to the guard, who pointed to the number on Randy's shirt and screamed out, "Now, you better remember that number! Whenever I call you, I want you to answer me immediately! Do I make myself clear?"

"Yes," Randy said.

The guard pointed to the cell and said, "This is your cell. Dinner is at 6:00 and lights out is at 10:00."

There were two double-decker bunks in the cell. Two men were in there already. After the guard slammed the door behind him, Randy sat down on one of the lower bunks. Almost immediately, one of the other men went up to Randy and said, "Who the fuck said you can take that bunk?"

Randy started to tell him that it didn't look occupied, and the man butted in and said, "Did I say you can have that bed? Now I'm asking you again—who said you can have that bed?"

Randy got in the guy's face and yelled out, "I did!"

Randy started to turn away, but the man grabbed his arm and whirled him around, shouting, "Hey! I'm talking to you, boy! There's an admission fee here!"

"I ain't got no money—they took it all. Besides, I already paid my debt to society."

"You got a real smart mouth, don't you, boy?"

"What's it to you?"

The man said, "Are you getting lippy with me, boy? I oughta ram that smart mouth of yours out the other side of your face!"

"Oh yeah? You and who's army?"

At that point he invited Randy to a fight.

Randy put up his dukes and said, "Okay, let's go!"

Randy made the first move, delivering a right hook and nailing the man in the jaw. He responded with a left hook that nailed Randy in the eye. What followed was an exchange of vicious upper cuts that lasted several minutes. Randy managed to grab the man by his shirt and fling him into the cell door. Before he had a chance to get in another punch, the guy put him in a headlock and using his free hand, started pummelling Randy repeatedly in the face. He somehow managed to punch the man in the balls, which forced him to break the hold. Randy then unleashed a flurry of upper cuts, which, for a brief while, had the man reeling. The man then gave him a karate kick in the side and head-butted him. Randy received several hard shots in the stomach. From there the guy grabbed him by the head and flipped him over. Once he had him on the ground, the man sat on top of him and, as he raised his fist in the air, Randy thought he was a goner. But instead of punching him, the man smiled, flashing a partially toothless grin. He got off of Randy and proceeded to help him up.

He then said, "Congratulations, you passed."

They were both quite a bloody mess.

The man shook hands with Randy and said, "Welcome to the club! My name is Bailey," then, pointing to the other prisoner, he added, "and this here is Carruthers."

"Hello, my name is Randy."

Bailey said, "Hey, there are no first names here—first names don't mean a damn thing! That number on your chest—to the guards, that's all you are to them."

Randy and his cellmates exchanged stories about why they were there. He told them he was in for armed robbery. Bailey was in for stealing cars and Carruthers for embezzlement. Bailey spoke of a fourth man in their cell named Thor (short for Thorson). The reason he wasn't there at the moment was because he was on kitchen detail. Incidentally, he was serving time for aggravated assault. Bailey complimented Randy on the way he had stood up to him. He asked him where he had learned to fight like that. Randy revealed that he had grown up in the town of Granby and it was quite a rough place. He had to start proving himself at an early age. In addition, he had a real slimeball of a stepfather who used to beat the shit out of him and his little brother. He told them he had been ready to start fighting back when his mother kicked him out. He added that he had been on his own since he was sixteen, and a lot of that time was spent on the road. He believed that his ability to fight was his best survival skill; it had come in handy on many occasions. Bailey said that he had handled himself better than any other new person who had stayed in their cell in the four months he had been there. Some of the new guys even cried and pleaded for mercy. They begged the guards to transfer them to another cell. But they wouldn't have been any better off, and there was no such thing as protective custody in that place. He told Randy that he should do okay there, but still, he had to watch his back.

An hour later, Thor returned to the cell. One of the first things he noticed was how Bailey looked.

Thor said to him, "Jesus Christ, what the hell happened to you?"

Bailey pointed to Randy and said, "Our new guy here passed his initiation with flying colours!"

Thor looked rather surprised—apparently he was familiar with Bailey's fighting ability.

He gave Randy a bewildered look and said, "You did that? Wow, you're tough, man! What's your name, kid?"

He wanted to say Randy, but since first names were apparently meaningless, he remembered to say "Watson."

"Oh, just like Dr. Watson! Pleased to meet you, I'm Sherlock Holmes! Watch out for this guy," he said, pointing to Carruthers. "He's Professor Moriarty!"

Now that all of his cellmates were present, Randy wanted to find out who the toughest man was in the prison.

Thor asked him why he wanted to know that, and Randy said, "Look, I'm going to be stuck in this shithole for two years, and I want to make sure I get respect while I'm here!"

Bailey said, "Jeez, man, what's the problem? Are you Rodney Dangerfield's illegitimate son or something?"

Randy said, "No, it's just something someone told me. If that's what I have to do, then that's what I got to do."

Thor said, "If you want to meet the toughest guys in this prison, you should go to the south or west wings. Those are remand centres for maximum security prisons. Hell, they got murderers, child molesters, mafia leaders and all the scum of society cooped up there. There's not enough room in the federal penitentiaries, so they keep them here until there is room. But here in the east wing there are some pretty tough guys as well. To my mind, the toughest guy in this wing would be Rico. That guy whopped my ass handily and I've got a black belt in karate!"

Randy said, "Point him out for me when you get a chance."

Carruthers said, "Wow, you're glutton for punishment, man!"

"I'm going to prove myself in every way possible."

When dinnertime came, the guards made the prisoners line up in an orderly manner and marched them down to the dining hall. To Randy, it seemed like they were herding cattle and he sensed a lot of tension. A tension so thick you could cut it with a knife. He saw it on the other prisoners' faces as they approached the dining area. When they were lined up, the no talking rule was strictly enforced; the guards were watching their every move. This added to the tension. He remembered watching on television the big riot that had occurred in the west wing last November. At that time he would never have imagined he would end up in the same place.

As for the food, it didn't look very appetizing. Some of the items looked like they were about to jump up and run away. When he sat down at a table, he recalled what his cellmate at the Remand Centre had told him about mealtimes. He avoided eye contact and conversation with any of the other prisoners. Even so, he didn't enjoy his dinner very much. The food tasted as bad as it looked and there were fights breaking out all around him. The tension was so bad that even if one prisoner looked at another one the wrong way, it was cause for a fight. He made a vow that if he made it out of that place alive, he was going to dine on steak and lobster at the Hotel Vancouver.

Later that evening the guards had a roll call. This was done every night just to make sure nobody was trying to escape. The prison was notorious for having lots of inmates escape; in the past year alone there had been thirty-two. That night everyone was accounted for. Lights out was at 10:00. Randy suddenly realized that the individual cells were not locked at night, only the main doors to the cell block. In a way that was a good idea, just in case there was a fire. But on the other, hand the prisoners were free to roam between cells. This made him feel very uneasy. Once again, he remembered some of the stories his cellmate at the Remand Centre had told him. There had been numerous incidents where inmates had the shit beat out of them when others had snuck up and attacked them during the night while they slept. He recalled three particular incidents of stabbings. He had told Randy it was a good idea to sleep with one eye open. Randy couldn't figure out how to do that. He decided that he better keep both eyes open that first night; he knew he was going to have a hard time sleeping anyway.

Even after the lights went out, a lot of the inmates made noise late into the night. He heard many loud arguments that often led to loud banging sounds, indicating the argument had turned into a fight. Considering the explosive situation there, anything could happen. A riot could break out at a moment's notice. Those weren't the only sounds Randy was hearing. There were moans coming from the cell next door that sounded like two guys having sex. He tried his best to tune everything out. He stared at the floor and noticed that every few seconds one or two cockroaches would scamper across.

As he was taking all of this in, he remembered something the judge had told him at his sentencing. He would be eligible for parole after serving one year. Randy knew that if there was any chance of that happening, he would have to be on his best behaviour. In this place, that was not going to be easy.

Randy had a choice of different types of work detail. He chose to work in the woodworking shop, building cabinets. He would be paid fifty cents an hour and he would most likely spend most of his money on cigarettes, despite the fact that inmates purchased them at a greatly reduced price. He started work on his second day. The power tools were still familiar to him. In his one and a half years in junior high he had been much better in wood shop than in metal shop.

Carruthers pointed Rico out to him, but Randy didn't get a chance to "introduce" himself that day.

The next day when Randy had some free time in the jail yard, he nervously walked up to Rico, tapped him on the shoulder and said, "Are you Rico?"

Rico said, "Yes, I am—what's it to you?"

Randy said, "I've got something for you!"

Before Rico had a chance to respond, Randy nailed him with a right hook, hitting him square on the jaw. He then drilled him in the forehead with a left hook. Both times Rico barely flinched. Before he had a chance to get in a third shot, Rico gave him a karate chop right across the throat. This threw Randy off guard and left him gasping for breath. Rico now took over. He nailed Randy with three vicious kung-fu kicks in the head and torso. Randy was on the ground by then and Rico repeatedly punched him in the face. Eventually Randy was a bloody mess and barely conscious.

Rico said, "Have you had enough?"

Randy barely squeaked out, "Yes."

"What the hell is your fucking problem, man? I could have killed you! I don't know what you're trying to prove, but if you know what's good for you, you better stay away from me! You understand me, boy?"

Randy was still lying on the ground, moaning in agony. But he managed to nod in agreement. There was a crowd of onlookers, but nobody offered to help him up. It took Randy quite awhile to get up and stagger back to his cell.

By the fifth day, he had slowly adjusted to life there. He compared the place to the Single Men's Hostel in Edmonton with one major exception. At the hostel he could leave whenever he wanted to. In prison he couldn't leave until the justice system said he could. One thing he still had not adjusted to, though, was the concept of sleeping with one eye open. He knew well enough not to sleep facing the wall, but he couldn't sleep unless he had both eyes shut. He figured that if he could make it through his sentence without making any real enemies, he wouldn't have to worry about anyone wanting to jump him during the night. However, there was one particular inmate that really gave him the creeps. He was a big, fat man with his hair cut like a marine corps drill sergeant. His cell was seven cells down from Randy's. Ever since he had been there, this man would stare at him for long periods of time in the dining hall and in the yard. Sometimes, late at night, he would walk to Randy's cell and take a long look inside. Randy wasn't sure what he was up to.

The night of his fifth day, Randy went to sleep as usual. He was fairly tired since he had worked for eight hours in the woodworking shop and he hadn't slept well the night before. At about 2 a.m. he felt a hand on his left shoulder; it felt like it was trying to force him onto his stomach. When he lifted his head a massive fist hit him on the back of his skull. He was momentarily stunned, and then he felt his gym shorts being pulled down to his ankles. Then he could hear and feel his underwear being ripped. He tried to lift his head up, but once again he was hit hard on the back of the head. Just then a huge weight landed right on top of him. Randy couldn't breathe, and the next thing he knew he had a homemade knife right at his throat.

A voice whispered into his ear, "One peep out of you, you little fucker, and I'll slit your fucking throat!"

He was lying face down so he couldn't see who was on top of him. Judging by the weight, it must have been the big guy who had been staring at him over the past few days. Randy could tell the man was stark naked, and his foul body odour was making Rabdy gag. The man used his right hand to hold Randy's head down and held the knife at Randy's throat with his left hand. Randy could then feel him sticking his male hardness up his ass. Judging by how painful it was, the guy must have had a big dick. He started making a violent up-and-down motion and Randy felt like the bed was going to break from all the weight.

The man began to moan in ecstasy and repeatedly whispered, "Oh, yes!"

Randy heard a voice from across the hall say, "Ride 'em cowboy!"

To Randy it seemed to go on for an eternity; he wished the man would stop. He felt completely helpless—he couldn't move or say anything. Eventually the man let out a loud groan and Randy could feel him ejaculating up his ass. When he finished, he kept the knife at Randy's throat.

He said to him, "If you rat on me, you're fucking dead!"

As the guy left the cell, Randy managed to lift his head and turn around. It was indeed who he had thought it was. He was putting on his shorts outside the cell, and when he noticed that Randy was looking at him, he gave a sinister grin. Randy was in excruciating pain; he could hardly move. He was still gasping for air. He could hear Thor snickering. All that was going through his mind was getting revenge. His only thought was, "The last laugh will be on you, fatso! I swear I'm going to get back at you!" For obvious reasons, he didn't go back to sleep.

The next day his mind was filled with revenge. Since the guy was quite big, Randy wanted to use something that would make a good "equalizer." He wanted to go into the metal shop and look for a metal bar or pipe, but since he hadn't signed up for that work detail, he was not authorized to go in there. Instead, while he was at work in the woodworking shop, he found a length of one-inch-thick doweling. He cut off about a two-foot length and stuffed it up his pant leg. After he finished work, he went over to the jail yard and looked for the fat guy. He wasn't hard to spot. Once Randy caught sight of him he tried sneaking up on him from behind. When he got close enough, he took the wooden bar out from his pants, swung his arm back and clobbered him right across the back of the head. He came down on the back of his skull a second time. In both instances the man didn't even flinch. He turned around and had a real mean look on his face.

When he realized it was Randy who had hit him, he yelled out, "Why, you fucking little piece of shit!"

Randy said, "Oh, shit," and began running.

The man immediately took off after him. He chased Randy from one end of the yard to the other. Randy couldn't believe how someone that size could run that fast. He eventually caught up to Randy near the main building. He grabbed him by his shirt collar and flung him like a rag doll. He picked him up and punched him repeatedly in the face. He then flung him into the building wall. Randy hit the wall full throttle. The guy gave him three hard shots to the stomach and flung him into the air once again.

Before Randy could get up, he grabbed him by the shirt lapel and yelled, "Get up, boy!"

He slapped him in the face, head-butted him and punched him repeatedly. Once again he flung him in the air. As soon as he landed the man began kicking him hard in the back and side.

From their vantage point overlooking the jail yard, two guards were observing what was going on.

When they saw what was happening to Randy, one guard said to the other, "Oh my god, he's killing him!"

The other guard said, "Where?"

"Over there! That big guy is beating the living hell out of that little guy! Cover me!"

While the one guard ran down to the yard, the other one fired a warning shot from his perch.

When the other guard reached the yard, he pulled out his gun, pointed it at the big man and yelled out, "Stop it!"

By then backup had arrived. They pulled the big man off of Randy, handcuffed him and took him to solitary confinement. Randy was out cold. He had been punched and kicked so many times that he was barely recognizable. His face was completely covered in blood. One guard called for an ambulance from his walkie-talkie.

Randy was taken to Burnaby General Hospital, where he was kept overnight. Some ribs and one kidney were bruised and he had some facial lacerations. His left eye was completely shut. He ended up staying in the infirmary for four days.

When he was well enough to return to his cell, Thor said to him, "So, I heard you got into it with Big Bubba!"

"Yeah, I did. Unfortunately, things didn't go my way!"

Thor said, "Just what the hell were you trying to prove?"

Randy couldn't believe his ears. He was absolutely flabbergasted that Thor would ask such a thing.

He said, "What was I trying to prove? What the hell do you think? He raped me! That fat fucker raped me! He violated my rights. For all I know, he could have some kind of venereal disease, or herpes or even that new homosexual disease AIDS, and you—you thought it was funny!"

Thor said, "I wasn't laughing at what he was doing to you. I was only thinking about what was going to happen afterwards. I know that I've only known you a week, but I've realized that you're quite the shit-disturber and I could tell you were going to do something to retaliate."

"Damn right I was!" Randy said, "I wasn't going to let him get away with it!"

Thor said, "Watson, I know you're trying to prove yourself here, but for god's sake, use your fucking head! Big Bubba is not even supposed to be here! He's a remand inmate and he belongs in the south wing. He is serving two life sentences for second-degree murder. He must be doing some favours for the guards or the warden because he definitely doesn't belong here. He's been doing that to a number of the other inmates in the cell block—he goes for the young guys. Nobody usually does anything about it. Even some of the tougher guys here are afraid of him. To put it bluntly, that guy is an absolute fucking psycho and should be locked up permanently!"

A deep feeling of uneasiness came over Randy as he came to terms with the fact that he could have been killed. He told Thor he was only standing up for his rights.

"Face the fact, Watson! You have no fucking rights here!"

It was at this point that Thor made Randy an offer. He was willing to watch Randy's back for him, which was good since he had a black belt in karate. He told him that he would make sure Big Bubba would never touch him again.

"Well thank you very much, I greatly appreciate that!" Randy said.

"Whoa there, big guy, I don't work for nothing!"

"Oh, you want me to pay you?"

"You don't have to pay me in money, but I do want something in return, if you know what I mean."

"Now wait a minute, here! Are you saying what I think you're saying? Come on, now, I am not a homosexual!"

Thor said, "That doesn't matter. You had better start facing reality, Watson! I have been here only two months longer than you have. Come to grips with the fact that we are going to be stuck in this fucking toilet for two years, and in that time you ain't going to get no pussy! Look around you, Watson! Do you see any women here?"

Randy said weakly, "No."

"That's right, it's just us guys here. At one time there were some guys here that were practically women, but they hadn't had the sex-change operation yet. There are a few guys here that are only eighteen and they make extra money selling their bodies. They have full protection and they're quite in demand. The bottom line is, I have needs and you have needs. There is no way around it. It is inevitable. So, the choice is yours."

Randy looked somewhat apprehensive. He thought about it for a minute and then said, "Thanks anyway, but if that's what I have to do in return, I would just as soon look after myself."

"You sure haven't been doing a very good job of it so far! You haven't been here two weeks yet and at the rate you're going, you are going to need protection! Look at you! Your face is all busted up and it could have been worse. I think you should give my offer serious consideration. Another thing you should know about me, Watson, is that it is better to work with me than against me. I can be your best friend, but I can also be your worst enemy. Believe me, you wouldn't want to get on my bad side. As you're well aware, I have a black belt in karate. That guy Rico, even though he defeated me, I gave him a run for his money. If I wanted to, I could snap your neck like a twig! So, if you don't accept my offer, you could be making a big mistake!" Thor paused. "But I'll be fair. I will let you think about it overnight. If you decide to accept it, meet me here at this same time tomorrow afternoon. We'll be all alone then. Bailey and Carruthers will be on work detail."

Randy thought about it long and hard throughout the night. He tried to decide which was worse—the exchange for protection or none at all. But after a typical breakfast and lunch in the dining hall and a morning spent in the jail yard, he didn't need much coaxing. That afternoon, he returned to his cell at the time Thor expected.

Thor said "I didn't think you would show up!"

Randy said "You win."

"I'm glad you decided to see things my way."

"All right, let's get this over with! What do I have to do?"

"First of all, don't sound so glum! Just let your inhibitions run wild. It's not really as bad as you think. We'll start out with you on the receiving end and after awhile, I'll let you have your way with me. You have a choice—oral or anal."

Randy thought about it for awhile, and then he remembered how painful his experience with Big Bubba had been.

He decided to go with the oral sex, and Thor said, "Good choice."

Thor began undressing by taking his shirt off first.

Randy asked, "What do you need to take that that off for?"

Thor said, "That will help get you in the mood."

Randy had seen Thor without his shirt on before, but had not paid that much attention. He now noticed how muscular Thor was and that he had a lot of tattoos. He then removed his pants, socks and finally his undershorts. Randy had never seen him naked before; they had never been in the showers at the same time. Thor's penis was not overly long, but was quite wide.

He lay down on his bunk and said to Randy, "C'mon, dig in!"

Randy was quite apprehensive. He stared at Thor's rock-hard dick for a few minutes and then he got down on his knees, closed his eyes and took it all in. He was a bit nervous at first, but then he gradually loosened up. He began making an up-and-down motion with his mouth and acting like he was enjoying himself. Thor moaned in ecstasy—Randy was really going to town. A few minutes later Thor came to a shuddering climax, blasting a salvo of come cream into Randy's mouth. Randy licked the tip of the iceberg, salvaging every last drop. Thor was still in a state of euphoric bliss.

He said, "Oh, Watson, that was fantastic! Are you sure you've never done this before?"

As for Randy, he was in a state of utter disbelief. He could not for the life of him believe what he had just done. Never in his wildest dreams had he ever imagined that he would give a blow job to another man. The fact that he had enjoyed it made things even worse.

For the next several days, Randy was in a constant state of confusion.

He asked himself repeatedly, "Am I gay?"

On the one hand, he had never felt any sort of attraction to a man before and he didn't recall ever fantasizing about making it with another guy. But on the other hand, why did he enjoy giving Thor head so much? He theorized that it was likely due to the fact that there were no women there and he was merely heeding Thor's advice. He figured that once he was out of there he would be back to his old heterosexual self. But then he wondered what he would do if he realized that he really was gay. He decided just to wait until after he was released and see what happened.

Another thing that was bugging him was how he was going to break the news to Mark that he was in jail. He finally got up the nerve to write to him. For Randy this was a very difficult task—it was about something he was definitely not proud of.

Over the next couple months, the number of sexual encounters between Randy and Thor became more frequent and practically got to the point where Randy was Thor's personal sex slave. What made things even worse was that Thor hadn't kept his promise of letting Randy be on the receiving end—he was still always on the giving end. The sex acts alternated between anal and oral. He wanted desperately to say something to Thor, but he was afraid of getting on his bad side. He knew he would have nowhere to run and nowhere to hide. So all he could hope for was that Thor would get early parole. However, Thor did keep up one end of the deal—on several occasions he helped Randy get out of a jam with other inmates.

15

Month five

It was visitors' day, a time when inmates could get together with family and friends, even though there was no actual contact (inmates and visitors were separated by a Plexiglas barrier). A middle-aged woman approached the gate house.

The guard said to her, "May I help you?"

The woman said, "Yes. My name is Carla McGuigan. I am here to see my son, Randy Watson."

The guard pointed toward the entrance to the main jail. He told her to check in at the front desk and then she would be directed to the visitors' area. He pointed out that she would have to go through a security check first.

In his cell, Randy was enjoying a day off from working in the shop. He was sitting on his bunk reading his latest copy of *Road and Track* magazine, when a guard approached his cell.

The guard said to him, "Watson! You have a visitor!"

"A visitor? For me? Who is it?" he asked.

"It's your mother!"

Randy looked really surprised. He had never imagined that his mom would come to see him.

He said to the guard, "What does she want?"

"Damned if I know! Get your ass down there and find out!"

As Randy entered the visitor's area, escorted by a guard, he noticed his mom sitting on the other side. This was the first time he had seen her in almost seven years. They sat opposite each other, separated by Plexiglas. They could communicate only through a two-way telephone.

His mom spoke first, saying, "Randy, it's so good to see you! How have you been doing?"

Randy said, "Well, I guess I'm doing all right, considering the circumstances!"

"You know, I never got a chance to tell you this, but I was really worried when you first ran away from home. I was concerned that something bad was going to happen to you. But when Gary told me that you made it to Edmonton and found a job, I was kind of relieved. He told me that you seemed happy there."

"Well, it's a little late, isn't it?"

"I don't blame you for being angry with me. I also don't blame you for wanting to run away. But whether or not you want to believe me, I was always concerned about you."

After a long pause, he asked her how the trip had been. She commented that it was a very long drive.

He asked her how things were at home, and she said, "All right, I guess."

He then asked her if William was still living there, already knowing the answer. He asked her if he had ever gone back to work.

"No."

Randy shook his head in disbelief as he said, "Gosh, mom, why do you keep letting that guy sponge off you all the time? All he does is spend your money! I wish you would kick the lazy bum out!"

"I don't really want to talk about this right now."

Randy said, "By the way, how did you know I was in prison?"

"Mark told me."

"So, how is Mark doing?" he asked.

It was then that his mom began to sob.

"Mom, what's the matter?"

When she regained her composure, she managed to blurt out, "Mark is in jail."

Randy was totally shocked by what he had just heard. When it finally sank in, he said, "In jail? Why? What is he in for?"

His mom continued crying, but she managed to squeak out, "Murder!"

"What? How did this happen? I can't believe this!"

When his mom regained her composure, she explained what had happened. Mark had received his first paycheque after his nineteenth birthday. It had been a Friday night, so he decided to celebrate. He had gone to a bar in a hotel in downtown Prince George. Over the course of the evening, he had noticed a man sitting several tables over who looked very familiar. He was a large native man with grey hair. He eventually clued in and realized that it was Larry Braithwaite, his mother's third husband. It had taken Mark awhile to figure out who he was—he hadn't seen Larry in over twelve years. In that time, the physical wounds had long since gone, but the emotional wounds were far from healed. When he realized it was

Larry, all those bad memories came flooding back and a rage began to build inside him. He approached him and asked him if his name was Larry Braithwaite.

When the man nodded, Mark said, "You don't remember me, do you?"

Larry indicated that he didn't remember who he was, and Mark said, "Of course you wouldn't! I was a hell of a lot smaller, the size of a person you like to beat up!"

Larry still looked surprised, and Mark yelled out, "I'm Mark Watson, you fat fuck! You used to beat the shit out of me when I was a little kid! You nearly beat me to death when I was only four years old! Four years old, for Christ sake! How did it feel, Braithwaite? Did it feel good, beating on a defenceless little kid? Well, as you notice, I'm not so little anymore and I'm going to kick your ass!"

Mark managed to give Larry a smack across the back of the head before two bouncers intervened.

One of them asked what the trouble was, and Larry responded, "I was just sitting here minding my own business when this little punk comes up and starts hassling me!"

Mark spoke up and said, "This man was once my stepfather and he abused the hell out of me when I was little!"

Larry said, "I never seen this guy before in my life! He must be mistaking me for someone else!"

"Then how come I know what your name is, Larry Braithwaite?"

One of the bouncers said to Mark, "I think you have had too much to drink tonight. I think you'd better leave."

As the bouncers escorted Mark out of the bar, he yelled out to Larry, "Don't try to deny it! You know who I am! You're gonna pay!"

After Mark had been ejected from the bar, he drove home, grabbed his .12 gauge shotgun and returned to the hotel. He waited outside the bar in the parking lot until closing time. When he saw Larry emerge from the bar, Mark got out of his truck, approached Larry and levelled the shotgun at him.

He said to Larry, "I've been waiting thirteen fucking years for this day to happen, you fat, worthless piece of shit! You're going to pay for all you put me through!"

When Larry had tried to reason with him, Mark fired a shot, hitting him in his ample stomach. All that managed to do was make him stagger backward. It must have been all that fat protecting him. Mark fired a second shot, hitting him in the chest. He then shot him in the neck, nearly blowing his head clean off his body. When the police had first seen Larry's body, all that was attaching his head to the rest of his body were a few muscle strands.

The police wanted to charge him with first-degree murder. If convicted, he could face life in prison.

Randy was in a state of shock. On the one hand, he couldn't believe that Mark would actually do something like that. But on the other hand, it didn't surprise him that, having crossed paths with Larry, Mark would react in that manner. Randy believed that he would have reacted the same way. As far as he was concerned, Larry had got what was coming to him. His mom told him that Mark was in the Prince George Regional Correctional Centre awaiting trial. He asked when the trial would be and she told him not until next November, eight months away.

He thought about it for a minute and then said, "Wait a minute! My parole hearing will be in October. If I get paroled, I can testify at the trial on Mark's behalf."

He asked for the name and address of Mark's lawyer. He could write to him or her and ask if he could be a witness for Mark's defence. She wrote it out on a piece of paper and asked the guard on her side to pass it on to him.

Randy said, "I would be a very good character witness. I could tell the court that Larry used to beat the shit out of us when we were just little kids, giving Mark a justifiable reason for killing him. I mean, I can help reduce the charge to second-degree murder or even manslaughter."

Randy noticed that his mom wasn't showing the same amount of enthusiasm as he was. He tried to convince her that they should give it their best shot and try to reduce the charge. After all, Mark didn't deserve to be locked up for twenty-five years after what he had been through.

His mom continued to stare blankly. Randy finally spoke up and asked, "What's the matter, mom?"

His mom said, "I don't know what I did to deserve this! I thought I raised you boys properly, but obviously I didn't. Look at this! Both of you are in jail! You, I might have expected it since you were always getting into trouble, but not Mark!"

Randy said angrily, "Maybe you should take a long look at yourself, mother! The main reason I got into trouble all the time was because I was bored. You were never there for me. You never cared about my well-being.

You were always off on your own! As for Mark, he did the right thing. Larry got what he deserved. If I had ever crossed paths with Larry, I would have done the same damn thing!"

"What is the matter with you and Mark? Larry was a good man! Don't forget he was a good provider. But he had a very dangerous job and he was under stress a lot. Before he came along, I couldn't handle you boys. At least Larry kept you and Mark in line!"

Randy yelled out, "Are you fucked in the head or something? Since when do you call beating the living bejesus out of us keeping us in line? You saw it with your own eyes and you didn't do a goddamn thing about it! What would you have done if he had killed one of us? For once in your life, mother, you should get your fucking head out from up your ass and face reality!"

She was absolutely seething by then and responded, "Don't you ever talk to me like that again! Don't forget, I'm still your mother!"

"You don't need to remind me! I just wish I never had such a fucking useless bitch like you for a mother! You never gave a fuck about anybody but yourself!" he shouted.

With that, his mom slammed the phone down, got up and stormed out of the visitor's area.

As she was leaving, Randy screamed out, "I hate you! I hope you burn in hell, you fucking slut! I never want to see your ugly face again!"

Randy had to be restrained by two guards because he was relentlessly pounding on the Plexiglas. One of the them threatened to spray mace into his face. The other one tried to get him to calm down by assuring him that his mom was no longer in the visitor's area. Eventually he did calm down somewhat, but the guards still escorted him back to his cell.

When they reached the tier entrance to Randy's cell block, one of the guards asked Randy if he was going to be all right

"Yeah, I'll be okay," he replied.

With that, the guards let him go back to his cell on his own. He didn't want to say anything to them, but he was still pretty angry. When he arrived at his cell, he opened the sliding door and slammed it full throttle.

Almost immediately Heatley, his newest cellmate, began yelling at him. "Hey! Did I say you could slam the fucking door?"

Carruthers had been released. In the month that Heatley had been there, he had proven himself to be a royal pain in the ass. He wouldn't say what he was in for, but knowing him, it could have been for any number of charges. It was believed that he was connected with the Satan's Angels motorcycle club, although he didn't really look like a biker. He wasn't very tall, but he sure was a mouthy bastard. Randy had been in several scraps with him since his arrival and so had the other guys in his cell. Still, Heatley never gave any of his cellmates any respect. He always acted like he owned the place. When he started yelling, Randy tried to ignore him.

Heatley said, "I'm talking to you, you fucking retard! Are you deaf or something?"

Randy was like a volcano ready to blow. He tried to stay cool, but eventually he completely lost it. He turned around and nailed Heatley in the jaw with a vicious right hook, quickly followed by a left hook to the forehead and several hard shots to the stomach. He grabbed him by the arm and flung him into the back wall of the cell. He hurled him into the cell door. He grabbed him by the hair and slammed his head full force into the cell door latch, opening a huge gash in Heatley's forehead. He threw him onto the floor, jumped on him and delivered numerous upper cuts to his head. One punch nailed him right in the mouth, knocking three teeth out of him. Randy wasn't quite finished with him. Under his mattress he kept a metal bed leg. It had come from the riot-torn west wing. Carruthers acquired it when he was on work detail cleaning up the mess there and had given it to Randy a couple months back. He kept it under his mattress for protection, and now he was going to make use of it. He took the bed leg and pummelled Heatley into oblivion. Bailey tried to restrain Randy (Thor was in the jail yard), but Randy fought him off, so he ran to get help from the guards.

When the guards finally came, Randy was still ruthlessly beating Heatley with the bed leg. He was acting like a man possessed, showing no mercy whatsoever. The guards tried to restrain Randy, but he wouldn't budge. When he started going at the guards with the bed leg, one of them sprayed mace into his face. Once he was subdued they put handcuffs on him and took him down to solitary confinement. As for Heatley, at first everyone thought he was dead. He was bleeding profusely from the forehead and mouth and showing no signs of movement. When the medical staff arrived, he was lying in a pool of his own blood and was completely unconscious. He was immediately taken to the infirmary.

Randy ended up spending four days in solitary confinement. Heatley had a concussion, needed sixteen stitches in his forehead and three hundred dollars' worth of dental work. He also suffered from numerous cuts, bruises and abrasions. He spent three days in the infirmary and was then transferred to the Ferndale Institution near Mission.

When Randy was taken out of solitary confinement, he had the uneasy feeling that he was now a marked man. He knew that Heatley had many friends on the outside associated with the Satan's Angels, and they would definitely have connections with people on the inside. Even Thor didn't think very highly of Randy's actions.

When he returned to his cell, the first thing Thor said to him was, "What the hell were you thinking of, man? Don't you know who that guy was connected with? That is one dangerous gang! Did you know they have access to fully automatic weapons? They have very clever ways of smuggling weapons into this place. You had better watch your back. You're on your own this time!"

For the next couple of weeks, Randy looked over his shoulder practically every second. He went out of his way to keep to himself and he tried to be on his best behaviour—his parole hearing was only seven months away (if he hadn't blown it already). He thought that if he could have a meeting with Warden Bjarnason and explain his situation, he might be able to persuade the board to grant him parole. One morning he asked one of the guards on his tier if he could arrange a meeting with the warden for him. Later that day, the guard told him that the warden would meet with him in three days.

When the time came for Randy's meeting with the warden, the guard from his tier escorted him to his office. Once inside, Warden Bjarnason asked Randy how he could help him.

Randy said, "Well, sir, my brother will be on trial in Prince George for first-degree murder next November. I was hoping that I could be a character witness. My parole hearing is in October and I thought that maybe you might be able to persuade them to grant me parole, given the circumstances."

Warden Bjarnason told him that he had no say in whether a prisoner was paroled. That it was entirely up to the Parole Board.

Randy said, "Well, just in case my parole is denied, would it be possible for me to be transferred to the Prince George Correctional Centre?"

"We are going to have to take that one step at a time. We will just have to wait and see how things go at your parole hearing and take it from there."

He looked over Randy's file for a few minutes and then said, "Judging by your file here, it doesn't look too promising that you will receive early parole. You were involved in an assault with another inmate in your first week here and just recently, you brutally assaulted your cellmate. In fact, you nearly killed him. It's a wonder that you didn't have your sentence extended!"

"I'm really sorry about that incident, sir. I guess that I was upset after hearing about what had happened to my brother. I wasn't thinking clearly. I was just angry, that's all. I know I should have just walked away. I hope and pray that Mr. Heatley will be all right."

The guard that accompanied him had to restrain himself from laughing. He felt that Randy should get an Oscar for his performance.

"There is nothing I can do for you now," Warden Bjarnason said. "All I can say is check back with me if your parole is denied and we might be able to arrange something."

As he was being led back to his cell, Randy asked the guard what he thought his chances were.

The guard told him, "To be honest, I believe Warden Bjarnason was thinking the same thing I was thinking—you are so full of shit that your eyes are brown! What was all this bullshit about hoping that Heatley will be all right? You hated the bastard! I bet that you really wished he had died!"

Randy didn't exactly appreciate the vote of confidence. He realized that for the next seven months it was going to be up to him to show the board that he deserved an early parole, so he had better try his best to keep his nose clean.

Month seven

Over the past two months Randy had been extra vigilant, anticipating that someone might retaliate for what he had done to Heatley. Fortunately, nothing had materialized. In fact, one prisoner had actually thanked Randy for what he'd done. It turned out that Heatley had been extorting money and cigarettes from him, threatening to sic his biker buddies on his girlfriend if he didn't comply. It seemed that you could have many friends on the outside, but it could be totally meaningless on the inside. As it turned out, Heatley was nothing more than a menace in the east wing. Thor had just been paranoid when he used those scare tactics on Randy. He'd been blowing things all out of proportion.

Randy had been trying his best to be a model prisoner, hoping it would influence the Parole Board to grant him early parole. He had been working diligently in the woodworking shop and was making a huge effort to stay out of trouble. However, he did have a bit of a setback the previous month. He had received a letter from Mark's attorney telling him that he didn't think Randy would make a very good character witness and his testimony would have very little, if any, influence on the outcome of the trial. Randy wrote a scathing letter back, stating that he knew Mark would be found guilty, but his testimony could make a difference as to whether Mark's conviction would be for manslaughter or first-degree murder. He pointed out that this could result in a seven-year rather than a twenty-five-year sentence. Randy then wrote to Mark and told him to get a different lawyer. He even offered to help out financially, although he didn't have much money himself. He told Mark to spare no expense and, if he had to, that he should try to get F. Lee Bailey to defend him.

One morning as Randy was getting ready to go to work, one of the guards came up to his cell and asked to speak to him. He said that the chaplain wanted to see him in the chapel. Randy asked what it was all about, but the guard didn't know. He would have to go up there and find out for himself.

When Randy entered the chapel, both the chaplain and assistant warden were present.

"You must be Randy Watson. I am Warden Bjarnason's assistant, Mr. Walters. This is our chaplain, Father Jenkins."

Randy recognized the assistant warden—he was often present at shakedowns (when they checked the cells for contraband). Mr. Walters told Randy to sit down. They both had sombre looks on their faces.

"What is going on here?" Randy asked.

Father Jenkins said, "Randy, I am very sorry to have to tell you this, but your brother Mark was found dead in his cell last night."

Randy was completely stunned.

After a few seconds of silence, he said, "No! It can't be!"

Mr. Walters said, "Randy, I'm afraid it is true."

As he fought back tears, Randy asked, "How did this happen?"

Mr. Walters said, "From the information I received, someone had smuggled some high-grade heroin into the prison and Mark had overdosed. Actually, they found him the following morning. There were several others that had taken the heroin the previous night, but they survived. Apparently, Mark had taken a lethal dose."

Randy was still in a state of disbelief.

After he had regained his composure somewhat, he spoke up. "I don't believe this! Mark didn't do drugs!"

Mr. Walters said, "Randy, I have very reliable sources. Officials from the prison and the RCMP from Prince George relayed the information. Right after the coroner examined the body he took a blood sample. It was found to contain a lethal amount of narcotics."

Father Jenkins asked, "Were you and your brother close?"

"Yes, when we were kids we were quite close. But since I left home, I have only seen him on two different occasions in the past seven years."

Mr. Walters said, "You see, you really don't know him as well as you thought, if that's all that you've seen of him in the past seven years." He went on to ask Randy, "During those times that Mark came to visit you, did the two of you ever do any drugs or did he even talk about drugs?"

"No, we didn't do any drugs, and I don't remember him talking about them at all."

"The official from the Prince George RCMP that I spoke to told me Mark had been charged with possession on at least three different occasions in the past year," said Mr. Walters.

"Even so," Randy said, "Don't they have surveillance cameras in the jail? Wouldn't they know if something was wrong? It seems strange they wouldn't notice he was dead until the following morning!"

Mr. Walters said, "I don't know what's going on there. They have been having a lot of problems with security lately. There have been a number of instances of people smuggling contraband inside, mainly drugs and weapons."

Randy asked if there was going to be an inquiry and Mr. Walters told him, "There's not really much point. It was pretty straightforward how he died."

Randy said, "I don't know. It sounds kind of suspicious. I think there was something they didn't tell you."

"Randy, I'm really sorry for your loss, but there's nothing more you can do. What's done is done," Mr. Walters said.

Randy said, "All right, but can I at least get an escorted pass so I can attend the funeral?"

Mr. Walters told him that there would not be any funeral.

"Why not?" Randy asked in astonishment.

Mr. Walters said, "Your mother requested that there not be any funeral."

"That figures! That cheap bitch probably didn't want to spend the money!"

As Randy got up to leave, Father Jenkins said to him, "Randy, if you ever need anyone to talk to about this or for anything else, I'm always here. My thoughts and prayers are with you."

"Thank you, Father."

Randy was still not convinced that Mr. Walters was telling him the whole story. He was certain that somebody was trying to cover up something. But he didn't have much to go by; in fact, it was only a hunch. It just seemed strange that none of the prison staff had noticed anything. He wrote to the RCMP in Prince George and demanded that there be an inquiry into Mark's death.

Three days after Randy learned of Mark's death, there was another shakedown in his cell block. As usual Mr. Walters was present. After they finished checking Randy's cell, he asked to speak to Mr. Walters alone. He asked him if he could make arrangements with the coroner in Prince George to do an autopsy on Mark's body. That way they would have proof if Mark had died by some other means.

Mr. Walters said, "I'm afraid that will be impossible because Mark's body was cremated. Now for the last time, Randy, it is over and done with. Give it a rest."

The news of Mark's death really hit Randy hard. It seemed like all that effort to be on his best behaviour those past two months had been for nothing. In the following weeks, Randy became a real problem inmate. He became more antisocial than before and was constantly getting into fights with other inmates. One day while at work in the woodworking shop, he beat another inmate over the head repeatedly with a two-by-four. Another day while having dinner in the dining hall, an inmate asked Randy to pass the salt and Randy beat him senseless. A few days after that during a shakedown in his cell block, Mr. Walters questioned Randy about his possession of a *Guns and Ammo* magazine. Instead of answering the question he got belligerent. As a result, Mr. Walters confiscated it. The final straw came when Randy took a swing at one of the guards, breaking his nose. He was taken—in handcuffs—to Warden Bjarnason's office.

The warden started out by saying, "I understand you assaulted one of our guards. Look here, Watson, I understand what you must be going through."

Before he could say anything else, Randy interrupted him by saying, "No, you don't!"

Warden Bjarnason said, "One more outburst from you, young man, and you will be spending the rest of your sentence in the south wing! Now, your behaviour of late has been totally unacceptable, and what you did to one of our guards was completely reprehensible. Also, that outburst you had in the visitors' area with your own mother disturbs me. Are you aware of that commandment of honouring your mother? Obviously not, since you are in here for breaking another commandment—thou shall not steal! Therefore, you will spend the next two weeks in solitary confinement."

Solitary confinement or "the hole," as it was more affectionately known, was not that much different than the regular cells. The only differences were that they were smaller, darker and had a greater abundance of rats and cockroaches. One advantage they had over the usual cells (or disadvantage, depending on how you looked at it) was that they were not shared. Therefore, the inmates had total privacy. This was Randy's second stint in "the hole," so the shock wasn't as great as it had been the first time. One way he looked at it was that his meals would be brought to him so he wouldn't have to go to the dining hall. In addition, for the next two weeks he would not have to be Thor's sex slave. But on the other hand, about all he would have to do all day would be to sit and think. At least that would give him lots of time to think about his actions.

At 3 a.m. on the fifth day, two guards came into Randy's cell and closed the door behind them.

One of them said, "We're going to teach you a lesson, boy! You're going to find out that when you fuck with one of us, you pay the price!"

For the next ten minutes, the guards took turns beating him senseless. While one of them held him, the other one beat him with his nightstick. Most of the time they hit him across the knees and back. They also jabbed him in the stomach. When they finished with him, Randy was lying on the floor moaning, barely able to move and in excruciating pain. The guards had known exactly where to hit him—where the bruises would be the least noticeable. Since he still had nine days left, they would be virtually healed by then. One guard said, "You see, boy, we stick together. We all watch each other's backs!"

The other guard added, "You will be wasting your time if you tell anyone about this, boy! Nobody will believe you, anyway! It's your word against ours. Nobody here gives a shit about you inmates. In here those guys," he pointed to two cockroaches on the floor, "get more respect than you!"

As they left his cell, Randy could hear them laughing as they walked away.

Randy ended up spending sixteen days in solitary, two days longer than he was supposed to. He wasn't sure if they had forgotten about him or if it was deliberate. He figured that the warden had done it deliberately just to make him suffer more. On the sixteenth day, Warden Bjarnason and two guards (not the ones who beat him up) entered Randy's cell.

Warden Bjarnason said to him, "Well, Mr. Watson, I hope we will see a change in your attitude during the remainder of your time here."

Randy said, "Yes sir, I will change."

"Good." He then ordered the guards, "Take him back to his cell."

As he was gathering his belongings, he overheard the warden talking to the man in the neighbouring cell. He said, "We are too overcrowded in the south wing, so I'll be placing you in the east wing for now. But I tell you, you had better hope and pray that none of the inmates find out the reason why you are incarcerated here. It's bad enough that you are in here for sexual assault, but she was only twelve years old, for god's sake! What on earth were you thinking of?"

As Randy was being led out of his cell, he got a look at the man that Warden Bjarnason was talking to. He was real short and skinny and quite ugly. Randy was thinking, "No wonder that guy had to resort to rape! But that's still no excuse!"

When he was returned to his regular cell one of the first things Thor said to him was, "So, how were things in the hole?"

Randy said sarcastically, "Oh, just fucking ducky!"

Bailey said, "Jeez, man, do you like it down there or something?"

"Look, I just wasn't coping well with my brother's death. I guess I will just have to live with it."

Just then two guards walked past the cell, escorting the prisoner that Randy had seen down in solitary.

Randy said to his cellmates, "That guy that just walked by with the guards—guess what? He's a skinner!"

"Him? Are you serious?" Thor asked.

"Yeah, I heard the warden having a talk with him down in solitary. Get this—he raped a twelve-year-old girl! The warden told him to keep his mouth shut."

Thor said, "Watson, you have just done your good deed for the day!"

Randy wasn't exactly sure what Thor meant by that. The rapist was placed seven cells down from Randy's. The other occupants of the cell knew Thor quite well. He was sure that Thor would be quite willing to pass that information along to them. That was most likely the case—Thor was noticeably absent for most of the afternoon.

That evening, about an hour after lights out, Randy heard yelling from the cell occupied by the rapist. He heard one of the inmates yell out, "Don't you fucking lie to me! What are you in for?" The rapist tried to tell them he was in for breaking and entering, but then one of the other inmates yelled out, "Don't give me that bullshit! You're in here for rape, aren't you? We have informed sources that tell us you're in here for raping a twelve-year-old girl. Now, we don't keep secrets around here. If you are honest with us and admit it, we won't hurt you!"

Randy could barely hear what the rapist was saying since he was talking in a very low tone, but it was something in the way of a confession. It sounded like his cellmates were tricking him into confessing, for barely a minute later Randy started to hear screaming. That was followed by one of the cellmates yelling, "You don't look so tough now, you useless piece of shit!"

The man's screaming was continuous and ear-piercing. Judging from the sound effects, they must have been beating him with some kind of object. The shrieking lasted for several minutes and none of the other inmates seemed to care about his plight. In fact, some were even encouraging it. Several times Randy heard someone yell out, "Give that fucker a hit for me!" After awhile Randy felt tempted to run over and tell them to stop, that the rapist had had enough. But he knew if he did that, they would turn on him. So all he could do was lie back and listen to the piercing screams. He put the pillow over his head to try to drown it out. Even though he felt that the guy deserved it for what he had done, in a way Randy felt guilty for blowing the whistle on him. If he were to die, Randy felt like it would be his fault.

Eventually the screaming was reduced to moaning and then silence. When everything went quiet, Randy wondered, "Is he dead?" The following day he learned that the rapist had barely survived. He was expected to recover, after which he would be transferred to protective custody at Kingston Penitentiary.

After his stint in solitary, Randy decided that he had just better accept what had happened to Mark and move on. He realized that no matter what he did, nothing would bring him back. If the circumstances of Mark's death had deviated in any way from what he'd been told, he would never know. He wondered what would have happened if Mark had had a chance to testify, but that was all irrelevant now.

A week after Randy was released from solitary, he was milling about the jail yard one afternoon when he heard a familiar voice say to him, "Well, hello there, stranger."

He turned around and was surprised to see a familiar face.

"Dave Sewell! Holy shit!"

"Randy Watson, what a surprise," said Dave.

Randy said, "Man, I don't believe this! How long have you been here?"

"I got here two days ago. Jeez, Watson, what the hell are you doing here?"

"What are you in for?" Randy asked.

"I asked you first!"

"Well, I'm in for armed robbery," Randy informed him.

"Jesus Christ, Watson! I never would have imagined that you would resort to robbing a place with a gun. What happened? Did you run up some gambling debts or something?"

Randy told him he had found himself mixed up with a group of bad-asses and one thing had led to another. He admitted regretfully that he had let them brainwash him and he had been led astray as a result.

Dave proceeded to tell Randy his story. For the past five years he had been working for his uncle's construction company in Kitimat. But even though he had left Granby, his reputation as a pool hustler followed him when he moved. When he turned nineteen he started playing for bigger money in the local beer parlours. But he soon found out that he was not really as good as he'd thought. He claimed he was good, but "definitely no Minnesota Fats!" There had been a lot more veteran pool sharks in the bar crowd, and he soon found himself racking up huge gambling debts, some to very unsavoury characters. In an effort to cover his ass, he deliberately began to write bad cheques, and a jail sentence was the result.

Randy said to him, "I probably made you look good. You helped me realize that billiards is just not my game. So, do you still play pool?"

Dave said, "To be honest, I have practically given it up. It wasn't just the gambling debts I accumulated, but when people start taking it too seriously and it's not a game anymore, I draw the line. For example, last year a friend of mine and I were passing through Telkwa and we decided to stop for a beer at the Telkwa Hotel. While we were there, two guys got into a heated argument over a pool game. One of them pulled out a gun and shot the other man in the head. After that I started to lose interest."

Over the next month Randy and Dave got together regularly and reminisced about the good old days in Granby. After all, they had a lot of catching up to do. Eventually Randy got up the nerve to make a confession to Dave. He asked him if he remembered what had happened to Kees Vandelaar.

Dave said, "Yes, I remember it clearly."

"Well, it was me," Randy admitted.

"Yeah, everybody I knew had a strange feeling that it might have been you. But lucky for you there weren't any witnesses, and Kees always claimed that he didn't remember anything."

"I feel bad about what I did to him." Randy added, "By the way, Gary told me that Kees made it into law school at York University."

"Kees—in law school? No shit? All I knew was his parents had sold the bakery and moved back to Holland. Somehow, I can't seem to picture him as a lawyer."

"Me either."

"I heard about what happened to Mark. I'm really sorry about it."

"Yeah, it came as a real shock to me too. But life goes on, I guess."

16

Month thirteen

Randy's first anniversary as an inmate in Oakalla came and went, and as promised, he had his hearing with the Parole Board. Unfortunately, the outcome didn't exactly go his way. As it turned out, his shenanigans in months five and seven did not go over well with the Parole Board, so his application was denied. However, the news was not all bad. The board did take into consideration the fact that for the past five months he had been a model prisoner and had never made any attempts to escape. So they came up with a compromise. He would spend the remainder of his sentence in a minimum security prison and would have another parole hearing in six months. Randy thought that it was better than nothing. At least he would be getting out of that hellhole. He asked which minimum security prison he was being sent to, and one of the members told him that it was Mount Thurston Correctional Centre in the Fraser Valley.

Randy said, "Well, I guess that sounds okay. When do I go there?"

Another member told him, "Tomorrow evening."

Randy spent the remainder of the day, as well as most of the following day, saying goodbye to his fellow inmates and packing his belongings. Both Thor and Heatley commented that he was lucky to be getting out of that shithole.

Randy said, "I'm going to miss this place like I miss a fucking hangover!"

Before he left, he got together with Dave one last time and told him, "Once you're released, I'll have to go up to Kitimat and visit you sometime. Maybe we can even have a game of pool. But this time, it will be just for fun!"

At 7:30 that evening a guard showed up at Randy's cell and told him that it was time to move out. He was escorted to a loading area in the basement of the main jail. From there he was loaded into a van with three other prisoners.

As they headed out, he asked one of the other prisoners, "So, are you going to Mount Thurston camp too?"

Immediately the guard in the passenger seat yelled out, "Hey! No talking in the back!"

Randy wanted to yell out, "Fuck you, asshole," but he knew that if he did that he would end up right back where he had come from.

The drive seemed to take forever and because it was dark outside, Randy couldn't see where they were going. Eventually the ride became very bumpy, indicating that they were on a gravel road. He could barely see the outline of trees outside and nothing else. It seemed quite a long time since he had seen anything that resembled a settlement. He kept thinking, "Man, this place must really be out in the boonies!"

Eventually the van pulled into a compound with several buildings. It stopped in front of the main building and Randy and the other prisoners filed inside. From there they were taken to their designated cells. Actually, they weren't really cells; they were more like cabins with bunk beds.

The following morning, Randy got a good look at the compound and realized that it looked more like a summer camp than a prison. But what really got his attention was the absence of a fence or a guard tower. In addition, the atmosphere was a lot better than at Oakalla. There wasn't a lot of tension among the inmates. In fact, with most of the inmates, it was difficult to imagine that they were capable of committing a crime. As an example, Randy's bunkmate was a lawyer who was serving time for contempt of court. The place also had one added bonus—the food was much better. He could also enjoy eating without worrying about someone potentially putting a knife in his back!

For the first week Randy was placed on work detail painting the outside of the recreation hall. Next he was assigned to raking leaves in front of the main building. After that he took a job in the woodworking shop building birdhouses and ornamental wishing wells.

For the first month everything seemed to be going okay there. Randy was getting along well with the other inmates and had managed to avoid getting on the bad side of any of the guards. But after a month he started to get restless. The absence of a fence was becoming a temptation to him.

He asked one of the other inmates why there was no fence was told, "That's quite simple. If you escape and get caught, you're sent back to a regular prison."

Randy said, "What if you don't get caught?"

"Do you know how far from civilization we are? There's only one road leading out of here, so it's not worth it."

A few days later, Randy asked an inmate who was from the immediate area where the road led to in each direction.

The inmate said, "Well, if you head east you will reach Chilliwack Lake, but then it's a dead end. If you head west you will eventually reach Vedder Road, which will take you to Chilliwack. But that's over twenty miles."

The inmate remarked on how strange it was that he had been sent there, since he knew the geography of the region so well, hailing from nearby Abbotsford. He pointed out that most of the inmates came from other parts of Canada, so escaping would be difficult for them because they would not know which direction to take. As an example, he pointed southward and told Randy that the Canada-U.S. border was only about three miles away. But in between there was nothing but mountains and wilderness, and once you crossed the border, it was the same thing. You would have to travel a great distance through thick woods before you reached a populated area. Randy found that quite fascinating, and then asked him what was directly north.

"Well, if you go up and over the mountain you will come out somewhere east of Chilliwack."

Over the next few days, Randy thought about what that local inmate had said about what was north of there. He remembered that whenever he had passed by Chilliwack on the Trans-Canada Highway, it hugged the foot of the mountain and was southeast of the city. He had hiked extensively in similar terrain in the heavily wooded mountains surrounding Granby. The combination of all of these factors was starting to give Randy weird ideas. He came up with a really hare-brained scheme. He decided to try to escape by climbing up and over the mountain, heading straight north. Once he reached the Trans-Canada Highway he would start hitchhiking. From there he would not stop until he reached Toronto. He hoped that if he got an early start and if he didn't have to wait very long for someone to pick him up, he could be well on his way to Ontario before they realized he was missing and sent out a search party. Roll call was at 7:30, so he would have to have at least a three-hour head start. He had this strange idea that once he reached Toronto, they would never be able to find him. Another advantage this place had was that he was allowed to wear his street clothes instead of a prison uniform. That way he wouldn't look suspicious when he was on the highway.

This hitchhiking odyssey would be very different from his previous ones. For one thing, he would have only the clothes on his back. His backpack and his other belongings were in a storage locker somewhere in Vancouver. Secondly, he had only twenty-five dollars to his name. How he was going to live on that all the way to Toronto was anybody's guess. Thirdly, he would be a wanted man. He remembered that during his first ever hitchhiking trip, he had thought he was a wanted man for his attack on Kees Vandelaar, but nothing had come of it. This time he really would be on the run from the law, and he would have to look over his shoulder practically every second. He wished himself well.

He waited until the right opportunity came along. He laid low for a few days and kept his mouth shut. He didn't want Paul, the inmate from Abbotsford, to get the idea that he was inquiring about the geography of the region with the intention of escaping, so he waited at least a week after their conversation. He was also afraid that if he said anything to any of the other inmates, they would try to talk some sense into him.

The morning of his escape, Randy woke up and looked at his watch. When he noticed that it was 4 a.m. he thought, "Great! This is my perfect opportunity!" He had slept in his clothes that night, so all he had to put on was his shoes and his heavy coat. He snuck out the door and made his way to the field at the north end of the complex. He bolted across the field and ran into the woods. Almost immediately, he began climbing up the mountain. From there he didn't stop. He climbed with great intensity, using every ounce of his strength. It was still pitch black out; daybreak was three hours away. He was constantly tripping over twigs and running into branches. It had rained the night before so the ground was quite wet. The slope was very steep, making the going even more difficult.

Randy eventually had to take a rest. He looked at his watch and saw that it was 10:00. He had been climbing and hacking his way through dense forest for six hours straight. He was completely exhausted and his ankles were killing him. He knew that they would have reported him missing by then, so his rest would have to be brief. He wasn't sure how much ground he had covered or if he was even going in the right direction. He didn't have a compass, so he could only guess that he was heading north.

By 4 p.m. he wasn't climbing as much and he could tell that he was approaching a ridge. He tried to find a clearing in the trees so he could get a vantage point and determine his position. He had figured that since it was November, the leaves on the trees would be gone, so that would make it easier to see. However, most of the trees around him were evergreens. He figured that was actually a blessing—that made it more difficult to track him from the air. A little earlier he had heard the sound of helicopters in the distance, and he had wondered if they were being used to look for him. There was only one hour of daylight left, so he figured that he had better cover as much ground as possible.

By nightfall he still had not found any clearings in the trees. He wanted to continue onward, but he knew that wasn't a good idea. He could end up going over a cliff or he could fall into an old mine shaft (if there were any in the area). Plus he could end up going in the wrong direction. He decided to take refuge in a grove of Douglas Fir trees. Despite the fact he was cold, he didn't want to start a fire; he was afraid that would give away his position. He tried to ration his cigarettes as he had only five left and he didn't know how long they would have to last him. It rained all that night so he didn't get very much sleep.

At daybreak he set off again. After an hour of hiking, he finally came to a clearing. But to his astonishment all he saw ahead of him was—more mountains! The Cheam Range was right in front of him, leaving him with only two choices: go over top of them or go around them. He decided to go around them by taking the east flank. Judging by the terrain that lay ahead, that would be no easy task.

Throughout the day Randy continued on, hacking his way through dense forest and climbing up and down. Occasionally he passed by a stream, so he was able to drink water. He didn't want to follow any of the stream beds since he could tell that they flowed in a southerly direction. He was afraid it would lead him right back to where he had come from. He repeatedly heard the sound of helicopters in the distance, so he knew that they were after him. Even after darkness started to set in, he still kept going. But then he saw in the distance a figure that looked like a bear. When it moved, Randy realized that it was indeed a bear. He hid behind a tree and hoped that the bear wouldn't notice him.

He said, "Holy shit! What is this with me and bears?"

Randy was glad that he had seen it in time; the last thing he wanted to do was surprise it. Eventually the bear moved on. He decided not to proceed any further until morning. He found another grove of trees and spent the night there.

That night it was very cold and it felt like it was going to snow. Randy wanted to light a fire in the worst way, but the logs were too wet. It was then that he faced the grim reality that he was truly lost. The one time he had been able to see into the distance, he hadn't seen anything that even remotely resembled civilization. He began to wonder if he was going to make it out of there alive. He even contemplated retracing his steps and heading back to Mt. Thurston Camp, but since he hadn't followed any trails, that would also be difficult. He thought that if he made it back there, he could just tell the staff that he had gone for a walk and got lost. He had not eaten anything since the night before he had left; all he had been living on was water, so he was absolutely starving. Even worse, he had been having a serious nicotine fit since he had been forcing himself to ration his cigarettes.

As expected, he barely slept a wink that night. He huddled under a large Douglas Fir and tried his best to keep warm. He was afraid that if he went to sleep, hypothermia would set in. The combination of lack of sleep and food was making him practically delirious. He wasn't sure if he was going to be able to carry on much longer.

He remembered that before he had left camp, he had stuffed three buns from the dining hall in his coat pocket. They were a bit stale by then, but he was so hungry he didn't care. When he took a drink from a nearby stream, he was wishing that it flowed with coffee instead of water!

He began hacking his way through the dense forest once again. After a couple hours he got a pleasant surprise. Lo and behold, right in front of him was a logging road! It looked as though it hadn't been used in awhile, but he figured that it had to lead somewhere. He wasn't sure whether to go left or right. Since it went downhill to the right he decided to take a chance and go that way. Once on the road he picked up the pace. Going downhill helped considerably. An hour later, after rounding a hairpin curve, he came upon a jeep parked in the middle of the road right in front of him. There were three men inside all wearing correctional officer uniforms. Two of them were carrying rifles.

The man in the driver's seat said, "Going somewhere, Mr. Watson?"

Randy was sent back to the hellish confines of Oakalla Prison. To add insult to injury, they added three months to his sentence for being unlawfully at large. He was not placed in the same cell as before. He was now in a cell two tiers below. The reception he got when he was reunited with his former cellmates was not very favourable.

When Thor saw that Randy was back, he said, "What the fuck are you doing back here?"

Heatley said, "Are you fucking crazy, man?"

And Dave Sewell said, "Do you like this fucking place or something?"

To those who asked why he was back there, he explained that it was because he had tried to escape from Mt. Thurston Camp. Their feelings were mutual. They all thought that Randy had completely lost his marbles.

He learned that in the month he had been away, tensions among inmates had increased to the point where it had become a virtual tinderbox and the place could explode at any minute. The problem stemmed from the mixing of remand prisoners and regular inmates, and the root of the problem originated from the federal penitentiary system. All of the federal prisons were experiencing severe overcrowding, so an increasing number of inmates that belonged there were being housed in Oakalla. With the riot-torn west wing closed, there was additional pressure on the south wing, which was bursting at the seams so they were placing remand prisoners in the east wing. Randy's cell was no exception. Two of his cellmates were serving life sentences for murder. The first prisoner, Sims, was serving two life sentences for murdering two children. He had broken into a house with the intention of robbing the place, and when he noticed there were two children there, he stabbed the ten-year-old girl and strangled the eight-year-old boy. The second remand prisoner, whose name was Kendall, was serving a life sentence for killing a cop. One night while attending a party at a friend's place, a lone RCMP officer had been called to the house because of a noise complaint. While the officer was interviewing the host, Kendall crept up behind him and shot him point-blank in the back of the head. He died instantly. Neither Sims nor Kendall showed any remorse for what they had done. In fact, Sims liked to brag in graphic terms about what he had done to the children. It almost seemed like he had enjoyed the killing. Randy found him sickening.

Another factor adding to the tension centred around the postponement to close Oakalla. Another promise to replace the ancient facility had fallen through, so it would be several more years before a new prison would be built. It seemed that the provincial government did not have the money for a new facility, so Oakalla would have to do. As far as the inmates were concerned, the government didn't give a goddamn that they were living in deplorable, overcrowded conditions.

The combination of these factors made Randy realize just how big a mistake he had made. With the place ready to blow at any time, he was very much on edge. The atmosphere at Mt. Thurston camp hadn't been anything like that. He had no one to blame but himself for blowing it. It was a classic case of "you made your bed, you sleep in it." In addition to Sims and Kendall, he also shared his cell with an obese, middle-aged inmate who wouldn't give his name. Nobody knew what he was serving time for since he would not give anyone the time of day. All anyone knew was that he was not a remand prisoner. Randy figured that as long as he kept his distance, the man shouldn't be any trouble. It was his remand cellmates that had him worried. Those guys were genuinely creepy; Randy knew they were capable of doing anything, and he had nowhere to run or hide. He wasn't exactly sure what their relationship with each other was. Sometimes they fought like bitter enemies and other times they acted like the best of friends. On some occasions they even behaved like lovers. Sometimes at night they would either masturbate each other or have anal intercourse.

One night things took a different turn, much to the detriment of Randy. Sims and Kendall were discussing trying something different. They were both agreeing that the same old sex was becoming passé. Then they both cast their eyes on Randy, who was sitting on his bunk reading.

They gazed at him lustfully for a few minutes and then Kendall said, "What do you think, Sims? Should we go for him?"

Sims said, "Fine with me. That boy sure has a nice ass!"

Randy said, "Hey, what's going on here?"

At that point Sims and Kendall both produced homemade knives that they had hidden under their mattresses.

"Boy, you better keep your fucking mouth shut and do as we tell you!" Sims said. He walked over to the cell door to prevent Randy from trying to escape. He ordered him to take his clothes off and Randy reluctantly complied. He told him to lie down on the bed face down. As Sims undressed, Kendall grabbed Randy by the hair on the back of his head and put his knife right up to his throat.

Kendall said in a sick tone of voice, "Sims, I wish I could slit this little fucker's throat wide open! I always wanted to watch someone bleed to death!"

After Sims completed undressing, he mounted his burly frame onto Randy, who could do nothing but lie helplessly. He proceeded to shove his male hardness up Randy's ass. As Kendall watched, he took his knife and pressed it right into Randy's cheek with the tip of the blade a mere inch from his left eye.

Kendall whispered, "How would you like me to cut your eyes out, boy? Would you like that, huh?"

Randy was absolutely terrified; either of these guys could kill him at any second and nobody would care. He tried nodding to indicate no and Sims hit him hard in the back of the head.

He yelled out, "Keep still, boy!"

As he rode up and down on Randy, both of them began to laugh.

When Sims finished, Kendall said, "Wow, man, now it's my turn!"

Over the next two weeks, Sims and Kendall raped and terrorized Randy on at least six different occasions. Each time, he was so traumatized that he had wished one of them would stab him to death and put him out of his misery. During each incident the fat man would just turn a blind eye and pretend nothing was happening. As for Randy, he wasn't sure how much more he could take.

One month after Randy was returned to Oakalla, the volatile situation finally exploded. It all centred around a remand prisoner who wanted to see his girlfriend when she came to the visitors' area. When the guards refused to allow him to see her, he became very belligerent. He began to yell and scream and bang on his cell door with a metal bed leg. He encouraged the inmates in the neighbouring cells to join in and before you knew it, at least twenty men were screaming their heads off. This was all happening three tiers above Randy's cell, but he could hear everything clearly. When two guards came to restrain the instigator, he punched one of them in the face and began kicking him in the groin. When the other guard came to his aid, the other inmates in that cell began beating on him. The two guards barely escaped the tier with their lives. After that all hell broke loose. All of the inmates on that tier grabbed whatever object they could find and began smashing everything in sight. The main objects of destruction were sinks and toilets. Randy's concern was for Dave Sewell. He was on that upper tier and he was badly outnumbered by the large number of remand inmates.

It didn't take long for the mayhem to make it down to Randy's tier. The inmates had complete control of the entire east wing and the guards were powerless to stop them. The RCMP and the Burnaby Fire Department were called to the scene, and there was even talk of the S.W.A.T. team being called in.

Randy's cell was not exempt from all of the chaos. Sims and Kendall began to attack the sink and toilet with metal bed legs.

Randy yelled out, "What the hell are you guys doing? How are we going to go to the goddamn bathroom?"

All around him inmates were screaming and smashing everything in sight. In the area outside the tiers, broken porcelain and other objects rained down. In at least three different cells inmates set fire to their beds. Smoke soon began to fill the entire east wing area. Randy pretended to be actively taking part in the riot by shaking his fist in the air and yelling out whatever the other prisoners were yelling. But deep down inside he was scared to death. He saw that inmates were turning on and beating each other, and he wasn't sure if he was going to come out of this alive. If he tried to run outside the tier, the guards would attack him. He realized that he was completely trapped, so he had no choice but to go along with the other inmates if he wanted to stay alive.

Eventually the RCMP emergency response team arrived on the prison grounds. Over a loud bullhorn, the commander announced that all of the rioters had a half hour to give themselves up or else tear gas would be deployed and the tactical unit would enter the cell block. A few minutes later, Randy and several other inmates made a run for the end gate. When the door opened, they were met by two heavily armed tactical team members.

Randy kept his arms above his head and yelled out, "I surrender!"

A guard ordered Randy and the other inmates to file down the hall in an orderly manner. From there they were led down to the old Segregation Unit. Over the next half hour, more inmates gave themselves up peacefully, including Kendall and the fat man. Sims and several other inmates remained defiant and stayed until the bitter end and had to be tear-gassed.

Randy and everyone else had to spend the night in the old Segregation Unit. They were not allowed back to their cells until the next morning. The unit was under heavy guard to ensure there would not be any more disturbances.

The following morning, Randy overheard the guards listing the names of the prisoners who had been the main troublemakers in the riot and who would be transferred to a federal penitentiary. Apparently this latest disturbance had been the last straw for Warden Bjarnason, who was finally fed up with Oakalla being a "warehouse" for prisoners who belonged in federal institutions. He had managed to persuade some of the federal prisons to take some of the remand inmates. Much to Randy's delight, one of those being transferred was Sims. He was being sent to Fort Saskatchewan Federal Penitentiary. Randy knew that the only time Kendall had acted tough was when he was hiding behind Sims. He could tell that, in reality, Kendall was nothing more than a coward. That was obvious from the manner in which he had killed the cop.

When Randy returned to his cell, Kendall was the only other person there. He was urinating in the toilet, which had managed to remain intact after the riot (the sink hadn't fared so well).

Randy said, "Hey Kendall, what happened to your bum buddy? Well, isn't that something? Yesterday you tried to destroy the toilet and now you're using it. Think about it! If you weren't such a fucking wuss, you would be pissing on the floor right now, wouldn't you?"

Randy gave Kendall a chance to do up his fly and turn around. But before he had a chance to flush the toilet, Randy sucker-punched him right in the nose. He gave him a brutal right hook followed by a left hook, grabbed him by the hair and shoved his head into the toilet bowl. He held his head under the water for at least a minute. Kendall tried flinging his arms and legs in an attempt to break free from Randy's grip, but to no avail.

He pulled Kendall's head out of the toilet bowl and yelled out, "You don't look so tough now, do you? You ever wonder what it's like to drown in your own piss? Here, let's find out!"

Randy shoved his head into the toilet bowl again and held it under for another minute. When he pulled Kendall's head out the second time, the man was starting to turn purple and was gasping for air. He reeked from his own urine. Randy then kicked him in the balls and followed that with a series of hard upper cuts. He flung Kendall hard into the cell door and repeatedly punched him in the stomach until he was spitting up blood. He once again grabbed Kendall by the back of the head and rammed him full throttle into what was left of the sink. From there he opened the cell door, threw Kendall out onto the tier and then proceeded to beat him up further. He landed a whole series of roundhouse rights and lefts, culminating with a vicious right hook to the head, which knocked him out cold.

Even though he was unconscious, Randy still yelled out to Kendall, "You can come back in when you show me some respect, you fucking worthless piece of shit!"

Afterward, Randy went up to the infirmary to check on Dave Sewell. Since he hadn't been down in the old Segregation Unit after the riot, Randy figured that something must have happened to him. Sure enough, his instincts were right. The doctor on duty told him that Dave had been brought up there after the riot, the victim of a brutal beating. He had since been transferred to Royal Columbian Hospital with severe head injuries. Randy didn't know what to make of that; he could only hope that his friend would pull through.

Over the following week, the situation had barely cooled down at all. The atmosphere was still extremely volatile, and another disturbance could erupt at any minute. Randy was still very much on edge and was looking over his shoulder practically every second. An example of the tense situation occurred one evening in the dining hall. He had just started eating dinner when two men at the next table got into a heated argument. It appeared as though one of them was a remand prisoner and the other a sentenced one. It escalated into a pushing and shoving match and eventually into an all-out fist fight. Then, without warning, one of them produced a jagged end of a toothbrush that had been broken in half (the end had been filed down to make it sharper). He took the sharp end and jammed into the other man's eye. The man started screaming at the top of his lungs and was bleeding profusely from his eye socket. Randy couldn't believe what he was seeing, as all of the other prisoners just sat back and laughed.

When the man staggered too close to any of the other prisoners, they would just say, "Get the fuck away from me, asshole," and would push him away.

Randy was absolutely horrified; he wanted desperately to help the man, but he knew if he made any attempt to do so, the others would turn on him. He couldn't finish his dinner. He got up and ran to the nearest garbage can just in time to get sick. He walked slowly back to his cell and was relieved to see that nobody else was in there; he wanted to be alone. Sitting down on his bed, completely broken down and starting to cry, he said over and over to himself, "I can't take this place anymore! Get me out of here!"

He made several efforts to arrange a meeting with the Parole Board. At first he didn't have any luck, but after two weeks of persistence, one representative agreed to meet with him. The first thing Randy told him was how sorry he was for his escape attempt from Mt. Thurston Camp. He promised that if he was given a second chance there, he would never try to escape again. He begged and pleaded for them to give him another chance.

But in the end the representative said, "You must think I'm crazy," and walked out of the meeting.

Over the next month Randy made a couple more pleas to the Parole Board, but they fell on deaf ears.

With all that had been happening at the troubled prison, it was refreshing to have something positive happen to Randy for a change. There was a new prisoner named Derek Chadsey who took a job working alongside him in the woodworking shop. Almost immediately he befriended Randy. At first Randy thought that was strange, since the name of the game there was to keep to yourself. Since his imprisonment, he had been having an increasingly difficult time trusting people. Derek, who was serving an eighteen-month sentence for drug trafficking, seemed interested in getting to know him. He often confided in him on matters pertaining to prison life and was very open about his background. Eventually, they hit it off and became friends. Randy was actually glad about this. After Dave Sewell had recovered, he had been transferred to the Prince George Regional Correctional Centre, and Randy had been left with no one to talk to.

Another event Randy learned of that gave him a new lease on life was that Doug had been arrested. While watching the evening news in the recreation room, the broadcaster read, "Eighteen-year-old Douglas Whitlaw, who fled to the United States two weeks ago after a warrant for cocaine trafficking had been issued, was arrested last night in Seattle, Washington. He has been charged with the brutal double murder of an elderly couple in their home in Bothell, just north of Seattle."

It turned out that Doug had broken into the house with the intention of robbing the place, but when he realized the occupants were home, he had bludgeoned the couple to death. As Washington had capital punishment, if convicted, he could face the death penalty. Randy thought, "Good! I hope they fry the bastard! It's too bad they don't have the death penalty in Canada!"

17

Month twenty-three

Over the past ten months, Randy had been going out of his way to be on his best behaviour. He had avoided getting into fights and had been working hard in the woodworking shop. Eventually it paid off. Three weeks before his second anniversary as a prisoner, he was granted a hearing with the Parole Board. This time the results were different—he was granted parole.

When he walked through the main entrance gate of Oakalla a free man, he felt like it was the happiest day of his life. However, it was kind of sad to say goodbye to Derek, but they agreed to get in touch once he was released. Derek said that his favourite hangout was the Patricia Hotel, so he suggested Randy look for him there in eight months.

Actually, Randy was not completely free. He had to report to a halfway house on Victoria Drive near Hastings Street. He would be under a strict curfew—he had to be back there by 11:00 at night. Drugs and alcohol were not allowed on the premises, and he had to report regularly to a parole officer. He figured he could live with that quite easily—at least he was free to leave the premises during the day.

The one thing he wasn't looking forward to upon his release was his visit to the doctor. He had to have a test for AIDS. With all of the sexual activity he'd had with the other male prisoners over the past two years, the test was necessary. Randy was worried sick about what the outcome might be. If he tested HIV-positive that would mess him up sexually for the rest of his life. Luckily, the test results showed up negative.

The timing of Randy's release couldn't have worked out better. There were still two weeks left of Expo '86. He had wondered if he would ever get a chance to see it. He remembered seeing the opening ceremonies on the television in the Oakalla recreation room, and he had hoped ever since then that he would be paroled before it was over. Luckily, that dream came true. He spent a total of three days taking it in and had a really enjoyable time.

One of Randy's other priorities was to get revenge on the four guys who had contributed to him ending up in jail. Although he agreed that he had to take some responsibility for his own actions, he felt that it was his upstairs neighbours who had influenced him into a life of crime, and then stabbed him in the back in the end. With Doug out of the way, that left only the four other guys to take care of. With a two-year accumulation of rage and hostility bottled up inside of him, Randy was willing to take on all four of them at once if he had to.

When he arrived at the house, he was in for a big surprise—it was all boarded up and there was a "For Sale" sign on the front lawn. Obviously perplexed by this, Randy decided to pay Jim Leung a visit to find out what had happened. He remembered where Jim lived but couldn't remember his phone number. Jim's place was a twenty-minute bus ride from the house.

When he arrived at Jim's place he knocked at the door and a middle-aged lady answered. He asked if Jim Leung was home. She said that he no longer lived there. In frustration Randy went to the nearest pay phone and called the real estate office where Jim worked. The receptionist explained that he had moved back to Hong Kong.

Randy knew of another lead. He remembered a friend of Chad's named Mike who regularly hung out at the Ivanhoe Hotel. The following day he paid a visit to the beer parlour at the Ivanhoe. Sure enough, Mike was there, and he still remembered Randy from his frequent visits to the house. He told Randy that Greg and Kelly had moved back to Ontario and he had no idea where the other guys were. In fact, he had not heard from Chad in over a year. Hearing that didn't help Randy very much. In addition, the only one of the four whose last name he knew was Chad. That wasn't much help either, since his last name was Smith. In the end, he decided that as long as he never crossed paths with any of them again he wouldn't worry about it. But if he ever ran into any of them, watch out!

Aside from his attempted vendetta against his former partners in crime, Randy had decided to adopt a new attitude once he got out of Oakalla. Instead of feeling sorry for himself all of the time and being angry at the whole world, he decided to make a strong effort to turn his life around. He figured the best way to start would be to leave Vancouver. He got this idea that as soon as his parole was completed, he would hitchhike eastward and not stop until he reached Toronto. He would start a new life there. He thought that in Toronto he would be away from all of his bad memories and that would help him start all over again. He brought this up at his meeting with his parole officer, Paul Bresseldorff. As he talked about his plans for the future, Paul shook his head in disbelief. He asked Randy what he thought he could accomplish by going to Toronto.

Randy said, "Well, the economy is doing really well there, and I should have a better chance of finding a job. Plus, there I will have an easier time forgetting about the mistakes I made in the past."

"Randy, you can't keep running away all the time. It won't do you any good to keep drifting from one city to another. There comes a time when you have to put down roots. Going to Toronto is not going to solve anything in the long run. You still have to face the fact that you are poorly educated and you do not have any viable job skills." Paul paused, then continued, "I see that you've worked on an oil rig. That job is definitely not in demand right now. I also see that you have operated a mixing machine at a feed mill. I doubt very much that there will be any positions of that nature in Toronto! To be honest, you need to upgrade your education and learn some type of vocation if you want to have any chance of making it in the real world. You'll be better off if you stay put here in Vancouver."

Randy realized that Paul was right, and he decided to take his advice to heart. He acknowledged that he had never learned any type of trade and didn't have a lot to offer employers. He also had to accept the fact that he had not held a steady job since January of 1982, over four and a half years ago. That was something he was definitely not proud of. He knew that he was going to have to make some changes if he was going to get anywhere in life. He also figured that Paul was right about staying put in Vancouver. He had never been to Toronto, and as was the case with all of the other cities he had previously ventured to, the idea to journey there was based solely on speculation. It was over halfway across the country and was much bigger than any of the other cities he had lived in. If he went there and things didn't pan out, then what? Maybe staying in Vancouver wasn't such a bad idea after all. One place he would definitely not relocate to was Granby. That evening while watching the news, he learned that the Bull Elk Mine was shutting down permanently, throwing two hundred people out of work. This made Randy feel like his decision to leave Granby eight years ago was one of the few good decisions he had ever made.

At his next meeting with Paul, Randy informed him of his change of plans. He told him that he wanted to go back to school next year and was interested in finding a job in the meantime. Paul, delighted to hear this, told him about a friend of his who operated a small printing shop.

His name was Morris McAlpine, and twenty years ago he had appeared to be heading toward a life of crime. He had been in and out of jail since he was seventeen for petty crimes, but then he had decided to turn his life around and had started a printing business. His story was truly inspirational. Actually, his printing business wasn't so small anymore. Many corporations had their annual reports printed by his company, and he had contracts with over seventy-five percent of the Chinese restaurants in the Greater Vancouver area to print their take-out menus. He now employed over fifty people. He had a program whereby ex-convicts who wanted to start over again were given an opportunity to work for him. Paul believed this was a very worthwhile program, since a lot of companies would not hire people with criminal records. Randy told him he would be interested in giving it a try. Paul warned him that if got hired, he would be under very close scrutiny. Morris would not put up with lateness, and absolutely no drugs or alcohol would be tolerated on the job. In fact, he would not even accept workers coming into work with a hangover. Randy said that he was cool with that.

When Randy had his meeting with Morris McAlpine, everything went favourably. Morris seemed quite impressed with Randy's past track record as a worker. He realized that the loss of his last job had not been his fault. He liked the fact that Randy had stuck it out on the oil rig for an entire drilling season, something not everyone could handle. He also received a positive report from Randy's supervisor at the woodworking shop in Oakalla. Overall, he was pleased with Randy's prior work ethic and was willing to offer him a position. Randy gladly accepted; he was to start the next Monday.

The first week on the job went very well; Morris was quite pleased with Randy's work. He started with the simple job of bundling together piles of take-out menus and placing them in boxes. After three months he was placed on permanent staff.

The following February, Randy enrolled in night courses through the Vancouver School Board in order to obtain his grade twelve equivalency. Before registering, he met with a counsellor to determine what courses he would need based on how far his studies had gone before he left high school. He had completed one semester of grade nine and had been halfway through the second semester when he dropped out. The counsellor told him that he could start off with grade ten courses and showed him the number of courses he would have to take in order to graduate. Randy figured that it would take him at least three years. He enrolled in two classes for the spring semester—English and math. He would be going four nights a week, Monday to Thursday, until the end of June. That would leave him Friday nights and weekends to study.

In March he completed his parole, so he was able to move out of the halfway house and into a place of his own. He chose a bachelor suite in an apartment building only two blocks from where he was taking his night courses. It was also only a fifteen-minute bus ride from work. This meant he had a little time to study after work and after class. Throughout the term, he pretty much kept his nose to the grindstone and kept the partying to a minimum. His attitude was, "I'll save my energy until the end of June." Usually, all he would do on Saturday night was walk down to a neighbourhood pub three blocks from his apartment and have a couple of pints. In the end, it paid off. His grades were better than any he had ever received when he was a teenager in school.

Attending night school proved to be more advantageous than he had expected. In addition to improving his education level, he met a girl in his math class who had taken an interest in him. Her name was Cassandra Peters and, like Randy, she was trying to obtain her grade twelve equivalency. She had a seven-year-old daughter named Ashley who was living with Cassandra's mother. Cassandra had dropped out of high school but under completely different circumstances than his (she had become pregnant). He wasn't sure if she had ever married (he didn't want to pry), but she assured him that her daughter's father was completely out of the picture. In addition to taking courses, she also worked part-time as a cashier at a Safeway store. Her eventual goal was to pursue a career either in accounting or as a legal secretary.

Early in the semester Cassandra introduced herself to Randy. She was looking for someone to give her some help with the math assignments and, since math was his strong point, he was able to lend a hand. Over the course of the semester they began to talk about each other's interests, their goals and aspirations and backgrounds. As it turned out, they found they had a lot in common. Randy was up front and honest with her about his criminal background. He admitted he had made a terrible mistake and that he was doing everything in his power to try and redeem himself. Cassandra said she was okay with that.

As the semester wore on, Randy tried very hard to work up the nerve to ask her out. He didn't want to let on that he was shy around women, but he figured that she could tell anyway. He found her very pretty, which was making the task even harder. He had never thought of himself as very good-looking, so he always felt that an attractive woman would never be interested in him. Of course he had developed that mentality while growing up in Granby, where boys had outnumbered girls by a ratio of at least ten to one. Any attractive girl in Granby was always extremely popular. Heck, even ugly women had men chasing them. Even Randy's mom, who was average looking, had men chasing her when she was between husbands. He had to keep telling himself again and again that he was not in Granby anymore. Even when he'd lived in Calgary, the situation seemed similar. But he finally realized, as the song implied, he was "looking for love in all the wrong places." He had no female co-workers at the printing shop and most of the women in his apartment building were married. There were a few single mothers living there, but they weren't interested in him. The dumpy hotel beer parlours he hung out in were not great places to meet girls. He remembered someone telling him once that the Ranchman's Nightclub was a great place to meet girls, but he didn't like country music. Randy figured he had just not put in enough effort to find a girlfriend while living in Calgary. But things were different now. He realized that this was the time to make a move.

With two weeks left to go in the semester, Randy walked Cassandra to her car after class as he usually did. But instead of saying goodnight right away, he asked her if she would like to go out that weekend. Lo and behold, she said yes.

She gave him her phone number and after she drove off the parking lot, Randy jumped what seemed to be ten feet in the air and let out a big, "Yahoo!"

He called Cassandra and asked her if she would like to go to a casual Italian restaurant near her place. He had no idea if the restaurant was any good or not. The reason he had chosen it was strictly for its proximity to Cassandra's place—he didn't want her to know he didn't own a car!

That Saturday night the date went very well. They both liked the restaurant and enjoyed each other's company. She agreed to go out with Randy again, but wanted to wait until after final exams were over. He was okay with that since, after all, he had to study too. The fact that she wanted to go out with him again was incentive enough.

One of Randy's first priorities was to buy a car—it wasn't very cool to go on a date and take the bus. His abstinence from drinking and partying over the past five months had really paid off. He had a substantial amount of money saved up, so he went to a used car lot on Kingsway and purchased a 1978 Oldsmobile Delta 88. The car was in fairly good shape and had low mileage. Randy figured that this car would be fine for the time being.

Randy and Cassandra wrote their last final exam at the same time.

As they left the school building for the last time that semester, Randy said to her, "So, how would you like to celebrate the end of classes this Saturday?"

"What did you have in mind?" Cassandra asked.

"How about I surprise you."

"Sounds good to me."

Randy asked her if 7 p.m. would be a good time to pick her up. She agreed, but was unsure how Randy would pick her up, since she had never seen him with a car. But Randy had deliberately parked his car next to hers that evening.

As they arrived at her car, she said, "Gee Randy, I didn't know you had a car!" Randy played it cool and said, "It needed some major work done so I had it off the road for awhile, but now it's good as new!"

The reason Randy had told her their date would be a surprise was because he didn't know where to go himself. He had to think of a place fast. He wanted to show he had some class, so that automatically ruled out the Sunrise Hotel! He also needed to do something about his wardrobe. He had never had any formal clothes. He went to Woodward's in Oakridge Mall and bought a pair of dress pants, a dress shirt and some dress shoes. While he was at the mall he went into Cole's bookstore and leafed through a copy of *Vancouver Gastronomic*, a local restaurant guide. Of all the restaurants listed, he decided upon the one at the top of the Sheraton Landmark Hotel. It looked like they had a wide choice of cuisine and the view was spectacular.

Before Randy picked up Cassandra, he stopped at Lobban's Flower Shop on Kingsway and bought a dozen roses. When he arrived at her apartment, she was wearing a white dress, had her hair done and had had a makeover. Randy flipped at the sight of her thinking, "Wow!" She thanked him for the flowers and complimented him on his attire.

The restaurant was a very fancy place. The meals were superb and the view was even better. However, Randy was more preoccupied with the view of Cassandra than the view outside. More than ever before, he realized just how beautiful she was. He felt like he had died and gone to heaven.

There was a live band playing so they were able to dance the night away. There was also a spectacular sunset that enhanced the setting. All in all, everything was going well until Randy got the bill. He totally freaked when he saw the total. He was relieved when he looked inside his wallet and saw that he had sufficient funds. He even had enough for a tip. He tried his best to play it cool and not act like the place was over his head. Fortunately, Cassandra was in the ladies' room when the bill arrived, so she never saw the surprised look on his face. As they left, she asked Randy if the place had not been too expensive for his budget.

He was very cool about it, saying, "Hey, no problem!"

When he dropped her off, she told him that she'd had a wonderful time and would love to see him again. Randy didn't want to invite himself into her apartment; he figured he would let her do that. When she didn't, he wasn't worried. He knew he would be seeing her again. He realized that the nice thing about being on his own and away from high school was that there was no peer pressure. He remembered back to when he was in high school. If he had ever gone out with Tracy Sanchez, the first thing his friends would have asked him the next day would have been, "Did you fuck her?" Randy didn't like that. He felt that his love life was nobody else's business. That was why he kept his personal life to himself among his co-workers.

Over the course of the summer, Randy and Cassandra began to see each other on a regular basis. Quite often he would have her over at his place for dinner, showing his culinary expertise (which had improved dramatically in the past year). She often returned the favour at her place. They liked to spend their time going for walks in Stanley Park and swimming at Kitsilano Beach. Randy really enjoyed it when they went to the beach—Cassandra looked sensational in a bikini.

One Friday night in August when Cassandra was working late at Safeway, Randy decided to go to the pub in the Patricia Hotel after work. When he entered the pub, he received a pleasant surprise. He saw his old friend from Oakalla, Derek, sitting at one of the tables.

Randy approached the table and said, "Well, hello there, stranger!"

Derek looked up and exclaimed joyfully, "Randy! How the hell are you doing?"

Randy said, "I'm doing just fine! So, when were you released?"

Derek said he'd been released three weeks ago. Like Randy, he had been granted early parole three months before the completion of his sentence.

Randy asked what was probably the most obvious question. "So, I bet you're really glad to get out of that shithole, right?"

"You better believe it! Man, that place was fucking horrible! It was not fit for a bloody dog!"

Randy nodded in agreement.

According to Derek, things had not changed one bit since Randy had left Oakalla. In the past year there had been two major disturbances and two escapes. Once again there was talk about closing the place down and opening a new facility in Maple Ridge.

When Randy heard that, he said to Derek, "I'll believe that when I see it!"

"So how have you been doing since your release?" Derek asked him.

"Well, I found a job, I'm going to night school to get my grade twelve equivalency—and I found a girlfriend."

"Wow, you've sure come a long way! I guess life is treating you pretty good now."

"I knew I needed to make some changes, so I did. So, Derek, what are you going to do with yourself now?"

Derek told him that he wasn't doing much of anything and he wasn't sure what he was going to do. For awhile he just wanted to savour his freedom.

They ended up staying the entire evening in the pub. They had a lot of catching up to do. They reminisced about their time together in Oakalla, and relayed their stories about how they had ended up there in the first place. At the end of the evening Randy was pretty loaded, so he had to take a cab home.

At 9:00 the following morning, Cassandra phoned Randy and asked if he wanted to go with her up to Squamish to visit her cousin. He was still in a drunken stupor and his mind was foggy, so he kept asking Cassandra to repeat her message.

Eventually he could tell that she was getting rather annoyed, so he finally clued in and said, "Sure, I would love to come. What time do you want to pick me up?"

"In an hour," she told him.

Randy struggled to get to his feet—he was pretty hungover. Even getting dressed seemed like a major chore. His first priority was to make some coffee. When the kettle began to whistle, he wanted to throw it clear across the kitchen. When Cassandra buzzed the intercom, he told her he'd be right down. He struggled down the stairs, still unable to walk in a straight line.

When he met her at the front door she said in a cheerful tone, "Good morning," and, turning to the girl at her side, continued, "This is my daughter, Ashley. I brought her along for the ride. I didn't think you would mind. Besides, I thought it was about time the two of you met."

Randy looked down at the girl and croaked, "Hi."

Then he muttered to himself, "Man, I sure hope she doesn't like to make noise."

As they got in her car, Cassandra took a long look at him and said, "My god, you look awful!" She then noticed the distinct smell of alcohol and said, "Were you drinking last night?"

Randy said, "Actually, I was. Do you remember that guy I was telling you about? We were friends when we were in Oakalla. His name is Derek. He was released three weeks ago and I saw him last night at the Patricia Hotel. To make a long story short, we ended up celebrating his new-found freedom."

Cassandra said, "I remember you talking about him. I'm not so sure it's a good idea for you to be hanging around him. He sounds like a bad influence."

"Don't pass judgment on him just from what I've said. He is the same as me. He made a mistake and he paid the price. Believe me, staying in Oakalla is enough to straighten a person out. If that place doesn't straighten you out chances are no place will. He deserves another chance."

Cassandra said, "Well, I've never met him, so I don't know what he's like. I trust your judgment, but you still should be careful."

Randy insisted that they stop in Britannia Beach so he could purchase a coffee to go. Luckily, by the time they reached Cassandra's cousin's place he had completely sobered up.

As summer wore on, the romance between Randy and Cassandra continued to blossom. Deep down inside, Randy wanted to take their relationship one step further, but not if she wasn't willing. He didn't want to force her to do anything she didn't want to do. Since this was his first real serious relationship, he wasn't sure what approach to take. He had the feeling that she thought he was old-fashioned. Some women like that quality in a man, but not all. He knew that he should just be thankful he had met a girl who was genuinely interested in him. But inside his hormones were raging. This was most obvious whenever they visited the beach. Just seeing her in her skimpy bikini caused a swelling in his swim trunks. He tried his best not to make it noticeable; he deliberately bought a pair of loose-fitting trunks.

With one week left to go before classes started again in September, Randy and Cassandra decided to celebrate the end of summer at the Town Pump nightclub in Gastown one Saturday night. While they were dancing, she whispered to Randy that she wanted him to come over to her place afterward. She said she had a "special surprise" waiting for him. Randy sensed it was what he had been longing for because she'd had her hands all over him practically all evening. He remembered back to a night two weeks ago when Cassandra was over at his place. They were lying on his couch and watching a very boring movie. She had allowed Randy to remove her blouse and her bra and let him caress her breasts, but it hadn't gone any further than that. Randy could tell that tonight his wish would finally be granted.

When they arrived at her apartment, she put on some soft music and offered him a drink. He requested a scotch and soda. She had the same thing. Actually, he ended up having three drinks. She went into her bedroom and said she'd be out shortly. Even though he'd had three drinks, Randy was still nervous. With every other girl he had ever made love to, all they had cared about was his money. They couldn't have cared less about him as a person. It seemed so unusual to Randy—a girl actually caring about him as a human being. It seemed sad in a way. He had always thought of himself as a nice guy.

When Cassandra emerged, she was wearing a white terry-cloth bathrobe. She took Randy by the hand and led him into her bedroom. She encouraged him to untie the belt and remove her robe. She was completely naked underneath. He could barely breathe as she helped him remove his shirt. She noticed that his tight jeans looked like they were ready to explode, so she helped him remove them, along with his socks and underwear. They kissed passionately for several minutes before climbing into bed. She moaned in ecstasy as Randy thrust his rock-hard penis into her vagina. Their rhythmic motion nearly caused the bed to collapse as they both unleashed months of pent-up sexual desire. Cassandra then rolled on top of Randy and rode up and down on him as if he were a horse. He soon came to a stimulating climax and she followed shortly afterward. They both flopped down on the bed from sheer exhaustion.

Cassandra said in a playful tone of voice, "You did very well—in fact, you were excellent! Those girls in Calgary didn't know what they were missing!"

As she ran her hands along Randy's chest, she informed him that she had taken the pill, so he had nothing to worry about. He was glad about that, but he thought that sometime in the future he would like to become a father.

He ended up spending the night at Cassandra's place. When they woke up the next morning they had one more round of lovemaking before getting up. It was then that they realized their destiny—they were made for each other. That evening at dinnertime they made a toast: "To us—forever!"

18

Eleven months later

Randy had achieved his grade ten equivalency. In September he would be taking grade eleven courses. On the personal side, last January, Randy and Cassandra had decided to move in together. Their individual apartments had been too small for two people, so they had decided to get a larger place. Since they both owned cars, they hadn't needed a place that was close to work and school, so they had chosen an apartment in a building near Oak Street and 16th Avenue.

As for the job, Randy was doing really well at the printing plant. In fact, he was seriously considering becoming an offset press operator. He was thinking that when he achieved his grade twelve equivalency, he would then enrol in a program at Pacific Vocational Institute for the necessary training. That was only one option. He would see what happened when the time came.

In July, Morris informed Randy that since he had been employed for over a year, he was eligible for two weeks' holiday. Randy was ecstatic about that, since he had never really had a paid vacation before.

When he informed Cassandra about it, she was also quite happy. She told Randy that she had some vacation time saved up at Safeway and suggested that they take a trip together.

Randy said, "That sounds like a great idea! Do you have any suggestions?"

"Well, you have told me so much about your hometown of Granby that I thought it might be nice to take a trip there."

"Hmm, that's a possibility. After all, I haven't been back there since I left home ten years ago."

"It would be nice to see where you grew up. I didn't know very much about Granby before I met you. It seems like kind of a fascinating place."

Randy said, "I know! Why don't we visit your hometown instead?"

"You're in it!"

"I see. Well then, I guess we're heading to Granby."

He had mixed feelings about travelling to Granby. On the one hand, it would be nice to see how the town had changed since he had left, and to see once again all of the places that were part of his childhood. The changes, however, would most likely not have been for the better since the mine had closed two years ago. But on the other hand, all of his friends had left and any visit there would surely bring back bad memories. He was not too anxious to see his mom. In fact, he was not even sure if he would get in touch with her.

Randy thought long and hard about whether they should take a trip to Granby. The following morning he decided to go along with it. They made arrangements with their respective employers, and for the next two weeks they made preparations for the trip.

On the first day of the trip they drove as far as Williams Lake. They took turns driving. All along the route, especially in Hope, Lytton and Cache Creek, Randy noticed people hitchhiking. He kept thinking, "That used to be me. That was the way I used to travel." He remembered back to all of the trips he had taken by means of the "thumbnail express," and he wanted to return the favour. But Cassandra would have no part of it. She pointed out that any one of those people could be escaped convicts, rapists or mental cases.

Randy said, "Look, when I was hitchhiking I was just a kid who was travelling from one city to another. The people who gave me a ride never had anything to worry about with me. I was never a troublemaker."

Cassandra said, "From what you told me, most of the people who gave you rides were men. It's different for women. I don't know what the person's background is and if one of them has a gun, you will not be much help. I don't care what you do when you're travelling alone, but when you're travelling with me, no hitchhikers. Got it?"

Randy agreed.

The next day they drove only as far as Burns Lake. They had originally planned to drive as far as Smithers, but it was getting late in the day by the time they arrived in Burns Lake. The pool in the motel they'd stayed at in Williams Lake was so inviting that they'd decided to go for a swim that morning before checkout time. It was late before they left. But neither one of them cared, since they were on vacation and they had two weeks. Randy actually enjoyed it when Cassandra drove. That way he could admire the scenery. Of course, he wasn't sure which scenery he admired more—the surrounding countryside or Cassandra wearing shorts and a tank top!

After leaving Burns Lake the following morning, Randy made an unscheduled stop in Smithers. Since the turnoff to Granby was about a half a mile before Smithers, it meant taking a slight detour. Once he was in Smithers, he stopped in front of the C.N.R. station. Cassandra asked him why he was stopping here. He got out of the car and looked over to the other side of the rail yard. He wanted to see the storage shed where he had spent his first night of freedom after running away from home. Alas, it was no longer standing.

As he turned onto Highway 55 for the remaining forty-two miles to Granby, Cassandra said, "So, are you excited about seeing your hometown again?"

Randy told her, "It's hard to say. You see, I left there on bad terms, and aside from my friends and my brother, I hated the place. Living there was an exercise in sheer boredom. Growing up there, you basically had three choices for the future, the mine, the lumber mill or you could get the hell out. I obviously chose the latter."

The scenery surrounding Highway 55 on the way to Granby had not changed a bit in the past ten years. There was still the same amount of development (or lack of it) along the highway. Right after they passed the "Welcome to Granby" sign, Randy turned left onto Smethurst Road. He continued until he reached the railroad tracks and parked the car.

He said to Cassandra, "Come with me. I want to show you something."

The first thing Randy noticed was that the railroad tracks were overgrown with weeds. With the closure of the mine, the rail line had lost over half of its revenue and was now completely dependent on the lumber mill for its income—as was the case for the rest of the town. He could remember when there had been three trains a day in each direction. Now the most traffic was two trains a week, sometimes only one. The line was slated for abandonment, but a group in Smithers wanted to turn it into a tourist railroad. The line passed through some spectacular mountain scenery and the many trestles and tunnels made it even more spectacular, especially in Sonora Creek Canyon. When Randy read the article in the *Vancouver Sun* about the efforts of this particular group, he'd wished them all the best.

As they walked up the tracks, Cassandra asked where they were going.

When they reached that infamous hairpin curve, Randy pointed to it and said, "That's the spot where I made my break for freedom."

Cassandra said, "When you say freedom, you mean freedom from what?"

"Freedom from a tyrannical mother and a deadbeat, opinionated stepfather. Freedom from a dead-end life in a dead-end town."

"Even though your home life was less than perfect, you still had a roof over your head and three meals a day. From what you have told me, you quite often didn't have that when you were on the road. If you had to do it all over again, would you have finished school and left town to go to college?"

Randy said, "Yeah, I guess so. I guess I didn't have that much ambition back then. That was the general feeling in the town then, and it must have rubbed off on me."

As they walked back to the car, Randy could sense that this would be the last time he would see the railroad tracks here; it would soon be just a memory.

The Starlight Motel was still in the same place and fortunately still in business.

When Randy registered for a room, the man at the desk said, "So, you folks here on business?"

After he'd finished filling out the registration form, Randy said, "You obviously don't remember me, do you, Frank?"

The clerk gave him a rather puzzled look, and Randy said, "I'm Randy Watson. My mom was Carla Watson, who is now Carla McGuigan. You may remember me through my friend Gary McAllum. You used to work with his dad on the C.N.R."

Frank thought about it for a minute and then said, "Oh yeah, I think I remember you now. I didn't recognize you because you're all grown up. So, how are you doing?"

Randy said, "I'm doing pretty good. I live in Vancouver now. I have a great job and I've met the girl of my dreams." He had signed the register as Mr. and Mrs. Watson. "So I guess you could say I'm doing quite well."

"That's great! But why aren't you staying at your mother's place?"

Randy said, "She doesn't really have enough room at her place." He didn't want to say that she didn't know that he was in town.

Before they left the office, Randy asked him if very many tourists ever came there. He was told that it got fairly busy there during hunting season and the Turgeon River had superb steelhead fishing.

As they went to their room, Randy said to Cassandra, "I know why this place stays in business. He has his old-age pension, his wife's old-age pension and his C.N.R. pension. Otherwise, this place would have gone belly up a long time ago."

Randy spent the remainder of the day showing Cassandra the sights of Granby. They went through what was left of the downtown. Amazingly, the King Edward and Granby Hotels were still in business, but the Cecil Hotel had not been so fortunate. He pointed out that people who were unemployed still somehow managed to have money to go to the bar. He showed Cassandra the Mountainview subdivision, where the earliest miners' homes were. From there they went north of the city to the site of the Bull Elk Mine. They found it all gated and padlocked. Randy could not adjust to the mine site being so eerily quiet. During his youth, noise from the concentrator building could be heard all over town, twenty-four hours a day. Afterward they went to the A&W drive-in for dinner. There were still some reminders of his younger days remaining and this was one of them.

The following day Randy would be performing what was perhaps the most difficult task of this trip. He would be paying his respects to his father and Mark.

He and Cassandra went into Tina's Flower Shop and purchased two bouquets of flowers. From there they proceeded to the cemetery. They walked up and down the rows of tombstones until they reached the one that read "James Gilbert Watson 1933-1967."

Randy placed the bouquet on the tombstone, and said, "Here's to you, dad."

They then walked up to the mausoleum building, where urns containing the ashes of people who had been cremated were encased inside the wall. They scanned the walls until they saw the marble slab that read "Marcus Allan Watson 1966-1985." There was a receptacle in front where flowers could be placed. Randy struggled to say something as his eyes welled up with tears.

Cassandra said, "It's all right, Randy. Mark knew that you loved him."

After they left the cemetery Cassandra begged Randy to go and visit his mom. She pointed out that his mom was about the only family he had left now. She told him that she and her mother had had their differences over the years, but they had always respected each other, and nothing would ever cause them to shut each other out permanently.

"All right, you win," said Randy. "We'll go and see her."

Randy wasn't too concerned about how he would react to seeing her again; he was more worried about how she would react to seeing him. He was afraid she would slam the door in his face.

When they pulled up to his old house, Randy noticed that the place had not changed one bit.

"Well, this is it. This is the house I grew up in."

He was quite apprehensive as he rang the doorbell. When his mom answered, she said, "Randy! What a surprise!"

She was no doubt surprised, but her tone appeared to be joyful.

"Hello, mother. We were in town. I should have called first, I guess."

"That's all right. Please, come in."

"Mom, this is Cassandra."

His mom extended her hand. "Hello, I'm Carla McGuigan."

"Hello, I'm Cassandra Peters."

The get-together was fairly cordial, which surprised Randy, considering their past tensions. His mom seemed much more subdued, probably due to Mark's death. One of the first things Randy asked about was William. His mom told him she had finally come to her senses and had kicked him out a year and a half ago. The Workers' Compensation Board had decided that he had fully recovered from his back injury, so he had been cut off from disability. Even so, he had never made any effort whatsoever to find a job and she had become fed up with supporting him. She didn't know where he was and didn't really care.

Overall, the visit went very well. His mom was actually glad to see him, which was a clear indication of how lonely she was. She hit it off very well with Cassandra, which was another good sign. As they were leaving, she asked Randy to keep in touch and told him to come up again sometime in the near future. Randy agreed.

The following day, Randy decided that the trip down memory lane was officially concluded. There was nobody else left there he knew or cared to see. Bill and Brad's parents had both been laid off when the mine closed, so they had sold their house (at a major loss), moved to Osoyoos and bought into partnership with the orchard. Gary's dad had retired from the C.N.R., and he and his wife had moved to Scottsdale, Arizona.

As they packed their bags, Randy said to Cassandra, "I doubt very much that I will try to look up Arnold Becker!"

Cassandra thought Randy was referring to the retarded guy on *L.A. Law*.

Randy said, "No, I'm referring to the retarded guy in Granby! He was my arch nemesis in high school. I pounded the crap out of him the night I left here, but my friends never gave me a chance to finish him off. Someday, I wouldn't mind finishing the job. Every time I watch that show I think of him. There's so much similarity between the two characters besides just their names."

They turned in their room key, and Frank wished them well and told them to come back sometime.

As they sped away, Randy said, "Man, that guy must be almost eighty by now. I just wish I could remember his last name."

Their next destination was Kitimat. Randy had promised Dave Sewell that they would get together if he ever got up that way. The two of them had been corresponding by letters ever since Dave's sentence had been reduced. His parents had also left Granby and they, as well as Dave, were living in a house on the property owned by his aunt and uncle. Randy wasn't sure what to expect. After the riot, Dave had spent a month in the Royal Columbian Hospital and had then been transferred to Prince George General Hospital. From there he'd been placed in the infirmary at the Prince George Correctional Centre. He had undergone extensive physical therapy, but apparently had not completely recovered.

After Randy and Cassandra checked into their motel room in Kitimat, they headed over to Dave's place.

When Randy rang the doorbell, Dave's mom answered, "Randy Watson! How nice to see you! I haven't seen you in ages. Won't you come in?"

Once inside she told them that Dave would be down in a minute and she called out, "David! Randy Watson and his girlfriend are here!"

Dave yelled back, "I'll be right down!"

When Dave came down the stairs, Randy couldn't believe his eyes. The right side of his face was contorted and he walked with a limp. His speech was slow and slurred. He was really glad to see Randy and invited them to pull up a chair and sit down—they had a lot of catching up to do. He offered Randy and Cassandra each a beer, which they both accepted.

Dave had suffered permanent brain damage as a result of the vicious beating he had received during the riot. He had been told (he still had no memory of that day) that three inmates had beaten him mercilessly with metal bed legs until he was unconscious and was given up for dead. The doctors who had treated him claimed that it was a miracle he had lived at all. But he might never be able to work again; he was not sure what he was capable of doing. Randy and Cassandra listened to him with a great deal of patience—he had difficulty talking. Randy could see the frustration in his friend's eyes as he struggled with every word.

Later in the afternoon, Dave's mom asked Randy and Cassandra if they could stay for dinner. They said they would be delighted. While they were having dinner, Randy could see that Dave even had difficulty with eating. He also noticed that his left hand had an uncontrollable twitch. Dave asked Randy if he wanted to go golfing the next day. Randy thought it was a great idea.

Dave asked Cassandra if it was okay if he and Randy went golfing, and she replied, "That's fine with me. Gee, Randy, I didn't know you golfed."

Randy said, "In grades eight and nine Dave and I were in the golf club in Granby Junior High, but I didn't pursue it after that."

Randy told Dave that he would have to borrow his golf clubs. After he had left, William had sold all of his belongings (probably to buy booze). It was a good thing they were both right-handed.

The next day, while they were on the third green, Dave said, "Randy, can I ask you something?"

"Sure."

He asked Randy if he had ever had sex with another man while in Oakalla.

"Of course, but not because I wanted to. It was because I had no other choice. You see, you're surrounded by four walls and you have nowhere to run and nowhere to hide. It was a constant game of survival, and I felt that if I didn't comply, I would be killed."

Dave said, "I really got messed up there. My girlfriend thought I wasn't interested in her anymore so she left me. I started to wonder if I was a homosexual."

"I felt that way too. But then I realized that in Oakalla, all you see all day is men, no women. Believe me, I am not proud of what I did. But once I got out, I felt no attraction whatsoever to other men, in a romantic sense that is. In fact, I made a proclamation that the only way I would perform a sexual act with another man is at gunpoint, and he would probably have to shoot me first. After I started dating Cassandra, it proved to me that I am indeed a bona fide heterosexual."

He tried to reassure Dave that he would get over it eventually.

When they were on the fourteenth green, Dave confessed to Randy that he wished that he had died in the riot. He felt that he would never be able to amount to anything, and that he would always be a burden to society. Randy tried to encourage him by saying that although he was impaired he could still walk, talk and think. If he continued his therapy he would eventually find something he was capable of doing.

Randy won by two points, and Dave said, "Well, I guess we're even now. Want your twenty bucks back?"

Randy said, "Don't worry about it. This one's on me."

The following day Randy and Cassandra said goodbye to Kitimat.

As they were leaving, Randy said, "It seems so unfair! All Dave did was write some bad cheques and they stuck him in that hellhole. I mean, look at me. I robbed a submarine shop at gunpoint. I deserved to go there. Why was it that I came out of there unscathed and he didn't? It's not right—he didn't deserve that!"

Cassandra said, "I know, Dave seems like a nice guy. I guess fate just works that way sometimes."

That day they didn't travel very far. They ended up at the hot springs at Lakelse Lake, twenty miles north of Kitimat. They stayed there for two nights and then travelled to Prince Rupert, where they also stayed for two nights before beginning the long journey home. Instead of taking the ferry to Port Hardy, they decided to retrace their steps and travel the same route home. The only detour they made was to Barkerville, where they spent four days. When they arrived back home, they felt happy and rested. Randy was not too anxious to go back to work!

One year later

Randy had completed half of his required grade eleven courses and was considering taking a leave of absence from work sometime the following year so he could continue with his studies full-time. That would speed up the process of obtaining his grade twelve equivalency diploma. As far as work was concerned, he had more responsibilities now along with some seniority. The long-term outlook appeared very good. But on a personal note things were not looking all that rosy.

Although Randy and Cassandra were still together and were supposedly still in love with each other, Cassandra had been acting very distant lately. She was frequently cold toward him, and she got annoyed with practically everything he did. Randy couldn't figure this out and had no idea what he could do about it. What made it even more difficult was that his mom was the only other female who had figured in his life, and she had acted like that all the time. He did everything possible to try and please Cassandra, but it seemed that nothing he ever did anymore was right. There had been no sex in over a month, which added to the frustration. It was as if she was completely losing interest in him.

Over the past year, he had brought up the subject of marriage on at least three occasions. Last Christmas he had even purchased an engagement ring and had formally asked her to marry him.

Her response had been, "Let's just wait and see how things go."

Every time he had brought up the subject she would avoid giving him a definite answer. Randy figured she was just not ready for a commitment yet, so he stopped bringing up the subject.

What was even more frustrating for Randy was that there didn't appear to be any major issues in their relationship. He had been faithful to her and had refrained from going to the bar with Derek for over a year. Even when it came to Ashley, there weren't any problems. He enjoyed all the times that Cassandra's mother had brought Ashley over for a visit. Quite often, the three of them would spend the day on an outing. He thought it was a great idea when Cassandra suggested that Ashley move in with them once they were both finished with school.

Since classes had ended for the summer, Randy was available to work overtime. The timing was perfect since Morris had landed three new contracts with the provincial government for the printing of various publications. As a result, Randy was putting in a lot of extra hours. On the positive side it resulted in much larger paycheques, but on the negative side, it added to the tension at home. Cassandra repeatedly gave him a bad time for always working late, but he emphasized that the busy stretch would not last forever. He also pointed out that working was much better than being on welfare. He felt that Cassandra should at least give him credit for having ambition and for his complete change of attitude since his stint in prison. He promised her he would arrange for two weeks' holidays later in the summer.

One Friday, he decided he would give Cassandra a big surprise. With Morris's permission he got off at 2:00 in the afternoon. On the way home, he stopped at a grocery store on Commercial Drive and bought a big bouquet of flowers. He was going to surprise Cassandra by arriving home early and telling her that they were going on a romantic getaway to a resort on Saltspring Island. Friday was always her day off, and she was not scheduled to work again until the next Tuesday.

When he arrived at their apartment, he decided to sneak in through the back door so she would not see him coming. He wanted to enter the apartment quietly and yell, "Surprise."

When he closed the door behind him, he could hear Cassandra giggling and moaning. He heard what sounded like bed springs squeaking, and realized the noises were indeed coming from the bedroom.

He heard Cassandra saying, "Oh, yes!"

Then, to his horror, he heard a man's voice, "Oh, Cassie! Where have you been all my life?"

All that was going through Randy's mind was, "What the fuck is going on here?" He walked into the bedroom and was shocked to see Cassandra in bed with Gordon, a colleague of hers at Safeway. His jaw dropped and so did the bouquet of flowers. Cassandra looked up and was equally horrified to see him standing there.

She shrieked, "Randy!"

Randy didn't say a word. He turned around, ran out of the apartment and bolted out of the building.

He spent the remainder of the afternoon driving all around Vancouver. He didn't have any specific destination in mind; he just drove around aimlessly. He continued this until well into the evening, without even stopping to eat. He ended up consuming about a half a tank of gas. He eventually decided that he needed someone to talk to, so he made his way to the Patricia Hotel. He knew that he could count on Derek being there. When Randy walked into the bar, sure enough, there he was.

Derek said in a jovial tone of voice, "Hey Randy! How's everything going? Pull up a chair."

Randy said nothing as he sat down. When the waiter came by he ordered a couple of glasses of draught beer.

"What's the matter, Randy? You seem down in the dumps," Derek asked.

Randy said, "Oh, it's nothing!"

Derek said, "C'mon, Randy, if something is bothering you, you can tell me."

Randy then piped up and said, "Well if you must know, I came home from work early today, only to find my girlfriend fucking a guy she works with!"

Derek looked somewhat stunned for a minute and then said, "Oh, I see."

He didn't know how to properly console Randy on this matter; he had obviously never been in this type of situation before. He figured that the best thing he could do was to offer to let Randy stay at his place. Randy asked if it was big enough, and he said it was rather small, but he did have a couch.

In the four years that Randy had known Derek, he had never seen his apartment. As it turned out, the "apartment" was a small suite on the top floor of a three-storey rooming house on Dunlevy Street.

As Derek opened his suite door, he said, "Well, this is it! It ain't the Ritz!"

"I sure hope not! They blew that place down!"

Derek looked puzzled and said, "What are you talking about?"

"Do you remember the Ritz Hotel on Georgia Street? It was blown down with dynamite awhile back." Derek finally clued in, and Randy continued, "Hey, even in a situation like this, I still have a sense of humour!"

Derek showed him the couch and allowed him to settle in. As Randy looked over the place he was thinking, "Man, I thought I was messy! This guy takes the cake!" Derek offered him a beer, which he gladly accepted. He also asked Randy if he wanted to smoke some pot.

"Sure, why not?"

As the evening wore on, Derek noticed that Randy was still looking dejected. He asked him if he would like to smoke some crack.

Randy said, "Gee, I don't know. I've never smoked crack before."

"Wow, man, you don't know what you're missing!"

He got out a funny-looking type of pipe mechanism and then took out what looked like a little white rock from his pocket. He placed the rock inside the pipe, took out his lighter and held the flame under the pipe until the rock was red-hot.

He handed the pipe to Randy and said, "Try this, it'll make you feel better."

He also warned his friend not to inhale too hard, but Randy didn't listen. When he took his first puff he nearly gagged.

"Holy shit! This is strong stuff!"

Derek said, "It takes a little getting used to."

A little while later Randy started to feel really mellow. It was a type of high he had never experienced before.

After a drug and alcohol infused weekend Randy didn't feel like going back to work on Monday morning, but he went anyway. He couldn't figure out how Derek could have money for beer and marijuana if he didn't work. He didn't want to ask him; maybe it was better that he didn't know.

As Randy was leaving work on Monday afternoon, he received an unpleasant surprise as he left the building. Cassandra was waiting for him outside the front door.

When Randy saw her, he said in a disgusted tone, "What do you want?"

Cassandra said, "Randy, I'm terribly sorry about what happened! I can explain everything!"

Randy started to walk away, saying, "I have nothing to say to you! Get away from me!"

Cassandra said, "Randy, please give me another chance! I love you!"

Randy stopped, turned around and said, "You sure have a fine way of showing it! Forget about it, we're finished! I'll move my stuff out at the end of the week!"

After that, he just drove off.

The following Thursday Cassandra was once again waiting for Randy when he got off from work.

When he saw her he said, "What is it now?"

Cassandra was practically in tears. "Randy, please listen to me!"

Randy said, "All right, let's go for a drive."

Once they were in his car, Cassandra said, "I am so sorry that I hurt you. I can't explain what drove me to do such a thing—you mean everything to me. I told Gordon I no longer want anything to do with him. I just wish I never met him in the first place. I'm begging you, Randy, please give me another chance."

Randy hesitated, then said, "Okay. I will give you one more chance."

She threw her arms around him and exclaimed, "Oh Randy, I love you so much!" She nearly caused Randy to lose control of the car.

That evening, he informed Derek that he was moving back in with Cassandra. Derek didn't think very much of the idea. He asked Randy if he was sure he was doing the right thing.

Randy said, "Cassandra begged me to give her another chance. She assured me that she is no longer seeing that Gordon guy. Let's face it, I have never been in a serious relationship before. It's not like I can just go out and meet someone else. I have to be thankful that she is interested in me in the first place."

Derek said, "I don't know, man. It sounds like she is playing you for a fool. I don't know if I would trust her anymore. But it's your decision. You do what you feel is best. If things don't work out, you always have a place here."

For the next three weeks everything went fine. But the old problems started recurring after that. The main issue still centred around Randy working very long hours. He kept promising Cassandra that he would take some time off before classes started and then they could take a holiday. He even went so far as to ask Morris if he could have a week off.

Morris told him, "I wish I could let you have a holiday, Randy. But it is absolutely nuts right now. We are having difficulty keeping up with the orders as it is, and if we are short one person, we will really be screwed. I'm sorry, but the answer is no."

If hearing that was not bad enough, Randy knew he would have an even more difficult time breaking the news to Cassandra.

With two weeks to go until classes started in September, Randy decided to resort to Plan B. He proposed that they travel to Victoria on Vancouver Island the next weekend and then go on a camping trip to Golden Ears Provincial Park on the Labour Day weekend. Cassandra did not seem too thrilled. He pointed out that it was better than nothing.

Two days after he had made the travel plans, his day at work proved to be exceptionally busy. He ended up working three hours of overtime. He felt fortunate that it was a Thursday and he was still optimistic that he would be able to get off work on time the next day to catch the 7 p.m. ferry to Swartz Bay. He had called Cassandra to let her know that he would be working late. She hadn't been home, so he left a message on the answering machine.

When he got home from work, Cassandra was still not there. He wondered where she could be—it was almost 8:00. He looked around the living room and noticed that it didn't look right. A number of Cassandra's personal items were missing. He then went into the kitchen and saw that all of her dishes were missing. He started to get frantic at that point. When he went into the bedroom, his heart literally sank. All the drawers that had contained her belongings were open and empty. When he looked in the closet he saw that all of her clothing had been removed. Then he noticed a piece of paper on the dresser. It turned out to be a note from Cassandra.

> *Dearest Randy,*
>
> *There is no easy way to tell you this, but Gordon received a promising job offer in Phoenix, Arizona and has asked me to join him. I came to realize that you and I are very different. Gordon is everything I've looked for in a man and we are very happy together. I hope you can understand this. Best of luck with your job and with your courses.*
>
> *Love,*
> *Cassandra*

Randy stood there, silent, holding the note in his hand. He was numb with disbelief. He kept wishing it was all just a bad dream; that he would wake up and find Cassandra next to him. A few minutes later he sat down on the bed and burst into tears.

After regaining his composure, he telephoned Cassandra's mother. He asked her if she knew anything about what was going on. She said Cassandra had told her that she was going out of town for only a few days. She had no idea that her daughter wasn't planning to return. What made her even more upset was that Cassandra had never said a word to Ashley about leaving. She wondered how in the world she was ever going to explain to her granddaughter that her mother was not planning to come back. She thanked Randy for letting her know. He assured her that he would call if he ever heard from Cassandra.

The following day he tried his best to be a real trooper, and he went to work as usual. But his heart and soul were just not into it. He had a difficult time staying focused on his work; he couldn't wait for the workday to end. After he left work, he went straight over to Derek's place. He wanted to catch Derek before he headed down to the Patricia Hotel. He needed to talk to his friend about this, but he didn't want everyone in the bar to know about it.

When he knocked on the door he felt lucky that he had found Derek at home.

"Randy, what a pleasant surprise! C'mon inside," said Derek.

As soon as Randy got inside, he said, "You were right, Derek. I should have listened to you."

Derek asked him what was wrong, and Randy told him that when he had arrived home from work yesterday, he'd found that Cassandra had packed up all of her belongings and fucked off with that Gordon guy. They had taken off to Phoenix.

Derek, looking very surprised, said, "Phoenix, Arizona?"

Randy gave Derek an annoyed look and said in a sarcastic tone, "No, Phoenix, B.C.! Of course I meant Phoenix, Arizona!"

Derek, looking rather perplexed, said, "I didn't know there was a Phoenix, B.C."

"It was an old copper-mining town in the boundary area between Greenwood and Grand Forks. There's nothing left of it anymore. The old man who lived across the street from us when I was a kid was born there."

He asked Randy if he would like to go to the Patricia Hotel and Randy said, "I thought you'd never ask. But whatever you do, don't mention this to anybody there. It's just between you and me."

19

The departure of Cassandra hit Randy very hard. For the next week he had a difficult time concentrating on his work. In addition, he had completely forgotten about registration for fall classes. By the time he remembered, all of the classes were full. Surprisingly, he didn't appear to be too concerned about it. His thinking was, "Oh fuck it, I can pick up the courses next February."

In the following months, Randy's drinking increased substantially. In fact, it was starting to get out of hand. To make matters worse, he was frequently buying marijuana and crack from Derek. Derek even gave him a custom-made pipe specifically used for smoking crack.

At first Randy and Derek only went out on Friday and Saturday nights to either the Patricia or Astoria hotels. Then it escalated to various weeknights as well, until they were eventually going practically every night of the week and staying until closing. Randy still got up and went to work every morning, even with a massive hangover. He hoped that Morris wouldn't notice, but being a recovered alcoholic himself, Morris was acutely aware of it. Besides, on some days it didn't take much to tell that Randy had been drinking heavily the night before. His eyes would be bloodshot and he would smell like a brewery. Normally Morris had a zero-tolerance policy toward employees coming into work hungover, but in Randy's case, he wanted to help. In the three years that Randy had worked for him, he had proven himself to be a dedicated, hard-working employee. On the one side, Morris didn't want to lose him, but on the other side, he knew he couldn't allow this to continue much longer.

One morning when Randy came into work late and was once again smelling of booze, Morris called him into his office. Instead of firing him, he gave him a long lecture and asked straight out if he had a drinking problem. When Randy said he didn't, Morris still gave him the name and number of a friend of his who ran the local chapter of Alcoholics Anonymous.

"Look, I can stop drinking whenever I want!"

"That's what they all say. Look, you've been a very good employee here, and I don't want you to blow it. If there is something that is bothering you, tell me about it. But I strongly suggest that you give this man a call."

As Randy left Morris's office, he still insisted that he was fine.

In the weeks that followed Randy was still not cooperating. With Christmas coming, Morris cut him some slack, unaware that Christmas was totally meaningless to Randy.

Three weeks after New Year's of 1990, Morris had finally had enough. When Randy came into work at 10:00 one morning, blitzed and acting like nothing was wrong, Morris called him into his office.

"Randy, I have been very patient with you, but I have now reached the end of my rope. You have done nothing to help yourself and your work performance over the last six months clearly indicates that. I'm sorry, but you have left me no choice. I am going to have to let you go."

Randy didn't seem overwhelmingly shocked by the news; rather, he appeared unemotional about it all.

"Good, see if I care! I don't need this fucking job!" he said as he walked out of Morris's office and the plant for the last time.

Randy didn't realize just how big a mistake he had made until he went to apply for Unemployment Insurance. With the new guidelines for receiving U.I. in effect, he had to fill out a report explaining why he was terminated from his job. He had to think of something quickly, so he concocted a story about being constantly harassed by his fellow employees because he was a half-breed Indian. He had finally decided to take a stand, and when he started beating a co-worker, his foreman had intervened. He ended up punching out the foreman, which had resulted in his termination. When he presented the report to his counsellor at the Employment and Immigration Canada office, he was told that he would have to return the next day as there wasn't time to process his claim at the time.

The following day, his counsellor told him that his claim had been transferred to another counsellor, who would arrive shortly.

A few minutes later, a man who appeared to be native came up to the desk and said, "Hello, Randy. My name is William Joe and I'll be reviewing your U.I. claim."

When Randy saw him, he started thinking, "Uh oh, now I'm in trouble!"

After looking through Randy's file, he said, "Judging by the name Watson, it must have been your mom that was Indian. What tribe was she from?"

Randy had to think of something fast, otherwise the gig was up.

All he could come up with was, "Actually, it is my father who is native. He was born on the Kispiox Reserve and was adopted by my grandparents, whose name is Watson."

William continued to review his claim. He pointed out to Randy that he was making very serious allegations. His foreman could get fired for this, and the company could have its business license suspended. Randy began to realize that what he was doing was not right. Leo, his foreman at the plant, was actually a nice guy. If Morris's business license were suspended, a lot of ex-convicts would not likely get a second chance. William said he took these kinds of issues very personally.

He said to Randy, "Us natives need to stick together, otherwise white men will always push us around!"

Right after that he told Randy that he had spoken to Morris over the phone and Morris had explained everything. William asked Randy about his arriving at work late and hungover after being out drinking all night. He made it very clear to Randy that since the termination of his employment was the result of his own negligence and because he had filed a false claim, he would not be eligible for benefits. His claim was therefore null and void.

William noticed that Randy was seething and added insult to injury by saying, "Oh, one more thing. You don't look the slightest bit Indian. Have a nice day!"

With Unemployment Insurance out of the question as a source of income, that left only one other alternative—welfare. It never occurred to Randy that he could possibly quit drinking and beg for his old job back. The monthly allowance for welfare was substantially lower than U.I. When he considered what he paid for rent on his apartment, he realized there would be very little left for anything else.

One of Randy's first priorities after getting on welfare was to sell his car. He took a fairly big loss by selling it for far less than he had paid for it. He needed the money right away, so he took the first offer that came along. The money he received did not go very far.

The meagre amount that he received from welfare did not stop him from indulging in drugs and alcohol. To him, they took priority over rent. After two months of coming up short with the rent money, the landlord, as expected, told him to leave. Randy didn't really care since Derek had offered his place to him again. Derek worked out a deal with his landlord whereby when he signed the rental forms that were required by Social Assistance, he wrote it out as though they were living in separate suites. Therefore, they each received the full rental allowance. That allowed Randy and Derek to spend half the rental allowance for their leisure.

In the following months, about all they did was sleep until noon and spend the rest of the day drinking beer and smoking crack. Randy was getting fairly addicted to it by then. On most afternoons Derek would step out for several hours, claiming he had some "errands" to run. Randy never asked him to elaborate; he didn't really want to know. Whenever Derek went out, Randy would head over to nearby Oppenheimer Park—most of his drug dealers hung out there.

One afternoon when he returned to the suite, Derek had a guest there. He introduced the man only as Tony and told Randy he had something he was willing to sell him. Randy asked what it was. Derek reminded Randy about the time when he had bought the .38 Special handgun from the biker.

"Well, Tony here has something even better!"

Tony reached into a duffle bag and pulled out a .45 calibre handgun.

Derek said, "What do you think?"

"It looks impressive!"

Tony said, "I'll sell it to you for a hundred bucks and I'll even throw in five rounds of ammunition. What do you think?"

Randy said, "That sounds like a good deal, but if you want the money right away, I'll be short for the rest of the month."

"Hey, with this baby, you'll get a hundred percent return on your investment in no time flat!" Tony told him.

With Randy's latest acquisition and his increasing addiction to crack, it didn't take long for him to pick up where he had left off just before his arrest. He started to go out at night and hold up convenience stores in his neighbourhood. As before, he always wore a ski mask so the store clerks were never able to identify him. He also left a fair amount of time between robberies in order to throw the police off his trail.

One afternoon in August, he decided to take a walk toward downtown Vancouver. He could not explain what motivated him, but something told him to head in that direction. Derek had been out since morning; it was almost 4 p.m. and he still had not returned. He headed up Hastings Street until he reached Burrard and then turned left. As he approached the main branch of the Bank of Montreal, he noticed a large crowd gathered around the entrance. There were a lot of police cars as well as two ambulances. He wondered what was going on. As he approached the front door of the bank, he saw what looked like a body lying on the ground. When he got a little closer, he realized to his horror, that the body was Derek's. Apparently he had been shot by the police while trying to make a getaway after robbing the bank. It looked as though he had been lying there for some time, as the blood had dried up. Yet they had made no effort to cover up his body.

Randy didn't have any time to grieve. He knew he had to get back home as soon as possible. The police would be coming by as soon as they found out Derek's address. If they got there before he did they would surely find his gun, his hunting knife (which he had recently purchased from a nearby pawnshop) and his ski mask. As well, they would discover all of their drug paraphernalia. He also knew that if the police talked to his landlord, he would tell them that Randy lived there too. So he immediately caught the eastbound bus on Hastings Street and hoped that he would make it home before the cops got there.

When he arrived back at the suite, the door was still locked, so that meant that the cops hadn't shown up. Once inside, he gathered his gun, knife, ski mask and all of their crack pipes and roach clips and loaded them into his backpack. He then took it downstairs and placed it in a storage room in the basement. Sure enough, two hours later two police officers knocked on the door. When he opened the door, one of them asked him if he was a friend of Derek Chadsey.

Randy said, "Yes. I'm also his roommate."

They asked if they could come in and he complied.

While one officer looked around the suite, the other one said, "I'm afraid I have some bad news. Your friend Derek attempted to hold up the Bank of Montreal in the Bentall Centre today. When he tried to escape, one of our officers told him to stop. He pulled out a gun and we had to shoot him. He died instantly."

Randy tried to act shocked and surprised, pretending to not know anything. All he could say was, "Oh, my!"

The officer that had been snooping around the suite eventually spoke up and asked Randy how well he had known Derek. Randy told him they used to hang out together at the Astoria Hotel. He avoided mentioning that they had been in jail together.

The officer said, "Did you know he had a rap sheet a mile long and he was the prime suspect in at least six different bank robberies in Vancouver in the past month?"

Randy did his best to act innocent by saying, "Gee, I didn't know that."

The officer commented that the suite seemed awfully small to be accommodating two people. Randy said that he slept on the couch and pointed out that they were sharing the suite in order to save money. Then the officer told him that Derek had been in trouble with the law since he was sixteen and had spent a combined total of ten years (not consecutively) in prison for a variety of offences.

He concluded by saying to Randy, "In the future, I strongly suggest that you pick your friends more wisely!"

The other officer added, "It looks like you have this place all to yourself now. It wouldn't have been any different if he had lived, because he would have gone to jail for a long, long time."

With Derek gone, Randy once again found himself all alone. It was now up to him to maintain the suite, which meant he was completely responsible for the rent. But he squandered most of his money on drugs and alcohol. When the first of September came around, he had already blown a large portion of the welfare cheque he had received only four days earlier. His dealer offered him a good price on some crystal methamphetamine so he decided to score some. As a result, he didn't have sufficient funds to pay the rent. His landlord was less lenient than some of his former ones had been; he kicked Randy out right away.

After he was evicted, he resorted to taking up residence behind a dumpster in an alley behind Hastings Street. It was under an overhang, so at least he would be covered from the rain. He made no effort whatsoever to try and find some cheap accommodation. His thoughts, when choosing the place in the alley, were, "At least the rent is cheap. I am free to spend my money on whatever I want."

As summer faded into fall, he became a shadow of the person he once was. His drug dependency had increased substantially and his weight had dropped to only 115 pounds. He was severely malnourished, for the majority of his meagre welfare cheques went to support his crack habit. He hocked his backpack and purchased a heavy winter coat from the Salvation Army Thrift Store. The coat contained two large inside pockets, which made it easy for shoplifting. Everything he owned (except for his bedroll) was contained in those pockets. That included his gun (with its five original bullets) and his hunting knife.

One cold evening in November, Randy paid a visit to his dealer as usual. His name was Tito and his base of operations was Pigeon Park at the corner of East Hastings and Carrall streets. Randy received an unpleasant surprise when he learned that Tito had almost doubled his price for a gram of crack for no apparent reason.

All Tito would say was, "Hey, I make the rules here! Them's the breaks!"

Randy begged him to cut him a deal because he needed his fix, but Tito wouldn't budge.

He said to Randy, "You get the money, you get your fix! No exceptions!"

Randy was very disillusioned. He didn't know what to do or where to turn. He started to walk up Hastings Street in a semi-daze. He was completely desperate and was willing to do practically anything to obtain the required funds to provide him with his fix.

When he reached the intersection of East Hastings and Columbia streets, he decided to cross over to the other side. While in the crosswalk, he looked over to a lone male in a late-model Honda Civic sitting at the stop light, with his driver's-side window open. This seemed strange considering how cold it was outside. Randy made an immediate decision to seize the opportunity.

He pulled the gun out from his inside coat pocket, pointed it at the man and yelled out, "Get out of the car!"

The man quickly complied, but was so shocked that he forgot to put the car into "park," so it started to lurch forward.

"Put it in park!"

The man tried to get out of the car, but he kept fumbling with the seatbelt.

"Move your fucking ass! Hurry up, get out of the fucking car!"

The driver eventually got out of the car. Randy told him to move back as he got in. He then told him to turn and run—which he did—as Randy sped away.

Randy drove eastbound a great distance along Hastings Street. He didn't know where he was going; he just wanted to drive. He eventually found himself driving erratically down a whole chain of side streets; he had no idea where he was.

After driving continuously for a half an hour, he finally decided to stop. He parked the car in front of a corner store that was run by a Vietnamese family. When he walked into the store, he saw a middle-aged Vietnamese woman behind the counter.

Without hesitation, Randy pulled his gun out, pointed it at the woman and yelled out, "Give me all your money!"

She yelled back in a thick accent, "Okay, okay! Don't shoot!"

She opened the till and began placing the money on the counter, her hands trembling with fear.

"Don't fuck with me, bitch!" Randy shouted, "*Move it!*"

Once the till was empty, she screamed in a hysterical tone, "Take it! Take it!"

As Randy stuffed the money into his inside coat pocket, it appeared as though the woman was lunging toward him. He reacted the wrong way, thinking that she was trying to grab his gun. He fired twice, striking her in the chest. Before he had a chance to react, her husband, who had come from upstairs to investigate the commotion, entered the store from the back. When Randy saw him standing there, he acted on impulse. He levelled his gun at him and fired two shots, also striking him in the chest.

Just then their son, who had also been upstairs, came from the back, yelling, "What's happening?" When he saw Randy standing there holding a gun, he cried out, "Holy shit," then he turned and ran.

Randy fired a shot at him, but missed. When he realized the chamber was empty, he took off after the boy. He chased him into the stockroom in the back, where he had him cornered. The boy tried to open the back door, but it was locked. Randy grabbed him by the back of the head and slammed it into the door. He then flung him into a stack of wooden crates. He grabbed a chair and cracked it over the boy's head. With the boy now barely conscious, Randy took out his hunting knife and slashed him across the throat. He flung him onto the ground, sat on top of him and began stabbing him in the chest. It was as if some raging force had completely taken over Randy; he was totally oblivious to anything around him. He just kept plunging the knife over and over deeply into the boy's chest as blood spurted into his face. A few minutes later, he realized that the boy was dead, so he got up and bolted out the front door.

He sped away. He still had no idea where he was. His face, his coat and his shirt were drenched with the boy's blood. Randy seemed to be more concerned about how he was going to clean it up than over the carnage he just had committed. He was driving more erratically than ever. He was running stop signs and he went through two red lights. A police car just happened to be near the intersection of the second light, so the officer gave chase. When he saw the police car coming after him with its lights and siren activated, Randy put his foot down on the accelerator. For at least ten blocks the cops chased him at speeds reaching seventy miles per hour. Three police cars coming in the opposite direction had blocked his path at an intersection ahead. Randy tried to drive up onto the curb in order to go around the police cars, but instead he ended up crashing into a lamppost. The impact busted open the radiator and the rear wheels were caught on something. Randy had nowhere to escape. Immediately, five police cars surrounded him. The police officers got out of their cars and converged on him with guns drawn.

One of them yelled out, "Come out and keep your hands where we can see them!"

Randy didn't waste any time. He came out of the car with his hands in the air. He was handcuffed, placed in the back seat of one of the police cars and taken to police headquarters.

The police officer who had initiated the pursuit had relayed the car's license plate numbers to headquarters, and they had matched those of the hijacked vehicle from Hastings Street. At police headquarters Randy was processed, fingerprinted and placed in a holding cell. Later he was implicated as the person responsible for the corner store robbery and murders, so he was denied bail. The next day he was transferred to the Surrey Pre-trial Centre.

Randy had to wait an agonizing five months for his trial to begin. As with his previous arrest, he was appointed a lawyer from Legal Aid. It seemed the lawyers chosen to represent Randy had made it through law school with the minimum grade-point average. The attorney, Mr. Bill Bloom, appeared very disorganized, and felt he must have drawn the short straw—it seemed like an open-and-shut case. He recommended Randy plead not guilty to the three murders, but guilty to stealing the car. The police had caught him red-handed in the stolen car, and the car's owner had identified him in a police lineup, so there didn't seem much choice about that plea.

Mr. Bloom's advice made Randy feel very uneasy. He felt the evidence against him was overwhelming. The bullets removed from the victims matched those in Randy's gun. The blood found on Randy's knife and clothing matched the blood type of the murdered boy. Despite this, his lawyer somehow believed that he had a legitimate chance of winning this case. There were no witnesses who had seen him leave the store, so that could work in his favour. The attorney suggested Randy not testify in his own defence.

After their first session, Randy questioned the competency of his court-appointed lawyer. The guy was either living in a fantasy world, or he had more gumption than brains. He couldn't believe that his attorney hadn't suggested a plea bargain. If they could prove that the murders were not premeditated, he would be willing to plead guilty to second-degree murder, provided the judge and the lawyer reached an agreement. That way, he would be eligible for parole in as little as ten years. He was afraid that if he brought this up, his lawyer would think he was telling him how to do his job.

In the days leading up to the trial, Randy debated whether he should make a request to change lawyers. He had a bad feeling Bill Bloom, but he didn't know where to turn. He didn't have the money for a decent attorney; neither did his mom. He idly wondered if Kees Vandelaar had his own legal practice by now, but even if he did, Randy figured he wouldn't represent him in a million years.

On the first day of his trial, Randy noticed that his mom was in the spectators' area. He waved to her and she waved back. He was not allowed to have a conversation with her. He could also see relatives of the victims in the spectators' area, including the couple's daughter. Perhaps the only reason she was still alive was because she had moved away to attend the University of Victoria. It must have been really hard for her to lose both her parents and her little brother all at once.

What really surprised Randy when he looked over at the spectators' area was that Cassandra was there. He wondered, "What the hell is she doing here?" He also wondered how she'd learned about what had happened to him from way down in Phoenix. He felt tempted to yell over to her, "You're the one who did this to me, you fucking bitch!"

As Randy was being led away after the first day of the trial, Cassandra tried to approach him.

She cried out, "Randy, I'm so sorry I hurt you!" Randy tried to ignore her, but as he was leaving the courtroom she managed to get close to him. "Randy," she pleaded, "please listen to me!"

He said, "Oh, all right," and asked the guards to hang tough for a minute.

With tears streaming down her face, she told him that she had left

Gordon and had returned to Vancouver last September. She had tried really hard to find him, but she'd had very little to go on.

Randy snarled back, "Well, it's a little late, isn't it? As far as I'm concerned, you can go to hell! Do me a favour. Don't ever let me see your face in here again!"

The next day, the prosecution presented its case. Mr. Bloom warned Randy that, in a meeting with the judge and the prosecutor, he had learned that the prosecution had an ace in the hole. They had a star witness. A woman who lived across the street from the store had heard shots fired the night of the robbery, so she had gone outside to investigate. She had hidden behind some shrubs in her front yard, and had seen Randy run out of the store and jump into the stolen car. She was easily able to identify him and the car. The lawyer assured Randy that he would put the witness's credibility to the test when she was brought to the stand for questioning.

During his cross-examination, Mr. Bloom focused on the quality of the witness's eyesight and the fact that it was night. She told him that her eyesight was 20/20, and the front of the store had been well lit. He continued to question her, but she remained positive, beyond a shadow of a doubt, that the man she had seen fleeing the store was Randy. She said she had gotten a good look at him—she had no problem identifying him in the defendant's chair.

When the cross-examination was over, Randy said sarcastically, "Good job, counsellor!"

The lawyer thought about making a last-ditch attempt to change Randy's plea to guilty, and go for a charge of second-degree murder. It appeared to be too late. When the prosecutor made his case, he explained that the boy had been stabbed twenty-seven times, and the man and woman had been shot with deadly accuracy. After several minutes, Randy was still waiting for an answer from his attorney about the change of plea. The lawyer gave him a look as if to say, "Duh, I don't know!"

Mr. Bloom and the prosecutor made their closing arguments—it was now up to the jury. It didn't take them very long to reach their verdict. Court reconvened the next day.

The judge said, "Will the defendant please rise? Members of the jury, have you reached a verdict?"

"Yes, we have, your honour," said the jury foreman. "For the charge of first-degree murder of Nuoc Minh Phuong, we find the defendant, Randolph Michael Watson, guilty. For the charge of first-degree murder of

Toan Lin Phuong, guilty. For the charge of first-degree murder of Terry Kien Phuong, guilty."

Randy's heart sank when he heard the verdict. Even though he had known that it was inevitable, it still came as a shock. His mom wept uncontrollably in the spectators' area. He braced himself as the judge delivered his sentence.

"Randolph Michael Watson, you have been convicted by a jury of your peers of the most severe of all capital offences, murder in the first degree. It is the duty of this court to issue the maximum penalty allowable for this offence under the Criminal Code of Canada. You are hereby sentenced to three concurrent terms of life imprisonment, with no eligibility for parole for twenty-five years. Your sentence will be served in a federal maximum security institution."

For the next few minutes Randy stood silently with his head hanging down. He was in too much of a state of shock to say anything. Then he burst into tears. Several members of the victims' family, who were watching the proceedings from the spectators' area, let out a cheer when the sentence was read. Randy's mom was not present. She had left a few minutes after the verdict had been read. She hadn't wanted to stay for the sentencing; enduring the trial had been hard enough on her. Hearing that her only remaining son was going to be put away for life would have been unbearable for her. To make things worse, the outcome of the trial would be plastered all over the media—front-page headlines in all newspapers, top stories on television and radio news.

Randy was taken back to the Surrey Pre-trial Centre. Two days later, a Corrections Canada van arrived to transport him and three other prisoners to Kent Maximum Security Institution near the town of Agassiz. As Randy got into the van, he remembered when he had been transported from the Remand Centre to Oakalla. At that time, he had thought of it as the longest ride of his life. Heading to Oakalla, he had known he would be getting out after two years (provided he survived living there). This time things were different—there was no comparison. This was the last time he would see the outside world for twenty-five years, so for the entire trip he took a good, long look at the surrounding countryside. He was thinking, "Here I am, twenty-nine years old, and I won't see the outside world again until I am fifty-four. What will I be able to contribute to society then?"

When the van arrived at Kent Institution, Randy noticed the buildings were fairly new. Inside was brightly lit and the main hallway was spacious—a far cry from the narrow tiers of Oakalla. But that's where the differences ended. The atmosphere was just the same, and the prison was having the same problems with overcrowding as Oakalla had when Randy had been incarcerated there.

Randy's cell was not much bigger than the one at Oakalla, but here he had only one cellmate. There was a sink and a toilet made out of stainless steel, for obvious reasons. As at Oakalla, the prisoners had to line up and file into the dining hall in an orderly manner for all meals, and lights-out was at 10:00 p.m. It took awhile for Randy to settle in, but he figured he'd better get used to it—he was going to be there for a long, long time.

20

Seven years later

The past seven years had been very difficult for Randy. Kent Institution had proven to be just as much a living hell as Oakalla had ever been. Since his incarceration at Kent, there had been four major disturbances and twelve stabbings. After each incident, there had been a lockdown which had lasted one or two days. During lockdowns, he wasn't allowed out of his cell except at mealtimes.

Randy had been involved in a number of skirmishes with other inmates. Now he pretty much kept to himself. He'd had three different cellmates over the past seven years, and hadn't gotten along with any of them. To pass the time, he worked in the prison woodworking shop—as he had in Oakalla. He seldom went to the recreation room, where there was a television and a pool table. It was an understatement to say that he had become very antisocial. He spent most of his spare time in his cell reading magazines. His favourites were *Rolling Stone*, *National Geographic* and *Time*. He had a transistor radio, but all it could receive was a radio station from Chilliwack, so he didn't listen to it much.

Randy's mom wrote regularly. He enjoyed getting her letters—the exception being the one she had sent five years ago telling him that Dave Sewell had committed suicide. That news had hit Randy especially hard. The previous year she had written that the lumber mill had shut down permanently. Granby was becoming a ghost town, and she was seriously considering moving back to Prince George.

Randy never received any letters from anyone else. He'd asked his mom to forward his mailing address to Gary, Bill and Brad, but he had never heard from any of them. It appeared they had completely deserted him.

During the past month, the prison chaplain had been encouraging prisoners serving life sentences to interact with each other. He felt it would help them cope better if they were to get the reason for their imprisonment out in the open. His focus was on prisoners who had committed multiple murders, and his main goal was to find a common denominator. He wanted to get to the root of what drove a person to commit such brutal crimes. He worked with troubled kids on the side, and he thought that if the prisoners shared their stories with others, it might help some of these young people turn their lives around.

One afternoon, the chaplain asked Randy if he would be interested in taking part in a "group session" with three other inmates. Even though Randy was still quite antisocial, he agreed. His response was, "What the hell, I have nothing else to do."

Randy, the chaplain and three other inmates serving multiple life sentences for murder gathered around a table in the recreation room. There were two big, burly guards keeping an eye on them just so they wouldn't get any ideas. They were mainly concerned that the inmates might take the chaplain hostage. The chaplain kept a journal and planned to record each prisoner's story. He took out his notepad and began taking notes. He asked the four inmates to introduce themselves, and then they began to tell their stories.

Jake's story

Jake was a bona fide racist neo-Nazi skinhead. He was a devout member of the Aryan Nations, and had lived at their compound near Rocky Mountain House, Alberta. He had been visiting his best friend, Wade, in Surrey, B.C., when he'd committed the heinous crime that landed him a life sentence.

Jake and Wade had attended the funeral of one of their fellow members, Hank, who had been killed in a car accident. The funeral had been held in Richmond one Saturday morning. Afterward, they'd come upon two little Jewish boys going home from synagogue school. Jake had asked the boys if they wanted a ride. When they'd refused, he and Wade chased them down an alley, carrying their hunting rifles with them. They eventually cornered the boys and killed both of them. The seven-year-old boy was killed with four massive blows to the back of the head with the butt end of Jake's rifle. The nine-year-old boy was shot point-blank in the back of the head.

What made the crime even more appalling was that Jake had raped the seven-year-old after killing him. Semen samples taken from the boy had contained Jake's DNA.

The murders had sent shockwaves throughout the Jewish community. Even hardened police officers were sickened by what had happened. Wade was serving time in Kingston Penitentiary in Ontario.

Richard's story

Richard, who hailed from Victoria, B.C., had an extreme, obsessive hatred toward Christmas. This went back to his early childhood. His mother had committed suicide on Christmas day—he had been less than one year old. His alcoholic father blamed Richard for the suicide, so every Christmas he would beat Richard and lock him in the tool shed. Eventually, Richard had run away. But his past eventually caught up with him.

Five days before Christmas, 1994, Richard, who had returned to Victoria only a month before, had paid a visit to Tillicum Mall. He had a sawed-off shotgun tucked inside his coat. He'd headed straight for the Santa's Village display and waited for the man playing Santa to take his break. As the Santa approached, Richard had shot him twice. He then turned the gun on a seventeen-year-old girl who was one of Santa's "elves." A young mother and her four-year-old son had tried to flee, but when they tripped, he shot them as well. A mall security guard was Richard's next victim. A bystander had grabbed him from behind, but Richard broke free and shot him point-blank. Richard was eventually wounded in an exchange of gunfire with police. In all, a total of six people had been killed.

Rudy's story

Rudy, who was from Williams Lake, B.C., had an obsessive hatred for cops. This was due to the fact that he'd been in trouble with the law since the age of twelve. Every time he'd been convicted of a crime, he blamed the police. He had never taken any responsibility for his own actions.

Three years ago, he had been released from Matsqui Institution after serving a seven-year sentence for manslaughter. He had returned to Williams Lake and had moved in with his best friend, Danny, and Danny's girlfriend, Lisa.

Rudy's number one goal upon his release had been to get revenge on the law enforcement agency that had arrested him—the Williams Lake RCMP. He had convinced Danny and Lisa to go along with a plan to set a trap and take some cops out. Danny and Lisa had fabricated a case of domestic violence to lure the police to their place. Rudy and Danny had hidden in the bushes alongside the heavily wooded driveway of the ten-acre lot. They had high-powered automatic rifles that Danny had smuggled from the United States. When the police car came up the driveway, Rudy and Danny had opened fire, instantly killing the two officers inside. They drove the police car to the back pasture, stacked some fallen trees on top of it and set the pile on fire.

When the officers had been reported missing, Rudy, Danny and Lisa had been obvious suspects. The next day, a large team of RCMP officers had entered the property with a search warrant. They eventually found the charred remains of the police car with the two officers inside. Rudy, Danny and Lisa had received life sentences.

It was Randy's turn to tell his story. His was drastically different. The other three inmates' actions had been premeditated, and they had been motivated by hatred. Randy didn't hate the people he'd killed; he hadn't even known them. He hadn't meant to kill them. He'd only wanted to rob the place and use the money to buy more crack.

None of the other three prisoners showed the slightest bit of remorse. Jake seemed especially proud of what he'd done. When he bragged that he would gladly do it all over again, Randy, in disbelief, commented, "They were just little kids, for fuck's sake! What did they ever do to deserve that?"

Jake sneered, "Little Jews grow up to be big Jews."

As for Rudy, he believed that all cops were cut from the same cloth. So to him, it didn't matter who paid the price. As far as he was concerned, they all deserved to be shot.

Although Randy didn't agree with what Richard had done, he did concur with him on one thing—they both disliked Christmas. To them, it was a fucked-up, useless holiday, and was nothing but a big waste of time and money.

Randy admitted he was sorry for what he had done, and would have given anything in the world to bring back the three people he'd killed. He was hopeful that he would someday be able to find a new lawyer who would be willing to take on his case and persuade the Court of Appeal to have him retried for second-degree murder.

Two years later

In the past two years, little had changed. Randy, now 38, had been incarcerated for nine years. He still had sixteen years to go before he was eligible for parole. Six months ago, he'd welcomed in the new millennium with very little fanfare.

He had given up hope on winning an appeal of his conviction. But suddenly two weeks ago that had all changed. Randy had received a visit from Mr. George Yerazelski, who was once one of the top-rated defence attorneys in Vancouver. In the last few years, he had been winding down his practice—he was planning to retire soon. He now spent a lot of his spare time at the University of British Columbia Law Library, reviewing transcripts of first-degree murder trials that had taken place over the past decade. When he'd looked over the documents from Randy's trial, he had noticed there were a lot of inequities. He then looked over the newspaper files of the case on microfilm at the Sedgewick Library at the same university. He took a special interest in the case, as he had a strong feeling that it could be reopened. He had decided to take a drive out to Agassiz and meet Randy in person.

At their initial meeting, the attorney could tell that Randy was very cynical about any chance of his conviction being overturned. He assured him that he understood how he felt—he had worked on many similar cases. A large percentage of them had been successful, so he told him to never give up hope. Randy asked why he was interested in having the conviction overturned. The lawyer told him that when he had read the transcripts of the trial, he had noticed that there were a number of flaws regarding the police investigation of the crime scene and the account of the eyewitness. But the most important and major flaw was that Randy had not been allowed to testify.

When Randy learned about Mr. Yerazelski's track record as a lawyer, he thought, "How in the world am I ever going to pay this guy? Good lawyers are definitely not cheap!" When he worked up the nerve to ask how he was going to pay the costs of the appeal, the attorney told him not to worry. If his appeal was successful and there was a new trial, and Randy was granted early parole as a result, he could pay him gradually—provided he could find a job. The lawyer asked Randy if he had earned any money in the nine years he had been in prison. Randy explained that he worked part-time in the woodworking shop, building cabinets, but most of the money he'd earned had been spent on cigarettes and magazines. The person in charge of the bookkeeping at the prison had set up a savings account for him, so any extra money had gone there. He had no idea how much was in the account, but he said he'd be happy to use that as a down payment.

"Let's see how things go first," the lawyer suggested.

At their second meeting, the attorney told Randy that he might have sufficient evidence to win an appeal. He said that if he could prove that there had been no malice or intent, the charge of first-degree murder might be dropped.

The attorney found it strange that Randy's first lawyer hadn't let him testify. Another thing he found unbelievable was that he had never brought up the subject of a plea bargain. That could be possible grounds for overturning the conviction, or at least for a mistrial. Randy said that his first lawyer had been chosen for him through Legal Aid. He had seemed very young—as though he had just come out of law school. He asked Mr. Yerazelski if he thought this Bill Bloom guy was a total idiot. The lawyer informed him that he was not at liberty to critique other lawyers. He had never met Bill Bloom, and had never worked for Legal Aid. Therefore, he had no comment on that matter.

At their next meeting, Mr. Yerazelski informed Randy of their subsequent steps. He had successfully arranged for a preliminary hearing with the Court of Appeal. At the hearing, he would present all of the evidence given at the first trial. His objective was to convince the judge that there had been no malice or intent when the crime had been committed. If he were successful at winning an appeal, the original charge of first-degree murder would be overturned, and there would be a new trial. He advised Randy to plead guilty to second-degree murder. His testimony might be necessary in order to prove the charge. If so, he would have to give minute details of what had happened that night, so he would need to remember as much as possible.

Randy agreed. He knew that if he could get the lesser charge of second-degree murder, he would be eligible for parole as early as next year.

As Mr. Yerazelski was leaving, Randy said, "Go for it," and wished him luck.

When the news of Randy's application for an appeal was made public, Lin Phuong, whose parents and brother had been murdered by him, took immediate action. She enlisted the services of Crown prosecutor Michael Blakely. She even went public by appearing on all of the local newscasts. She expressed her outrage as to why anyone would want to reopen the case. Lin, now married with two small children and living in Victoria, stated that her children would never know their maternal grandparents, or their uncle. Her life had been changed forever, and Randy deserved to remain in jail. She was hoping that this would persuade the general public to be on her side. Michael Blakely vowed to fight the appeal tooth and nail. Realizing this, George Yerazelski knew that he would have his hands full.

The hearing with the Court of Appeal was scheduled for September 15, 2000, or as Mr. Yerazelski called it, "D-Day." One week before the hearing, he bought Randy a white shirt, dress pants and some good shoes. He wanted Randy to look as presentable as possible.

Early on the morning of the appeal, Randy dressed quickly and felt optimistic in his new clothes. He was transported from Kent Institution to the law courts building in Vancouver in a Corrections Canada van. He met up with his attorney, and they filed into the courtroom. Lin Phuong was unable to attend the hearing, so her cousin Tran took her place. He planned to present the court with a victim's impact statement.

Once everyone was inside the courtroom, the bailiff bellowed out, "All rise! The Court of Appeal is now in session. The Honourable Cornelius Vandelaar presiding."

When Randy realized who the judge was, he completely freaked out. His eyes bugged out, his jaw dropped and he became as white as a sheet.

While Michael Blakely was presenting his opening arguments, Mr. Yerazelski looked over at Randy and whispered, "Jesus Christ, man, are you all right? You look like you've seen a ghost!"

"Right now, I would be happier if I had seen a ghost."

The lawyer gave Randy a puzzled look—he couldn't fathom what his client was talking about.

It was Mr. Yerazelski's turn to give his opening argument. He presented the court with the transcripts of Randy's trial and outlined the flaws with the defence and the eyewitness accounts. Randy and Kees made eye contact several times, and Randy could tell by the look in the judge's eye that he remembered everything. Still, Randy vowed to keep his mouth shut. He didn't want to let on that the judge was someone from his past, and even worse, someone from his past with a dark secret. The last thing he wanted was to have that incident brought out into the open again.

After all of the arguments had been presented, court was adjourned. Once they were outside the courtroom, Randy told his lawyer that the whole thing had not been a good idea. He should never have tried to get an appeal; this was all a waste of time.

"What the hell is the matter with you?" interrupted the attorney. "You've been acting weird ever since we've been here! Now, let's not give up. It's not over until it's over."

After only an hour, court was reconvened. Mr. Yerazelski seemed quite surprised that the judge would make a decision so quickly. Little did he know that the judge had most likely made his decision before court had even been adjourned. When everyone reassembled in the courtroom, the Honourable Cornelius Vandelaar issued this statement:

"Your application for an appeal has been denied. The original charge of first-degree murder will stand."

He said nothing more after issuing his statement—he simply got up and walked out of the courtroom, avoiding any further eye contact with Randy.

"I'm very sorry, Randy," Mr. Yerazelski said. "I tried my best. I really believed that we stood a good chance."

Randy didn't say a word. He was taken from the courtroom to the Corrections Canada van parked outside and transported back to Kent Institution. He would remain there until at least 2016, when he would be eligible for parole.

About the Author

Photo by Katherine Marion, www.3rdEyeFoto.com

Born in Vancouver, Robert Boyd grew up in Chilliwack, British Columbia. He majored in Business Administration at Southern Alberta Institute of Technology in Calgary, Alberta. He has travelled extensively throughout Western Canada—many of the places he visited are documented in this book.

His short stories are published in Canadian Stories. He now lives in Aldergrove, B.C.